The Deadly Discord

Marc B. DeGeorge

MuseMarc Studio, LLC.

ISBN: 978-1-956487-12-1 (digital), 978-1-956487-13-8 (paperback)

First Edition: **December 2022**

9 8 7 6 5 4 3 2 1

Acknowledgments

On this journey to write, not just a novel, but a series, I have not walked alone. Many have been involved in it's making, and to them I owe a great deal of thanks.

First, my dedicated and awesome reading group, Ben Pick, Salone More, Tracey Canole, E. Marie Robertson, Michelle Darnell and J. Logan Rice. Thank you for your critical commentary, positive support, and friendship.

My amazing editors, Joanne Machin and Ariel Anderson. You have been a huge help in making this book a reality. Thank you.

Also to my wife for giving me the time to forge this work...and all the ones that come after.

And finally, to my parents, who are not only proud of their son for his efforts, but actually read what I write!

Chapter One

I know if I keep pushing like this, something bad is bound to happen.

That, eventually, luck will catch up with us and we'll have to pay our dues. That one of these days, one of us is going to get seriously hurt, or worse.

Somehow, that doesn't stop me.

"Prepare to meet your end, Ransom Quigley He'," Nayla, the ex-princess extraordinaire, says with a narrowing of her eyes.

I drop to a crouch, my body tensing. This is it. The big test that will determine everything. Whether we win or lose, or if we even survive. I've been waiting for this moment, and I will not fail.

"Quit the talk and serve already!" Afton, Nayla's paramour and chaos in a female body, shouts, pounding her fist into her racket. Nayla looks at her and pouts. Afton's face goes apologetic and soft. "Please, babe?"

"Okay, last round! Let's go easy, players," Kayley, the love of my life, says. "It's just for fun, yes?"

"Says you," Parrish, resident knight in shining armor and team captain, replies with a smile. Kayley throws him a warning look, and he shrugs it off.

After yet another near-death situation on Canis Ludis, it's been great to just relax and play a few games of shinkoball on the makeshift court we built on the beach. It's almost a square deck, with the longer side running between the two teams. There's a net about head-high in the middle and a back wall on each side as tall as half the length of the court. We did a good job piecing it together with Teddy parts from their ship. I hope they didn't need any of them.

Afton and I are facing off against Nayla and Parrish, with Kayley as the judge. We've been rotating the teams, though this is by far the best matchup yet. For all her dislikes of things physical, Nayla is quite nimble. I've had to really stay on my toes just to keep the score even.

But now I'm ready to finish this round and take set advantage.

Nayla tosses the plastigraph ball just above her head and winds her arm back. When it drops to shoulder height, she swings and thwacks it over the net. I let out an exclamation. It's got some serious velocity to it.

"Let it go!" Afton shouts. She's right. I let it hit the back wall and bounce, then lob it over the net with only a little lift.

"Oh, shoot!" Parrish says, dashing up from the rear of the court. He just gets under it before it hits the ground.

It's Afton's turn now. She snarls and slams the ball with a loud pop. It shoots straight at Nayla's head. Nayla yelps and throws her racket up to protect her face. The ball bounces off it and hits the net, landing on the ground.

"Eleven–ten, ours!" I say and high-five Afton while Nayla attempts to cool her displeasure with inhales and exhales. She may not be royalty any longer, but she's still the queen of calm aura—even when she looks like she's ready to smash her racket over Afton's head.

"Well, someone's sleeping on the sofa tonight," Grady, our genius in residence, says.

"Yes, darling," Nayla says. "Perhaps some meditative insight might clear your spirit of such aggressive behavior. I expect the sofa would be a perfect place for such contemplation."

"Or maybe I should just give her team a one-point penalty for unkind play," Kayley adds, "and for announcing the score when that is the *judge's* job, Rance."

"Are you serious?" I say. "Just because I beat you last game doesn't mean you get to take it out on me!"

"I'm just adhering to the rules. Judges make the announcements, and may I remind you, you've got to get to nineteen before you win the round, so there's no reason for you to celebrate just yet."

"Oh, she's so totally pissed at you," Afton says with a smirk.

"Yep, looks like we're both stuck in the gravity well," I reply. "But I'm used to it."

"Hey, chill out, everyone," Grady says. "We left the conflict back on our last mission, right?"

Grady means our takedown of the notorious and former Bailiff Daughtry, who was dead set on sending our souls to a new realm, one where we could not meddle in her illicit affairs. Or anyone's. After our crisis on Canis Ludis, we tracked her down and brought her in to face justice.

"Yeah, about that," Afton says, moving into position to receive Parrish's serve. "We didn't even get a friendly letter, a thank-you card, or the *huge reward we deserve* for saving the Chamberlin from total failure!"

"You're not expecting one, are you?" Parrish asks as he tosses the ball, sending it whizzing across the net so quickly that Afton can only blink as it flies by her.

"Hey, I wasn't ready!" Afton moans.

"Thirteen to eleven! Parrish still serving," Kayley shouts, cutting off any further complaints. I really hate the part about this game where the serving team gets two points and the receiving can only get one. With Parrish pounding away like that, they're going to win this round with ease.

"The Chamberlin could at least thank us," I say as I ready myself for Parrish's onslaught. "It's not cool that he won't pay us just because we missed his arbitrary schedule. We risked our lives! Afton even got hurt!"

"Which is why you should go easy on me!" Afton says as she feigns agony by rubbing her side and putting on as pathetic of a look as she can. Only Nayla gives her any sympathy.

If Parrish was going to back off a little, his next serve doesn't hint at it. It's fast and hard, driving towards my rectangle of the court. I just get the tip of my racket on it. The ball spins sideways, curving in a graceful arc towards Nayla.

Who then pounds it into the ground on my side.

"Fifteen to eleven! Nayla to serve!"

"You know, KayKay, I think your score announcement has just a hint of joy behind it."

"Judges don't play favorites." Kayley waves a dismissive hand at me with one finger pointing up. Now I know she's lying. That's her telltale sign.

I slump my shoulders and take a moment to share my despair with Afton. She's right there with me but tries to keep her spirits up by offering me a low five. I'll take it since it's the only support I seem to be getting from anyone at the moment.

We should have pressed for that one million jorins, though I'd take anything, even some recognition. He could toss us some medals we could hustle off on some collector. At least then we'd have some funds for a nice dinner or something.

"Are you ready, soulmate?" Nayla asks, pressing the ball against her racket. "I promise to be as gentle with you as you were with me. It is the right way of things."

"Bring it, babe," Afton shoots back.

The ball flies. Afton catches it in midair and thwaps it back at Parrish. He returns it with a load of topspin. I dodge left and let the ball smack the back wall and bounce, then I drive it across the net, in between the two of them. Nayla and Parrish reach for it but can't get their rackets to it in time. The ball taps the back wall, then lands.

"Yeah! That's the way to do it!" Afton pumps her fist and raises her racket to the sky.

"Fifteen–twelve. Nayla still serves," Kayley mutters. I throw her a suspicious look. Her nonchalant shrug makes me open my mouth, ready to protest, but Afton pulls me into a huddle before I can speak.

"Listen, if we want to close this one up quickly, we've got to get more proactive like that last shot. No more of this passive stuff. Let's take more risks!"

I nod as I crouch. It's a solid strategy, and not just for shinkoball. We might be better off taking matters into our own hands if we want anyone to give us credit for all the hard work and sacrifices we've made. That won't be so easy. Few people know what we did, and telling more could backfire on us. The conspiracy could put us on their *new people to hate* list, and that could put us in more danger than we're already in.

"Heads up!" Afton shouts.

Nayla's serve comes right for me. I can only react to block it from hitting me. It's still enough to get the ball over the net. Parrish volleys it back over to Afton. She's got to reach wide to pat it back, putting the ball in a position where Nayla can smack it back at us.

Instead, Nayla lobs it high, aiming the ball over our heads. I push back, lifting off my feet and swinging hard. It works, but I'm still moving backward and only stop when I smash into the wall with a heavy thump.

"Easy, dude!" Grady cries. "The court isn't strong enough for that!"

"So *the court* is what you're worried about," I say. "Thanks, dude."

"Fifteen–thirteen," Kayley says. "Parrish to serve."

"Nice hustle! That's the way to nail the points!" Afton says, reaching out a hand to help me up.

Parrish rockets the next serve right down the sideline. I can't move anywhere near fast enough to return it. That's another pair of points for his team. Another serve like that and Afton and I lose the round, the set, and the game. Kayley would just love to see me lose, though I'd get payback by making her console me after.

Which makes me realize that the only way we're going to get paid or get anything is to demand it from the ones who can make it happen. Like the Chamberlin.

"I think we should contact the Chamberlin and tell him we want a reward," I say. "Doesn't matter what it is—money, authority, assistance. We deserve to have something."

"Now that's proactive," Afton says. "I vote we do it!"

"Let us not be hasty, darling," Nayla echoes. "Let me at least consult the oracles first."

"Let's discuss that later," Kayley says. "I would need to think about it. We can't just decide this on the spot."

"Yeah, serve already! I'm getting bored here," Grady says. "What's the score?"

"Seventeen–thirteen. Round point! Actually, set and game point, too."

"Okay, here we go!" Afton jogs in place and swings her torso back and forth to psych herself up. I don't think she needs it. Afton is already burning enough adrenaline for all of us. "Come on, Parry, do your worst. We're ready to take control of this round!"

Take control. That's exactly what Kayley did with my suggestion. She was too hasty to push the discussion off. There is no better time to talk about this than now, while we're all here. It's not like it will be a big debate. We just say what we think, and then, like always, we take a vote and—

"Rance, wake up!" Afton shouts.

Shoot, the ball is coming right at me!

I slip sideways and swing. The ball connects with my racket and flies towards Nayla. She panics, shutting her eyes and swatting at the ball, yet hitting it with amazing accuracy. It comes to Afton, who pounds it over to Parrish. He pulls his arm back and grits his teeth, ready to fire it back at us.

But instead of putting on the heat, Parrish just taps it. The ball lifts and arcs, heading towards the line. It might be out. Or it could still be in. Should I go after it? Should I let it just drop? This could be the last point. What do I do?

"Play it, play it!" Afton cries.

I go. But it's out of reach and getting lower. I've got to dive for it—it's the only way. I jump and stretch my arm out. Too far! All I can do is flick my wrist and hope it's enough.

Grady screams as I go airborne. I say a prayer to Durga as the ball contacts my racket. With a yell, I push at it, using all I've got.

Then my face meets the sand. I throw my arms out to stop from sliding. My body hits hard, the edge of the court digging into my shins. The air goes from my lungs. A flash of light hits my eyes.

"Whoa!" Parrish shouts.

Someone turns me over as I gasp for air. Kayley drops next to me, her hands coming to my face, to look me over. She relaxes when she sees me breathe again.

"Did I get the point?" I ask, looking up at everyone's faces. Afton presses her lips together. Grady rolls his eyes and looks away. Nayla raises an eyebrow. "Did I?"

"Nineteen–thirteen," Kayley says softly as she pats my cheek and smiles. "Round, set, and game to Parrish and Nayla."

I let out a sigh. I tried—and failed, of course, but I think the effort I put in was worth it. Still, it's just a game. We've got something else more important to do.

"Alright then. So back to the Chamberlin," I say. "I think the easiest way to—"

"Uh, no," Kayley says, putting her finger on my lips. "That's not happening now."

"Why not?"

"Because I'm the judge, the leader, and your girlfriend, and I say you need to relax for a moment after such a hard fall."

"After that, then."

"No." A smolder builds behind Kayley's eyes. "We are here to have fun, and that's what we are doing today. Leave it for another day."

"Why? We could get rich from this!"

"You're really pushing it," Kayley says, her voice going dark. I wonder why she's so against it, but I'm getting the vibe that this is not the place to discuss that, either.

"Come on, guys, back me up here!" I say to rally the others.

Afton, Parrish, and Grady walk away. They know better than to get involved. But Nayla stays for a moment, watching me. I give her a hopeful look, but she just shakes her head.

"Ransom Quigley He', you really wish to end your life early, don't you?" she asks, then turns to follow Afton.

"What did I do?"

Chapter Two

"See now? Isn't this better?" Kayley asks as she leans into me to feed me a piece of her sandwich. "Nothing but a pleasant breeze, good friends, and some tasty food. What do we need besides this?"

Kayley and I share a smile, and she leans her head on my shoulder while our rivals for cutest couple, Afton and Nayla, do a near mirror image of us. And so they won't be left out, Parrish offers a piece of his sandwich to Grady, who pretends to swoon and takes hold of Parrish's arm, clutching on to it like a mite to skin.

We left the court behind in favor of a shady row of palm trees that line the secluded cove known only to the locals. The people of our town refer to it as the Furatus Vault, because it kind of is, in a way. It's a place for the townspeople to lock away their precious natural habitat and keep it out of the destructive hands of tourists. It's rocky out by the water, so not a great place for water sports, but the cool breeze that comes in off the ocean and the quiet of the area make it one of the best places on the coast to relax.

"Yeah," I say with a relaxed sigh. "You're right. We haven't done something like this in a while. At least not together. And we have a new member of the gang to share this glorious moment with. I wouldn't trade this for anything, not even if the Chamberlin himself were to come here and beg us to help him again."

"Ransom He'?" a male voice asks.

When I look up, I see a young military officer staring down at me. A young Imperial officer. My first thought is to wonder how he found me. The next is about how he's wearing dress shoes in the sand. But what if...Yes! He's here to give us our reward!

Kayley clears her throat before I can get too excited. My shoulders slump then. There's no point ruining our pleasant moment with business from the Empire. I still have half a sandwich to finish.

"No." I wave him away with my hand. Yes, it's rude. It's also on purpose. "No, absolutely not. We're on break. No meetings."

The officer blinks, then stares. "Listen, I don't know what that's about, but I'm just here to deliver a telegram." He pulls an envelope from his bag and holds it out to me. It's made from actual paper and dressed up with several layers of elaborate design. I think the seal may even be made of gold. "From His Lordship, Chamberlin Tyrwhitt Sitwell Egerton, with his compliments."

It's my turn to stare. What happens if I accept it? What more Imperial entanglements do we get into?

As if to answer my unspoken question, the officer pushes it at me.

"You have to take it," the officer says. "Also, I'll need a DNA sample to prove I delivered it to the correct person."

I sigh and accept it from him, examining the seal closer. Even if I toss the letter, this little nugget might be worth enough to take the entire gang out for a fun evening. Maybe our parents, too.

"Ow!" I jump as a fire burns my arm. The cause of my pain is a needle that the officer drops into a small vial.

"Sorry. It's the only acceptable way." He shrugs. "Anyway, I've fulfilled my mission. Have a nice day."

I grumble, and Kayley glares at him as he leaves, then she consoles me by rubbing my stuck arm.

"What's that?" Afton asks, pointing at the envelope.

"Imperial correspondence," Nayla answers, her face turning sour. "It is likely not good news. I will check for a sign in the stars for the answer."

"Or you could just open it," Grady says.

"Or better yet, throw it out," Kayley says. "I agree with Nayla. It can't be good."

"Well, it won't be as bad as this," Afton says. She's looking past me to something behind my back. Nayla follows her gaze and frowns while Grady and Parrish attempt to hide their faces. I have no idea what's going on, but now I'm dying to know.

And regret it the second I turn to find out.

A man in a standard business suit and raincoat, wearing sunglasses and a permanently unhappy face, is walking up to us. My muscles tighten, and heat rises inside of me. Kayley must feel my tension, because she clasps my arm with both her hands, stopping me from taking any rash action.

"Mr. Cavalcante!" Grady yelps. There's good reason for his outburst. He wouldn't have expected to see the man responsible for the prosecution of his parents. The man who skirts the line between loyalist and conspirator with strange ease.

The man who can also be called my father.

"I know you," Nayla says, grabbing my father's attention away from me.

"Princess de Avila?" He takes his sunglasses off and squints at her. Afton moves in front of her, her face impassive. I don't think Afton will do anything stupid, but she's made it clear that Nayla is off limits.

"I am no longer known by that title, but yes, you have guessed correctly."

"I see." My father throws a glance in my direction before returning his attention to Nayla. "And now you're friends with my son?"

"Son?" It's Nayla's turn to blink. Her open-mouthed glance at me and my father is enough for me to know what a surprise it is for her to learn that.

"Why did I not foresee this?" she says to herself.

"What do you want?" I say, my voice pointed. There's no need for small talk. The sooner he says what he wants, the sooner he leaves. I rise to add to my show of annoyance.

"To have a chat with you, son."

He shrugs when I don't reply. If he wants me to go somewhere to talk with him, I'm not interested.

"Well, perhaps this is as good of a location as any," he says. "Your friends should join us as this concerns them, too."

The others stand along with me. For support, I think. Kayley slides her hand up my arm to give it a supportive squeeze as I stare at my would-be dad. My father has betrayed everything I believe in by pretending to make amends with me, then crushing any hope of that ever happening. He put Grady's parents in jail, not because he thought they were guilty, but because they were in the way of his ex-lover's ambitions.

"So here we are," I say, waving a hand around. "Talk so you can stop ruining my day."

My father opens his mouth, then shuts it as something catches his eye. Shoot—he sees the Chamberlin's envelope! I didn't even think about hiding it. Not that there was time.

He knows what it is, of course, which just adds to the unease of the moment. At least I can't tell him what's in it, even if he asks.

"From the Chamberlin?" my father asks, pointing to it.

"What if it is?"

He sighs. "This is the very thing that I wanted to warn you about."

"What do you mean, warn us?" Kayley asks.

"Bailiff Daughtry was a serious person for you to bring to justice. I'm impressed that you pulled it off."

"Well, she sent an assassin after us!" Grady yells.

My father startles and turns to Grady, eyes wide. So he didn't know. After his mention of the bailiff, I would have expected he knew everything we were up to. Perhaps his little spies have had some difficulty following me around.

"You aren't hurt." My father inspects us as he speaks. "I'm glad for that, but this is why I'm here. Bailiff Daughtry is not only a powerful figure in the Empire, she is very important to what you call the conspiracy. You and your friends here just took out one of their senior leaders, and they will want revenge."

"We can protect ourselves," I reply. It's not unexpected to hear this. If we made a serious dent in their organization, of course they'd want to get back at us. Fine. Let them try.

"I'm not so sure you can, Rance." He shakes his head. "This is a highly organized and dangerous group, and you've gotten their attention on more than one occasion. I'm not surprised to hear they've targeted you for assassination. You've got to back off, or they will find you, and their next attempt won't fail."

"They won't get a next attempt." But as I speak, a chill runs down my back. As selfish as my father is, he doesn't wish me dead. If he's warning me about this, he's got to be serious about it.

Still, that he's telling me at all is surprising. I haven't made things easy for him. I forced him to dump his girlfriend by threatening to get her arrested if he got in our way of helping Grady's parents. It wouldn't be much of a stretch for me to believe he's doing the same thing to me here, except this would be a threat of death, not of ruining my social status.

"Listen." He points a finger at me. "I'm going to give you some advice, and I suggest you take it."

"Why should I listen to anything you have to say?"

My father grits his teeth and exhales. That's my cocky comments and negative attitude having their effect. Good. He's welcome to leave anytime he wants.

"Rance, if you take the Chamberlin up on whatever offer he is giving you, I can almost guarantee you and your friends won't make it another two weeks! Is that what you want?"

"And if you keep making threats like that, you won't last another five minutes," Afton growls, taking a step towards him. "I stopped that assassin, and I can stop another."

"Darling, please," Nayla says, reaching out to her and drawing her back.

My forehead wrinkles. How does he know it's an offer? We haven't even opened the envelope yet.

"Take my advice," he says. "Before someone gets seriously hurt, publicly announce that you are ending your pursuit. If you do that, I promise I will do what I can to stop anyone from coming after you."

Well, that sounds sincere, at least. I don't doubt that he has enough connections inside the conspiracy that he can have some influence, and I believe he would do what he says. What his benefit is in all of it, I can't be sure. He could have some deal that's pending his ability to convince us to stop.

Now that would be more his style, and I don't care for it. I'm not happy for my buds and me to be pawns in whatever power play he's got going on behind the scenes.

A part of me worries that he's right, because he probably is. That's a risk we've got to consider, though I have no intention of doing that today. Or tomorrow. Danger of that kind is far away from my list of think-abouts for a long while.

"So, what do you say?" my father asks, watching me.

I look at him for a long time, not because I'm considering taking his advice, but because I want him to feel uneasy, just like he's made me feel for most of my life. I was good for a short time when Kayley and I became a couple, but when he took up the case against Grady's parents, he broke that peace. Now, despite our efforts, they're in jail for at least two more years. I hate him for that.

"I say you're full of it," I reply, to his frustration and my glee. "We already know we're in danger. Or were. We solved that problem with ease! If there's more like the bailiff, then that makes our work even easier. Let them find us. We'll toss them to the Chamberlin's guards, just like we did Yvonne Daughtry! There won't be any overthrowing of the Emperor! Not while we're on the job!"

"You're being a fool!" My father waves a finger in my face. "Quit your fantasy and listen to me! I can protect you!"

"No, thanks."

"Rance! You are going to die!"

"I think we've heard enough, Mr. Cavalcante," Kayley says, stepping in. "We appreciate the warning, but I think we're old enough to make our own decisions."

My father stares at her, shaking his head. He can't understand how he isn't the important part of this situation. How he doesn't get to save the day. It's just like when he left my mom and me in pursuit of his career. He thought everything would be alright. It might have been, had he returned to us. But he never did.

"I can't get through to you anymore!" He throws his hands up. "Fine! It's your life. End it if you want to so badly!"

And with that, he turns on his heel and stomps away.

"Sorry," I say to Kayley, but I really mean it to all my buds. She embraces me as I feel the pent-up tension draining from my body. I squeeze her and put my head on her shoulder.

"It's not your fault," Kayley says, soothing me. "He had no right to say that to us."

"No, he didn't. So let's forget he was even here and enjoy the rest of our day."

Everyone nods, and I smile, but it's forced. My father has ruined my day, no matter how much I'll try to push him and his warning out of my mind. I guess that's what it means to be cursed with a parent like that.

Chapter Three

With our enjoyment of the outdoors wrecked by my father, we head to the spaceport early to meet Doc Elizabeth and Original Teddy. Afton and Nayla decide not to join us. They want to get their afternoon meditation in, so they head back to Grady's parents' house, promising to meet us later for dinner at Wylde Thyme. I'm sure they just want some alone time. Kayley and I were the same way when we first started dating.

The spaceport is in a new phase of growth, which is good for Angelcanis, I suppose. They're constructing a new terminal and a new launchpad. That'll double the capacity of the port, which means more people coming to the planet. I'm not sure if that's such a great thing, especially if they're citizens of the Empire. We're better off without them.

We wait just outside the arrivals gate in the main hall of the terminal, which is just a gigantic dome with some box-shaped rooms dumped in the center that radiate out in a single line to the edges of the space. A few are two stories tall and almost as big as my house. It's impressive, but I wouldn't want to live here.

"Hey, you okay?" Kayley asks as she leans on me. I put my arm around her and give her a squeeze. She's likely wondering why I've been so quiet. Kayley knows, I'm sure. It's just her way of starting the conversation.

"Yeah, I'm fine," I say, with no attempt to sound convincing. I will be fine. I just don't want her to worry, even though I know she will. She's got enough on her mind, and I'll bet what my father said is on her mind, too. This is just not the place to discuss it.

Kayley knocks into me and glances over at Grady and Parrish, who seem to be sharing images of something. I'm a little envious because they're way excited about whatever they're looking at.

"Really, I will be," I repeat.

"Liar."

"I'm not. I just know that everything will be okay because you're here with me."

"Now that's the right way to lie to me." Kayley pivots to face me, grinning. Her hands slide up to grab my jacket, and she pulls me into a kiss. I'm not ready for it, so I make a few muffled sounds of surprise before I relax. We've shared plenty of smooch time, but now and then, Kayley catches me off guard, and it's like we just touched lips for the first time all over again.

I wrap my arms around her and pull her into an embrace. It's my way of showing my appreciation for her concern. Of course, I'm trying to comfort her, too, but she probably needs it less than I do. Kayley's always been stronger than me when it comes to emotional fortitude.

As we share the moment, I look out at the crowd of people waiting for passengers. Most are like us, idle, biding their time until their friends or loved ones arrive. It's always in these kinds of moments I find I get a lot of deep thinking done. I wonder if they're the same.

Except for that guy.

A man with short, spiky hair in a black jacket made of animal flesh stares at us. He's creepy on several levels, and I am very wary of creepy dudes, especially when they look at Kayley like they're about to gorge themselves on some piece of meat. It was bad enough when she first became famous, but now we can't even trust the lovesick stalkers to be harmless.

"What? Don't enjoy holding on to me anymore?" Kayley teases, feeling me tense.

"No, not that. There's someone watching us," I reply.

"Where?" Kayley spins, searching. I slide to the side, trying to get around her, but by the time I do, the man is gone.

"Not there," I say. "Not anymore."

Kayley shrugs, used to the leers and distasteful comments she's had to deal with. I don't know how she stays so calm when I'm about to freak out every time it happens.

"Hey, there's Elizabeth!" Grady says, standing up and waving at her. Parrish does, too.

Kayley and I turn to face the gate, searching for the obvious pair of blond hair and pink fuzz. It's not too long before I spot them. Doc Elizabeth is holding Teddy's tentacle as they walk. They spot us and wave back.

Then it happens.

Kayley screams, falling to her knees. I reach out to her, but someone rushes past, slamming into my shoulder. I spin and crash into a bystander. They grab me and keep me upright until I get my feet under me again.

"Kayley!" I drop next to her as the others crowd around.

Kayley's face warps in anguish as she presses a hand against her side. She's been stabbed! Blood seeps between her fingers as she tries to stop the flow. I search my jacket for anything that I can use to help, but Doc Elizabeth is already on it.

"Did you see who it was?" Grady asks me. "Did you see them?"

"No!" I shake my head. But then I remember something. A smell. A foul smell—animal skin. Like from a jacket. "Goddesses, it was that guy!"

"What guy?" Parrish asks as he scans the area.

"Go after him!" Grady shouts.

"No...Kayley!" I look between them.

"You're the only one who knows what he looks like!"

Shoot. I am. But I don't want to leave Kayley. That guy might come back and try something worse. Plus, the constables are going to show up, and they're going to want answers. Doc Elizabeth doesn't even have an ID card, and Grady's the son of convicted criminals.

"Go," Elizabeth says, pushing at me. "I've got her. Take Teddy with you."

Even with the push, I hesitate. Kayley got hurt, and I was standing right next to her. Was my father right? Can we not protect ourselves?

"Come on," Parrish says, grabbing my arm. "Let's get him before the authorities do."

We split up, Original Teddy with Grady while Parrish and I take the passageway that someone saw the man head down. I press forward with my legs flying under me, but my brain is still back with Kayley, worrying how serious her wound is. No good. If I can't focus, this guy is going to escape.

The passage turns into a bridge heading towards the exit that leads out to the street—and the taxi stand! We have to stop him before he gets one.

I pick up the pace, but my legs are already burning. Parrish is right beside me, not even puffing. I do a quick upload to Teddynet to give the others our location.

As we blast from the exit, my head darts to both sides, searching for any sign of a man wearing a dead animal on his back. If I find him, I will take my anger out on him every second before the constables show up.

There he is!

"Hey, you!" I shout, charging at him. I know he's got a knife, so I grab an unused post and raise it above my head, ready to do some damage.

The guy's eyes go wide. Then he digs into his jacket.

In a flash, his hand comes up. In it is a gun, small but no less deadly. Now it's my turn to panic.

I step back into a defensive posture, dropping the post back on the ground, but there's little I can do if he shoots. My hands can't block bullets or plasma bolts, and as fast as Parrish is, he can't stop the man from firing.

"Stay back, or he gets it!" The guy keeps his eyes on me, but he's talking to Parrish.

Parrish tenses, ready to jump if he has to. His eyes dart back and forth, searching for an opportunity to tackle the man and take him down. Maybe if the Goddesses aren't bored with helping me yet, they might find a reason to save me.

Forever is not as long as the time I wait for him to make a move. He's got the advantage, and he knows it. The sneer across his face tells me all I need to understand.

"Thought you had me, didn't you?" the guy says, pushing the pistol into my face. "Well, the shoe's on the other foot now, isn't it?"

"That's got to be uncomfortable," I say, shaking my head at him.

"Think you're funny? How about a big hole in your head?" He snickers. "That'd be funny, now wouldn't it?"

I swallow hard and press back against the doors. I wasn't trying to make a joke. It just came out that way.

Parrish slides forward, and the man swings his gun towards him, backing away from my reach. His eyes narrow, and I hope that means he realizes his advantage is slipping. He won't be able to track the both of us at the same time.

"You'll get yours soon enough," he says and whips me across the face with the butt of his gun. My head snaps back, and I crash into the door and tumble through it. He bursts through the next one and races back down the corridor towards the terminal.

Parrish is picking me up in a second. I shake him off, adrenaline racing through my veins.

"What are you doing?" I shout. "We've got to go after him!"

He just stares, and the longer we delay, the heavier my body gets as I watch our opportunity to capture him slip away.

Chapter Four

I TAKE OFF WITH Parrish calling after me. I can't wait. That swipe across my face took a lot out of me, and he's nearing the end of the bridge. But I've still got some reserve. Plus, he's trapped in the corridor until he gets to the other end. We can still capture him before he gets lost in the crowd.

"Rance, hold up!" Parrish calls again. His shout catches the attention of the guy. A few shots from his pistol force us to drop. Security is going to hear that. If they capture him instead of us, we still lose the chance to get our payback.

Parrish catches up with me as I jump to my feet. The guy is through the doors, but he goes for a maintenance door rather than into the mass of people. I send an update through to Teddynet and race after him.

The maintenance door leads to a luggage routing system. The room is a complex of snaking conveyor belts and automated trailers. They're crossing the space at an accelerated speed, making it dangerous for humans to be here.

He sure picked a great place to get hurt.

A shot glances off the belt above our heads, sending sparks down on top of us. We bolt from under the conveyor, only to be fired at again. Fine. Let him keep shooting and waste his ammo.

The guy is just ahead, attempting to weave his way through the trailers. He's not doing well. One wrong move and—

Bang! The guy cries out, dropping to the ground as an auto trailer smacks him from behind. He's fast enough to pull himself out of the way before he gets run over.

"Let's go!" I shout and charge after him.

But before I take two steps, Parrish grabs my shoulder and pulls me back.

"Dude, wait!" Parrish says. "He's still got a gun!"

"I know, but he's down! This is our chance. He can't have many bullets left. I'll go one way, and you go the other."

"All he needs is one to kill you."

"He won't hit me." I turn to run, but Parrish keeps a firm grip on me.

"Are you willing to bet your life on that?" he asks, looking me in the eye.

I just stare back, shaking my head at him with my mouth open. We've been in plenty of situations like this. The risk of getting hurt, or worse, has always been there. I don't get why he's so cautious.

"He hurt Kayley," I say, trying to keep calm. "You know better than anyone what that means to me. This guy is not getting away."

Parrish presses his lips together and glances at the guy, then looks back at me. He breathes out, then nods. "But let's keep to cover until Teddy gets here."

I frown. "How do you know he's coming?"

"Because I know you." Parrish pats my arm and spins to watch the auto trailers. A second later, he's off, with me right behind him. I'm fatigued, but I try to keep up. For Kayley's sake, I won't mess this up. This guy is going to feel just how wrong he was to hurt her.

He's going to feel it badly.

We match the speed of a trailer running parallel to our target, keeping down and out of sight. No matter how many bullets he has left, he can't hit what he can't see.

Parrish is right. Original Teddy and Grady are headed our way. I can't tell where they are, but I know they'll be here soon. We've just got to keep this guy from escaping until then.

The trailer makes a turn. We jump, just making it to the next one before our cover slips away, but this one is heading past the spot where I saw the guy. I tap Parrish and point, motioning to where we need to be. He gives me a thumbs-up and scans for the next trailer.

One's coming, but it's far. We're going to lose this one before we can get to that one. That means we'd be in the open for as long as we take to run from here to there. It might be too long. Still, if we want to catch this guy, we've got to do this.

"Hold up," Parrish says. "There's no way we make it there now. Wait."

"We can't wait!"

A shot fires, ricocheting off the other side of the trailer. Dummy! I should keep my voice down. Not that it matters now that he's heard me. We've got to wait now, but not for long. I'm going the moment I think it's right. It still could be wrong, but I won't know until it's too late.

"Not yet," Parrish says.

"Yes yet."

"Dude, it's still too far. Even I can't make that."

I'm no match for Parrish in a sprint, or any kind of race. If he doesn't think he can, then there's no way I will. But then a vision of Kayley in pain crosses through my head.

"I'm going," I say and take off. I won't wait anymore, not while this guy has a chance to get away.

Two shots come from the side. The first one skips off the floor. The second—

A fire drags across the back of my arm just as I dive behind the next trailer. It stings something bad. I touch the area and jerk my hand back. The tips of my fingers are red, but I think I may have gotten off easy. The bullet must have just scraped me. Still, I'll need to stop the bleeding.

Parrish makes it with no shots fired after him. Either the guy is out or he was reloading while Parrish made his move. I'm thankful either way.

"He got me," I say, showing Parrish my arm. His eyes go wide, so I elaborate. "Not bad."

He grabs his shirt and tears a piece off, wrapping it around my arm as I wince.

"You rang?" Original Teddy says, dropping from the conveyor belt above us. I high-five his tentacle as he settles in behind the trailer with us. The unit has stopped for the moment, which is fine. We need to figure out our next steps.

"Where's Grady?" Parrish asks. I point towards the back of the room, but he frowns and shakes his head.

"He's blocking the door that goes out to the launchpads," I explain.

"And what does he expect to do, trip the guy?"

"He's just there as a deterrent. We'll have this guy popsicled in no time. Or Teddy will, anyway."

"And how are we going to coordinate with him now that Teddy is with us?"

"Don't worry about it. We won't have to."

Parrish sighs. I get his frustration. He doesn't have Teddynet or built-in Teddy comm like I do. To him, there's no plan, because we haven't discussed one. To be fair, I'm the one who hasn't told him yet.

"Why don't we just hold here and wait for the authorities?" he asks.

"Dude, no! We've almost got him!" I put my hand on his arm. "Just trust me, okay?"

"Trust you to do what? Get shot again?"

"I didn't get shot."

"Rance, your arm is bleeding!"

It's my turn to sigh. Of course he has a point. I can't let that stop us, not when we're so close to getting this guy. We just need a quick distraction, which I need to explain to Parrish that he will be taking part in, and then Original Teddy surprises him from above with a popsicle attack. It couldn't be easier.

So maybe I should explain it to him, then.

"Let me get this straight," Parrish says once I'm done. "A distraction in your mind is running back and forth to the other trailer while that guy takes shots at us until Teddy gets into position?"

"Yeah, that's pretty much it."

"Dude, that's insane."

"Do you have a better idea?"

"Yes! We *wait for the authorities* like I said we should."

"Believe in me. I know what I'm doing. I've got this all figured out. Just follow my lead."

"No offense, Rance, but you're not the leader Kayley is."

I feign a pout at him and signal Original Teddy to get moving once I run. He gives me a tentacle salute, then lifts off into the conveyor system. I nod to myself and inhale, suddenly getting this sense that I don't know what I'm doing. Maybe I'm going to screw this up and get myself killed.

No, I've got to shake that off. If I can take down one of the top leaders in the conspiracy, then this guy should be a simple task.

Right?

"You go first," I say to Parrish.

"No," he replies and points to himself. "If *I* go first, he'll be ready for you, and your slower pace will be easy for him to hit. You go first."

I consider that for a moment—more like a second—before I realize Parrish is right. I bite the corner of my lip, trying to not freak out and lose all my confidence.

"Okay, I'll go first," I say.

My mind races as I peek around the edge of the trailer, scanning for the guy. He's there, straight ahead, about fifty paces away. I can't see his condition, because, like us, he's hidden. Somewhat. His feet are sticking out, and one of them hangs at a strange angle. Is it broken? That would be ideal. We'd almost be guaranteed to get him then.

Without warning, our trailer moves, heading in the wrong direction. Parrish yelps and shoves me forward. I take off just as the guy pops his head over the edge of a conveyor and spots me.

Bullets fly, pinging off any nearby solid object while bits of graphcrete and metal spray forth. They pelt me like a swarm of angry bees as I barrel towards the closest place to take cover. I can't tell if Parrish followed me or not, and I'm not about to stop and look back. I'm already more of a target than I want to be.

No bullet holes in me—good. Now to see about Original Teddy. I upload an image of a popsicle. A second later, I get an image of a human hand doing a thumbs-up. Good. Teddy is ready.

I search for a sign of pink fuzz on the conveyor system, but I see nothing. I know he's there, just not where. He should be able to see the guy from wherever he is. I hope.

Time to make myself a distraction again.

A second later, I'm racing towards the next stationary trailer. It's closer to the guy. That's risky, but I've got to make sure Original Teddy's got a good bearing on the man.

Three shots impact a trailer right where I was two seconds ago. One bullet bounces and shoots right past my face. I drop to a slide, praying I've got inertia to make it all the way to safety.

I've got eyes on the guy now. He's leaning against a wall, closer to me than I want him to be. I've got to risk calling Teddy on comm to give him the go-ahead. The guy'll hear me, but he already knows where I am.

Oh...and he's coming towards me.

"Teddy! Popsicle now!" I shout so loud I don't need the comm.

A pair of bullets fly over the trailer. I peer under the unit and see a pair of feet, one dragging behind the other.

"Teddy, where are you?" I cry. Two more shots are the reply. I jerk my head up, scanning for Original Teddy. Found him! He's in the conveyor system.

On the opposite side of the room. Near a refrigerator box.

That's when I consider I might have really screwed this one up.

Doors bang open. Constables pour in from every direction. They're armed and armored as much as any soldier, and they look like they want to take someone's head off. The moment they spot me and the guy, they swarm towards us, shouting.

"Drop it!"

"Hands up!"

"Do it now!"

Not wanting my head taken off, I do as ordered. The guy must, too, since the constables lower their weapons. He's the property of the law now, and with all the surveillance cameras in the spaceport, they'll have the evidence to throw the guy in jail for a long time.

Which means we don't get to ask him anything. Or get my revenge.

I sigh and drop my arms once the constables allow it. My thoughts turn to Kayley. Doc Elizabeth is with her, so I know she's getting the best care, but she's hurt, and I was helpless to do anything about it. That can't ever happen again. Not to the love of my life. I couldn't bear to see her hurt again.

That's it. Starting now, I'm going to make sure Kayley is well protected—as soon as I can come up with an idea of how to do that.

Chapter Five

"WHY ARE YOU LOOKING at me like that?" Kayley asks as she lies in bed—her actual bed in her actual home. We're never here. Almost never. That's because it's a lonely place. Kayley's parents are never home. Just like Grady's parents—before their incarceration—their lives revolve around their work, except for weekends. Then the place is as packed as a convention hall, full of everyone who either cares about them or wants something from them. That's why Kayley spends so much time at my place. Well, that, and t he food.

Since the last time I was here, she's redecorated. The canopy bed has transformed into a low-slung affair with muted tones replacing the bright pinks and blues that Kayley likes. All the pillows are still super fluffy, and she's kept one stuffed animal, which sits on the night table on the left. I'm disappointed that I don't find the body pillow with my image on it anywhere. I'd ask if I wasn't afraid to hear the answer.

Other than that, there's a long desk that stretches along the wall with her laptop, a light, and not much more. All the posters have come off the walls in favor of a few choice abstracts of nature and a framed photograph of her parents that sits next to the stuffed animal.

"Like what?" I reply.

"Like you think I'm about to die?"

"I do not!" I reply, but I know my face just gave away my total unease about her condition. Doc Elizabeth said there was nothing to worry about, that the stab wound wasn't that deep, and she removed any chance of infection. Still, Kayley is here, recovering, and I can't help but feel a lot of guilt for that.

"You are a totally bad liar. You know that, right?" Kayley says, tilting her head.

"Yeah." I sigh, my shoulders slumping. "But doesn't it bother you to see someone you love hurt?"

"So…" A small smile appears on her lips. "Does that mean you love me?"

"You know I do."

"Good. Just checking."

"But KayKay." I kneel next to her and take her hand. "This is something that could have been avoided. You're more of a target than the rest of us, just because people know who you are. We need to get you more protection, or else it could happen again."

"I know what the risks are." Kayley gets serious then. "But that won't stop me from doing what's right."

"Still, we should get you a bodyguard. Maybe two."

Kayley frowns at me as her head dips. "No, I don't want bodyguards."

That's Kayley's way of saying there's no more to discuss. But I've got more to say, even if that means she gets a little annoyed with me. I just need to approach this with a bit more of a delicate touch than I have been. I had to put my heart out there first so she understood this really bothered me. Now I can make every attempt to have this conversation without having this conversation.

Of course, Kayley is way better at that sort of thing than I am. And she'll likely know when I try to do it to her. I can hope and pray to the Goddesses that she's got too much painkiller in her system to be really on point, but that is just fantasy. Kayley could outdebate me in her sleep.

"So how do you feel?" I ask, going for the roundabout approach.

"You just asked me that," Kayley replies.

"Did you answer me?"

"Do I need to?"

This is what I mean. Her ability to talk circles around me is second nature to her. I'm fighting against every reality that I can imagine. If Afton was here, she'd back me up, but she's got different priorities these days. I can't blame her—I remember what it was like to fall in love for the first time. That's because I'm still in the middle of doing it.

"I'm just worried about you, KayKay," I say and give her my best cute little innocent animal look.

"*That*, you can keep saying," she replies, patting the bed next to her. I don't wait for a second invitation. I was concerned about getting too close to her because of her wound, but if she's asking, there's no reason to hesitate. Plus, Doc Elizabeth isn't here. That means she can't yell at me for doing it, and it also means that Kayley is healthy enough to leave her in my c are.

Kayley leans into me, tilting her head to rest it on my shoulder. She loves being like this, and I'm more than happy to let her. As much as she gets from doing it, I get back. We've got some kind of mutual sharing thing going on, and I will never say no to being near her.

"I want to protect you, KayKay," I say, keeping my voice soft.

"You do."

"Maybe, but I don't feel that. I just want to make sure you never get hurt again."

"You can't ensure that." Kayley rubs my arm. "We take too many risks."

"I can. At least I think I can. And I haven't even tried yet. I've got some ideas that I think might work."

"Like what, bodyguards?"

"Sure, like bodyguards."

"You remember I just said no to that idea, don't you?"

I nod, remembering with all clarity. That was what made me want to press this conversation in the first place. Just because she's refusing to accept the idea doesn't mean it's wrong. I still have to convince Kayley of that fact, but at least I believe I'm on the side of right in this conversation. The others will back me up, too. I think.

I also know that right means nothing when it comes to Kayley. She'll bend things to fit her beliefs, and she's often not wrong in doing it. It's a personal trait I wish I had. It's also why she's the boss and the leader of us. Kayley's willing to make the decisions the rest of us try to avoid.

It also makes my job of convincing her to listen to me all that much more difficult, because when I do, Kayley thinks I'm not listening to her. She gets annoyed with me, and I have to go on the defensive. It's not her fault. I'm just an idiot for not being able to explain what I mean.

Now, I could just drop the subject and let her do whatever she wants, but that would be hard for me to do. I love her way too much to just forget that some random dude was able to sneak up on the four of us and stab her. What if he'd used his gun instead? I'd be at her funeral instead of here talking with her.

I need to push this. For Kayley's sake.

"KayKay," I say, squeezing her hand. "You'd never want anything to happen to me, right?"

"Of course," she replies. "And may I remind you plenty has happened to you already. So I'm sure you know how much I worried about you then."

"I do, and I'm sorry about putting you through that."

"Well, now that you know how it feels, I hope you'll be a bit more understanding of my orders."

"What do you mean?"

Kayley sighs. "It's not easy being the leader. Especially of you. I've got to make decisions that can affect everyone, and no one but me can take responsibility for that. All of you look to me to make the hard choices, and I'm willing, but if one of my orders puts you in trouble or gets you hurt, I feel that. I really feel that.

"And you"—Kayley knocks her head on mine in a way of expressing her frustration with me—"don't listen. You think you know better—"

"That's not true!" I interject, but she just glares at me.

"Rance, the others watch what you do, and if you're defying me, they notice. That really makes it hard on me when I'm trying to keep us focused, and I'm tired of that. I don't want to fight with you to get things to happen the right way. You always promise to follow what I say, and then you still do what you want. I don't want to do that anymore. It's getting in the way of us having a good relationship, and if I have to choose, then I say I'm done with it."

Wait, what does she mean by that? Does Kayley want to break up with me?

"KayKay, give me one more chance. Please? I'm not ready for this. All I wanted was to see you safe. I didn't think things were this bad between us. Were you holding this in all this time? I'm sorry, Kayley, I had no idea. Can you reconsider?"

Kayley's forehead collapses into a sea of wrinkles as she lifts her head up to stare at me. I'm not sure what else I need to do to get her to forgive me. I'll get down on my knees if I have to. In fact, I should do it now.

"Rance." Kayley holds me from moving with her arm locked about mine. Her hand shoots out, grabbing my chin and turning it towards her.

I stare, ready and not ready to hear the confirmation that will end our romantic relationship.

"What in the Goddesses' holy names are you talking about?"

"Aren't you breaking up with me?"

If I had a camera, I could record the steam coming out of Kayley's ears. I suppose that response is both good and bad for me.

"That's what you think? That I'm dumping you because I'm exhausted of your nonsense?" She closes her eyes and shakes her head. "You really are the biggest idiot in the entire Empire, aren't you?"

"Well, maybe."

"Do you really think I'm giving up on us?"

I'm not even sure anymore. Kayley's got me so confused that I can only hope what I think is all wrong. It usually is when it comes to her.

"All I want to do is protect you, KayKay," I say.

She smiles then, bringing her hand up to touch my cheek. Then she leans in and plants a kiss on my lips. Now I'm even more lost.

"And that's all I want to do for you," Kayley says, looking into my eyes.

I lose my words. I always do when I get lost in her gaze. It's like I'm seeing her for the first time every time I do. I could want for nothing else for the rest of eternity and still be happy. And that is all I want—to have the chance to look at her forever and know that she's safe. That she's okay. And that I've done everything I can to make that happen.

"Please, KayKay," I say. "Let me do this for you. I know you don't want it, and I know you think I'm trying to go against you, but I can't live another day knowing you're not safe."

Kayley's smile gets wider. She kisses me again, holding my face in her hands.

"You're cute when you try to beg, you know that?" Her face goes stiff then. "I know what the risks are, Rance. I know what I've gotten myself into, and so far, it's all been worth it. If we could someday stop this conspiracy, then even a little hurt is acceptable. You, of all people, should know that."

"I'm not the only one who's been hurt. Parrish destroyed his leg. Grady had his parents taken away from him—"

"And you have been to jail, gotten beaten up more than once, and sacrificed so many other things for us and for the Empire that you don't even see it anymore. All I'm asking from you is to understand that I worry about you as much as you do me, and that's why I ask you to follow my orders. They're to keep you safe, not stop you from achieving your goals. They're my goals, too!"

She did it, all right. Kayley spun the conversation around me so fast I thought I was losing her. I'm glad, extremely glad, it wasn't that, but any point I wanted to make is gone now, and all I want is to know is that we will be together until the end of the universe.

"So...no protection, then?" I ask, my voice full of uncertainty.

"I already have all the protection I need." Kayley kisses my nose and flicks it with her finger, and all I can do is smile and be happy that we are still together.

And then I realize I must do everything I can to keep us that way.

Chapter Six

After a day or two, Kayley is feeling better, so much so that she is bugging me to take her outside. We go for a walk to Grady's house to get some exercise and see the others. Parrish says he'll meet us there, which means it's going to be a full team meeting.

Not that we have much to meet about. It'll be more of a hang, which I'm just fine with. No stress, no parents weighing us down with talk of someone wanting to hurt us, and no one actively trying to hurt us. It's bad enough that I keep looking over my shoulder while clinging to Kayley as we walk. She doesn't mind; she says she feels a chill. It's never cold in our town, however. I make a note to ask Doc Elizabeth to check on her when we arrived.

"Hey, dude and dudette. Welcome," Grady says as he opens the door.

We step into the foyer, confused smiles on our faces. *Dude* is a definite term of endearment used by Grady, but *dudette* is a new one. I suppose the joyful surprise on Kayley's face is a sign that she likes the new label.

Grady escorts us into the front living room, with its two long sofas, matching coffee table, and large window that lets the morning sun illuminate the space with a glorious golden beam of light. Afton, Nayla, and Doc Elizabeth are already there, and they've prepared a comfy section of the back sofa for Kayley to relax on.

As I lead her to the spot, a sparkle from the coffee table catches my eye. The Chamberlin's letter. Right. I had forgotten all about it. But now, as I gaze at it, my curiosity grows by astronomical values. We've got to open it, if for no other reason than to read what it says.

"Did you guys read it?" I ask as a way of starting the conversation.

"Huh?" Afton follows my look and spots it. "Oh, that. No, why? Is your desire for self-abuse that high today?"

"You're not even curious what's in it?" Kayley asks as she settles into her nest between Doc Elizabeth and Nayla. She winces when she sits but holds me up from helping her with a lift of her hand.

"Some things are better left unopened," Nayla says. "However, if you must know, I will draw three cards to see if there are any portents. This is the safest way. Anything else will be trouble."

"Or, as I said last time, you could just open it," Grady says.

Nayla sighs, rolling her eyes up to look at me with an expectant gaze. That means I get to decide. Great. Just what I want to do.

Afton might be right. I may be itching for some bad news. Or I can think positively and believe it could be the best possible thing to ever happen to u s.

Nah, probably not, but I can't just leave it be now. I need to know.

"Let's open it," I say with an apologetic smile to Nayla. "If we're going to roll the dice, it's better just to get it over with."

I slide my finger under the seal to pry the envelope open. If it's official correspondence from the Chamberlin, it's likely not all that bad. Even if he's only telling us how dissatisfied he is that we've failed to complete his Canis Ludis mission, nothing will come of it. Something would already have happened if that were the case.

"Ouch!" I pull my hand back from the seal as the envelope's paper edge slices the side of my finger. It stings worse than the Imperial officer's arbitrary gene sample.

"I told you, Ransom Quigley He'. You will only get trouble from opening it," Nayla says. "One day, you might decide to listen to me."

Grady holds his hand out and shakes it, motioning for me to hand him the envelope. I'm glad to get rid of it. It's caused me more pain in half a minute's time than any conspirator ever has.

"So what does it say? Anything about money?" I ask.

"Hold on, it's kind of difficult to read. The Chamberlin writes the same way he talks—in riddles," Grady says, glancing over the telegram. As he reads, his forehead grows more and more wrinkled. "Well, so far, he congratulates us for rooting out a traitor in his office, says some stuff about us being the core of the Empire, and then compares the core of an apple to the fruit of our youth, whatever that means."

"So not so bad," Kayley says. "At least he's not threatening to take our heads off."

"But no money," I add.

"Wait!" Nayla's hand shoots up. "There is more."

I look at Grady for an answer. He nods.

"He's...I think he's offering us...or maybe ordering us...to capture the rest of the conspirators," he says. "Apparently, there's a meeting of their big bosses somewhere on Herdewyke."

"Great," Afton mutters. "I hope he's willing to pay like a *trillion* jorins for a job like that."

I give Kayley a hopeful smile as Grady reads on. This could be what we've been waiting for.

"No...no pay," Grady says, "but he'll clear our records and write recommendation letters for anything we want."

"Anything?" I snatch the letter back from him to reread it because I can't believe that the Chamberlin would do anything other than pontificate about how great the Emperor is and that we should just do all of this as an honor for him, even though we're not, nor have any interest in becoming, citizens.

I want the conspiracy gone, though. All they're doing is creating an unstable situation, where one of the Central Planets gets cocky and decides that they should be the ones running the show. Then we've got a galactic civil war on our hands.

What's more enticing is the idea that with a letter from the second most powerful human in the Empire, we'd have a free pass to do whatever we want. Not only could Kayley have real time to address Parliament, she could scold them like the little children they are, and they'd have to sit there and take it. Grady could get his parents out of jail, and Parrish could get his mom into the best hospital on Albion. My mom could quit her job and not only spend her days gardening, she could be the head of any garden in the Empire!

Now, I'd be stupid to think that this isn't a massive trap. First, it would be a major undertaking to uncover and arrest all the conspirators. It could take us years to get them all, not to mention the angry reaction these people have had to our attempts to snatch them up. The knife attack on Kayley is just another sign of that. It's a miracle that none of us are dead or permanently wounded.

Which makes me wonder if my father was telling the truth about the threat against us. I got the vibe that he was, and this only supports that feeling. The conclusions I draw from that are not anything I am happy with. If we do this, we better be really careful.

"We're not going to do this, right?" Grady asks. "Let's just melt that seal down and go spend a weekend on Littus. The Empire can solve its own problems. They already know where to go."

"Wouldn't you want your parents to be home?" Afton asks. "You could have that with a letter from the Chamberlin."

"Littus sounds like a better idea," Nayla says, sliding her hand into Afton's. "I do not wish my soulmate to experience any more pain."

"That makes two of us," Afton replies.

"Yeah," Grady says, "I didn't get to go to Littus last time. I'd totally be down for a weekend trip."

Grady pokes me when I don't reply to his question. Then he glares when I remain silent. My mind isn't on planet-long beaches and endless sunshine. I'm thinking of an ambition I once shared with my father, and I'm thinking how I could achieve that with an all-access pass, direct from the Chamberlin's hands. But more important that any of that, I'm envisioning how all my buds get to live a life they can only dream of.

We can have a pleasant weekend, or we can sacrifice a little and really achieve our goals. Really get down to work and create an Empire that everyone, citizen and non-citizen alike, can benefit from. Sure, there will be trouble. My father is right about that. I just don't know to what degree.

"What do you think, KayKay?"

"I think..." Kayley presses her lips together and leans her head against one of the extra pillows by her side, her eyes half-closed. Our trip here took a lot out of her. Now that I see that, I regret making her walk all that way. She was happy to do it, but I have a feeling she was pushing herself more than she knew. "I think I need a nap."

"How about you, Ransom Quigley He'?" Nayla asks. "What is your wish?"

"I really wish you would just call me Rance," I reply. "We don't call you princess anymore, even though I wouldn't mind it. Could you try it, at least?"

"Very well," Nayla says, though she looks like she's got ants crawling up her back. "I will attempt it, though I relate the shortening of your name to limiting your potential."

"That's not what she meant," Afton says. "She's asking about your opinion of the Chamberlin's offer."

"Yeah, I got that much."

"Then...Rance." Nayla says my name as if it's caught in her throat. "Share with us your opinion."

I look to my two old friends and my one new one, and my heart fills with the desire to see them more than happy. I want to see them fulfilled and loving life so much they have not even a single worry in their heads.

I would do anything to achieve that.

"I think we need to make a solid plan about how we answer this call. Forget the Chamberlin. It's the people of the Empire who need a future that they can look forward to. If the conspiracy gets stronger, then we're all in trouble. It doesn't matter if we're citizens or not."

"Stop trying to be a hero, dude," Grady says. "Yeah, I want my parents out of jail, but there are safer ways to do that than poking a nest of traitors."

"I don't care about being safe. I want to be happy, I want Kayley to be happy, and I want all of you to be happy, too."

"I'm happy," Afton says and rubs her head against Nayla, who smiles at her and snuggles her back. "But I get your point. We won't be worry-free until this conspiracy thing is done. There could still be an assassin out there searching for us, and I don't want to keep looking over my shoulder. I'm down for it."

"I will go where you go, darling," Nayla says. "In this life, our destinies have become one."

Everyone's eyes fall on Kayley, who's staring at me with thoughtful eyes. Now I'm feeling nervous about what I said and wondering what she thinks about it. Maybe I went too big with my grand plan and she's about to crush it down to a much smaller size. I'm praying she doesn't, though.

"Rance, we just talked about this," Kayley says, frowning. "You might not care about being safe, but I want you safe. I want you to have a future, too. A happy one. You deserve it." A small twinkle appears in her eyes before she says, "Of course, I'm hoping I'm a part of it, too."

"I want a future with you, too, KayKay," I say, the words bursting from my lips. I couldn't get them out faster, but if that's her confirmation of our engagement, well, I already knew that. Still, it's great to hear it again. "And I want you to be safe, so if this scares you, I'll understand. Just tell us what you want us to do, and we'll do it."

"No." Kayley shakes her head. "This is for everyone to decide on their own. It's your future, not mine."

"No, KayKay." I smile. "It's *our* future."

Grady rolls his eyes, but Doc Elizabeth gets teary and rubs at her eyes. What she's upset about, I don't know. Maybe they're tears of joy. Again, from what, I'm clueless.

"You already heard our choice," Afton says to me. Then she looks at Grady. "What are you going to do, dudette?"

Grady glares at her, but he looks resigned to agree with the rest of us. A solemn nod from him confirms it. Out of all of us, he's the one that had the biggest and most recent scare. The assassin got him bad, and we almost lost him forever. I can't blame him for being reluctant to jump back into any dangerous situation.

There's a knock at the door, then Parrish opens it and comes in. When he sees our faces, his grin disappears and his forehead wrinkles.

"What did I miss?" Parrish asks.

"Nothing yet," I say, raising my arm to welcome him in. "In fact, you've arrived just in time for your future."

Chapter Seven

Kayley and I walk arm in arm, headed to my house, with Nayla and Afton in tow. They are just tagging along with us until we get there, then they're going to sit at this pond that Nayla saw the other day. She believes there might be some spirits there in need of direction, so she's thinking of doing a séance to commune with them.

Their company is welcome, as Kayley keeps to herself as we walk. Maybe she's just in a food coma after a round of Parrish's amazing chef skills. I'm feeling it, too. That third helping probably did us in. I offered to get a taxi, but Kayley insisted on getting some physical exercise to help our digestion.

"Do you think they will find anything?" Nayla asks, meaning Parrish and Grady, who stayed back to look into this alleged meeting on Herdewyke that all the conspiracy bigwigs would be attending. I figured if we could capture all of them, that would take the head off the monster and achieve the Chamberlin's mission in one shot.

"Of course they'll find something. It's not just Grady that's on it. He's got the Teddys and whatever stuff Colonel Cortell can offer us."

"Colonel Cortell? The one who single-handedly stopped the war between the humans and the...what did you call them?"

"Teddys."

"Yes. Your little friends. They have been so very helpful, have they not?"

I couldn't agree more. Without them, we wouldn't have accomplished even half of what we have. Plus, their technology has been a literal time-saver. If we had to travel around the Empire with human tech, we'd all be a few years older already.

I'll let Afton correct her girlfriend about who actually stopped the war—or not. It's not all that important to me that she knows the truth. Besides, Colonel, then Sergeant, Cortell is on our team, so it's kind of accurate to say he was responsible. Just not solely responsible.

"What do you think, KayKay?" I ask.

I frown as I notice her bow her head. Her hair falls over the side of her face, blocking sight of any emotion she might be feeling. She's leaning on me heavier than usual, so she must be tired. I stop and turn her towards me.

"Hey." I keep my voice gentle as I rub her arms. "Let's get you a taxi, huh?"

After a moment, she lifts her head and gives me a smile. It's a little forced, but the remainder is sincere.

"No, it's okay," Kayley says, squeezing my arm back. "We're almost there, right?"

Afton and Nayla are giving me dubious looks behind Kayley's back. I know they'd prefer we get her off her feet. But Kayley is right. It's not far now. Just a few more blocks and she can rest in the guest bed for as long as she wants. My mom will cook her anything she requests, too.

I smile back and nod, so she takes my hand and pulls me along, doing a small hop before continuing down the graphcrete sidewalk. Afton shrugs and takes Nayla's hand to follow along. I think the three of us are of the same mind: allow Kayley to do what she wants and stop her just short of her hurting herself.

Then Kayley falls.

I don't see it happen. Her foot must have caught on something. All I feel is her hand slip from mine, and then she yelps. Kayley tries to laugh it off as she turns to us, a look on her face that is half embarrassment and half distress.

"KayKay!" I'm down and next to her before she can refuse me. Afton is too, a worry in her eyes that is unusual for her normally disaffected look.

"I'm fine, I'm fine! I don't need to be treated like a child," Kayley replies.

Yet, as she says it, her hand presses on her side, right where the guy stabbed her, and her expression devolves into agony.

"I shall request a taxi," Nayla says, pulling her Sergo out from her dress pocket.

"No!" Kayley manages to say in between sharp inhales through her teeth. "I'm fine."

"You are not fine," I say. "We're taking a taxi home, and that's final."

Kayley pulls back, her eyes widening as she stares at me. I'm surprised by my intensity, too. Only Afton seems fine with it. Nayla takes that as her cue to hail a taxi. She flips her Sergo open and scrolls to her ride request app.

"I don't need a taxi," Kayley says, pushing us away. Even if she does it gently, her message is clear—*back off*. I throw Afton a glance in hopes of more support, but Afton only scrunches her mouth up. I guess I'll have to wait. Kayley and I have already battled over this, and I'm not looking to lose another fight.

I could carry her if I had to. It's more like if she'll let me, which, based on her last motion, seems very unlikely to happen. Still, Kayley's hesitation over getting back on her feet only makes me worry more.

"Okay, well," I say. "Let's get you home, yeah? Mom will whip up some congee for you tonight."

"Thanks." Kayley smiles through her pain. "But after that lunch, I don't think I could eat any more for the rest of the week."

"Agreed," Nayla says.

I push up and offer Kayley my hand. She gives me a grateful look and takes it, attempting to pull herself up. Afton moves behind her to take her under her arms and help lift.

"Wait, wait, wait," Kayley says, her eyebrows squeezing together as if she's concentrating hard. A whimper slips from her lips as Afton struggles to keep moving her up. Then Kayley's knees buckle. I catch her before she falls, but her limp weight is tough to keep upright from my half-crouched position. If it wasn't for Afton and then Nayla helping, we would have crashed to the ground.

Kayley gasps in my ear as I move to sit her back down. Afton supports her back as I come to her side. There's a darkening stain on her shirt. I lift it to see the bandage on her side blossoming red.

"KayKay, your wound's opened again," I say, "and you can't even stand. We're getting you back to Doc Elizabeth. Now."

"It can't be that bad," she replies. "Let's just go home. I'll take the taxi."

I can feel Kayley's heart pounding in her chest. Her breaths come faster, too. I do want to get her home, but I'm not sure that's the best place to take her.

Afton gives me a pointed look. She means to tell me that home is not the option I should choose. Doc Elizabeth left Grady's house with the Teddys just before we left. It wouldn't take too long to track her down, but it might to get her there. An ambulance would be faster, plus they'd be able to care for her the moment they got here.

I look at the bandage again. Maybe her bleeding is slowing down, but I can't tell. She may have internal bleeding, too, though Doc Elizabeth said she made sure that couldn't happen. I want to believe that, yet I'm two seconds away from calling emergency services.

"Remove the bandage," Nayla says. "I will examine her injury."

"What do you know about medicine? Or knife wounds?" I point a finger at Nayla. "And don't tell me you were a doctor in a former life. That doesn't help her now."

"Hey, easy," Afton says. It's not a threat, but it could be with a small amount of force put behind it.

Nayla's eyes narrow, but she only adjusts her skirt and crouches down next to me, reaching out to slowly peel Kayley's bandage back. I feel Kayley tense, and I tighten my hold on her. She leans into me and lays her head on my shoulder. I hope whatever Nayla is doing, it tells us if Kayley is in danger.

"Since you wondered, Ransom Quigley He'," Nayla says as she presses against Kayley's side, "I was a doctor in a former life, but that is not why I know how to do this. Mother requires all members of the court to have a knowledge of wound care. That includes her, though none of us have ever let her practice her skills."

"So can you tell if she's bleeding internally?"

Kayley squirms a little under Nayla's touch. For someone who must be in a lot of pain, she's being more courageous than I could be.

"I am unsure," she says. "I do not suspect so, but perhaps it is better to bring her to a hospital or to your friend Elizabeth."

"Okay," I say and nod. "Okay. Let's call an ambulance."

"No," Kayley says, her voice stronger than it has been. "No ambulance, no hospital. And if you insist on taking me there, I'm breaking up with you. Elizabeth can come check me at your house."

"KayKay!"

"Please, I just want to lie down."

Afton looks troubled. I am too. I would feel a lot more at ease if Kayley would allow me to take care of her. She's made it clear that's not happening, and I don't even want to test how serious her threat of breaking up with me might be.

But if she's more hurt than she's telling me, I'll never forgive myself for giving in to her demand, even if it seems okay. Kayley's not leaving me a lot of room for choice here.

Maybe if Doc Elizabeth can get there fast enough, everything will be okay. Maybe.

"Alright, KayKay," I say with a sigh. "But we're taking a taxi, even if it is just three blocks, and I'm putting you in bed the moment we get there. We'll call Elizabeth on the way."

"My hero." Kayley presses her lips to my cheek for a kiss, then lowers her head to my shoulder again, content with my decision.

She's the only one of the four of us who is.

Chapter Eight

KAYLEY IS OKAY. HER bleeding was only superficial. One spot that Doc Elizabeth had trouble getting a good seal on popped open when Kayley fell. A small liquid stitch—human tech—sealed it back up again. Now Kayley's confined to bed for the rest of the day and the next. She doesn't seem overly upset about it, provided I give her my every waking moment. I agreed, of course. I'd do anything to give her all my time.

Parrish and Grady are coming over soon to give us their report. They didn't tell us anything when they called, but I suspect we're in for a challenge.

"Wake up, sleepyhead," I say as I sit next to Kayley on the guest bed, brushing her hair from her face. I slept in my bed last night, mostly to give her a peaceful rest. My mom probably wouldn't object to us staying in the same room together, but I still feel uncomfortable making that assumption. And forget about me ever bringing it up for discussion. I'd choke before I could finish my first sentence.

Kayley stirs, her hand sliding up to take mine. A moment later, her eyes open and search for me. She smiles at me with that dreamy look she has when she wakes up. I think it gives her this aura of total beauty. There's this glow about her that makes my insides drop out whenever I see it. That I'm wide awake at this moment to experience it just makes it all the better.

I am so very lucky to have her as my girlfriend.

"How are you feeling?" I ask as I help her sit up. She winces a little as she moves, but it's better than yesterday. Anything is better than yesterday.

"Like this," Kayley says, an irresistible, sultry drawl slipping from her lips. Her arms come around me, and we kiss. I close my eyes and let my entire being enjoy the moment. We hold each other after that, simply happy to be with each other.

Halfway through our embrace, or at least what I think is halfway, there's a knock at our door. I want to ignore it, but Kayley calls for whoever it is to come in. That doesn't stop her from keeping her arms around my neck, but now that we're interrupted, that's all that is going to happen.

"Hey," Parrish says as he pokes his head in the door. The moment his eyes fall on us, he averts them. "Oh, sorry! I thought I heard…"

"You did," Kayley replies. "I said it. Don't worry, we were just talking."

"You were?" Parrish peeks up.

"Of course we were." Kayley gets her words out before I can even take a breath. "Come in. Let's hear what we're up against."

As she says it, I feel my muscles tighten. Kayley is giving me the vibe that she's treating yesterday like a chance occurrence, and that she's going to go into this conversation with the idea that she'll be leading whatever mission we're about to embark on. I'm not sure I'm okay with putting her in harm's way, even if she's better. I'd be fine with her just staying here.

Though I doubt that will be the case.

"So," I say, "how's Herdewyke?"

"It's bad," Grady replies, pushing past Parrish and dropping himself into the one chair in the room. "There's no better way to say it. We're going to be up against some serious stuff."

Another knock at the door brings Nayla, Afton, and Doc Elizabeth in. They might be here for this discussion, but I suspect they came for my mom's breakfast. I warned her this might happen, so we went to the market early this morning to stock up on the ingredients.

Afton drops herself on the opposite side of the bed, but Nayla demurs and just leans against her, while Doc Elizabeth comes around it to check on Kayley. It's a large enough room to hold all of us, but it was never meant to be a meeting hall. Everyone will make do, I suppose.

Once we are all settled, Grady begins.

"As we know, there's the Imperial staging base that orbits Herdewyke. They've built up its defenses significantly since our last visit," he says. "It now includes special sensors for detecting Teddy ships. So no sneaking past them like we did last time. We'll have to use a more standard form of subterfuge."

"Which is what?" Kayley asks.

"Spoofing their security to think we've got official access to the planet. Between Colonel Cortell's info about Imperial codes and my talks with the Teddys—"

"Speaking of," I say, glancing around, "where is Teddy?"

"He said he was going on a nutritional rendezvous," Parrish replies. "I guess he was hungry."

To my left, I hear Nayla wretch and clear her throat. It hasn't been long enough for her to get used to how the Teddys eat. Then again, she may never. We should probably keep that in mind for future excursions, especially the longer ones.

"So do you have a solution?" Kayley asks, putting Grady's presentation back on track.

"Yeah," Grady replies. "We've put together a signal that will appear like an older code, but it should check out."

"Have we found the location of the meeting?" I ask.

"Sort of," Parrish says, rolling his eyes. "We've got it narrowed down to an area about the size of our town."

"*Our* town?"

"Parry," Afton chimes in. "Do you remember we tried to jog around our town once?"

Parrish shrugs and nods.

"Do you remember we didn't even make it halfway?"

"The area that we need to search is smaller than that," Grady explains. "It's in a mountainous region, and the only buildings there belong to a resort. There's a high chance that the meeting will be there."

After hearing two of our problems, most likely our biggest, my freak-out level is fairly low. This sounds like the start of every other mission we've gone on. There are no issues so far that we can't overcome. Kayley might be okay to go if she hangs back and doesn't get into the fight.

Still, I think there might be more to this than Grady is telling us.

"Okay, so what's so bad about all this so far?" I ask. "We can get on-planet. We know where to land and where to find them. What's the big deal?"

Grady holds up a finger, then pulls out his Sergo and projects an image of the mountain and the resort that sits on the southern side of it. The five buildings that I can see are mostly covered by the tree canopy, and there's no obvious place to set a shuttle down.

"As we can all see, the only way to get us anywhere near this place is to rappel down a rope into the forest and hike to the buildings. To keep anyone from spotting us while we're doing this risky maneuver, we'll have to drop on the opposite side of the mountain and hike for a good five or six hours to get to the resort. Then, after that grueling fun, provided we don't run into any guards hiding out in the area, which we absolutely will because the military trains on and around the mountain, we've got to infiltrate the resort."

"How many people do you think will be at the resort?" Kayley asks.

"Not sure, but more than a hundred attendees, security, and staff. And that's just the ones Parrish and I could come up with. There could be more."

"We're also assuming they'll have all the top surveillance equipment that the military uses," Parrish adds. "Harry—"

"Who is Harry?" Nayla asks. "What is his birth sign?"

"Colonel Cortell," Afton explains.

If Nayla responds, I don't hear it. My thoughts are on the significant amount of hiking we're going to have to do to even get to the location. Kayley would struggle with that, even in perfect health. Maybe it's better to get her to hang back.

"Kay—" I start, but Kayley interrupts me.

"Okay," she says. "This sounds more like what I expected. Assuming we could make everything else happen, how many of the top leaders do we expect to capture?"

"If we go in with everyone except for me—" Grady says.

"Or me," Doc Elizabeth says. "I tried that last time. The field is not the place for me."

"I will also not be hiking," Nayla adds.

"Right, everyone except for me, Nayla, and Elizabeth. That leaves you four, plus Teddy and his buddies, for a total of nine. So if each of you could manage one prisoner, we shouldn't capture more than nine. Any more than that, we'd be risking one escaping or them overpowering you. Don't forget, you'll have to hike back to the other side of the mountain again. With captives."

I throw a glance at Kayley to catch her reaction, but she's steady, running through the mission in her head just like she always does. This could be a good time to mention my concern.

"Kayley," I say. "Maybe you should hang back, too."

She just glances at me and continues to contemplate our actions. I look at Afton, who just purses her lips.

It's not good, just like Grady said. We're going to have an impossible time getting to the resort, avoiding both roaming security and active military who will be holding live-fire exercises. Then, if we're not already exhausted, we're going to have to fight our way into the meeting and grab as many of the head honchos as we can.

If I was Kayley, I wouldn't want to go. I might even delay the entire mission for the extreme level of risk we're going to face. She can't be on the ground. Not in her condition.

"KayKay," I try again. "You should sit this one out."

Again, she ignores me. But Parrish and Doc Elizabeth shift. They heard me. Why they aren't speaking up is beyond me. I guess they don't want to step in when I've already tried to broach the subject. Twice.

"Any other concerns?" Kayley asks Grady and Parrish.

"Of course. Where do I start?" Grady responds.

"How about the fact that they'll just be three of us on the ground since Kayley will be staying on the ship?" I say. That gets a response. Finally, Kayley frowns at me, processing my words. She was so focused on creating the details of the mission, she didn't hear my protests against her participation in the active part of the mission.

"What are you talking about?" Kayley asks, shaking her head.

"Perhaps this is too much to handle," Nayla says. "Perhaps you need help. A larger force to approach the location with. If his chart aligns with all of yours, you could ask Harry."

"Adding more people only increases the risk of us being caught before we even get there," Grady says. "These may be conspirators, but they're also some of the top leaders in the military. It wouldn't take much for them to order whatever number of battalions are in the area to stop us. Then we've suddenly gone from a hundred to more than a thousand soldiers armed with the military's best equipment we'd have to fight. That's what makes their location and timing so perfect. They're practically untouchable."

"Hold on, hold on." Kayley raises a hand, then turns back to me. "What do you mean, there's only going to be three?"

"Me, Parrish, and Afton. That's three," I reply. "You'll be back on the ship, directing us from there."

Then she gets it. And it doesn't make her happy.

"Um, no, I won't be," Kayley says. "We need every able person to be down on the ground, and that means I'm going."

"But you're not."

"Not what?"

"Able, KayKay. You're still recovering!"

"After today, I'll be fine. That's what Elizabeth said. So I'm cleared to go. And I will."

Kayley's sharp gaze says she's daring me to say more. She thinks she's so right about this that she will obliterate any concern I bring up. And I know she will, because Kayley always wins, whether or not I let her. Not that I do a lot of allowing her to do anything. Kayley's the leader. She gets to decide who stays and who goes. That's what makes this even more difficult for me

I scan around to the others, but they're all avoiding my look. Even Doc Elizabeth isn't willing to contradict herself on this one. We're going on this mission, and this discussion isn't about the *if*. It's about the *how*. I can keep putting up a fight if I want to get verbally beaten up by my girlfriend. She might even be considerate enough not to do it in front of everyone. That doesn't make it any better.

"You got anything more to say about that?" Kayley asks, still staring at me.

I sigh. "Only that I love you and I care about you, KayKay," I say, giving her my best pleading face.

The sides of her mouth curl up a little, and her eyes soften. At least she's not overly mad at me. Still, I failed to stop her from going, and I'll worry about that every second we're on the mission.

Goddesses, please don't let me regret giving in to her.

Chapter Nine

THE ONE THING GRADY forgot to tell us about Herdewyke is how unbearably hot it is here. Sure, we're hiking on the side of a mountain, in the shade, but the humidity is about a thousand times wetter than our town ever gets. Perspiration is dripping off my head in torrents, and my shirt is already soaked through. My arms are sticky, and my stun gun strap keeps slipping down my arm. This is the absolute pits. We could take a long dip in the ocean and still be dryer.

The good news is that we're close to the final navigation point before we reach our primary target—the resort. I've prayed to each Goddess about ten times over that our success will be as uneventful as our five-hour hike has been so far. There were a few scary points where traps and sensors could have ended our mission, but Kayley's decision to have the Teddys in the trees saved us. We were extremely happy to have them along, and the Teddys were having a ball.

"Where is it?" I whisper to Kayley as she passes by.

"Over the ridge." Kayley wipes away a lock of hair that's pasted itself to her face and points straight ahead. "Grady, can you see anything?"

"No. I'm trying to keep the drone away enough that it won't be spotted."

"Wait, I thought it had Teddy tech to make it invisible," I say.

"It does, and it is invisible to scans. Someone could still see it or hear it."

"I'll look," Parrish says and hustles through the trees to climb the ridge. Before he gets to the top, he drops to crawl and peeks over the edge.

A few seconds later, he gives us a thumbs-up. Afton pushes forward, with Kayley following and me taking up the rear. I turn my head to the green canopy above, wondering where our Teddy buddies are. I'd expect pink to stand out against such a conformity of color, but Original Teddy, like all Teddys, is also a master at camouflage. They are born hunters, and their senses, especially their hearing, are far better than a human's.

Which makes it absolutely strange that they didn't hear several hundred soldiers marching over the next ridge straight towards us.

"Down, down!" Afton hisses as she drops and takes cover behind a tree. I grab Kayley's arm—only to have it slide out of my grasp. She waves me off and dives behind another tree just behind mine.

"What is it?" I subvocalize over Teddy comm. I also do my best to upload an image of a soldier to the Teddys, though if I can now hear the ruckus an entire battalion makes, they're likely covering their pointy ears from all the noise.

"We just ran into a live-fire exercise," Parrish replies, his voice rumbling in my head. "But I didn't get the sense they were about to shoot anything."

It's true. Boisterous laughter and shouting float over the ridge, along with the relative hum of sound that occurs when so many people are close together. There's even more than usual because I suspect they're about to take a break. I hope it's a short one.

Then, I get an image from Teddynet. Of a sandwich.

"Oh great," I mumble.

"What's going on?" Kayley asks.

"I think the Teddys see that they're about to have lunch."

"That's not a bad idea," Afton says. "I'm starving."

Kayley just leans around her tree and gives Afton a nice *no way in hell* glare. I'm a bit peckish myself. It's been six hours since our last meal. We're traveling light, so none of us have much to eat, just a snack bar or two and a lot of water. I've been worried about Kayley, but she seems like she's recovered. This hike hasn't worn her down any more than the rest of us.

"They're settling into the furrow between the ridges," Parrish says, "and it looks like they're going to be staying for a while. What do we do?"

"Eat and wait them out," Afton says, pushing her food agenda again. "We'll be rested, full, and ready to move on."

"It's not a bad idea," I add.

"Fine, but someone needs to monitor them," Kayley says. "And be quick about it."

"I've got a good view from where I am," Parrish says. "And I already finished my two bars."

Upon hearing that, the rest of us get to chowing down. We don't want to be caught with mouths full of energy bars. That would be an embarrassment for as long as we got to live after that. If they figure out who we are—which isn't difficult these days—they'll be eager to dispose of us quickly.

"So what are we going to do?" I ask. I've got a few ideas, but in keeping with my promise, I'm letting Kayley run the show.

"Go around them?" Parrish suggests.

"That could take us a long time," Afton says. "We'd be better off staying put and letting them move."

"And risk them moving right on top of us? No, thanks." I give Afton a firm shake of my head.

"Well, we can't fight an entire battalion." Afton, once again with the obvious. Fighting wasn't even part of the discussion until she brought it up

.

I think they're nothing more than an enormous obstacle, one with eyes and ears...and guns, of course, but still just an obstacle. We could go around them, go under them, or go around the other side of the mountain—none of which we have time for. The meeting could be over by the time we showed up, half-melted by the heat and so exhausted that we wouldn't even be able to walk, much less capture a squad of prisoners.

"Could we distract them? Like with an explosion or something?" Parrish asks.

"Nope," Kayley replies, sounding glum. "An explosion would shut down the meeting and evacuate everyone we want to get our hands on."

"That's perfect!" I say. "Then we grab them while they're running. It'll be total chaos as they try to escape. No one will even notice us!"

"What cine did you steal that from, buddy?" Afton's dead serious, and she could be right. I kind of remember one where the hero blows up a bridge or something, and that gets all the bad guys to head towards it to save their fellows. Then the hero sneaks past and captures their boss. That won't happen here. We'd be complete fools to believe it would.

"I stole nothing," I mutter with a sigh. "And what idea have you come up with so far?"

"I suggested we sit and wait."

"Yeah, also a bad idea," Parrish says. "They won't be there forever, and for us to stay static like this is waiting for them to find us. We might as well just go over this ridge and ask to join in their war game."

"Well, anyone else, then?" Kayley asks. "Rance, anything from the Teddys?"

"Nothing. They understand the problem, but no suggestions."

"Guys, I hate to suggest it," Kayley says and shifts, clearly uncomfortable with what she's about to tell us, "but we may have to consider scrubbing this whole thing."

The four of us get silent then. It's probably something we should have done in the first place, given it only takes one of nearly a thousand soldiers to spot us or hear us. Add our failure to find a way around to the time ticking down on the meeting, and it's no wonder we're feeling the stress of the situation. We're about to turn back on Kayley's orders with nothing to show for our grueling trek through the forest.

"Goddesses, it's so hot," Afton says, running her water pouch across her forehead.

I lean back on the tree trunk and turn my head up, hoping for some rain to reach us through the leaf barrier above. I don't even know if it is raining. There are too many branches and leaves blocking the sky from view. The canopy is so thick above us, I might be better off climbing a tree—

"Wait...I have an idea!"

"Rance, keep it down!" Kayley hisses, then leans forward with an eyebrow raised. "What's your idea?"

"The trees." I stab a finger towards the sky. "We can't go around them, but we could go over them with help from the Teddys."

"Oh boy," Parrish says. "I never really liked heights. Can't we find another way?"

"No," Kayley says. "I like it. How soon can the Teddys get here?"

As if answering her question, a blue buddy drops in the middle of the three of us, followed by another, then another. Parrish makes a startled noise, likely because the fourth blue buddy came down next to him.

"Okay. They're here," Afton says. "Now what?"

With no warning, the blue buddies fling a tentacle around each of us and launch up a tree with impossible speed. All I see is a blur as the forest drops beneath us. I feel weightless, as if I'm spacewalking, and my senses freak out. It's like I'm making my way to the *Mursilis*, and I've got no control.

Then, gravity returns, and I land on a tree limb with a muffled yelp, thirty stories up from the ground.

"Holy Sophia," Afton says, breathless. "Warn us next time you plan to do that!"

"Nonsense," Original Teddy replies. "Teddy does not speak Common."

"Yeah, but *you* do!"

"Teddy did not want to shout."

"Yeah, probably a good idea," Kayley says, her eyes wide as she stares down at the ground. "We don't want to alert the soldiers."

With a hard gulp, I glance down and realize we're right above the battalion. The soldiers are about as large as my Sergo is long. That's the one redeeming factor here. They might notice movement, but they won't recognize us as humans unless someone uses a scope or some other visual enhancement. We'd look like large birds or unusually plumed primates to their naked eyes.

"Time to make the pastry," Original Teddy says, directing us to go farther out on the tree limb. Afton, the bravest of the three of us, climbs out with a heavy helping of reluctance. Teddys may be at home in the trees, but humans belong on solid ground.

A blue buddy grabs on to her pack with his hands and toes and swings to the next tree using his tentacles. Afton is nothing more than a package to him, and I'm sure she's hating her straight-down-to-death view.

"Watch the claws!" Afton hisses.

Next it's Kayley's turn. She does her best to accommodate an easy lift, but the female Teddy that takes her picks her up like Kayley is nothing more than a pile of feathers. Kayley's light, but her Teddy doesn't even grunt as she lifts her up.

Then, before I know it, I'm suspended high above a thousand heavily armed people who would likely use us for target practice if they noticed us up here. I wonder how Parrish is handling this. Heights aren't his worst fear, but he's the heaviest out of all of us. I guess my real question is, how is his Teddy handling Parrish?

Our progression is slow. Slower than I want it to be. It would only take one of these soldiers to lie back and stare up to notice something strange going on above them. We may look like animals from down there, but we'd be the strangest animals anyone would ever lay their eyes on.

Halfway across, Afton's Teddy snags a branch that's too small. It snaps, sending part of it down to crash in a group of six men.

"Hold still!" Kayley orders. There's little I can do to make that happen. We're at the mercy of our transporters, who do their best to stop us from swinging. We're half-camouflaged by leaves, and I really hope that's enough to stop us from being seen.

One soldier glances up, and my heart skips a beat. I hold my breath for fear of them hearing air escape my lungs. It's a ridiculous thought, but that doesn't stop me from thinking it. All that solder has to do is realize something is not right above him, and we're done.

So when his buddy slaps him on the arm and he forgets us, I thank the Goddesses three times over. And then I do it again.

"Okay, let's go," Kayley says, her voice shaky. It's bad enough we're in danger of becoming human pancakes if the Teddys lose their grip. We need no more reasons to push our risk.

It's a good thing, then, that the rest of the way is free of eventful moments. We clear far to the other side of the ridge, and then our terror returns when the Teddys return us to the earth. Afton and I both land hard, as I bet our weight pushed the limits of Teddy strength.

"Guys," Grady says over Teddy comm. "Are you okay? Did you make it? What did you see?"

"We're fine," Afton replies with a cough. "Mostly. Goddess, my stomach hurts."

"Do you think anyone saw you?"

"Not sure," Kayley says. "My eyes were closed the entire time."

Chapter Ten

AFTER A HARROWING TEN minutes suspended above potential death, the next half hour of crashing through the forest is like a casual nature stroll. We come across a handful of motion and sound sensors, as well as a patrol, but we avoid them with skill. Those obstacles were the ones we prepared for. None of us were thinking we'd run into an entire battalion.

The wooden fence that marks the perimeter of the resort is a joke. The humans of the group vault over it in only one second more than it takes the Teddys. Then we take cover in an ideal spot for surveillance—a hedge. We can monitor the staff from there, and they'd never suspect a thing.

"Grady," Kayley says. "Any movement nearby?"

"Not that I'm seeing. Just a few patrols outside the perimeter. None inside. Either they're confident in their outside security, or there are soldiers around that I can't see."

"That's not very encouraging."

"Sorry. I'm not an oracle. Ask Nayla, maybe."

Kayley takes a few minutes to observe our surroundings. She's looking for that unknown variable, that hidden element that always trips us up. There's always one, and usually, we can't see it until it smacks us hard in the face. It can't be helped. We'll have to deal with it when it happens.

"Okay, let's go." Kayley nods to Parrish, and he and Afton take off. The two of us are next. Kayley squeezes my shoulder, and I turn to her. The look in her eyes says enough. She's as ready as she can be for this. Still, we need to be careful, or we'll be dead.

With well-rehearsed skill, the two of us break from the hedge and sprint to the edge of the nearest building—the one where the meeting is taking place. We scan the area, then chase after Afton and Parrish, who are already up a set of stairs that lead to a maintenance door.

I can't see them, but I know the Teddys are forming a guard around us. Only Original Teddy will be coming in with us.

Parrish unlocks the door with a small Teddy device. It's silent as it disables the sensor and lock with nothing more than the flash of a light. Good. Our plan is moving smoothly now. The rest should be second nature to us.

Not that I'm counting on that.

Kayley raises her stun gun and gives the command to proceed. Afton takes point while Parrish waits to let Kayley and me pass by. The moment I touch Afton's shoulder, she goes, and I go with her. We move like a couple dancing, our movements synchronized and innate. It couldn't be better.

An empty hallway leads to a kitchen. We stun the unlucky chefs and sous-chefs in seconds and keep moving. They'll be fine once they wake up, though dinner might be a little late.

We move like water, flowing into the hallway surrounding the conference room. I find it strange that there are no guards here, but I won't discount whatever blessing I may receive. What's in front of me is what I have to contend with. If that's nothing, then I'll count myself lucky.

Kayley and Parrish slide around the corner while Afton and I take the main entrance. I can hear the mindless drone of an officer pontificating about some aspect of his command. His lucky audience is about to be given a reprieve from his dull speech. In a matter of seconds, they'll all be our prisoners.

"Ready?" Kayley whispers over Teddy comm. "In three...two...one...go!"

We burst into the room, shouting for the people around the table to put their hands up. Only a few do, but Afton makes our insistence known by dropping an admiral with her weapon.

It was the wrong move.

"They've only got stun weapons!" one of them cries, and suddenly a plethora of handguns appear in everyone's hands. In microseconds, we've crashed into a stand-off.

"Drop them, or we drop you!" Afton shouts.

"No! You drop yours!" a woman, who I guess might be a minister, shouts back. "We're not afraid of your little toy guns!"

I exchange glances with Kayley. We were lucky up to this point, but now I know why there are no guards inside the perimeter. They aren't needed. It's clear that this group can defend themselves.

"I don't have to stun you," Afton says. "Our weapons can fry your brains just as easily."

That's no lie. Safeties off, our guns could do just that. It's not the plan, but it's better than getting killed by this group of overpromoted buffoons. Maybe a solid jolt into their skulls might improve their outlook on things.

The woman who attempted to sham us takes a hesitant step away from Afton. We won that round. I just wonder how many more there will be. I'm sure they've got some way to alert security, and we can't let them use it.

I try to catch Kayley's glance, but she's too focused on covering those around her. With a little more luck, we might still get a good number of captives, though I'm not betting on it. If we can get out of here with no wounds, that'll be a bonus.

Before I can react, a man dives towards a device in the middle of the table. He's going for the alarm! I raise my gun, but he goes stiff and falls onto the table. The others gasp in surprise, and I grin. Original Teddy is just out of sight, keeping tabs on the situation.

"Drop your weapons, or you'll suffer the same fate!" Kayley shouts. It's a good bluff. A few of the conspirators appear ready to do just that.

But the others hold firm and give those nervous ones the courage to keep their guns.

"Do you really think we're going to give up just because a bunch of kids want us to?" The general at the end of the table stands up straight. "We're going to take the Emperor down, you little brats. We're not afraid of you."

"Yeah," another officer with a jacket well decorated with medals says. "You can't beat us. So drop your guns, and we'll consider sending you home with just a spanking."

That gets a laugh from a few of them and a frown from Kayley. There's no way they'll let us walk out of here. We can't give up. The only question is, how many of them can we drop before they kill us? That's not a question I'm ready to hear the answer to.

We should give up on getting any prisoners, though my brain is fighting that realization. We've risked so much to get here, and now that we're in this room, pointing weapons at the big leaders of the conspiracy, we've multiplied our hazard level exponentially. To get nothing out of this but our lives somehow seems like a poor trade.

There should be some question why we care if the Emperor gets deposed. We're not even citizens. What he does or doesn't do won't affect us. Still, it's my fault for us being here. I had to dream big and worry about the people who do count themselves as loyal subjects of His Majesty.

I know I'm not the only one. That's why all of us are involved in this grab and go mission. We all want the Empire to be fair for all who live in it, including us, even if we don't get all the perks.

"We'll give you ten seconds to make a choice," Kayley says, her gun pointed at the general who spoke. "After that, I don't care whether you live or die."

The general grins and returns her threat by aiming his pistol at her. Shoot. Why'd she say that? Bile climbs into my throat, and I fear she won't survive this encounter. The rest of us might not, either.

"Do you think any of you are getting out of here alive?" a female officer says, though I notice a tremor in her voice. Fear is prevalent in this room. Neither side has a monopoly on that.

If I have time, I need to come up with a practical solution. There's fourteen of them, and four of us, plus one. Original Teddy can take out three at once, which means we can drop seven before they shoot back. It's not enough. At least one of us is going to die.

I won't accept that as our fate. Maybe there's a way to hit a few and run. Maybe we can grab at least one conspirator on our way out.

Perhaps we can.

A quick upload to Teddynet gets the foundation of my plan solidified. I wish I could communicate it to the entire team, but I'll just have to hope that they follow along once things happen.

My eyes catch Kayley's, and a quick exchange occurs. She adjusts her stance and the grip on her weapon. I notice others shift in the room, too. They're going to make a move. We'd better be faster.

Out of the corner of my eye, I catch the general jerk his arm. A millisecond after, I squeeze my trigger. Electricity erupts from my weapon, zapping the lighting in the ceiling. All goes dark.

There's a flash and a bang from a gun. Energy zaps from Afton's weapon. Bodies drop. Chaos spreads through the room. A pair of guns go off, but their plasma just hits walls.

"Go, go!" Kayley shouts. A shot fires in her direction, but she's already gone.

I drop to the floor and reach out for the nearest body. I grab an arm and yank it along with me. Then I'm out the door, dragging my captive with me. Guns continue to go off inside the meeting room, covering the space with flashes of light and smoke. But we're already gone. I hope.

Someone, probably Afton, grabs the legs of my prisoner and runs. I follow—out the door and down the steps. We run to the back of the perimeter and hurdle the fence. Then, rather than back the way we came, we head in the opposite direction.

I take stock of our team—we're all there. Four humans and likely five Teddys, two of which are now carrying our popsicled captive as they fly through the trees.

Parrish holds his shoulder and winces as he runs. Afton helps him. Kayley must be somewhere ahead, but I can't see her. I just know Teddynet says she's with us—and unharmed, I pray.

And me? When I get a second, I check myself over. Nothing. I'm fine, save for my nerves.

It's a five-hour return to our pickup point. The shuttle should still be there, hidden from view by the copious amount of branches we used to cover it.

It'll take a few minutes for the conspirators at the meeting to organize themselves. They'll be after us the moment they do, and they'll scour the mountain to find us.

But they won't.

We didn't come anywhere near achieving our goal for captives, but we leave with one...and our lives.

In my mind, that still spells success.

Chapter Eleven

THE MOMENT WE CLEAR the last branch from the shuttle's canopy, we pile in and launch. Grady sends us a new code to broadcast, and we escape the planet with no issues. If anyone checks the telemetry from the area, and I'm sure they will, they'll see our launch, but we'll be long gone by then. Besides, I want them to know who it was that crashed their meeting. Putting a little fear into our enemy will only work in our favor.

"How's the shoulder?" I ask as Afton puts a bandage on Parrish's wound. He winces, sucking air through his teeth as if answering me. I flinch right along with him, knowing full well what it feels like to get hit with a plasma blast. It was only a graze, but even so, it's got to be painful.

"Don't worry," Afton says as she finishes up. "You're still young. It'll heal over, and you'll never even remember they shot you."

"Still young?" Parrish's brow wrinkles. "I'm not five years old, you know."

"But you're in good health," I say, trying to be supportive.

"I like to think so," Parrish says with a smile that turns pained when Afton pats him on the arm.

"Don't worry," she says. "You'll be okay in a day or two. Mom won't miss anything."

Afton's talking about Parrish's mom. While he's here, she's undergoing a deluge of tests to determine what might be wrong with her. I'm sure he's wanting to return home as soon as possible.

"Speaking of okay, how's our hostage?" Kayley asks me.

"Secured and, for the moment, sedated with the stuff that the doc gave us. She'll sleep the rest of the trip and will just be waking when we turn her over to Colonel Cortell's team."

I'm not sure who we snagged, but the lack of a uniform on the petite woman makes me think she's an aide or other minor Imperial official. Still, she was at the meeting. That means she's someone important to the conspiracy.

"Hey, heads up, guys," Grady says over Teddy comm. "I just intercepted a priority message that was sent to Rance's Sergo. No, wait...Kayley just got the same message."

"Why are you looking at our Sergos?" Kayley asks. "We didn't leave them on the ship for you to sneak a peek at. There's private stuff on there, you know."

I throw a curious glance at her. Of all the things that she could ask about this potentially important message, she chooses that?

"Who's it from?" Afton asks.

"It's from..." Grady gasps. "The Chamberlin! There's a link in here to an encrypted line. I think he wants us to call him."

"Call him, then," I say. "We've got nothing to hide."

"Uh"—Afton motions to our sleeping hostage—"we've got lots to hide."

"It's fine," Kayley says. "If he wants to talk, we'll talk to him."

Grady takes a few moments to scan the link and the line to ensure it's not some kind of sneaky counterattack by the conspiracy. Then he connects the Teddy globe in the shuttle to the call. As the call comes through, I wonder why the Chamberlin is calling us. Maybe to follow up on his earlier message? We haven't given him the courtesy of a reply yet. That's because we didn't have one.

When the Chamberlin appears on the vid, he spreads his arms wide and gives us as honest a smile as I think he can come up with. I'll take that as a compliment. It's not likely he gets to do that much. Be honest, I mean.

"I give you my congratulations, young crusaders. You have accomplished much in a short time. And time is short. The length of—"

"Okay, okay," I say, waving my hands to stop him. We don't need another one of his cryptic statements. "Thanks, but what do we owe this call to, Lord Chamberlin?"

I instinctively cringe as I wait for the bailiff to pinch me—then remember she's locked away, on Exodus, the worst jail in the Empire, I hope. That's what she deserves for trying to have us assassinated.

"You have accomplished something of worth, and your worth has increased to His Majesty. His Majesty remembers those who serve him. Remembrance by His Majesty is a luxury, and you have indeed allowed him to have a splendid memory."

So far, nothing is difficult to understand. I'm not sure how the Emperor remembering who we are and what we've done for him is going to benefit us. I'm not even sure if it will. It certainly hasn't yet.

"We were glad to arrest Bailiff Daughtry on your behalf, Your Lordship," Kayley says. "If the Emperor appreciates it, then we're glad to hear that, too."

"You are mistaken," the Chamberlin says. "I do not speak of what you did. I speak of what you have done."

Okay, now I'm lost.

"Herdewyke has been a challenge for my office, but not for yours," he continues. "Where I have faltered, you have thrived. We did not know where we should find the occurrence, but it has occurred to you where it was. Your infiltration was a success, and success you shall find with the right choices. Choose right, and you may name your wish."

"So if we choose what you want us to, you'll give us something we ask for?" Afton asks. She's just ahead of me on the Chamberlin comprehension scale.

"Yes. This, I wish for you."

Kayley throws up a hand. She's right to. We've only got one chance to get this right, and the Chamberlin just gave us a planet's worth of information to unpack. If I heard him correctly, he just told us he knows what we just accomplished.

There's only one way that I can figure the Chamberlin could know something like that. He had someone on the inside. Someone who not only witnessed our attack, but lived to communicate what happened.

The Chamberlin may know what we did, but I'm not ready to admit it. Neither is Kayley.

"What makes Your Lordship think we were on Herdewyke?" she asks, her face impassive. The Chamberlin smiles again. I guess he likes our attempt to be evasive.

"His Majesty requires to be knowledgeable," he says. "This is an office of knowledge. It is our duty to provide His Majesty all that is knowable. If there is such a thing that can be learned, we shall uncover it, and there is nothing in our Empire that can remain covered for long."

He's trying to get us to admit what we did. Kayley won't be so easy to influence. Still, I wonder if there's some benefit in acknowledging the mission and its success.

Kayley's eyes narrow as she begins his tricky negotiation. And that's exactly what it is. "Even if we were there, how does Your Lordship know we did anything worthwhile?"

"To make admissions is meaningless." The Chamberlin waves a dismissive hand. "You understand my meaning. There is no point to confirm or deny. This office has already communicated the question I wish to confirm. This is the reason for my communication."

So he's impressed with our work, and he wants to know if we want more. We're already doing what he wants, so I don't know what the benefit is of telling him we'll let him be our employer again. It wasn't the Chamberlin's fault it didn't go all that well last time, but I doubt any of us would be all that excited to work for him a second time.

Though when I consider it, the Chamberlin may have some use for us. He is the second most powerful person in the Empire, after all. He might be willing to provide us with whatever we want—weapons, armor, a nice swimming pool. All we'd have to do is ask. That could be of some actual use to us.

Of course, it would mean professing our loyalty to the Emperor. He's the only one who has yet to offer us anything. We might have trouble gaining cooperation from some people if we went around flying an Imperial flag.

It would make it easier for us to work with Colonel Cortell, however.

"I'm sorry, Your Lordship," Kayley says with a shake of her head. "But there is—mmph!"

"Actually, Your Lordship," I say, clapping my hand over Kayley's mouth, "if you give us a moment, I'm sure we can come to an agreement with you."

Kayley throws me a glare of molten metal, which I acknowledge with a single nod. Then I whisper my idea into her ear, and her body relaxes. She still digs her nails into my hand when she rips it off her face. I snatch it away, waving it to rid myself of the sting.

"You deserved that," Afton says under her breath.

"Apologies, Your Lordship," Kayley says. "Something just came to light. Perhaps we can clarify some things before we give you our answer."

The Chamberlin acknowledges his willingness to listen with a flourish of his hand. It's unusual that he has no words to add, but I'll count that as a good thing.

"Other than our records expunged and a letter of recommendation to anywhere we want, will you be willing to provide us with material and personnel support?"

The Chamberlin regards Kayley for a long moment, a small frown growing on his face. She's asking for a little more than I suggested, and maybe that's just her tactic. I hope it doesn't lose us the deal.

"This office accepts your proposal," the Chamberlin says with a nod.

I let out a sigh but then have to catch myself as the Chamberlin raises a hand.

"However, may I also be the one to remind you that this office does not tolerate disloyalty. Should you act improperly, then the Emperor will respond in kind."

"Meaning he won't be kind to us any longer," I add. I guessed where he was going with that, and by the pleased look on his face, I got it correct. He nods once to me, then opens his palm in my direction.

"Precisely."

Chapter Twelve

IN A FEW MINUTES, Colonel Cortell and a few of his aides will arrive here at Kayley's house. It's been more than a few months since we saw him last. He was only a lieutenant then. Now he's even surpassed the rank of his former commander. Not that his rank matters all that much to us. Harry Cortell is a friend. We're all looking forward to seeing him.

We had to change the normal venue because my place is too small and we know someone's been watching Grady's house. Our work with the colonel has to be kept under wraps. It would be bad if the conspiracy found out before we could put any plans into action.

Because of its sophisticated hosting ability, I suggested we use Kayley's place. Kayley agreed but reminded us we needed to be careful. Her parents are very strict about the tidiness of their domicile. Even their daughter is required to keep her room museum-neat. It's been easy for her to do since she hasn't been here, save for those few days when she was recovering.

"This is all wrong," Nayla says. I suspect she's not talking about our situation. Afton comforts her with a caress down her cheek. Nayla continues to pout as she eyes the sofa where Grady and I sit.

"Sorry," Kayley says. "We're not moving any furniture today. There are more important things to do."

"That is a genuine tragedy," Nayla mumbles and crosses her arms. It's loud enough for Kayley to hear, but before she can reply, the door chime rings.

Kayley springs up and darts to the door. The moment the door is open enough, she bursts through it and disappears. Meanwhile, a man and a woman a few years older than us step in. They separate and scan the room with suspicious eyes, ignoring us until they get to Original Teddy. Their eyes linger on our fuzzy friend for a minute before they continue into the rest of the house.

"Yes, nice to meet you, too," I mutter as I make my way to the front door to find out what became of Kayley.

I find her releasing Colonel Cortell from what must have been quite the embrace. He's all wide-eyed and lethargic, as if Kayley had just slapped him across the face. I might like to see that someday. He's the only one who has ever made me jealous because he's a good-looking dude and he spent six months with Kayley—six months that I didn't get to spend with her.

Okay, well, his former boss spent time with her, too, but Lieutenant Colonel Nelson sacrificed his life for us, so he gets a pass. And he was a mentor to me, so it's a bit more than a pass. I feel an ache in my heart thinking about him. It seems so long ago that he was yelling at Grady and me because we had hitched a ride on the Teddy ship before any other human. That first ride was supposed to be his.

"Hey, Rance," Colonel Cortell says, coming out of his smother-stupor. I forget my adolescent feelings then and open my arms to hug him. He's been with us from the beginning, and even though we haven't been able to see him much, he has given us a huge amount of support. I count him as a member of the team.

"What's with the civvy outfit?" I ask, noticing the fact that he's not in uniform.

"Don't want to bring any suspicious eyes our way," he replies. "I'm just a normal person today."

"Yeah, and with that, we should get inside," Kayley says and ushers us in.

After a few introductions and a little staring—it shocked Colonel Cortell to learn who Nayla was—we all move into the rather sizeable Garmonichnyy dining room and begin the briefing. Colonel Cortell's two aides—Lieutenant Pahina, the woman, and the man, Master Sergeant Vinnai—remain standing and alert while the rest of us sit.

"So we got little intel from the first guy we got our hands on," Colonel Cortell says as he begins his review. "As we suspected, he's just a foot soldier and has no access to any confidential information. We're holding on to him for now, because we don't want him telling his bosses what he's learned."

"Can you do that?" Grady asks. "Can you keep him for as long as you want?"

"Sure. We're not the police. And if this situation gets any worse, there could be a civil war. That gives me the authority to do pretty much whatever I want." The colonel grins. "And with your free pass from the Chamberlin, we're fairly unrestricted."

"So what about the woman?" Kayley asks, leaning forward in her seat. "What has she told you?"

"We're just getting started with her, but you were right. She's a council member on Pectafortis, and as the communications officer for the conspiracy, we think she is going to provide us with a wealth of information."

So we scored big after all. This woman could lead us to all sorts of intel on these seditionists. I bet she could lead us back to the rest of the bosses. Then all we need to do is snatch them up, and that will be the end. We get our records clear, and then the future is ours.

"Have you found out anything from her yet?" I ask, eager to learn more.

"Yes." Colonel Cortell nods. "She's given us the location of an address list, which allegedly contains the names of anyone who has ever been a member of the conspirators or has helped them achieve their goals."

"That's it!" I clap my hands together, and the sound reverberates through the room. "We get that, and they're done!"

"It won't be that easy," Afton says. "You know that."

"What are you talking about? This is exactly what we need!"

Leave it to Afton to find the negative in our opportunity. I'm wondering if she wants to do this at all. Nayla has given her plenty of reason to live for, but she's also dulled Afton's edge.

"Afton is right," Colonel Cortell says. "The—"

"Surela," Nayla corrects.

The colonel gives her a curious glance, but then continues. "They keep the list in a vault within a special secure facility on Albion. I don't have the authority to search the facility without proper authorization from the minister who supervises it."

"So? No problem. We'll just get the Chamberlin to order whichever minister it is to open up for us."

Afton just shakes her head.

"What?" I bark. She just gives me that *I already told you* look of hers. When Kayley does it, at least there's a hint of sympathy for me. Afton's gaze is bereft of any compassion.

"Well, this is where the problem comes in," the colonel replies. "This is a privately owned vault that caters to the ultra-wealthy. The Chamberlin has no authority over it. However, the minister who manages it is a member."

"So who is this minister?"

When Colonel Cortell keeps his mouth shut, I get an itch all over my arms. Whoever it is, I'm not going to be happy about it. I realize now that this is what Afton was talking about. She must have called on Nayla's power of divination to know it before the rest of us.

"Who is it?" Kayley asks, shifting in her seat.

"His name is Crowley."

"Well, there goes that idea," Grady says.

Minister Crowley is the original menace. *My* original menace. He's the one who first ordered the military to fire on the Teddys and create a fake war so the Empire could steal territory from them. We put a stop to his plans, but not before he captured me and threw me in jail. We tried to do the same to him, but his friends in the government gave him a free pass. Still, I bet he's got a light-year-long grudge against us.

The feeling is mutual.

"No. Absolutely not," I say and fold my arms. Grady and Afton both slump in their chairs. "Not him. No way."

Kayley rubs my shoulder in an attempt to calm my nerves. It helps a little. Still, we're going to need more than a light massage to solve this issue.

"Harry, I don't see how we could convince him to help," Kayley says. "You know his history with us."

"He's probably part of the conspiracy!" Grady cries.

"Listen, I understand all of your concerns," Colonel Cortell says. "But I can assure you, Minister Crowley is loyal to the Emperor, and he doesn't know what the vault holds. Now, you'd be correct in thinking he won't just turn over the contents of the vault locker if we tell him what's in it. This is a very private business. If the members found out that the minister gave us access without question or process, every one of them would pull their valuables out of there in a nanosecond."

"There's got to be a better way," I say and sigh. I really don't want to see this guy again. He was the first one to throw me in a cell and threaten to keep me there for the rest of my life. At the time, I fully believed that was going to happen to me. All I want from Minister Crowley is to see him get what he deserves. He's the real criminal.

"Perhaps there is a subordinate that might...handle this for the minister?" Nayla suggests. "Mother would never become involved in something so routine. So should it be with this Crowley, no?"

"I tried that," Colonel Cortell replies. "The vault has a manager of operations who runs things from day to day. He said there was no procedure for letting an outsider dig through a member's property. Not even with supervision."

All eyes turn on me. They're staring at the last obstacle we need to overcome before we move forward with meeting Minister Crowley. I can't bear to look back. I hate being the one thing that's causing problems.

"Rance," Kayley says in my ear in a soft voice. I know what she's about to suggest; I was considering it a microsecond ago. "Why don't you—"

"You know I can't." I turn to meet her gaze so she can see I'm serious. Kayley catches her breath when she notices. Her face turns wistful with sympathy for my dilemma.

But before she calls off the entire plan, I beg her to wait. Kayley nods with an understanding smile. Then she has to watch me struggle through this decision.

This is the only way, and I know it. We could spend the rest of the day making suggestions, but none will be as simple or as safe as negotiating with Minister Crowley. Kayley and Afton should handle this. I won't. I can't. I get I'm being selfish. The amount of clarity I have about it makes my stomach hurt.

There should be a better way, but there isn't. I'm going to have to hold my breath and jump into water that's well over my head, hoping I won't drown in my traumatic memories.

"We've got to shut this conspiracy down," I say, "as quickly as possible. If meeting with Crowley is the most direct route, then..."

Everyone holds their breath as I take a deep one of my own. I've never told anyone how afraid I am of drowning. I'd accept any other way to die besides that. Yet here I am, about to jump into a depth I'm not sure I can swim.

"Goddesses, watch over me." I clench my fists. "Okay. I'm in."

Kayley wraps her arms about me and kisses my cheek, then stands and says, "Okay, let's get the details straight."

"Hey, buddy." Afton slides her chair next to me while the others form a separate group away from me to give me a little space. "I get how hard that was for you. Don't worry, I won't let you fall, okay? I'll be right next to you the entire time. That's a promise."

As she embraces me, I catch Nayla watching us. Her eyes find mine, and she nods with a smile. Her approval isn't just for my courage. It's for Afton's compassion. She's always had it in her, but she's never expressed it like this.

Realizing that gives me strength. Maybe I can face my nightmare, after all.

Chapter Thirteen

"And remember, hands off the fries!" I give my dining companions across the table a harsh look to make sure the three of them understand how hungry I am.

"Easy, buddy," Afton says. "This isn't our usual hole. You can get fancier than fries."

"What's wrong with fries?"

To de-stress a little, Nayla suggested a double date. Kayley, Afton, she, and I went downtown to a snazzy new place that Nayla had her eye on. I don't think I'd ever come here on my own, but seeing the level of excitement that appeared on Kayley's face when we first walked in, I decided I would come back as long as they have taro fries on the menu.

This place is definitely a Nayla pick. It's got her ethereal sense of style all over it. Long, semitranslucent curtains run from floor to ceiling, connecting the transparent metal dividers that both isolate each glass dining table and give the sense of being in a wide, expansive space. There's lots of indirect light from sources around the room, some of which are shaped like stars. Our table has a low-hung chandelier that is both a light fixture and a floating work of art. The serene music being piped in just adds to the feeling we're floating on clouds.

I hope they have taro fries in the clouds.

"Too bad Harry couldn't come," Kayley says, playing with the straw in her juice cocktail. I know she doesn't mean what I hope she doesn't mean. Yet the jealous streak runs down my spine. There is and never has been anything between them. I just accept that I'm a paranoid fool when it comes to Kayley and other more successful, better looking, and more well-groomed guys.

"Grady or Parrish either," I add. Parrish is taking care of his mom, and Grady had no interest in being a fifth wheel, so he headed up to the ship with Original Teddy to work on something with Doc Elizabeth. I worry I will become the test subject for whatever they come up with.

"We'll bring them here next time," Kayley replies and turns to studying her menu. I should do the same.

Before I can examine it, something about the light falling on Kayley's face captures my attention. Its soft quality makes her skin glow. The highlights on her head accent the soft texture of her scarlet hair. I see Kayley as if for the first time, and I fall in love all over again.

Afton catches me staring, but instead of taking advantage of the moment to humiliate me, she just smiles and nods, her hand sliding over to interlace fingers with Nayla, who lifts it to her lips and places a soft kiss on Afton's knuckles.

The moment fills me with warmth, and I sigh, content. This was a stellar idea. We're all sharing in the enjoyment of some quiet time with our significant others. I'm a little sad that my buds can't join in. Still, I hope they can the next time.

I'm so enthralled with the moment, I almost miss the movement over Afton's shoulder. A man in a long, dirty overcoat roams through the diners, who are enjoying their experience so much they don't notice him. His eyes are wild as he scans the room, looking for...what?

A waiter approaches him, frowning. There's no doubt he doesn't belong here, so why did they let him in? In that filthy outfit it's clear he didn't come here for the cuisine.

"What are you going to have? Rance?" Kayley asks, but I'm too focused on this guy to answer.

Then he turns my way. A manic grin covers his face. He reaches for the edges of his coat, and my senses scream in alarm.

"Death to the Emperor!" he cries.

There's a flash. I'm thrown back as a shock wave shakes my body. I go airborne, flying until I smash into a divider. It cracks under the impact, sending shards of metal out the other side.

Then I'm on the floor. My head is spinning so fast I can't tell which way is up. A thought fills my head. Kayley. Afton. Nayla. Are they okay? I've got to find them and get out.

A rumble comes from across the room, then a scream and a thunderous crash. Dust bursts from the ceiling's collapse, filling my lungs before I can think to hold my breath. I choke and cough, my eyes tearing up from the foreign particles trying to invade my eyelids.

I roll onto my side, my back aching with every slight movement. Still, I force myself up onto my hands and knees and move in the direction I only hope is toward those I care about.

I pull out my Sergo and turn on the light. It's gone pitch-black inside the building. The blast must have destroyed every light fixture in here. Not even a peek of illumination from the streetlights makes it inside.

"Kayley!" My hoarse croak goes unanswered. I try again, but it only adds to the fear filling me. My ears are overpowered with the ring that fills them. I might miss hearing her if she can't yell. She may not hear me, either.

"Help! Help me!" A young girl's voice breaks through the constant din. She might be on the other side of the collapse, and by the sound of it, I don't think she's hurt. I should go get her—right after I find Kayley.

A sharp pain like a needle slides into my palm. I draw a ragged breath through my teeth and remember all the glass that surrounded us. Most of it is on the floor, and a piece is now in my hand. I'll have to go through the unpleasant motion of pulling that fragment out. Then I should get up so it doesn't happen again.

"Kayley!" I try a third time.

Our table, or what is left of it, comes into view through the smoke and dusty haze. There are blotches of red smeared across the remains of the top. No! I panic, shoving half-smashed chairs and a fallen chandelier out of my way, no longer caring if I get cut. If Kayley's hurt—or—no. I don't want to think it.

A groan comes from the ceiling. Chips of glass rain down as if someone had just tossed a handful from the top floor. That's a bad sign. The entire building could be unstable. I won't have much time.

"Is someone there?" the young girl calls. "Please! Help me! I'm stuck!"

"Hey!" I shout. "Can you hear me?"

"Yes! Yes, I can hear you! Please help me!"

Some well-chosen curse words would be appropriate right now, if I could think of any. I don't want to upset the Goddesses, though. I'm already begging them to hold the remainder of the ceiling up.

Every second more I search for Kayley and can't find her is a second my panic grows. Afton and Nayla are no less critical. The sight of that blood across the table keeps replaying in my mind. That could be all that remains of the girl I love.

No. I've got to think with some level of positivity. Otherwise, I'm going to curl up in a ball and cry. Maybe the three of them already got out. I don't know if I blacked out or not after I hit that divider. Maybe they couldn't find me. Or maybe someone else pulled them out.

All I know is that they're nowhere to be found, and there's someone I'm sure needs my help.

"Okay! I'm coming!"

I stumble through the wreckage of what was to be a night of happiness. A pair of bodies, limp and bloodied, come across my path. I check for a pulse and get the unfortunate answer I expected. What bothers me more is that I don't see more of them.

"Mister, can you see me yet?" the girl calls.

"Not yet, but you sound closer!" Or my ears are ringing less.

The smell of burning...something fills my nose and makes me wretch. I don't want to imagine what it could be. It's not coming from the kitchen. That much, I'm sure.

"Hey, kid, what's your name?" I shout.

"Christa."

"Christa. I'm Rance. Just hang on, okay? I'm coming."

The collapsed part of the ceiling appears before me, and I scan it with the beam from my Sergo until I find a potential spot to climb through. It's large enough to fit my body, but it's seriously risky. Live electrical wires could be hanging down. I could miss one with my light and grab it by accident. Then Christa has no one to save her.

I put my leg through a pair of fallen supports and test the stability of the floor beyond. It's safe, or at least seems so to me. Then I grab hold of a support and bend down to slide the rest of my body through.

As I put weight on it, the beam flexes, and the entire ceiling shudders. I freeze, hoping that I didn't just make a fatal mistake.

Everything stays in place, and I continue, wishing I had Teddy-like climbing ability or, better yet, the Teddys were here to help. I could upload something to Teddynet, but it wouldn't make a difference. They'd never get here in time. There should be a rescue squad coming soon, anyway.

My left leg gets through to the other side. Now for the right. I grab hold of the next crossbeam in my path and raise my foot to pull it through.

But the moment I pull, my shoe catches on something and stops me from moving through. I shake my leg, attempting to free it, but no luck. This is going to require a more forceful, and risky, maneuver. I drop my Sergo in my pocket and grab hold of the crossbeam with both hands.

With the beam to keep my balance, I plant my left foot and, with a hard yank, try to break the lace on my right shoe. It's tough, so I turn up the force, increasing my kick.

With a pop, the lace snaps, but I've overdone it. The extra force throws me off-balance, and I fall back, crashing into a chair. Pain shoots up my side. I've got to take a moment to recover before I pull the Sergo from my pocket. My eyes lock on the crossbeam, and I pray I didn't just bring the rest of the ceiling down on me.

"Are you Rance?"

The nearness of the girl's voice breaks my attention. I roll over, flashing the light towards where I think Christa could be.

A squeak and a pair of small arms confirm I've hit my target. Good. At least I can save one person today.

"Yeah, that's me." I turn the light back towards me so she can see who I am. "Are you hurt badly?"

"No, not really. My leg is stuck under something."

"Okay. I've got it."

I stand and dust myself off, then examine how to get Christa free. Despite the worry on her face, she's a cute five- or six-year-old with dark hair and big eyes. She reminds me of what Afton looked like at that age.

There's a sizeable chunk of tabletop across her foot that must weigh more than she does. No wonder she can't get herself free.

"Alright, I'm going to lift the edge of this up, and you pull your leg free, okay?"

Christa nods, and I bend down to grab the edge.

"Here we go, ready?"

I tighten my muscles and pull up with as much force as I think is necessary. But it's not enough. I pull harder and, with a grunt, lift the glass up. Christa squirms, placing her hands on the ground and tugging with all her might.

She's free! Now to stop myself from getting a hernia.

"Stand back, Christa. I'm going to let go of this."

The glass tabletop hits the ground with a thud and cracks in half. I feel the vibration of the impact in the floor. That was a lot heavier than I thought. I wipe a sleeve across my brow and start scanning around for a way to get out of this death trap.

And that's when the rest of the ceiling collapses.

Chapter Fourteen

I'm okay. I'm still breathing...nothing broken...no gaping wounds. I think. There is a weight pressing down on my legs, causing me not a little discomfort. I dropped my Sergo, which must be buried under a bunch of rubble now, so I can't see what's crushing down on my thighs, but I bet it's that crossbeam I so naïvely clung to on my way over here to rescue Christa.

"Christa!"

"I'm here."

She's not far away from me by the sound of her voice. I can also tell by the tremor in her speech that she's terrified.

"Are you hurt?"

"No." Christa coughs. "I didn't get hit."

"Good. That's good. But listen, I still want to get you out of here, but I'm stuck. Can you help me find my Sergo so I can see what's fallen on me?"

A light blinks on and shines on my face. I squint and hold up my hand to block the glare. Behind it, I can see the silhouetted edge of a young girl.

"I've got mine," Christa says. Why didn't that possibility cross my mind? Kids get Sergos as soon as they can walk these days. I think they're a little spoiled, though, for this moment, I'll be happy about that fact.

"Great. Can you bring it over here and shine it on my legs?" I ask.

Christa moves towards me, taking hesitant steps over the chunks of broken glass that impede her path. She falls once, yelping with such a high pitch that I clap my hands over my ears. If she didn't just shatter all the glass in here with that squeak, I'd be surprised.

"Hey, you okay?"

"Yeah. I was just scared. That's all."

When she turns the light on my legs, I do my best to hold in all the curse words I want to blast out. That'd be a bad influence on Christa, and I'm trying to rescue her, not corrupt her.

There's a crossbeam on my legs, alright, just not the same crossbeam I put my hands on. This one is attached to a graphcrete plank the size of me. It's got to weigh a good deal more than I do, too, and I've put on some pounds, the way I been eating lately.

I won't get this beam off me on my own, and Christa isn't going to be much help. She makes a great light stand, however.

Which reminds me.

"Christa, can I borrow your Sergo? I want to call for help."

Christa thrusts the device towards me, its light still blazing. It blasts me in the eye, and I fumble the Sergo a few times before I get a solid grip on it. I take another few seconds to remember Kayley's number. Then I punch it in and hope she picks up.

As the line rings, a few crumbles of graphcrete fall on my head. Christa reaches out and wipes it off me.

"Hello? Who is this?"

It's Afton. Her voice sounds desperate, as if she was waiting for a call to come through.

"Afton! It's me! Where are you?"

"Hey! It's Rance!" Afton calls to someone nearby, then returns to the call. "We're outside! Where are you?"

"Inside. Under a chunk of the ceiling." I swallow hard before I ask her the one question I'm fearful to ask. "Where's Kayley? Are you guys okay?"

"She went for help." A pause. "She's okay. Mostly. We're all banged up a b it."

The sigh that escapes me makes Christa stare at me as if my spirit just left my body. It almost did. I've been focusing on my and Christa's rescue, so my panic about Kayley went to the back of my head, but the moment I made the call, it dropped front and center again.

Thank you, Goddesses, for looking after the love of my life. Afton and Nayla, too.

"So I'm going to need help to get out of here. Did the rescue squad arrive yet?"

Another pause. Afton sounds like she's arguing with someone too far away for me to hear.

"They're here, but they won't go in," Afton growls as she gets back on the call. "The building's too unstable."

Oh great. This place can collapse any minute, and the people responsible for getting everyone out before that happens don't want to do their job. I shouldn't blame them for not wanting to come into the space that I'm trying to escape from. Still, it leaves me with not-so-stellar options.

"What's that mean?" Christa asks.

"Someone there with you?" Afton says.

"Yes," I reply. "A young girl. She's not hurt, but I've got to get her out of here before something else falls down."

"Can you see a way out?"

"Not from this position."

"Kayley's going to meet the Teddys, but I don't think they'll be here before..."

"It's that bad, huh?"

There's silence from the other end, and that's all the answer I need. I may have to accept the fact that I might not make it out of here. I'm not done yet, and before any tragedy befalls me, I've got to get Christa out.

I turn the light of the Sergo on the walls. The light flickers as I move it. Shoot. It's down to only fifteen percent power. Leave it to a little kid not to have good battery discipline. She could have charged it right on the dining table if she wanted to. Likely she was too busy playing games to be bothered with a recharge time-out. It's happened to me a few times.

I'd better be thriftier with my energy use.

"Afton, call you back," I say and hang up before she can get her protest out. There's no point wasting precious battery while she argues with the rescue squad.

If I could find an exit for Christa to crawl through, I'd hand her the Sergo and let her get herself out. That'd leave me with no way to talk to the outside world, and no light, but now that I've got an idea of my situation, I could still try.

I try to get leverage under the plank and test it to see if I can even move it. Graphcrete is sturdy stuff, but this piece is so broken that it only bends as I push up on it, which weakens my leverage. I press a little more to see if

I can fold it off me like a blanket, but here's where the material's stiffness comes in. I can flex it a bit, but then it just quits being cooperative. I'd have to use more force to bend it than I would to lift it.

"Hey, Mr. Rance," Christa calls. "I think I see outside."

"Where?" I swivel towards her voice and find her close to the back of the dining room. That's where the kitchen is. There might be a door or vent over there that she can climb out of.

Christa points to a space just under a fallen ceiling tile.

I call Afton back, and she picks up right away.

"We're still working on it. What you got?"

"Come to the side of the building where the alleyway is. I think you can pull Christa out from there."

"What about you?"

"Still working on that."

"Well...Hold on, Rance. The chief of the squad wants to talk to me...What? You've got to be kidding!" Afton mutters a few choice words. "Buddy, you've got to get yourself free and over to that alleyway exit. The chief just said there's a fire in the kitchen. They didn't notice it before because it was small, but now they think it's growing."

Christa and I share a look of horror. The young girl overheard every word that Afton just said, and her face is twisting into a sob. I'd cry too if this was the first time I was in a situation like this.

"I'm giving Christa the Sergo," I say to Afton as I motion the girl over to me. "There isn't much battery left, and maybe it'll be easier to find her with the light."

"How are you going to see to get yourself out?"

"Maybe the fire will help."

"Not funny, buddy." Afton sighs. "Alright. Do that. We'll keep working outside to get to you."

"And, Surela," I say with all kindness and seriousness. "If I don't get out...please, tell Kayley..."

"No," Afton replies. "I'm not promising that, because you're going to tell her whatever you want herself. And don't get all sappy on me with that Surela nonsense."

I laugh. "I love you, Afton."

"Shut up and get your ass out here."

I hang up and hand the Sergo to Christa, who takes it as if it is some kind of poisonous animal. I try to reassure her with a smile, but the sniffle she responds with tells me I'm not successful.

A whiff of smoke touches my nose, and I glance towards the kitchen. There's an orange glimmer flickering there that's growing. Christa's got to move, or she's going to freak and not be able to escape.

"Hey." I reach out to touch her hand. "You've got to do me a favor, okay?"

Christa presses her lips together and nods. Maybe she's expecting me to lay some heavy responsibility on her. I'm not. I just want to ensure my effort in coming to rescue her won't be in vain.

"Don't think about anything but getting yourself out. That's the best thing you can do to help me right now. Squeeze through whatever hole you can over there, and once you're halfway out, start shouting and waving your Sergo around. Got it?"

"Got it."

"And don't let my friend scare you. She acts all tough, but she's actually very nice."

"Okay."

"Alright, get going."

Christa gives me one last forlorn look, then scrambles over to the hole she found and starts shoving herself through it. I watch her until I can't make out her small body any longer.

Now to get myself out, if I can.

I might have been joking, but the glow of the fire is illuminating the space a little. There's also heat wafting forward from the kitchen, and smoke is billowing into the dining area. I can only hope that there's a big hole somewhere in the roof to let the smoke out. A fire doesn't need heat to kill me.

My eyes squeeze shut as the fumes from the fire sting them. There's got to be a ton of toxic chemicals floating in the air right now. I'll try not to think about it. I don't need another hazard to overcome.

I try to slide my legs out from under the panel, but any movement only presses the plank down on them more.

The smoke is becoming thicker, and soon I'm going to have trouble breathing.

Maybe I can wedge a beam or something under the plank and lever it up that way. If I can jam it under the crossbeam, rather than the plank itself, I could lift it up enough to slide my legs out. All I need now is something to lever it with.

But there isn't anything.

Christa cries out and kicks at the fallen debris that surrounds her. I didn't know she was still here! Why hasn't she gotten out yet?

An enormous boom shakes the building. Bits of metal and glass explode from the kitchen and fly towards me. I try to cover my head and duck. Too slow. The blast hits me and tosses me like I'm a piece of scrap paper. Slivers of glass impale my arms, and I smash against a divider. It cracks and crumbles, falling down around me.

I'm free, but at what cost? My arms and legs sting with the intensity of a thousand needles sticking into them. I've sprained, perhaps broken, my ankle, too.

A jet of flame shoots out from the kitchen—the gas line! If that hits the main valve, the entire building will turn into a fireball.

There's a groan from the ceiling above me. I don't think. I just move, diving under the fire. The entire front wall of the building crashes in. Now there's a way out!

Christa screams again, and I'm moving to her on my hands and knees, feeling pain at every step. It doesn't matter. I push through my agony and get to her.

"Christa! What's wrong? Are you stuck?" I call, shaking her foot. It's the only part of her I can still see.

"Yes! The hole is too small!"

"Forget it! I'm pulling you out!" I grab her ankle and tug. Christa cries out, but her body moves an inch.

The blast of flames coming from the kitchen is searing the area, turning it into a smoldering pile of potential combustion. The heat is so intense that I can feel the hairs on the back of my neck burning.

I pull Christa again, and this time, she assists me. A second later, she's free and grabbing on to me.

"That way!" I point to the hole in the collapsed wall. There's a pair of rescue squad members gawking in from the outside.

Christa takes my hand, and we find any way to get to safety. We still have to climb over the debris of the wall. I help Christa get up and over, then I try to stand. Burning rips through my hurt leg, and I collapse to the ground.

One rescuer climbs in and grabs Christa, pulling her out.

The other offers his hand to me, and I reach for it. It's a good thing he's wearing gloves, or all the glass in my palm would give him an unwelcome surprise.

With a grunt, the rescuer lifts me, and I pull myself the rest of the way. I roll out, and then several pairs of hands grab me and haul me away.

A second after I'm placed on a stretcher, Afton's and Nayla's faces appear over me, their eyes wide. They look as I must—faces full of soot and blood, hair all over the place. Nayla's trademark turban hangs off her head, only half wrapped. She reaches out but is hesitant to touch me.

"I made it," I say with a voice that sounds like I just drank sand.

Afton pats my cheek.

"I never doubted you." Then she smirks. "You're getting to be almost half as good as I am."

Chapter Fifteen

After spending a day in the hospital so they could check me over, I'm back home, enjoying the special meal my mom prepared for me this morning. That was the only stellar meal I've had in two days, given we didn't get to eat anything at Nayla's fancy place, thanks to that idiot with a bomb.

Mom had to go out—she's playing croquet with Kayley's mom—so no more great dining for me today. The one bonus is that Kayley agreed to trade spots with my mother while she's enjoying her day on the lawn. I think she said that Original Teddy might join them, but I find that hard to believe. He doesn't know how to play croquet.

There's a knock on the front door, then it opens. That's Kayley now, though I hear two pairs of footsteps. Maybe Grady came with her to see how I'm doing. He was the only other one who wasn't preoccupied with something else today.

"I'm upstairs!" I call.

Thirty seconds later, Original Teddy strolls in, looking...different. Something is strange about his appearance, but I can't—

Oh, wait. It's the hat.

He's wearing a straw boater hat with a black-and-red ribbon around its crown. If that wasn't odd enough, one of his tentacles is wrapped around some kind of mallet.

A croquet mallet.

"Dumbass," Original Teddy says as he hops up on my desk chair. "Creation of reckless is not prescribed."

I'm glad he's worried about me, but he could do a better job of expressing it.

"You really have to cool it with calling people that, Teddy," I say. "It's not nice."

"Muckraking is required. Skill honing is necessary. Expiration for opportunity is forthcoming."

"Are you guys ending your cultural study?" Kayley asks, walking in behind him. She pauses to examine me, then smiles once she sees I'm okay, even if my hands are still wrapped up in bandages. Doc Elizabeth promised she'd check out the doctor's work once I came up to the ship. She'd come down, but her project—she wouldn't explain what it is—is nearing completion.

"That is accurate," Original Teddy replies. "Abandon is arriving. Study is approaching conclusion. Departure will arrive posthaste."

"Wait." I think I got what he was saying. I just can't believe it. "You're returning home?"

"That is not accurate," Original Teddy says, swinging the mallet.

Kayley and I sigh. We would miss the Teddys something serious if they left us. They've been with us through every moment, happy and sad. They've lost friends just like we have. Teddynet isn't the only connection I have with them. We've got a powerful emotional bond, too.

"Teddy has never been home."

Kayley gasps. So do I. It's true. Original Teddy was born on one of their ships, and he's spent his entire life cruising the stars. He's probably explored so many planets. Seen so many amazing things. It's a wonder that the Teddys stayed as long as they did. I wish Teddynet could tell me more, but once something is uploaded there, it loses all connection to the individual that uploaded it. The one thing that I don't need Teddynet to tell me is that Original Teddy has always wanted to see his homeworld.

"So you're leaving us?" Kayley asks, coming over to sit on my bed.

"That is not accurate. Rancid cannot be left."

I still find it amazing that I can be light-years away from the nearest Teddy ship and still have a connection to them. It won't be the same, though, no matter what Original Teddy says. There's no substitute for him being here.

"When will you leave?" I ask.

"Specificity is unknown. Teddy will endeavor to remain for potential maximum length."

"But once your mission is over, you've got to go."

"That is accurate."

Original Teddy's tentacles slump. It's his attempt to mimic our own disappointment. It's effective enough. I don't even need to check Teddynet to understand his feelings. They're the same as mine.

I want to ask him to postpone his departure for a little while more, but I don't want to be the one to pressure him to stay. But once he's gone, no one will have any sort of connection to him other than me, and even that won't be very specific. It's only because the Teddys have uploaded situation-specific information to Teddynet that I've known it was from our Teddys. I've never been to their homeworld, so I've got no way to know if Original Teddy is trying to send me something or not.

"Is there no way you can delay? Just for a bit longer?" she asks.

Original Teddy swings the mallet and pretends to inspect it. It's very much a borrowed human habit—avoiding the question. He doesn't want to tell us no, but that is the only answer he can give. Even though Teddys are individuals, their society and culture are all about what's best for them as a whole. As far as I can tell, it's never been an issue—until they met humans.

I wrap my arm around Kayley's and draw her near. I'd prefer to hold her hand at this moment, but all the wrappings on my hand make that near impossible. She presses closer to me to make up for that lack of connection. It's enough.

"You know that won't be the same, even with Teddynet," I say.

"Rancid," Original Teddy says as he looks at me. "This is inaccurate. Teddy does not designate 'Teddynet.' Rancid should endeavor to make a more accurate reference."

"Okay, I'll try."

I guess if I had to think about it, "community knowledge center" would be the way the Teddys might describe it. It's not wrong, but not entirely accurate, either. I can't find the words in Empire Common to name it with any sort of accuracy. I understand it, but it's hard to explain in human terms.

"We don't want you to go, Teddy. *I* don't want you to go."

"Vocalization is unrequired, Rancid. Teddy understands."

Of course he knows. So does that mean I should fall on my knees and beg him to stay? Would he if I did?

It's not right for me to hold him back, but I know once he's gone, a piece of me leaves with him.

"What is Elizabeth going to do?" Kayley asks. I hadn't considered that. Not yet. She's got no way to communicate with us if she leaves. I don't think she will. Still, I won't know until I ask her.

"Unknown," Original Teddy replies. So he hasn't spoken to her, either. Maybe he hasn't even told her they're headed home. That's unfair. Doc Elizabeth should have time to consider her options.

Though, if I try to convince Original Teddy to stay, I won't have to do the same to Elizabeth. I don't know how long she's been alone with the Teddys, but from what I've seen as of late, she is truly enjoying human company.

"Couldn't you wait just a little longer?" I ask, repeating Kayley's request. "We need you guys."

"Yes," Kayley adds, "this is a critical time. We're on the verge of ending the conspiracy. We can't do that without you."

Silence from Original Teddy again. He can't answer a request like that. It's not up to him. Only Captain Teddy could decide that, and it's likely not up to him, either. I doubt I could get Captain Teddy to change his mind. I'm not even sure if I should try.

I sit up and lean my chin on Kayley's shoulder. As much as I want to convince him, I also know that it's selfish of me to do so. If I make him stay, then I hold him back from his dream. I can't do that, not when he's done everything he could to help me achieve mine. While I'm not there yet, I wouldn't be where I am without Teddy.

"Rancid. K-K-Kayley," Original Teddy says, "departure is not conclusive. Teddy will remain. Always."

I get he means that he'll be back again. That could be fifty years from now, though. The Teddy sense of time differs from humans. They understand we only live for so long, and so do they, if just a bit longer.

"I know, Teddy," I reply. "I just hope you understand how hard it is for us to see you go. Probably it's just as hard for you, too. You're...like family."

"No," Kayley corrects, "you *are* family."

"Teddy understands family."

I hang my head. There's no sense in trying to get him to do something he cannot commit to. It's just best if we can enjoy the time we have left together. The only problem with that is we're caught in this battle to save the Empire. There's no enjoyment in that. We only get to relax once the fight is won. If we can win it, that is.

Original Teddy hops off my chair and waddles over to us, extending a tentacle to us as he does. Kayley and I reach out and accept the offered connection. We're two completely different species, yet there is no substitute for the communication of touch. Perhaps it's universally understood by all creatures that exist. I've got no way to confirm that, but it's a nice thought. For now, all we can do is accept that our physical connection to Teddy can only be temporary.

"Teddy will also wish for future contact."

All we can do is smile and hope that we'll be able to handle missing him and all the Teddys that have done so much for us. It makes me remember how vast the universe is and how we consist as just a tiny part of it. It's humbling and inspiring at the same time.

We'll have to learn how to deal with things without Teddy help, if we can. Maybe we can manage it. They haven't always been here. The conditions that forced us together were harsh but were critical for our successes over the last two years. No one can bond with someone else, even if they're aliens, over extreme circumstances and not expect to have a permanent connection. I'm more than willing to accept that. And that's what makes this so difficult.

"Time to make the croquettes," Original Teddy says, swinging his mallet.

"That's not the same thing, Teddy," Kayley says with a giggle. "Croquettes are food. You're going to meet my mom to play a lawn game."

Teddy stares at Kayley with his big disk eyes. I don't know what his reaction is, but I think he's disappointed.

"Preference for nutritional is recommended," Original Teddy says.

"Don't worry," Kayley says. "I'm sure my mother will have a nice array of stuff for you to enjoy while you play."

"Define the quantity of array."

"Teddy, did you ever consider not being so food-focused?" I ask with a grin.

"Nonsense, Rancid."

Chapter Sixteen

"Well, that sucks," I say, staring out the window to watch Original Teddy depart.

"It does," Kayley replies, "but we couldn't expect them to be here forever. They've got responsibilities just like we do, and looking after the Empire isn't one of them. It's better if they go."

I look over at her and blink. What she says is true, yet I never expected something so...direct from her. Kayley's always been the nurturer, the supportive and caring leader type. Plus, her friendship with the Teddys runs as deep as mine does. It can't be that easy for her to let them leave. Can it?

"We still need their help, though, KayKay," I say, stating what I believe to be the obvious.

"We do, and we don't."

I feel the skin on my forehead squeeze together. She's almost in full Afton mode right now. Maybe I should recommend she hang out with Nayla less. Or is it more? The ex-princess did a lot of good for Afton. If Kayley's sliding down into a bad place, she might benefit from whatever hocus pocus Nayla can conjure up. I may have my doubts about it, but it's helped Afton.

"Kayley, is something on your mind?" I try. If I can uncover what's bugging her—if anything is—then I can talk through it with her. That might relieve a little of her tension.

"Yes. The same thing that's on your mind," she replies. Her tone is flat, which means she's not giving me the full answer. Okay. I'll play this game for a moment.

"Oh? What's on my mind?"

"The Teddys, of course."

So she's going with that. Fine. I'm up for a challenge. I reach for her shoulders and turn her towards me. She resists, then lowers my hands down gently. I try to catch her glance, but she won't look at me.

"Don't do that. You'll hurt your hands again."

This is absolute proof and confirmation that something else is on her mind. Time to dive in and sort this out.

"KayKay, I can't believe that after all this time, you'd rely on the same avoidance tactic you've been using since you were ten. Are you going to tell me what's up, or am I going to have to tickle it out of you?"

Kayley's shoulders slump as she sighs. There. I've struck the jackpot. Now I'll be able to do some Nayla magic and make her feel better.

"No, I need to talk to you."

"Good, then talk to me. If you can't talk to me, then who can you talk to? I'm your boyfriend and, maybe one day, more than that. We've got to be open and honest with each other, right?"

"It's not that easy." Kayley levels her gaze on me then. Now I get why she's been struggling for the last few minutes. She has to tell me something, something that won't make me happy, and she's been fighting with herself to bring it up. Whatever it is, it can't be that bad.

"KayKay, tell me. Don't keep whatever it is inside. That's not healthy."

I don't like the look of pity she gives me after I say that, but I put myself out there, so I've got to accept whatever it is she tells me. She's already confirmed we're not breaking up anytime soon, so I'm safe there.

With a breath, she reaches out, taking my face in her hands. Then she kisses me. Softly. Sweetly. And for a really long time. After a minute of our lips pressing together, I've got to come up for air. I stare at her, dazed. Now I'm afraid of what she'll say. No one kisses someone like that without bad news attached to it.

I wait in anticipation, my heart beating faster, and not only from the kiss. My skin starts to itch, too. I can't think of what she's about to say, but with all this buildup, I know I'm not going to be ready for whatever it is.

"Don't go to meet Minister Crowley," Kayley spits out. "Let me handle it."

"Oh, Goddesses." I release my breath and cover my bandaged arm over my heart. "I thought you were going to tell me something terrible...Wait, what?"

"I know, I know." She raises her hands in apology. "I should have stopped the others from pressuring you into it, but that was before someone tried to blow us up."

"People have been trying to blow us up for a while now, Kayley. How is this different?"

"It's not, but this is yet another disaster that you've been involved in, and I don't want you getting hurt anymore. Not physically and not mentally. You need a break. So...sit this one out, okay?"

Kayley's eyes plead with me to say yes. It's hard for me to resist when she looks at me like that. Yet I don't get why she's decided that I'd be better off resting. I feel like I'm always resting. Always recovering from something or other. That's nothing new. We've got a mission to accomplish. I'll rest when we're done.

Then I realize that I just did the same thing to her before our last mission.

"Hey, I appreciate what you're wanting to do, but the four of us were in that blast. Not just me. We were just trying to enjoy each other's company. You, Afton, and Nayla may not have gotten more than a few cuts, but don't tell me you haven't had nightmares about it."

"Yes. You're right. I did. Just last night. But no one has gone through more stress and more pain than you have, Rance."

"What about Parrish? They shot him. Three times now! He can't run like he used to. And Grady almost died! Don't forget the torture we put Afton through, having to choose between Nayla and us. All of us have wounds. It's unfair for you to pull your boss card out on me like this. Nobody else should take any more risks than I do."

"But that's just it, Rance. You have taken more risks than anyone else. Whether you wanted to or not. Anytime we've had a serious complication, you've been in the middle of it."

"Except when it was just you and Parrish trying to get on Exile."

Kayley gives me a look, then she turns away. That wasn't a point I wanted to score. I did it anyway, likely because she hurt me first. I'm not proud of it. She was only stating a fact, and so was I, but mine was meant to wound. I didn't realize that's what I was doing. I just reacted, and now I regret it.

"I'm sorry, Kayley. I didn't mean—"

"Yes, you did." Her voice remains calm, amazingly. "But I don't blame you. You've been through a lot these past few days. I understand how fragile you are right now."

"Fragile?" I'm a little stressed, sure, but not fragile.

"You're suffering from post-traumatic stress, and you don't even realize it."

"Now wait a second." I'd hold up a finger, except I can't. They covered my entire hand in bandages, so the only thing I can do is hold that up. "If I'm stressed, so are you. So are Afton and Nayla."

"Afton and Nayla aren't meeting with Minister Crowley. They're doing the intelligent thing and taking a break."

"So then why shouldn't all of us do the same thing?"

"Because the meeting is set, and someone has to be there."

"So why do you get to go and I don't?"

Kayley huffs and folds her arms. We're going around in circles with our argument. I get she's trying to care for me, but her reasons don't hold up. I could throw everything she's put on me right back at her.

"I see now why you didn't want to bring this up," I say.

"Yes! Because I knew you would be a complete dumbass about it!"

"Hey now...Calling me a dumb—"

"You. Deserve. It!" Kayley's words are accented by her finger being thrust into my chest. "You've got no sense of how to keep yourself safe! You jump into the middle of a disaster even when I beg you not to! You can't always be the hero, Rance! This idea that you're the only one who can solve things is naïve and juvenile. You're just like your father that way!"

My mouth drops open. Did she really just compare me to my father? To him? The man she knows without a doubt I never want to be like? If I wounded her with my words, then she's gone in for the kill.

I feel my chest get heavy. This is almost worse than her saying that we're over. Until now, Kayley's been reasonable and considerate. But I won't sit back and take this. Not even from her.

"Hero? I'm not the who got a gigantic head from six months of everyone on the planet bowing to them. And I didn't go to the Imperial Parliament thinking I was so important that I could change their minds."

She pulls back, a grimace taking over her face. It remains as she stares at me, silent as my body gets weary. I went too far with that one. But she picked a sensitive wound and rubbed on it. Hard. Kayley knows better than to compare me to my father.

I still regret saying it. I wounded her, too, likely just as bad.

"You see?" Kayley says in a quiet voice. "You see what your trauma makes you do?"

I sigh. She's still pushing me, though nowhere near as hard as she did a minute ago. If I push back, we're going to end up hating each other. Neither of us wants that, so one of us has to surrender. I'll let it be me. This time.

"I'm sorry, KayKay." I hang my head. "Maybe you're right."

"I am right. You just can't see it."

My hands tighten. She's not apologetic at all, but I've got to let that go. At least for now. She's stressed about everything, and I'm not helping.

"So what do you want from me, then?" I ask, leaning my hands back on the bed.

"Right now? Nothing. Stay in bed today. Sleep. Don't think about the meeting tomorrow. Just rest."

Sheesh. Kayley's asking more of me than she realizes. I've rarely been so immobile. Grady and I have spent only a handful of days where the only thing we did was play games on his system. That was back when we were in school. That was over two years ago at this point.

She's asking—I think she's only asking, that is—so I should make myself comfortable. Maybe even consider whether that bomb stressed me out. I won't rule out that idea. Who can survive an explosion like that and not be affected?

Still, if I'm going to stay here and play the obedient patient, I deserve to get something out of it.

"If I do that, will you let me go to the meeting?" I ask.

Kayley crosses her arms, and her gaze gets hard again. She can't keep it up, though. Our fight has exhausted both of us, and I get the feeling she's willing to capitulate a little. None of us can remain so strict for very long.

"Fine. But you stay back and let me do the talking. If you open your mouth, I'm sending you home. Got it?"

I nod.

"Stand up, then."

I do as requested as I wonder why she wants me to.

The moment Kayley's arms wrap around me, I get my answer. My embrace of her is automatic. When she's near, I always find myself wanting to hold her.

This hug feels different, though. It's soft and close, like always, but I notice she's tense.

Kayley kisses my cheek and leans back. Our eyes connect, and I relax a little. There's the girl I know, minus the smile. I try to coax it out of her with a curl of my mouth. Instead, I get her hands running though my hair as she looks at me. It's comforting, but I wish she'd show me everything is o kay.

"I love you, KayKay," I say.

Silence is my only answer. Then, "Rest. I mean it. We're starting early tomorrow."

I watch her leave, still shocked at our fight. Maybe she is, too. We've had disagreements before, but we've never tried to hurt each other over them.

Kayley wants me to rest. That's going to be impossible. I'll never be able to relax until we make up for real. This wasn't that. This was just a truce.

Chapter Seventeen

We await Minister Crowley on the balcony of his district office, on his homeworld of Magnus Dolus, capital of all things commercial. They are so proud of that title that they cover their world with advertisements. Anywhere you go, including the toilet, is sure to have a bevy of petitions for every unnecessary item one can buy. It's a noisy, raucous place, and anyone who is a light sleeper would equate it to being in the seventh level of hell.

Still, I'm glad this meeting wasn't on the military station above Herdewyke. I couldn't have handled being back at the site of my first imprisonment, not with the way things are. As it was, Kayley said very little to me the entire way here. She was in constant conversation with Colonel Cortell. I don't think she was avoiding me, but every time I watched the two of them talking, it made my chest tight. My own seventh hell would have descended on me if Afton wasn't sitting next to me and doing her best to keep me distracted. I'm glad she changed her mind and came with us.

Minister Crowley's balcony is about as high up as it needs to be to avoid any of the floating billboards that harass apartment owners on the lower levels. I guess money and power give him that privilege. It gives me a chance to clear my head and prepare to see his face again.

The view is beautiful. Beams of the sun cut through the morning haze in a ribbonlike pattern, reminding me of the edges of Kwanon's golden robes. Beyond those rays, the walls of the buildings sit in muted grays and blues in comparison, fading into the dark of the streets below. Soon enough, those same roads will be emblazoned with the light from a thousand vid screens playing product ads.

I'm glad I'm not down there. Being up here is tough enough for me.

Afton puts a hand on my shoulder as Minister Crowley arrives, followed by a pair of assistants. Two guards arrive with him but stay inside. I guess that means he's limited his trust in us to the three steps required for one of them to get to him, should he need protection.

"Minister." Colonel Cortell bows and receives the proper nod of the head in return. "Thank you for accepting our meeting."

"Yes, well, always happy to meet with fellow citizens." Minister Crowley forces a chuckle while he eyes all of us warily. His gaze falls on me and stops. I squirm under his appraisal. Then he says, "Ransom Quigley He'. You look well."

I bow my head with a sharp inhale. Afton reacts with a squeeze of my shoulder. She knows I'm looking away, not attempting to honor him. Just the sight of him sent chills down my spine. I almost lost it when he addressed me. It's a good thing I've got the person who drop-kicked a child's toy into his face supporting me.

"Minister." Kayley steps up to him, taking the spotlight off me. "We understand your time is valuable and limited, so we will make this as brief as we can."

"That's appreciated," Minister Crowley replies. "However, I will hear you out. Colonel Cortell said this was a serious matter of Imperial security. As the newly appointed chair of Imperial oversight, I am, of course, concerned with issues concerning threats to His Majesty. Whatever information you give me will be kept discreet, so please, take your time, and let me know what you've found."

"Well, actually, Minister." Kayley pushes herself up to stand straighter. "We have more of a request, rather than just information to share."

He regards Kayley for a moment, looking unsure of how to respond.

"Very well. What is your request?"

"We need access to the Furatus Vault."

"Why?" He draws the word out as he rubs a knuckle on his chin. Let's see how this goes.

Kayley, with the help of Colonel Cortell, describes our capture of the conspirator lady and her subsequent interrogation by the colonel. That part Kayley isn't supposed to know, so Colonel Cortell does all the talking there.

Minister Crowley listens with growing interest—and annoyance. Now he's back to the sinister man I remember. I recall the moment he ordered his men to beat me up, and my skin prickles. Afton must have noticed my change, as her hand moves from my shoulder and drops to wrap around my waist, pulling me closer.

Maybe Kayley is right about my mental state, but it's not some explosion that's doing this to me. It's Crowley. I've been through a lot, including an escape from the deadliest prison in the entire Empire, yet that didn't make me break out in a cold sweat the way this vile man does.

Kayley needs to be careful.

Once they finish their explanation, Minister Crowley clasps his hands behind his back and paces around the balcony. He's got plenty of space to do it. There's enough room up here for a few dozen people. That includes keeping the eight-seat dining table and the bar here.

"I wish you had brought this to me sooner," Minister Crowley says. "I could have mobilized the entire oversight ministry and the Emperor's guards to arrest every one of these seditionists. Then we would have removed the danger to His Highness already. Now there could be an infiltrator in his palace. I will have to send an emergency communication immediately."

"We didn't have this information sooner," Kayley counters, "and the urgency of the matter is why we've come to you directly. Because we've had some experience with this situation, it is best that we continue to handle it."

"*You* handle it?" Minister Crowley stops and turns a narrow-eyed gaze on Kayley. "You are not even citizens, if I remember correctly. Perhaps I should have you arrested for interfering with Imperial business."

Afton's fingers dig into my side. It's a caution—stay put and stay silent. Let Kayley handle this. Afton was right to do it. I don't know if I can handle him threatening us like that. I also don't know what my reaction would be—attack him or run. Neither of those options would be good.

"Minister," Colonel Cortell says, "they were the ones who uncovered Bailiff Daughtry's deception and arrested her. I can honestly say my team would not have been able to achieve the same in such a short time. We need their help."

"Perhaps your team needs better leadership," Minister Crowley replies.

"Minister, we all want the same thing—to stop these conspirators," Kayley says. "I promise you, we can get it done faster than anyone. We have the support of the Chamberlin for anything we need."

"The Chamberlin knows about this?" The minister rubs his chin and keeps his eyes on Kayley. To her credit, she remains brave and unmoved in the face of his superior attitude.

That last piece of news changed his attitude, however. I expect that means he will look to profit from that somehow. I knew from the day I met him he was only a politician for his own benefit. How he wants to gain from this remains to be seen.

"I will give you access on one condition," Minister Crowley says, moving forward to stand over Kayley. "Before you go to the vault, I want you to retrieve something from the Chamberlin for me."

"Of course." Kayley shrugs, but my muscles tighten. "What is it you need?"

"I want you to get Bailiff Daughtry's seal of authority."

"The Chamberlin demolished Bailiff Daughtry's home after we brought her to justice," Colonel Cortell explains. "They left nothing there. Certainly nothing as important as that."

I know why he wants that seal. Anyone would. It would allow its possessor the ability to requisition all sorts of things, piles of money included. All in the name of the Chamberlin.

"It's not at her home," the minister corrects. "I said I wanted you to retrieve it from the Chamberlin, because that's where it is...in his office. Since you already have such a rapport with His Lordship, this should be an effortless task for you. Or, if you can't ask, I'm sure the same amazing skills that enabled you to capture that conspirator should get you in past his security with ease."

Kayley's eyebrows nearly smash together. She's ready to refuse with severe outrage. I'm right there with her. Crowley wants us to break into the Chamberlin's offices? No way! If we get caught, we're done! The Chamberlin will break off his deal with us and then throw us in prison if he doesn't execute us first.

I should have known he'd do this.

"Easy, Rance," Afton whispers in my ear. "She's okay. Let her work."

I'm not sure if I can. This whole meeting was a bad idea. I should have listened to Kayley and stayed home. I'll vomit all over the minister's nice outdoor rug if I stay here any longer.

Then I let Afton's words seep into my brain. Kayley deserves a chance to solve this, and she needs my support, even if that means I stand here and stay quiet. It's harder than I thought it would be, but if I just breathe slowly, maybe I can do it.

"I'm sorry, we can't do that," Kayley says, keeping her voice calm. "Betraying the Chamberlin is the wrong decision for us. If there was something else we can help you with, perhaps we would consider that—"

"So you think you can now negotiate with me since His Lordship dangled a few precious stones in front of your greedy little faces?" Minister Crowley shakes his head. "No! There is no deal to be had here. Either you accept my terms or you can go back to your little backwater planet with nothing."

My slow breaths turn into fast ones. Afton does her best to calm me, but I'm ready to explode. He's worse than anyone in the conspiracy. At least they don't pretend to be on any side other than their own. This jerk uses his authority to take what he wants.

I shut my eyes for a moment and let Afton keep me upright. She has never been closer to a saint than now, handling me like this. I've got to hold on just a little longer. Kayley can do this. I've just got to avoid becoming the distraction.

"Minister, I think you should reconsider what you are asking us to walk away from," Kayley says. "If we do not stop these traitors, they will strike and do irreparable harm to the Empire. Surely you aren't willing to let that happen?"

"You question my loyalty to the Emperor? It is my sworn duty to repel any threat to His Majesty, and I will do that duty, whether you assist me or not. You want access to the vault? Bring me the seal!" Minister Crowley smirks. "I even know where it is and will share that information...if you agree to get it."

My hands are visibly shaking now, and I'm feeling faint. I'm ready to push this bastard over the edge of his balcony and watch him plummet all the way to the bottom.

Kayley's struggling with this, as any of us would. I'm not sure I would be much help to her, even if I was thinking straight. Now I understand why she asked me to keep silent. I set my jaw and hold my breath. If I don't, I will mess this up for her.

"We'll get it," Kayley says, her face set. "But you won't lay a finger on it until you show us proof of access to the vault."

"Of course." Minister Crowley smiles and inclines his head toward her. "Threats to His Majesty must be eliminated."

We just made a deal with the devil, and Kayley knows it. I only hope we can actually pull off what we've just agreed to do.

All this, just for our futures.

"Okay," Afton whispers as I draw in a ragged breath and lean on her. "Home for you. Let's go."

Chapter Eighteen

"Are you sure this is going to work?" I ask Original Teddy as I stare at the new device that looks a lot like the gates we found chasing after Cecelia Nilsson-Lim. About three Teddys tall, it reminds me of an oval doorway, minus the door, and like most things on the ship, they've built it out of that moody dark gray material that's always cool to the touch.

"Unknown," he replies. "Concern is unrequired. Mechanical is confirmed."

"Sure," Grady says, patting the side of the device. "We know what the tech does, but shouldn't there be another one of these things on the other side?"

"Nonsense."

"Dude." I stare at my bud from across the Teddy ship's hangar. "You built the thing. Don't you know?"

"I didn't build it. I just helped design it."

I roll my eyes at him. This is no time to be concerned about words. We're about to jump through a brand-new device that's only been tested once before, and that was with a Teddy, not a human. And even if it works, we're going to be dropping into what is likely the worst possible place for us to be at the moment—the Lord Chamberlin Egerton's office.

I'm feeling not all that great about our chances.

"Is this really the only way to get this done?" Parrish asks. "Can't we just break in like normal? Maybe smash a window like we've done before?

"Smash a window in the Chamberlin's office?" Afton says, looking at him with uncertain eyes. "Buddy, the second most powerful person in the

Empire is bound to have better security than...let's just say, everywhere else in the entire galaxy."

The plan is for Parrish, Afton, and me, plus two Teddys, to sparkle-drive into the room, snatch the seal, and be gone before anyone even notices we were there. We've got on these funky jumpsuit outfits covered in wires and Teddy tech that are supposed to help blink us in and out when we're ready. If we're fast enough, security will miss us when they come to do a visual check of the room. And they will check, because the cameras and scanners will fuzz out the moment we arrive.

I'm supposed to be there only as backup in case something goes wrong. We've gotten sharp enough with stuff like this that we actively create a plan B for when things don't go as planned. And, as we've learned, that's almost a guarantee.

"Okay, everyone ready?" Kayley says over Teddy comm. She and Nayla are acting as eyes and ears, as Grady needs to be down here with the Teddys to make sure we're good to go.

Kayley and I are back on speaking terms, though I still think something is wrong. She thanked me for keeping my mouth shut during our meeting with Crowley, though she admitted she wished she had my support rather than Afton supporting me. I confessed I was in no way, shape, or form to do anything other than hold myself back from puking all over the minister's boots.

"Teddy will initiate," Original Teddy says. That's considerate of him to try out their device first. I really hope it works.

With a wave of his tentacle, our fuzzy pink friend bounces through, followed by one of his blue buddies. A bright light, like lightning, flashes as each Teddy passes through the device. I'm disoriented by the afterimage floating across my retinas and fling my arms up to block the effect. It's silly, and I know it. What's not is my fear that our two Teddy buddies just became dust.

"Afton, Parrish, Rance, go!" Kayley commands, and there's no more time to worry about the functionality of a potentially sketchy device.

I jump through, my arms staying up. The flash hits my peripheral, and then I'm through. A pair of tentacles grab me and stop me from crashing into a glass-paned cabinet straight ahead. I slide to my right, getting out of the way so I don't become a crash pad for my buds. That would be painful. To me.

But as we wait, the seconds tick by, and there's no sign of Afton or Parrish.

"Kayley, do you read?" I call through Teddy comm. "What's going on? Where are they?"

A string of shouts and curses is the reply. Then Grady gets on.

"The device stopped working! I don't know why! Goddesses! Why did this have to happen now?"

All sorts of terrible thoughts rush through my brain. Did the device zap my buds? Are they stuck somewhere in between here and there?

"Where are Afton and Parrish?" The words fall out of my mouth as fast as I can think of them. I cringe as I await the reply.

"We're here, on the ship," Afton says, "and fine, other than feeling a little stupid that I just jumped through that thing and nothing happened."

Well, that much is good, though now I realize I'm stuck here with the Teddys, and they're too busy picking through all the shelves in the room to be concerned about our situation. Maybe they just have more faith in their technology than we do.

"Standby, Rance," Kayley says, attempting to provide some comfort. "We'll pull you out as soon as it's up and running again."

Hold on. If they get the device up and running again soon, that means I'll get pulled out of here without us accomplishing the mission. If we don't, then the Teddys and I are going to get caught for doing nothing more than trespassing. The Chamberlin won't execute us for that, but he will terminate our deal. And then we won't get access to the vault, and well, that's just an awful state of affairs.

"I'm going to search for the seal," I say.

"Rance..." Kayley warns but then sighs and says, "Just be careful, okay? There's a good chance guards are on their way to you right now."

"I will. Just do me a favor and get that device up and running soon? Like in thirty seconds soon?"

"We're already on it," Grady says. "The Teddys think it's an easy fix."

"Yeah, let's hope so."

Now for that authority seal. Minister Sinister—I mean, Minister Crowley said there should be a wooden chest of small drawers somewhere in the room. Bailiff Daughtry's seal is in one of those drawers. All I need to do is figure out which one and pick the lock.

"Shoot, I don't have my Sergo!" I say. It would have had the one tool I need—a light. Afton and Parrish were the fully equipped ones. I'm supposed to be the backup guy.

The room lights suddenly flicker on. I freeze. The guards!

No. It's just Original Teddy turning the switch on.

"Thou art illuminated," Original Teddy says.

"What language is that? And where did you learn it from?"

"Historical documents," is the only answer he gives. Whatever. Now I can look for that cabinet.

And I find it in record time. It's sitting on a table next to a glass display case at the end of the row of shelves. This entire room is a secure storage area full of confidential documents, valuable relics, and likely a bunch of data to blackmail every royal and politician in the Empire. I bet I'd find some real juicy stuff if I had the time to search through it.

But I don't.

"How's that device coming?" I ask.

"We've found the problem," Grady replies. "They're printing up a replacement part now."

"Teddy," I whisper to my pink buddy, "hear any footsteps?"

"That is accurate."

Thank the Goddesses for sensitive Teddy hearing. The guard could be minutes away, and they'd still hear them.

I waste no time in examining the drawers on the chest. They've each been labeled with some number I can't figure out the meaning of. They're just codes, but they don't provide even a hint of what the contents of each drawn could be. All the drawers are also inconveniently locked, so I can't just rummage through them until I find what I'm looking for.

"Footfall is receding," Original Teddy says. I let out a sigh. Good. I'm not out of time. Yet.

What logic might someone use to place items in this thing? All the drawers are the same size with the same lock, so that won't dictate importance. Maybe location? The top drawers could be where they put the most critical items. That would certainly be Imperial thinking. Then again, the Chamberlin is a smart man, and he might know that someone could realize that's the way he arranges things. That would put the seal down on the bottommost row.

Wait, I'm overthinking this. I don't need to be so sophisticated in my approach. This is supposed to be a smash and grab. I should just, well, smash. The chest's made of wood, so it'll crack if I can hit it hard enough.

"Rance, you still there?" Kayley asks.

"Yeah, still here," I reply as I scan the shelves for something heavy and hard enough to pummel this cabinet.

"Hang in there…We'll…bring you back as soon as we can."

Kayley sounds more like she's convincing herself of that fact than trying to comfort me. She's likely doing both, but it still reminds me that the two of us have some talking to do. We need to solve our problems before they get worse.

Now back to smashing.

"Teddy, I need something to smash this cabinet. Help me look."

"Dude," Parrish says. "Smashing something is going to bring way more than one guard to that room. You're already on limited time."

"That is accurate," Original Teddy says. "Footfall is approaching."

"We're back up!" Grady shouts loud enough to hurt my ears. "Once we identify each one of your coordinates, we'll start pulling you back one by one."

I stare at the chest as the sound of my heart thumps in my ears.

"Forget it. Let's just pick it up and throw it on the floor."

"Rance, no!" Kayley shouts.

"It's okay," Grady says. "We'll have them out in ten seconds."

The Teddys lift the chest like it's a bedsheet for them to fold. A second later, they're up on the top of a shelving unit, hurling it down at the floor as I duck and cover.

The entire room reacts to the shattering boom of the box. Shelves rattle, wood splinters fly, and the floor shakes. I'm filled with a sense of impending doom from the aftershock.

"Goddesses, I heard that up here," Afton says with a gasp.

As we scour the wreckage, Blue Buddy winks out. Original Teddy's doing his best to sift through the rest, but his tentacles didn't evolve for such tasks, and his short arms and legs aren't much help, either. He is going as fast as he can.

Then Original Teddy winks out, too.

"Rance, you're next," Grady says. "Stand by, we're recalibrating."

"No, wait! I can find this thing. Just give me ten seconds more!"

"Do you even know if you have ten seconds?" Kayley asks. "Grady, bring him back as soon as you can. If we miss it, we miss it. I'm not taking any chances."

The seal shouldn't be too hard to find. It's got an obvious cylindrical shape, and one for someone as important as a bailiff is bound to look the part.

That's when I spot it, peeking out from under the remains of its drawer—on the bottom row.

"Found it!" I snatch it up, drop it into a pocket, and spring up, ready to disappear. No, wait—the lights! I stretch my arm to the switch and pound my fist on it. The room goes dark again, and I hope that'll be enough to throw anyone off our path.

"Grady, now!" Kayley cries.

"I can't! The device is down again!"

"May I suggest in the future we set a minimum of one year to test any seriously critical equipment we plan to use in the field?" I say.

"I second that," Parrish says.

Still, it could be worse. I could be stuck here, face-to-face with a guard.

Chapter Nineteen

It's worse.

The latch to the door clicks. I duck behind a shelf. It's a terrible hiding spot. If someone comes in, it's only a matter of time before I'm found. Grady better get a move on with that device.

As the door opens, I crouch down, ready to spring on my would-be discoverer. Either I can get lucky and slip past them, or I might try to knock them down before they can aim a weapon at me. Anything that buys me time would work. I just have to be careful that they don't see my face.

A beam from an electronic torch shoots in from the doorway along with the luminous spill from the hallway. It's enough for whoever's out there to catch the shards of wood spread out across the floor.

"Durga's lion! What happened in here?" a woman's voice hisses. She springs through the door and quickly shuts it with a sigh. I tense my muscles, ready to jump. But something is strange. She's the only one who came to check the room. And why did she shut the door so fast?

I should be careful not to take too much of a risk here. I've only got to delay my capture long enough for the team to sparkle me back to the ship. Maybe I can get the shelving unit to topple over and cause more of a ruckus.

She switches the lights on, turns to check the debris on the floor, then gasps. I catch sight of her face and stop myself from doing the same. The guard is too engrossed in the smashed chest to notice me, but I recognize her. I know exactly who she is.

Bailiff Daughtry's aide.

So that could explain the solo visit. She saw the cameras go out and assumed the worst. Maybe she knew exactly what someone might be after in this room of secrets.

"Where is it?" the guard says to herself as she crouches down, spreading what remains of the contents around. "It's got to be here."

"Rance," Kayley says in my ear. "We're almost there, just a few minutes more. Are you there?"

I can't respond. That would give me away, but I might just do that, anyway. This guard might be someone worth capturing. She's got to be on the ex-bailiff's side. I'm sure of it.

Time to uncover the truth.

I step out from behind the shelf, startling the guard. She falls back with a yelp and tries to push herself away from me. I get as close as I can, in case she pulls out a weapon. I don't need any new holes in me today.

The guard looks up at me and stops. Once her eyes meet mine, her jaw drops open and she blinks.

"You're with the conspiracy, aren't you?" I ask with a grin. "Well, not anymore."

The guard's eyes widen. It's like she's seen a spirit of a former Emperor come to accuse her of being a traitor. Good. I can use her fear to my advantage.

"You!" She points. "I'm going to make you regret sending Bailiff Daughtry to prison!"

Oh, that's not good.

She reaches behind her. Does she have a gun? I take a step back, putting my hands up to protect myself, and realize that's useless. If it's a gun, I'll need to react quickly to avoid being shot—and killed.

What comes out is a stun baton. Not deadly, but very painful. If she subdues me with that, she could arrest me and take me to the Chamberlin, or worse, she could bring me to her conspirator bosses. They would want to see me more than the Chamberlin would. They'd also want to exact revenge on my body.

"You have it, don't you?" she seethes.

"Have what? Your future in my hands?"

"Don't pretend like you don't know what I mean. I'm going to get it back, and then I'll break both your legs for what you did to the bailiff!"

"Try it."

We stare at each other for what seems like hours. She's at a disadvantage on the floor, but she's also got the weapon, hence the stalemate. Each one of us is waiting for the other to make the first move.

Perspiration drips down the side of her head. I'm no better. We can't keep this up forever, but I shouldn't have to. Hasn't it been a few minutes already? Why hasn't Grady—

"Rance!"

Kayley's voice makes me flinch. The woman takes it as my first strike. Her baton swings and crunches my arm. I crash into the shelf and crumble. She springs to her feet and attacks again, going for my head.

I duck and roll past her. Sparks fly as the baton contacts the metal shelf. The guard throws her arms up, and I take the initiative, diving into her midsection to knock her down.

As we fall, she brings her baton down on my back twice. I cough as the impact blows the air from my lungs. The advantage turns back to her, and she launches me off her, pushing with her legs. My body tumbles into a chunk of the broken chest, and I arch my back in pain.

She's got me now.

But rather than press her attack, the guard stares at her baton, flicking a button on the handle with her thumb. That's when I realize I never felt a shock. Did her baton break from the hit on the shelf? No—she hit me before that. Does that mean my sparkle suit absorbed the energy?

"Rance," Grady's voice sings in my ear, "we're ready. Three seconds."

"No! Hold on!" I shout. The guard raises an eyebrow.

"Why should I? Are you ready to give up?"

"Here we go!" Grady says. Shoot. Too late. There's no way I'm going to grab her in time.

But three seconds pass by, and I'm still here. So much for that. I get up and dust myself off, examining myself for wounds.

"Uh, I think my suit got fried," I say.

"What are you talking about?" the guard asks. Then she looks at her baton as she figures out what I mean. She bares her teeth and growls. "Doesn't matter. I can still pummel your bones to dust!"

"Fried?" Kayley asks. "Is someone there with you?"

"Yes!" My shout gives the guard pause, but not for long. She raises her baton and charges. I press my feet into the floor and bolt forward, meeting her halfway. My hands fly up, and I catch her arms before she can swing. The momentum throws her back, and we land hard, with me on top. We struggle for control of the baton, rocking back and forth.

"Get off of me!" the guard cries and tries to flip me away. I spread my feet out and push down on her. It's not very gentlemanly, but there are other things to worry about.

"Rance, can you talk?" Kayley asks. "What's going on?"

Before I can respond, the guard wraps her legs around my waist and rolls, taking me by surprise. Now she's sitting on me, in a better position to keep me on the ground. The guard raises her baton over her head. I try to block it as it comes down on me, and I cry out as the solid weapon cracks my forearms. She raises her baton again, ready to break my bones.

I struggle to escape, but her fighting experience is far better than mine. Every swing hurts a little more, and I cringe, anticipating each new hit. There's got to be some way to get free. I push at her, even buck my hips to get them off the ground, but none of it is effective.

"You are such a pervert. Is that what you're into?" Afton says.

Wait, that wasn't Teddy comm...

She's here!

Afton's words startle the guard. She twists to search for the voice and meets Afton's foot with her face. The guard's body convulses, and then she topples over, hitting the ground with a thud.

"I hope you've got a new suit for me," I say, pushing her off. "And one for her."

"Why would we need one for her?" Afton asks, coming to look at the unconscious guard. "Who is she, your new girlfriend?"

"No time for bad jokes," Kayley says. "Get the suit on."

"Don't you recognize her?" I say as I make haste and change. "She worked for Bailiff Daughtry."

Afton frowns, then rolls the woman over to get a better look at her face.

"Now that you mention it, she does look familiar."

"Yes! She's a conspirator! She needs to come back with us!"

"We don't have time for that," Kayley says. "We're way past our timetable! More guards will come to check on this one."

"We don't have another suit anyway," Grady adds. "The one you're putting on is Parrish's."

"Oh, is that why the sleeves are too long?" I say as I attempt to roll them up. Then I shake my head. "No, wait. We can't leave her here."

"Why not?" Kayley asks.

"Because she recognized me!"

"And you recognized her," Afton says. "If she tells the Chamberlin, you can tell him she's a conspirator like her former boss. He'll believe that over the idea you broke in here to steal the bailiff's seal. That just sounds crazy."

When Afton puts it that way, it makes sense. I just hope the Chamberlin believes that, too.

"Okay. Grady, get us out of here."

Chapter Twenty

MINISTER CROWLEY WAS SO shocked that we got the seal, he all but handed us the pass codes to the vault—once we gave it to him, that is. All we had to do was show up, and the manager on duty escorted us straight to the main vault room. We made a copy and split.

Of course, they had encrypted the list, so it took a little more stress to get it unlocked. Thank goodness for Teddynet. Grady's all-powerful workstation would have taken over a hundred years to come up with the key. We didn't have that much time to wait.

Once it was ready, we gathered in Doc Elizabeth's room to go over it. Even though it's a little cramped with eight of us in here, it was still the largest room on the ship with a screen that didn't include the curdling screams of dying prey.

I sit with my back against the wall next to Parrish, with Kayley resting on my legs. Grady is opposite us, cross-legged, next to Afton and the plants. Everyone else is standing or leaning, except for Nayla, who reclines on the exam chair as if she was the Goddess of leisure. Maybe she is.

"Okay, give us the scoop," Kayley says to Grady. "Any obvious names on there?"

"Not that I recognize," Grady replies, tapping on his Teddy-made laptop. He's thinking of commercializing it, if he can get the Teddy quirks out of it. "Plenty military of all ranks."

"Yeah, we expected that," Colonel Cortell says. "As it is, I'm not sure if I can trust everyone in my division. I've kept knowledge of this list to my close aides, just for that reason."

I can only imagine what would happen if someone found out we had duplicated the list. Grady thinks it's still possible that there could be a copy log embedded in the memory card it was on. He also said there could be a trace program on it, too. The Teddy tech that cracked the code wasn't able to find any hint of either, so I'll just add that to my nightly prayer to the Three Goddesses. My list of asks is getting a little long.

"So the message addresses are all there, right?" I ask.

"Yep," Grady replies. Then he blinks and looks up. "Yeah, good point, dude. We can trace all the domains to the planets they originate from. I'm sure they spoofed some, but I bet most of the lower ranks on here are just fake addresses. Their domains are real, so it wouldn't be that hard to locate t hem."

"All we need are a few real ones," Kayley adds. "That guard at the Chamberlin's office could be an easy way to check. Finding out her name shouldn't be difficult."

"Yeah, just ask Rance. He was all hot and heavy with her when I got there. If he's any kind of gentleman, he should have asked her name at least."

Afton grins when I throw an *I'm going to get you back for that* look at her. Kayley only sighs, but the comment is enough to get Nayla and Doc Elizabeth to eye me with curiosity.

"I'll find out," the colonel offers, saving me. "That should be easy enough for me to do."

"Ooh..." Grady says, his eyebrows raising.

"What'd you find?" Parrish asks.

"It's a subtle division, but I think I found the list of the bosses. We would have lost this with decryption on one of our machines. There's bound to be a few names on here that we know."

"Let me see," Afton says, reaching for Grady's laptop, but Grady keeps a firm grip on it and glares at her. Afton pouts and tugs harder, pulling it from his hands.

"Hey! Give that back!" Grady cries.

"Surela," Nayla says in a calm voice, "remember the flow of the universe. You must allow others to do their part."

Afton is too absorbed in the list to respond. She scrolls through it like an apex predator ready to devour its fresh catch. I can almost see the saliva dripping off her canines. Yuck. The thought makes my stomach ill.

Then she gasps, leaning in to look closer at what I can only assume is a name on the list. Her jaw goes slack, and her eyes widen to an extreme degree.

"Holy Sophia," Afton whispers.

"What? What did you find?" I ask, pushing off the wall and unsettling Kayley, who turns to me, surprised. It takes a lot to disturb Afton, so whatever she sees has got to be mind-blowing, because her brain just exploded into a million pieces.

Afton turns a stunned look at me, speechless. I'm surprised she even heard me with the way she is at the moment.

Grady snatches the laptop back from her and stares at the screen, his eyes taking a moment to adjust to the small type.

"Great Durga," Grady says, his face becoming an exact copy of Afton's. I'm getting the feeling that whatever it is, I won't like it very much.

"What?" Kayley demands, standing. "Whatever it is, just tell us!"

Grady looks at me, every sort of apology or word of sympathy deep in his eyes.

"Rance's dad is on the list," Grady says.

"That's it?" I shrug. No actual surprise there. Likely he's playing both sides to see which one comes out on top. Then he can ride along with them. Bastard.

"No." Grady shakes his head. "That's not it. Dude...he's a boss of the conspiracy."

There's a collective exclamation/query from everyone in the room, save for me. I'm not shocked—I'm much worse than that. My breathing gets fast and shallow, and my heart thumps hard through my chest. My upset stomach twists itself into a knot that only gets tighter.

"His warning was real," I say, the worlds slipping out of my mouth like sandpaper on cement. My father knew exactly what the conspiracy was up to because he was a part of the meetings that discussed going after us. He offered to talk to them because he had a direct connection to those in control.

The one small thing in all of this that gives me a microgram of relief is that he wasn't at that meeting on Herdewyke. My father may be a boss in the conspiracy, but at least he's not a big boss.

"Well, we've got our first target," Afton says, then presses her lips together.

"Not the best moment to suggest that, darling," Nayla says.

"Suggest what? Better we take him down than Minister Crowley. At least then we can plead for leniency. Otherwise, they'll execute him for sure."

"Surela!" Nayla hisses. "Be considerate!"

Despite her typical blunt comment, Afton is right. The Emperor will have no mercy for traitors. He can't. If he lets one slide, all that does is open up the gates for others to try going after him, and that could lead to civil war.

Kayley turns and puts her hands on my arms, looking at me with a wistful smile. Despite the heaviness of the moment, I welcome her attempt to comfort me. She's always been good at knowing when I need her, which is always. Even before we were dating, Kayley was sensitive to when something was bothering me. It's obvious to everyone how distressed I currently am, but she is also the first to do anything about it.

"You okay?" she asks.

"No," I mumble, then try to return her smile to assure her I'm not about to collapse.

Kayley lowers herself to look at me directly. "Rance, I know it will be tough, but I think we should at least discuss your father. If we don't answer that question, someone else will, and then we lose the opportunity to protect him."

"Why would I care about protecting him?"

"I know you have a lot of reasons to be angry with him, but I don't think you want to see him executed, do you?"

I turn away, though there's nowhere to hide. I can't escape everyone's questioning glance. Even Doc Elizabeth, who I can often count on to remove her ego from the discussion, has an expectant look on her face.

"I think everyone here agrees you should choose how we move forward," she says. "This is more than personal for you."

I nod. I'm as close as anyone could be to this. He's my father, and while I hate him for a good many things—the biggest being him walking out on my mother and me when I was twelve—I'm not sure I could make the right decision. There are too many feelings connected to a choice like that. I can't be objective about it, and I'd regret any choice I made.

There was a time when I wanted to be just like him. Now everything about him is poison to me. Kayley's even accused me of being like him, and while she may have forgotten about that, I never will. Her words will haunt me forever. I really want nothing other than to find the farthest place in the universe from him and remain there until he disappears.

Yet, if I don't choose, that will put his fate in someone else's hands.

As I stare into Kayley's steel-blue gaze, I feel the compassion she has for me. After all the hard decisions she's had to make, Kayley understands where I am, and I wish I could just get lost in her eyes until this is over. I can't. Everyone is relying on me to be strong.

Okay. For their sake, I will gather my strength and push through to a decision. But when I try, my body and mind don't respond. Everything in me screams to run as far away from anything related to my father, right down to the smallest detail.

"I'm sorry. I can't," I say. "Maybe it's the right thing for me to do, but I don't want to have that on my conscience. Let someone else make that choice."

"You understand that means losing control of his fate, right?" Kayley asks. She wants clarity, not an argument. I nod a confirmation.

Kayley nods back, her acknowledgment that she accepts my answer. Her arms go around my neck, and she embraces me, squeezing with a gentle touch. Somewhere during that connection, I feel her lips on my cheek, and it sends warmth through my body.

"So...we're going to leave him alone?" Grady asks. He sounds almost happy about it. I'm sure my bud is acting that way for my sake. If it were up to him, Grady would do everything he could to ensure the man who put his parents in prison gets what he deserves.

"Yes," Kayley answers. "I'm sure there are many more on that list. Higher priorities. Easier targets that we can go after. We need to get the practice of this down well. Any mistakes could cost us more than we want to pay. Understood?"

Everyone acknowledges with a single word. They're all in sync with the idea that any more wounds are too many. We've certainly had our share of hurt, and each gunshot, broken bone, cut, or bruise leaves a permanent scar on our minds. We're not superheroes of the cine. We're barely adults. This was not the future we wanted.

That has never stopped us from charging straight for it.

"Alright," Grady says, cracking his knuckles and digging back into the list. "Let's see who the lucky winner is."

Chapter Twenty-One

WE HIT THE EDGE of the general's compound as a precision strike team. Each one of us is skilled in our roles. Our task is simple: raid the compound and capture our first conspirator from the list. We will be in and out before our target's tea is ready.

Pectafortis is the planet, Cockalorum is the city. The general lives on its outskirts in a secluded area. All the better for us. No help will arrive before we're long gone.

I won't say it'll be easy. We've done this too often to be that naïve. Still, I'm confident. If walls and bored security guards are all that's facing us, this won't be difficult. We've brought enough Teddy power to get the job done twice over.

"Signal when you're in position," Kayley says over Teddy comm. She, Grady, and Nayla are all doing their part to keep us out of trouble. Colonel Cortell and his five men are here in case they can't.

"Five seconds," Afton says at point. Like Parrish and me, she's flanked by two blue buddies who will popsicle anything that moves.

I flip down my infrared goggles and check my surroundings. It's clear. Ten quick steps and I'll be where I need to be on Afton's left flank. My blue buddies get airborne, climbing a tree that overlooks the entire compound. From there, they'll fly over the fence and take care of the guards at the gate.

Parrish is at the front for a change. He's the distraction if we need it. If not, he's the guarantee for our quick exit. If all goes well, and I'm expecting it won't, we'll have pulled the general from his comfy chair and be on our way home in ten minutes.

"Ready," Afton says.

"Good. Right on schedule," Kayley says. "Grady, you go with counter-measures?"

"Yep."

"Nayla, you go with surveillance?"

"As long as I do not need to see any violence, then yes, I am ready."

"You won't see anything," Afton says. "It's dark down here."

It won't get any darker than the midnight sky we're experiencing now. The general could already be in bed. It's Afton's job to find out and mine to ensure the Teddys subdue him. No searching for info, no data to steal.

"Okay. Go," Kayley commands.

Afton is off first, headed straight for the servant's gate. Of course it's secure. Two guards. Lots of light. But Afton doesn't care about being seen. Grady's already hacked the cameras and the sensors. There weren't many. This man may be a general, but he's the lowest kind there is.

"Ten seconds, Rance," Kayley says. "Keep your eyes open, and if you see anything strange, don't wait for me. Get out. Got it?"

"Yes, darling, sweetie, love of my life."

"This isn't playtime. Stay focused."

Kayley's using that tone of hers that tells me she's scared but doesn't want anyone to know it, except I know it, and I get she's more worried than she usually is. I can't figure out why, but I'll talk to her once the mission is over.

"Dammit!" Afton says. "Hold!"

I signal my Teddys to pause. It's strange that we've got a problem this early on. Maybe Afton is being overly cautious, but that's not Afton at all. It only deepens my suspicions. There's little I can do until we figure out why Afton is calling for a pause.

"Why? What's going on?" Kayley demands.

"There's way more than two guards at the gate," Afton replies.

"How many is way more?" I ask.

"There's seven here."

"I'm seeing ten at the front gate," Parrish says.

Great. That could mean there's a full platoon here—thirty or forty soldiers altogether. We're only eleven. Even with the initiative, we can't take out enough of them to get through with any sort of ease. It could turn out to be a protracted battle, and that's just not the plan. We're here to capture, not to fight.

Kayley's got to be thinking we shouldn't even try this, and she'd be right. But she's silent in that regard. After the last few lectures from her, I'm more than a little reluctant to take any action without checking with Kayley first. Besides, she's worried about something she hasn't shared with me yet. I'd be an idiot to jump in without knowing what's got her nerves on edge.

"What do we do, KayKay?" I ask.

"Hold on, I'm thinking."

I drop my goggles down over my eyes and check the surrounding area again. It would be bad if part of that platoon sneaked up on me. I won't be the liability this time.

"All that thinking done yet?" Afton asks. "We're getting short on time."

"Last I checked, Surela, I'm not the only one with a brain in this group," Kayley shoots back.

Not good. We don't need the two of them arguing. That'll end our mission for sure.

Kayley's got a point, though. She's not the only one who can come up with a plan. All of us can, so we should help her out. Of course, coming up with a new tactic right on the spot isn't all that easy. I'm not great at that kind of coordination. I just act, and the others handle the rest.

Whatever we come up with, it has got to be simple and easy enough to execute. Maybe I could do something that would get their attention and let Afton slip through. I don't have a clue what that might be. All I've ever been good at is getting captured.

Wait a minute.

"Hey, I've got an idea," I say.

"Okay," Kayley responds. "What is it?"

"If I can cause a diversion big enough to pull a good amount of them away, Afton can get in, and she and Parrish can go get our guy."

"Not me," Parrish says. "Running is kind of a problem, remember?"

"I'll go in with Afton," Colonel Cortell says. "I remember most of the floor plan."

"Good," Kayley says. "What kind of diversion did you have in mind?"

"Well, if I set a few charges—"

"No explosions."

"How about—"

"Or fire. We can't risk anyone in the city seeing it. We'd have a lot more than a platoon of guards on us if that happened."

"Why is there a platoon here, anyway?"

"Not the time to discuss. We still need a diversion from you, Rance, or this is done."

Shoot. My idea is about to fly out the air lock if I can't put something together.

"Alright, I'll be the diversion," I say. "I'll get them to chase me, and then Afton can slide in after them."

They meet my suggestion with a chorus of sighs. I should expect as much. It is a dumb idea. As if they wouldn't see that plan coming from light-years away. I give it very low odds of success. I'll get captured, and even though that *would* be a diversion, the rest of the platoon would be on high alert.

"No way you're going to get even five of them to come after you," Afton says.

"Yeah, I don't see that working," Parrish adds.

"Well, do either of you have a suggestion? Because if you don't, I'm calling this mission over," Kayley says. I can't believe she's backing me up!

"My cards predict a better-than-average outcome," Nayla adds. "You should do it. But be careful."

"That's great, darling," Afton says, "but could you do us all a favor and stick to watching the drone vid?"

"But this is more accurate," Nayla pouts.

"Alright!" Kayley's voice channels the tone of Colonel Nelson, stunning us all to silence. "This is what we're going to do. Rance, you get as many as you can from the servant's entrance to give chase. Then Afton, once he's out of sight, you and your buddies zap the rest and go in. Parrish, switch places with Harry, and Harry, be ready to follow Afton. We'll be in and out within five minutes, max. Are you with me?"

"Um, what do I do about the guards who chase after me?" I ask, ducking my head a bit as if both Kayley and Colonel Nelson were right in front of me.

"This is your plan. Figure it out."

We rearrange our positions, and once Kayley gives the go signal, I take a breath and stand up. This isn't the stupidest thing I've ever done, but it's definitely up there with the best of them. I pick up a few rocks and step around the corner and into the light of the entrance.

"Hey, you big jerks! You think you can fight me? I bet I can beat you with just this stone!" I hold it up so they can see it in my hand. My thought gets uploaded to Teddynet, and I get an image back I interpret as them acknowledging readiness for my idea. Good. That'll be critical to getting them to come after me.

I hear some muddled conversation between a few of the guards at the gate. Yeah, I didn't think that would work on its own. I was hopeful, though. On with the plan.

"Come here and say that," one of them shouts back. "Then we'll see how tough you are."

"Wrong answer!" I shout and throw the rock at the closest guard, hoping my aim is good. It is.

The moment it pelts the man in the shoulder, the closest blue buddy—one of mine—popsicles him. He goes stiff and topples over. The other guards step back as they stare at their fallen comrade. I upload an image of a tentacle high-fiving a human hand. *Great timing, Teddy.*

"What the hell?" a guard shouts. "He killed Kenneth! Shoot him!"

"No, wait," another says. "I know who that is! We'll get a big reward if we capture him!"

Oh, so there's a bounty on our heads? What a surprise. Still, it's perfect. Between their thirst for revenge and their greed, I've got them right where I want them.

"You three go after him," their captain says. "I'll call this in and get B squad to join you. He won't escape."

I pivot and break into the trees, headed towards the Teddy shuttle. It's on the other side of the compound, opposite the city. I won't go all the way there, just enough to get my pursuers far enough away from the compound.

"Afton, go!" Kayley says. "You've got two minutes. Someone's going to come around once they don't hear from that gate captain."

I close my mind off to the chatter and focus on running, like Parrish taught me. Even with the occasional flash of light behind me, the dark of the forest is closing in. There's more here than just guards that I need to watch out for. Bare roots and undergrowth will take me down in an instant. I've got to be careful.

A branch smacks me in the face. I stumble, then recover, but I've lost some distance between me and the entire squad of guards giving chase. One of their spotlights finds me.

"There he is! You two, go there! And you head the other way! Get around him and trap him in!"

There's enough of them to pull that off, and that's a problem. I still haven't figured out what I'm going to do to shake them off my trail. My blue buddies are following, but they can't stop twelve guards at once.

A stun bolt flies past my head. It's not meant to hit me, only drive me straight into the others who lie in wait. They've likely surrounded me by now, and my situation is getting dire. All they need to do is tighten their circle, and then I'm caught.

Wait. The guards are spread out. They won't need to popsicle all of them!

I upload an abstract of my plan to Teddynet and dodge left. I just need to give my blue buddies a little time to get into position. If I can shake off my pursers, I might be able to help them.

As the seconds tick by, my lungs ache with increasing irritation. I can't keep this up. Soon enough, they're going to notice I've been running them in circles. Then they'll trap me for sure.

My leg gives out and I fall, smacking my head into a tree. A roll gets me back on my feet, but then I'm blinded by a light in my face. I throw my arm up to block it and get a kick in my ribs for my efforts. I go flat on my back, coughing.

"Got you now!" the squad leader snarls as he comes to loom over me, his prey. I wince and try to push myself up. His foot presses on my chest and shoves me back down. I chuckle then, remembering another situation where I was definitely the sucker.

But this time, I've got the advantage.

"Nope," I reply with a grin.

The squad leader frowns. Then he realizes that he's the only one here with me. He grabs his radio to reach his team. When no one responds, he tries checking the settings on the device to no result.

My blue buddies drop from the trees, flanking the squad leader on both sides, their antennae out and ready. It distracts him long enough for me to pull out my stun gun.

"Thanks, Teddy," I say, "but this one is mine."

Before he realizes I've got a gun, I raise it up and zap him hard.

Chapter Twenty-Two

I ENJOY WATCHING OUR arrival to Angelcanis from the Teddy solarium. Nothing feels more like coming home than seeing our green-blue planet with my own eyes. The fact we scored our first conspirator on our first try only adds to the excitement.

Kayley, Afton, and Nayla are here with me, along with Original Teddy. He's also grown attached to our homeworld, as he's never been to his own. Angelcanis has been a surrogate for him. He'll enjoy it as much as he can. Until he goes home, that is.

Home means an all-I-can-eat feast of my mom's cooking, too. That's the thing I look forward to the most. That, and seeing her. My buds may be my extended family, but my mom is the only nuclear family I have. Well, until Kayley and I get married, whenever that happens. We've got a minor problem to fix before we can even think about that. The minor problem being me, of course. She's still a bit annoyed by me but is trying not to let it show. Still, I plan on going slowly until we can talk.

"Teddy, before you go, we've definitely got to take you to see the Winged Dawn," I say. "It's something you can't miss."

"That's a great idea!" Kayley says. "I've never been. Have you?"

"Actually, yeah." I'm sheepish about admitting it. Grady, Afton, and I went on a class trip, but Kayley and Parrish couldn't go. She had a big recital, and Parrish was playing a finals game. That was back when they were dating, so it worked out for them. Still, I'm sure they would have liked to have gone.

"Teddy will endeavor to view," Original Teddy says. "Archival is paramount."

"It's more than just documenting it for Teddynet," I say. "You'll see the 'wings' of Angelcanis. It's a life-changing event!"

"Indeed," Nayla says, leaning her head on Afton's shoulder. "I expect it to be quite romantic."

"Teddy does not wish to alter existence any further. Rancid has already done enough."

We all laugh. The release of tension has been great for all of us. Our mission succeeded, but the few snags that we had were enough to drive all of our heartbeats up for a while. Now we've put another serious dent in the enemy, and Colonel Cortell has another person to gather intel from. Between that and the communications list, it'll only be a matter of time before the conspiracy collapses. Maybe it was better not to go after my father.

Kayley's Sergo rings, and she digs it out of her pocket, surprised she can get a call this high up. As she's checking her message, Afton jumps and pulls her Sergo out as well. I wonder if Grady modified them to use a carrier wave to connect to the planet-side network. If he did, then why didn't he do mine as well?

Then my Sergo goes off.

I pull mine out and thumb over to the chat screen, half expecting to see a message from my mom asking me what I want for dinner. Likely, she's already bought all the ingredients for my favorite dish, but she just wants to get my confirmation. Not like that would be difficult. I love any meal that's got noodles in it.

"Kwanon," Kayley whispers, and I pull my attention from my Sergo to look at her. That's when I hear Afton gasp. Nayla glances at her Sergo and goes stiff. Kayley's the same. Now I'm reluctant to look at my screen. Have I received something that will make me freak out, too?

Only one way to know. I take a breath and look down at the message.

It's from my neighbor. I have to read it three times to understand it. Even then, I can't believe it.

BOB: Rance, there was an explosion in your house. You should come home.

"Kay—" I start.

"I have to go home. Right now." Kayley's words fly from her lips. When I look up, I see fear in her eyes. She's breathing heavily as she reaches out to me. "They bombed my house, Rance."

Then the realization hits me. It wasn't just some accident at my house. It was a deliberate attack. Anyone who was inside, or even nearby, could have been killed.

Mom!

I try to call her, but we're still out of range. Chat text is our only option. It could be enough.

I pound away at my Sergo, just like Afton and Kayley. We're sending messages as fast as we can tap them out—to our parents, our neighbors, the local authorities. Whomever we can think of that might reply.

"You should go," Nayla says to Afton as she rubs her shoulder. Afton just stares at her device, waiting for—anything.

"You too, Afton?" I ask, my voice breaking.

Afton nods with an unconscious movement. She may dislike her mother, but there's no way she would wish for her death. It's not just her mother. Her father and two brothers might have been home, too.

There's a pounding of feet just outside the solarium. Parrish bursts in, breathless. Grady is just behind him. When they see our faces, they know, and now so do we. It's happened to all of us.

"Shuttle is available," Original Teddy says. "Instant departure possible."

Kayley and I squeeze each other's hands, and we spring up, racing to the elevator along with the others. We pile in and take a collective breath, leaning on each other for support.

As we descend to the hangar, the loudest silence pervades the tiny space. I can hear everyone's thoughts. They echo my own. If only this elevator could go straight down to the surface or, better, to our own houses. Instantly. Right now is too long to wait to learn the fate of our families.

Doc Elizabeth meets us at the shuttle door. She watches us as we pile in, eyes like a concerned parent. I am grateful for her to come, but I hope we will not need her skills today.

"I know this isn't a question any of you want to answer," she says as the shuttle begins its launch, "but we need to decide whose house we will go to first."

Several looks of disbelief respond to Doc Elizabeth's suggestion. She's right, but no one will give her an answer.

"My place is empty," Grady says. "We don't have to go there."

"Who says we have to stay together?" Afton asks. She's not trying to be cruel. All of us are having selfish thoughts, I'm sure. I know I am. Everyone's families are important to me, but the only question I want to know the answer to right now is about my mom.

I pray to the Three Goddesses that she is safe. Then I do it again. And again. All the while, my arms keep Kayley comforted as she sits in front of me. I can feel her unease, however. Even strapped in, she shifts in her seat, her hand clutching my wrist. The lack of information is torture.

"It will be better if you stay together," Doc Elizabeth replies. "If we need to provide some rescue assistance to the crews, one or two of us won't be much help. Ask your neighbors to find out if any of your parents were home."

"I did," Afton replies. "They don't know."

Kayley and I are still waiting for responses. Anxiously.

"Parrish? What about you?" Kayley asks. Maybe she's trying to take her mind off her own worries. If it's working, she's not showing it.

Parrish just shakes his head and looks down. The only chance for his mother to not be home is if she had gone for her medical treatment or to a doctor's visit. Otherwise, she's been too sick to go anywhere. He almost stepped back from this mission. I was glad he didn't. Now I'm not so sure. Who knows if he could have prevented someone from bombing his house if he was there? He might have become a victim, too.

My mom could have been home, she could have been out, or she could have been over at Kayley's house with her mom. All the possibilities are making my head spin, and my heart is torn between the action I should take.

I desperately want to know about my mother. Seeing her smiling face is the only thing that will cure my twisting insides. But I don't want to leave Kayley, either. The vision in my head of her alone when she finds out her parents are gone is enough to break me. I can't do that to her.

There is no reasonable solution to any of this. It is all bad. All wrong. We shouldn't be selfish. Yet I have no will to forget about my own needs and support Kayley in hers. I just have to choose and pray it's not the decision I learn to regret.

"KayKay," I whisper in her ear. "Let's stick together. I will go with you to your place."

"I want that," she replies and sniffles. "I want that so badly...but I can't. I can't ask that of you."

"You're not. I'm deciding." And I will pray and keep praying that my mother is unharmed until I see her with my own eyes.

Kayley unbuckles her harness and turns to throw her arms around me. She squeezes hard and buries her head between my neck and my shoulder. I can do nothing more than place a kiss on her head and hold her. I've got no words to say that will comfort her.

Doc Elizabeth glances at me as she presses her lips together and shakes her head. Her attempt to keep us together failed. She's resigned to do what she always does—stand by until someone needs her. Maybe no one will, and that would be the best thing that she, or any of us, could hope for.

Kayley's Sergo buzzes, startling the two of us. It's in her hand a microsecond later, and she's thumbing open the new message in another one after that.

I hold my breath as her eyes scan the message. Kayley's face betrays none of its contents, and I try to keep my level of unease from getting out of control.

"It's from my mom! They weren't home!" Kayley throws herself back into my arms, crushing me with her embrace. The others make small sounds of contentment and lay hands on her shoulders or arms. They're happy for her, but their own worries limit the amount of joy they can muster.

Kayley pulls back, her hands coming to my face. Our eyes connect, and I see her pure elation turn to solid determination.

"We're going to your place," Kayley says. "We're going there, and we'll find out Mom's okay."

I push a small smile onto my face for her, though the need to know about my mom still burns a hole in my chest. I'm sure Afton and Parrish are no different. Still, Kayley's become more optimistic, so I try to be there with her and for the sake of my buds. We need to keep our hope from fading. That's the only way we get through this. Together.

"We're going to find out everyone is okay," I reply. I don't believe it yet, but I desperately want to.

Chapter Twenty-Three

If I saw my house only from the front, I would assume it was fine. The chunks of wood, glass, and graphcrete strewn across the yard are the first signs that something is wrong. The next hint is the kitchen sink in my neighbor's yard across the street. Smoke wafts by from somewhere close, calling me to investigate further.

A quick glance at the side of the house explains everything. It's not there. The start of the living room all the way back to Mom's winter garden is just gone. It's like some enormous animal decided it was hungry and took a gaping bite. My upstairs bedroom—what's left of it—is severed in two, and my mattress now lies in the spot in the living room where the vid screen used to be.

I exhale the breath I'd been holding for the last half minute. I don't get the sense my mother was here when this happened. The only way to be sure is to check before the rescue team gets here. I'm amazed they're not. Maybe the destruction of our five houses are stretching their personnel resources to the limit.

Despite warnings from the neighbors not to, we step into the living room and search for any sign of anything. They're not willing to help, so their opinion means little to me. I'm also not concerned about messing up any criminal investigation. I know who did this, and until we bring them down ourselves, they will never stand trial.

Kayley's Sergo rings. It's Afton. Kayley wastes no time in asking if everyone is okay. I watch her, waiting for any sign from her that confirms it.

The grimace that she makes tells me otherwise. She takes her Sergo from her ear and puts the speaker on. At least I won't have to wait to find out the unfortunate news.

"They took her to the hospital," Afton says about her mother. Her tone is subdued and matter-of-fact. I wouldn't expect her to be anything but worried, even for her mother. "She was in the back of the house when it happened, so..."

"What about your dad? Brothers?" Kayley asks.

"Far away on patrol."

"Do they know?" I ask.

"Not yet," Nayla answers. "We will tell them once we know Mrs. Jee's condition."

Kayley and I share a look of relief, however temporary. Afton's mom isn't safe yet, but she's got a much better chance now that she's in the care of medical professionals.

"What about your mother?" Nayla asks. I tell her what we've found so far, which is nothing. No sign of my mother or the rescue team, even though the neighbors have called them five times. I'm staying hopeful, but there's a ton of debris to sift through. And it needs to be done under threat of the rest of the house collapsing on us.

"So you're going to the hospital now?" Kayley asks.

"No," Afton says. "No, we're coming to help you first."

Kayley frowns, her eyes sliding over to glance at me. Maybe she's waiting to see if I'll accept their help or not. That's easy for me to decide—anyone who will make the burden of finding clues easier is welcome to join in.

"Alright, see you soon," I say, and we disconnect the call. Kayley pockets her Sergo, then grabs my wrist before I can walk away. I flash her a curious glance, wondering what's going on in her mind.

"Rance, this is not the time," she says, "but I need to tell you something. Something Mom told me about your father. It's...I should have brought this up before."

"Why not tell me now?" And why didn't my mother tell me herself?

Glass crunches under someone's foot. I turn, expecting to see the neighbor checking on us. Instead, no one's there. Maybe I was just hearing things. I try to release myself from Kayley's grasp so I can head to the back to check. For some reason, Kayley doesn't let go.

Kayley shakes her head and motions for me to get down. It's strange that she doesn't want us to be seen. Everyone around knows we're here, so why would we bother hiding from them?

There's another scrape of glass against the kitchen floor, and I realize whoever might be there could have bad intentions. Is it the bomber? That would be strange. Why would anyone return to the scene of their crime? Unless they were looking for proof of its effectiveness.

In which case...

I nod towards the kitchen and put myself up against the wall that shares a side with the oven and stove. Kayley stays with me, balancing deftly on the soles of her feet. She may not be dancing much anymore, but she's lost none of her skill.

I'm not as nimble, however. A wrong placement of my boot on something slippery sends my leg shooting forward to kick a chunk of the end table across the room. It crashes into the wall with a loud crack.

Three blasts erupt from the other side of the wall, spraying splinters of wood over our heads. Kayley dives on top of me, pulling me down to the floor. I cover my face, expecting more bullets. When none come, I push back up to my knees, ready to run or fight.

Boots pound across the kitchen floor, heading away from us. No! We can't let them go! They may know something about my mom!

"We have to capture them!" I jump up and dig my feet into the floor, but Kayley throws herself into me, and we hit the wall together. I spin on her, my brain filling with rage.

"Rance, no!" Kayley yells.

"Are you serious?" I shout back.

"They've got a gun. We don't! Get that into your head!"

"We can stop them! Trust me!"

Kayley takes a breath, putting her words in check. She's shaking her head no, but I can see in her eyes she wants to take down this bastard. They might not have lit the fuse, but they're just as guilty as anyone who did.

"I'm calling the Teddys," Kayley says, pulling her Sergo out. "Keep close to me, and we'll follow them from a distance. We're not engaging anyone until they arrive. Those are my terms. Got it?"

I nod and keep quiet, not wanting my words to provoke her. It's enough we're going.

We sprint out the kitchen door, headed towards the yard behind mine. There's a narrow walkway that runs between the neighbor's houses. We've used it before for our own escape, so I know it well. We'll catch up with our target in no time.

As we hop the fence, I catch sight of the retreating offender. It's a man. He's fast...and familiar. I need to confirm who it is and make him pay for the damage he's done.

Kayley and I get halfway down the walkway before I stop and consider a way to cut him off. By the time I figure it out, she's made the call to the Teddys. Once they're here, there's no way for that guy to get away. Maybe doing it her way isn't so bad.

"Come on," Kayley says. "We can't lose sight of him!"

The two of us pound down the walkway and break out onto the street. Our target is missing, however.

"Shoot! Where is he?"

"There!" Kayley points.

The man hears us and turns. It's him! From the spaceport! The one that stabbed Kayley! We drop to hide, but he pivots and keeps running. I don't know how he escaped custody, but I'm going to make sure he goes back there and stays. Permanently.

In a microsecond, we are up and after him as he burns down the street towards the old industrial park. If he goes in, it'll be to his harm. Kayley and I know that area well.

Which is why she holds me up when we see him enter the area.

"Careful," Kayley says between breaths. "There're a lot of places to hide in there."

Mr. About to Get Caught goes into a side alley, and we take up a steady pace just behind him. I know Kayley wants us to use a healthy dose of caution, but he had the chance to fire at us before, and he didn't. Either he's out of bullets or he's only interested in getting away from us. That's to our advantage, and I intend to press it. I missed getting my revenge on him last time. I won't miss it again.

It's dark and creepy in here. Save for the front row of shops and restaurants, the rest of the area is closed at night. The double- and triple-story walls of the former factories tower over us, creating a canyon of corrugated metal. The small amount of light that comes in is from the streetlights just outside the zone. It won't get any brighter as we go deeper inside this labyrinth.

Kayley keeps close, her hand on my back as we tread forward. We stay silent but vigilant for any noise. The background hum of environmental systems masks our hearing. I hope we'll be able to catch the sound when he moves.

The answer comes sooner than I expect. When footsteps echo through the alley, Kayley taps me on the back and points. I nod, and we head off. We're about to trap him in a dead end.

I try to upload as many images as I can to Teddynet, giving them tons of mental notes about the sense of the place. The more they know, the better they'll be able to zero in on us and our suspect.

We come to a junction and pause. Shoot—this isn't the direction I wanted him to go! One way leads to the street on the other side of the industrial park. The other heads deeper into the factory alley. There's still a chance to trap him, but now we need to figure out where he went.

"Which way?" I whisper.

"Be quiet and listen for a moment," Kayley says.

We wait in darkness for what seems like an hour. There is nothing but the sound of compressor motors pumping away the remaining toxic air inside the abandoned buildings. That's one thing we have going for us. He won't try to go inside for fear of being poisoned.

I hear a shout. That came from the back alley! I'm sure of it!

"That way," I hiss and take off, but Kayley grabs my shirt. I'm forced to stop.

"No, that came from the street!" Kayley says. "Let's go!"

I shake my head and follow as Kayley darts off in the opposite way I want to go. We can't split up, though. That would be dangerous. I'll have to trust her guess and hope it's right.

"Wait up!" I call after her. She waves a hand back at me—a signal to keep quiet. I do, even though I'd prefer to voice my objection about how far ahead of me she is. Kayley's about to exit the alley onto the street while I'm still a good fifty paces away. I don't know what happened to staying together, but getting into an argument with her now is a bad idea.

To my relief, she stops and scans the area as she waits for me out on the street. I pick up the pace, worried we could have already lost the guy. The Teddys really need to get here. Like now.

"Come on!" Kayley hisses, waving her arm as if that will make me go any faster than I'm capable.

Then a shot rings out. And then my world comes to a halt.

As if on slow-motion vid, Kayley's body convulses, her arms floating up to the sky. Her head rolls back as if some powerful unknown force just railed into her. I run faster to get to her, but the alley seems like it just grew to twice its length.

Another shot. Kayley's torso twists, and her knees buckle. She collapses to the ground like a leaf falling off a tree. Her head hits the pavement, and she goes still.

"Kayley! No!" Every cell in my body screams to deny what I just witnessed. It's not possible. It couldn't have happened! No—she's not dead. No way!

This can't be the way she dies.

As soon as I get to her, I'll see. She'll be fine. Then I'll save her. Everything will be fine. I just have to get to her.

I know I shouldn't break cover, but I can't keep away. She's too much a part of me. I need to know. I have to know she's still alive.

Please, Kwanon, show her mercy.

I drop to my knees before her, scooping her limp body up in my arms. My fingers find the spot on her throat where it meets her jaw, and I press, praying with all my heart that I feel a pulse. Any pulse. Slow. Fast. I don't care. Just give me a sign she's still alive!

But there's none.

A sob bursts from my throat. I pull her closer, clinging to her, with hope drifting away from me. Kayley's body is still warm. It still smells like her. Yet nothing else gives me the sense that she's still alive. I press my face into her hair and pray with all my might that some miracle or blessing will come. Technology won't save her now. All I have left is faith.

"How convenient," a voice says. An eerie and familiar voice. I spin, searching for its owner.

When a figure in black steps out of the shadows, a rifle in her hands, I understand everything. This was a trap. For us. I made a huge mistake, and now my life is over. I'm not sure I care. Kayley's gone, and I'll be joining her soon. If that's the way we can be together, then I welcome it.

"You got me good back on Canis Ludis," the assassin says, pulling off her hood to reveal a woman with short blond hair, not that much older than me. "My jaw is still sore from where your buddy roundhoused me. I owe her payback for that. And that was some trick, paralyzing my legs, too. I'm still wondering how you did that. Gas maybe?"

Her words don't register. I'm too focused on the thousand other thoughts rushing through my head. Is my mom still alive? What will she do when someone tells her I'm dead? Or Kayley's parents? What about Parrish's mom? What about Parrish? Afton? Nayla? Grady? Is the same thing going to happen to them?

"Yeah, I learned my lesson," the assassin says, showing me the rifle. "I went too easy on you—no blades this time."

I come out of my mind blitz to glare at her. I don't understand how anyone could kill so willingly. A tear slides down my cheek. It's not for me—it's for Kayley. It's for everyone I failed by getting caught.

The conspiracy better not get away with their plan.

"Hey!" She snaps her fingers in front of my face. "You listening? I'm trying to make conversation here. Maybe give you a few more minutes to live? This is a pretty lonely job, you know. It would be nice to have a chat once in a while."

"I could not care less about what you want," I growl through my teeth. "Just shut up and do it already."

The assassin gives me a disappointed pout. Good. At least I can hurt her a little before she takes my life.

"Have it your way." The assassin raises her rifle and takes aim. Then, before she shoots, she says, "Life sucks, doesn't it? Consider yourself lucky."

Then everything goes black.

Chapter Twenty-Four

I dream.

I dream about floating. Floating in a sea of pure white with a bleak sky above. The sea is not water, and the sky is not air. All I recognize is a horizon some distance away. I feel the gentle sway of my body, like waves are rocking me. Maybe this isn't the sea, but I don't know what to call it other than pure comfort.

This can't be heaven, either. No Goddess or angel has come to judge me. I have no sense of anything but this state of suspension. Wherever it is, I'm stuck here in this in-between, not saintly enough for salvation and not evil enough for damnation.

My thoughts drift, like this endless sea, never focused on any one thing, nor forgetting to remember everything. I see images. People's faces with names I can't remember. They're important to me, somehow. Perhaps I miss them, and maybe they miss me. If I only knew who they were.

Then, one face becomes distinct over all the others. A girl with red hair. She smiles at me, and a memory returns. I remember her, my scarlet girl. My love and my life. But where I should feel happiness, I only feel pain. A twisting, heavy pain that takes my heart and squeezes it until I feel as though I can no longer bear it.

Tears come then. A sadness that seems infinite. I sob and moan for what must be days, though I don't understand why. There is a great sense of loss connected to this girl. Who was she to me?

I attempt to force recall upon my memory and get nowhere. Maybe it doesn't matter. I have been here for days, perhaps months; time is unknowable. Nothing has changed. I still exist in this limbo, with no hint or idea of when I will move on to another state. It doesn't matter to me. I feel no emotion other than the grief that hits me when I see her steel-blue-eyed gaze. Is this my punishment? What have I done wrong?

No answer comes.

Gradually, after a greater length of time, I gain an awareness of body and limbs. I wriggle my fingers and toes as if it is a novel action. It is like the first time that I've ever done it, though I know at one time, long before this, I could.

Memories slip into my consciousness, too. My name—Rance Quigley He', son of Benicio Augustus Cavalcante and Tzu-Yu He'. There's more than that, but it's just beyond my mind's reach. I stretch to grasp for it with a desire to know more about who I am and why I am here.

A name comes to me, like a strike of lightning into my mind. Her name. The girl with the red hair and blue eyes. The one I've been aching to see this entire time.

Kayley. Kayley Scarlett Garmonichnyy. My girlfriend. The girl I'm going to marry.

The girl who died.

My throat wells up, then realize I have a throat. Something's stuck in it, choking me. I lash out, my hands and feet hitting something solid. The sound of water splashes in my ears. I am floating in the sea!

But now I'm drowning!

I twist and flail. The thing that's jammed down my throat is also covering my face. I can't breathe anymore. Panic is taking over. I'm going to die. I'm going to die, and there's nothing I can do!

As I struggle, a thought strikes me and I pause, my body relaxing a bit. I'm not drowning. I can't. I'm already dead.

A pair of hands grab me underneath one arm, followed by another on the opposite side.

"Whoa, steady, dude." Parrish. It's Parrish! Did he die, too? "I've got you."

"Hold on, don't struggle. I've got to remove the intubation tube." Another familiar voice—Elizabeth. Doc Elizabeth.

I hear a click, and the thing choking me rubs against my throat. I gag and double over. The palm of someone's hand pounds me on my back, and I vomit what must be a bathtub's worth of milky fluid.

Exhaustion comes to me, and I rest against the hands that hold me. Whatever this existence is, I much preferred the one before it. This one is torturous.

"Welcome back, Mr. He'," Elizabeth says in my right ear. "I am so very glad you made it."

"Mmmade...it?" My voice comes out as a mumble of syllables as fluid continues to drain from my lungs.

"Yeah, we found you and Kayley just outside of where the Teddys said you would be," Parrish says. "Just in time, too. Any later and we might not have been able to rebuild you."

"Reebillud?"

"Ah, yes," Doc Elizabeth says, rubbing her hand on my back. "I never showed you what I was working on, did I? Well, you remember the nanotech we used to heal Grady? You might not right now, but hopefully your memories will come back."

"Graad-ee." My best friend's face comes into my mind, and the edges of my mouth turn up a little.

"He's been worried about you. We all have been. I wasn't sure if our fuzzy friends had copied the technology well enough for this tub to work, but thanks to Mr. Grady, he translated the design for them." Doc Elizabeth pats me on the back. "Don't worry. I'm about to explain.

"That technology isn't a Teddy design, you see. It's of human origin. The tub is a means to enable humans to travel very long distances through space, during a time when it would take them centuries to go to the nearest star. I'll spare you the finer details, but the bath is full of nutrients and nano machines that constantly replace dead or dying cells. While in suspension, you don't age, you don't get sick. You simply float."

My mind fills with questions, none of which I can focus on long enough to ask. She's going to need to repeat all of that again to me, but from what is making sense to me right now...I'm...

"I'm alive," I say.

"You totally are, Rance," Parrish says.

Which means—

"Kayley."

"Yes." I can hear the smile come to Doc Elizabeth's lips. "We saved her, too. But—"

"I want to see her!" With all the strength I have, I throw my body up straight and flop my hands around, searching for something to lift myself up by. Doc Elizabeth and Parrish scramble to restrain me, their hands slipping off the slimy liquid in the tub.

"Not the best time to do that," Doc Elizabeth warns. "She needs to heal more, just like you do."

"Get me out. Get me out!" My hands find supportive shoulders, and they let me rest on them. "Please! I have to see her!"

"You will, but perhaps you'll want to wear some clothes first. A blanket, at least."

"What?" As her words reach my brain, they become sense. I realize that there is no reason for me to be wearing clothes in the tub. That I am naked doesn't bother me all that much. All that matters is Kayley. I just need to see her face so I will know she is really alive.

Wait. I can't see anything at all.

"Why can't I see?" I demand.

"Relax a moment, and I'll take the rest of the mask off," Doc Elizabeth says. "Your sight is still going to be blurry for a while."

She's right. Once the mask comes off, my eyes sense brightness and shadows but no definition of anything. Parrish and Doc Elizabeth are just blobs of darkness that move. That means I won't be able to see Kayley's face, but it doesn't matter. I need to see with whatever eyes that I have that Kayley's alive.

I try to get my feet planted on something solid to push myself up, but my muscles don't respond. I'm fatigued beyond belief.

"Why can't I stand?"

"You've been mostly dead for three months," Doc Elizabeth replies. "Your muscles need time to strengthen again. Don't worry. You'll be on your feet again sooner than you think."

Something lands on my shoulders and wraps around me. Doc Elizabeth's suggested blanket. I realize that I've been shivering—from a chill or from weakness, I don't know.

"Help me lift him to the bed," the doc says to Parrish. They swaddle me like a baby, then raise me out of the fluid and over to something not nearly as gooey. The pressure of the mattress against my back is more irritating than it is comfortable, however. I tolerate it, as it brings me one step closer to seeing Kayley.

"Please let me see her," I beg with what's left of my voice. It sounds small, even childlike, in its tone.

Doc Elizabeth sighs. "I'm against it, but what do you think, Parrish?"

"Let's ask Afton," Parrish replies. "She's in charge now."

Afton? In charge? What happened while I was in that tub?

Parrish goes to get Afton and brings her back with Nayla. I know they're back when I see an Afton-shaped blob come over me and I hear Nayla murmur something. Once Afton embraces me, I'm sure it's her.

"We missed you," Afton says. "How do you feel?"

"I need to see her," I reply.

"That's not what I asked."

"Please, let me see her."

"She's not ready, and neither are you."

"Guys," Parrish says softly, as if he doesn't want to disturb my rest. "It's that time. I have to go. I'll tell Grady he's awake."

"Where are you going?" I try to call after him, but all my throat does is croak louder. "Where's he going?"

"He's...got something to take care of," Doc Elizabeth answers. "Don't worry. He'll be back later."

I'm disheartened by the tone of her answer. It's not just her, though. I may be sense-limited at the moment, but I feel like I've woken up at a funeral. No one is jumping for joy that some crazy Teddy tech just brought be back from the nearly dead. Not just me. Kayley too. Yet every time I ask to see her, they deny my request as if it was something beyond reasonable.

"Why?" I ask. "What's wrong with her? Why won't she see me?"

Silence meets my question. They shift on their feet and do whatever else they need to so they can feel at ease over their lack of response.

"Nayla is here, Rance," Afton says. "Say hello."

"Hi."

"Ransom Quigley He', I do not think you understand the miracle that you are," Nayla says, her hand coming to rest on my shoulder. "I am sure there is much we must explore, but for now, I believe rest is the proper recommendation."

As she leans down to plant a kiss on my forehead, my spirit sinks. They're keeping something from me, and I fear that something might be bad. Very bad.

"Do not fear, you have more time than you think," Nayla whispers and walks away.

"Is Kayley really alive? You're not lying to me just to make me feel okay, are you?"

"Yes, she *really is* alive," Afton says and sighs. "This is getting silly. Rance, trust me, okay? I'm doing this for your own well-being. Just rest. You'll see her soon enough."

It's not what I want to hear. Afton is asking for me to trust whatever she thinks is best right now. I've little choice but to accept. The only other thing I can do is whine at her, and that won't change anything.

"Just tell me. Did she ask about me?"

"Yes. Every day. Now do what Elizabeth tells you to and rest." Afton turns to go, then pauses. She looks at me for a minute, then reaches out to wipe my wet hair away from my face.

"Just remember, Kayley loves you. Very much."

Chapter Twenty-Five

"Hey, you look good," Parrish says as he comes into my room. His face wears a humble smile, and he bows his head a little, as if the ceiling is too low for him. It's standard human height, however, so his act comes off as odd. I'll chalk it up to every other space in the Teddy ship, save for Doc Elizabeth's room, being much lower.

"Yeah, for a guy who just took a three-month-long bath," I reply with a smirk.

"How are you feeling?"

"Like that question has been seriously abused ever since I woke up."

Parrish laughs, then pulls up the one stool in the room. Other than the tub, the bed, and a counter with a bunch of drawers under it, there's nothing else in here. It's as sparse as can be without becoming nonfunctional. It also cannot be any whiter.

"I bet," Parrish says. "Don't take it personally. We just want to make sure you're okay."

"Dude. I'm alive. After being dead, I couldn't be more okay."

I have no memory of anything from when the assassin pulled the trigger until I started dreaming. I don't know how long ago that was. I had no sense of time, nor did I really care about it. I was content. Happy even. Until I remembered something to be concerned about, I had no worries. There's something to be said about that when compared to life.

I'm glad that it was Parrish who was there when I woke up. There is no one stronger, more stable, or more grounded. I needed to have all of that or else I might have lost my sanity. I only wish he could have hung around longer.

Which reminds me.

"Hey, where'd you go yesterday?" I ask.

"Well…" Parrish tries to hide his face from me. There's no way I'm going to accept that as an answer. If he's got something he needs to tell me, he's got to get it out.

"Come on, dude. You can tell me. It doesn't matter what it is. I'm listening, okay?"

Parrish's head hangs lower. I grow concerned, but I'll try to be patient with him. He's always given me the time when I needed it.

"Mom's not doing well," Parrish says as he clenches his hands together.

"Yeah, I know." Then I blink and remember that they bombed our houses. I never had time to ask him about that. "Was she hurt in the attack?"

"No. It's not that."

"Then?"

"They took her in after the explosion and checked her out. That's when they found the reason she hasn't been feeling well." Parrish swallows. "The doctor gave her only a few months left to live."

My jaw goes slack. What do I even say to that?

"Wait, have you talked to Doc Elizabeth? What about this thing?" I point to the tub. If it could fix me, then it could heal Parrish's mom, too!

Parrish's brow wrinkles, and he stares hard at the floor, as if there is something there he can't make out. Then, after a moment, he shakes his head.

"I asked," Parrish replies. "She explained it, but I couldn't really follow. There was something about the nanos not being programmed to see her condition as a problem to fix."

Whatever worries I had before he stepped in here get pushed aside by my concern for him and his mom. I got another opportunity to live my life. Parrish's mother doesn't get that chance.

"Where is she now?"

"In the hospital. The doctor is still running some tests to see if she could benefit from a new therapy they're testing."

"Then why are you here?"

"Because I felt bad about leaving you like that yesterday." Parrish raises his head then. "And I need to talk to you about something."

The look in his eyes makes the back of my neck itch. I get the feeling he's about to tell me something that is going to change things between us.

My hands grip the sheet that covers my legs as I try to prepare myself for whatever he's about to say. Maybe he's going to ask me for something that I can't give him. But there isn't anything like that. He's saved me more than once. If he asked me for the universe, I would give it to him.

"Okay." I try to give him a supportive smile. He should feel like he can talk to me about anything without hesitation. He's there for me. I'm there for him. Save for when I was dead, of course.

"I'm quitting," Parrish says.

"Quitting...school?"

"No." Parrish shifts in his seat and looks away again.

"Running?"

"No, nothing like that."

"Then what?"

Parrish leans forward to rest his elbows on his legs. He takes a breath, and I watch as his knuckles go white. That he's struggling so much with this is getting to me. What could bother him this much?

"I can't help you fight the conspiracy anymore, Rance. I need to go take care of my mom. There's no one else who can. Or should."

I stare at him, feeling the intense pressure inside of me drop. I thought he was going to tell me he was terminal, too. Or out of money. Anything but what he just said.

"Dude, that's what's got you so wound up? You need to go take care of your mom, I get it. You should. And if you need help, well, I'm there for you. Then once she's cared for, you'll come back, right?"

I wasn't sure how to say *after your mom passes away*. He's going to need people around him after that. Maybe getting back into conspirator-hunting would help to take his mind off losing her. I know if my mom died, I wouldn't want to be alone even for one second.

No one has said anything about my mom. Not since I got out of the tub. I'm certain she wasn't home during the blast. But then, where is she? She must be worried about me. It's been over three months since I've talked to her. We talked, or at least communicated, nearly every day anytime I was a way.

"No, I won't be coming back," Parrish says.

Parrish's words bring me to a full stop. I didn't think he could shock me twice in one sitting, but he's done it. My brain needs to restart before I can even figure out how to respond to that. I know I heard him correctly—I'm just not sure I believe him.

"You...you're not?" I ask.

"I have to finish school so I can start coaching," Parrish explains. "The house is still under mortgage, and someone needs to pay for that."

"Money? We can get that, dude!"

"No." Parrish raises his hands. "I don't want to accept money from anyone. I just want to work an honest job and get paid for it."

"What we do isn't honest?"

Parrish presses his lips together. Maybe he regrets telling me now. I suppose I'm not making it easy on him. It's difficult for me, too. Parrish is asking me to let him go...forever. Sure, we'd still be friends, but it wouldn't be the same. His life will head in another direction. We will see less and less of him after a while, and then one day, one of us will just stop calling.

Our team would feel wrong without him, too. There would be an enormous gap that the rest of us couldn't fill. It's not just his strength or athletic ability. He keeps us all connected to the ground, even when we're out in space.

It's hard not to think selfishly about this. I could say that it would be better for him to stay with us. That he needs to be with his friends, and we need him, too. That's always been the greatest benefit of our little gang. Our interdependence. We rely on each other, which is why, when one of us asks for support, we don't hesitate.

Or maybe making Parrish stay is the absolutely wrong thing to do. Maybe I would ruin his future potential if I held him back. I could be the obstacle in the way of his ability to prosper. I always thought that we would only achieve great things together. Maybe I'm wrong about that.

I wish I could see it that way. I wish I had the courage to just let him go. But I can't. After being returned to this world, I'm still trying to figure things out.

I'm not proud about what I'm about to do, but I don't have it in me to do anything else.

"Parrish, you can't go," I plead. "Not like that. You can't just leave us. We need you. We can find a way to pay for your house. An honest way, so you can feel like you're working for it. But you can't go. Please. Don't be unreasonable like this."

The anguish that comes to his face makes my heart drop. I just did that to him. My friend.

Parrish struggles to find a reply, one that he believes won't hurt me. Even when I'm the one being unreasonable.

"Rance..." Parrish sighs. "I wish I could. I really wish I could. But I've realized that this isn't for me. Not anymore. It's taken too much out of me. I doubt I'll ever get back. I just want to live a quiet life now."

"You can! We won't do this forever! Please. This is a critical time. I need you. *We* need you. Once it's over, I promise, we'll all have quiet lives. Together!"

His deep brown eyes, full of sadness, settle on me. The look chills me to the bone. I know my words haven't swayed him one bit.

Now all that's left is goodbye.

"You can't promise that, and I can't expect you to." Parrish stands. "I wish there would have been a better time or a better way to break this to you. I'm sorry it had to go down like this."

He steps to the door and turns back.

"I hope you find your mom," he says. "I know how much she means to you. That's something we've always had in common."

"Yeah." I close my mouth. There is more to say. A lot more. But I can't find it within me to say any of it. Whether it's him, my mom, or all of it. I'm stunned to silence.

What do words matter when they've lost their meaning?

Chapter Twenty-Six

Despite my pleas, it was still five more days before I could get to see Kayley. It wasn't her. It was me. After's Parrish's bad news, I had what Doc Elizabeth called a "negative reaction" to the nanos in the fluid because of the nanos that were in me before. There was an incompatibility, and my body bore the brunt of that microscopic battle.

"So one side won?" I ask Doc Elizabeth as she puts on my socks. I can walk now, but my coordination is still a little awkward.

"Unfortunately, yes," Doc Elizabeth replies. "I think you can guess which one it was, since you are alive and talking to me."

I consider that for a moment as she wiggles a pair of slippers on my feet. With the Teddys' help, I'll shuffle next door to the room where Kayley is. Just the thought of seeing her has pushed my pulse up and kept my hands fidgety.

"Unfortunately? So if the old nanos are gone...what does that mean?"

"You already know that answer."

"Maybe, but help me out."

"Try downloading something from the net."

She's talking about Teddynet. Which means...

My hands stop their twiddling and squeeze together as fear seeps into my body. I try to connect to Teddynet, but there's nothing. I'm cut off from the collective conscious. Alone. My chest gets tight, and my breaths come shorter and faster. I feel like I've fallen into a deep hole with no exit.

"Hey, hey. It's okay. I'm here." Doc Elizabeth takes my hands and squeezes. "I know what you're going through, Rance. I've been there, too."

"Huh?" Her admission shakes me from my panic. I'm sure I heard her right, but if that's true, I should have known that. Did I forget everything I learned while connected to Teddynet?

"I also was connected to Teddynet once," she says with a wistful smile. "The Teddys were looking for a way to help me recover some of my lost memories. They hoped that the connection would fill in the gaps. It didn't work, obviously. I miss that feeling, though. Perhaps that is why I stayed with them."

"Does that mean you know how you lost your memories?" I ask.

"Yes! But that's a story for another time." Doc Elizabeth hops up and pats my leg. "Let's not keep you from your first date."

I feel my cheeks get warm. She's right. It seems like I'm about to go on my first date with Kayley. Even though my heart is longing to see her, my body shakes with schoolboy jitters. I know we've both been through a great deal, but once we see each other, everything will be just like it was before.

That will be a true blessing. I will need all the support I can muster to get over this sense of isolation. I don't know why I didn't notice my lack of Teddynet connection before. Maybe I was just too focused on getting better so I could see Kayley.

Original Teddy and one blue buddy come to spot me as I make my way to the next room. As I step out of my white sanctuary and into a larger space, I recognize that all of this is new. The Teddys must have built it for us. I'm confused about where we are on the ship. Maybe in the lower decks where I've never really been? Until now, that is.

Before we enter, Doc Elizabeth stops us by turning and putting her hands on my shoulders and makes sure I'm giving her my full attention.

"Rance, I want you to go slow, understand?" Doc Elizabeth presses her point by looking at me straight in the eye. "As excited as you are to see her, remember that you're both still healing. Be patient."

"I'll try," I promise. That's about as much of a guarantee as I'm willing to give. Doc Elizabeth doesn't realize the last time I saw Kayley was when I was holding her lifeless body in my hands. I can't pretend that image isn't permanently scarred into my mind. I need to use anything I can to erase it.

Doc Elizabeth nods and opens the door. She's there, sitting on the edge of the bed with Nayla, Afton, and Grady around her. I go still, taking her in and letting my brain accept that the person I see before me is real.

She's got on a loose-fitting sleeveless tunic over a long-sleeve shirt—one of Grady's. I'm in something similar, except my shirt is my own. On her head is a knit cap, also one of Grady's. Like me, her hair—all of it—dissolved in the tub. Doc Elizabeth promises it will grow back.

"Hey, you," Kayley says as I shuffle in. She stands and spreads her arms around me. It's all I can do not to throw myself at her. I said I'd go slow, so I'm trying, even though it's killing me to do it.

We wrap our arms about each other, and I hold on to her for what could be eternity but still seems too short. I shut my eyes and just listen to her breath in my ear. With her so close like this, it's impossible to feel that moment when she was gone. Maybe if I keep holding on to her, that memory will never return.

"You're real," I whisper.

"You too."

My hands come up to cup her face. She smiles, and I become lost in her eyes. As it finally sinks in that she is alive and in my arms, I'm filled with joy. I want to feel her lips on mine and to show her just how much she means to me.

But before I can kiss her, Kayley jerks back, pulling her head away from mine. Confusion covers her face. I blink, stunned by her reaction.

"What...what are you doing?" Kayley asks as she shakes her head.

"Okay." Afton pushes her arms between us, separating Kayley and me. "That's enough for today."

Too many things just happened for me to make sense of them all. The one that tears through the others and stabs me in the heart is Kayley's rejection. I want to ask her why, but she's as baffled as I am. Only Afton seems to know something about it.

"What's going on?" I demand, glaring at Afton.

"That's my question," Kayley says, still staring at me. "Did you just try to kiss me?"

"Rance, don't answer that!" Afton says.

"Why not?" Kayley and I ask in chorus.

Afton curses and looks to Doc Elizabeth for help. She sighs and steps forward, placing her hands on Kayley's and my backs and moving us forward.

"Alright, alright," the doc says as she leads both of us over to the bed. "The two of you, sit, and I will do my best to explain."

"I knew this was a bad idea," Grady mumbles as Kayley and I settle in. Our shoulders bump, and Kayley slides away from me, putting space between us. It's painful for me to notice it. I feel tears welling up.

Does Kayley not love me anymore? If that's true, then bringing me back to life is the worst thing anyone could have done to me.

"Now listen," Doc Elizabeth says, pulling up a stool to sit in front of us. "I had no way of testing it, so I couldn't be sure of the extent of it, though it's a little clearer now."

"Extent of what?" I ask.

"Kayley has lost a good portion of her memory from the last three years. Or thereabouts. I think she realizes it, too. She has no recollection of what happened just before you were both assassinated. I don't think she remembers what all of you have accomplished over that time, either."

"She doesn't," Afton says. "Nayla and I have asked."

"So she doesn't remember...that we were dating?" I try to pick my words carefully. The wrong ones will trigger me, and I will just collapse into a sobbing mess. They could do the same to Kayley. She's already under a world of stress hearing this.

"We were dating?" Kayley throws a look at me. I don't want to see it. I know that the disbelief covering her face will devastate me. "And what do you mean assassinated? Afton only told me I was shot."

"Well, you were," Doc Elizabeth replies. "They shot you twice. And you died."

Grady sits down behind me on the opposite side of the bed and drops a hand on my shoulder. I welcome his touch, but I have to stare at the floor. It's the only place where my eyes won't meet anyone else's. All this is turning into a veritable hell. Maybe it would have been better if they had left me to float in that tub.

I am trying hard to see the positives in this nightmare. I'm alive. So is Kayley. Such a miracle should elate me. It doesn't. Kayley and I, being just as we were before, would have been the perfect ending to all of this. That can't happen now.

"Then how am I alive?" Kayley glances between Afton and the doc, her voice rising in pitch. "And why haven't you been telling me all of this already? It's been three weeks since I woke up!"

"We knew there could be some side effects with the original unit—" Doc Elizabeth says.

"Then you should have put me in it," I say.

"And then Kayley would be feeling what you feel right now," Afton replies. "Is that what you want?"

"We tried," Grady says. "But the unit was rejecting you, and we were running out of time. We had to swap you before your brain activity went to zero."

"You said you knew about the side effects," Kayley says. "How did you know? Aren't we the first ones to use these things? They don't exist in the Empire, right?"

"You're not the first to use them," Doc Elizabeth replies. "The Teddys found me floating in it inside an emergency pod, and we've used some of the technology to fix Mr. Grady, too."

"That's why you lost your memory," I say as the realization hits me. I look up at her. "How long were you in it?"

Doc Elizabeth presses her lips together and shakes her head. She may never remember her past, but she has created a future for herself here with the Teddys.

Kayley likely won't remember, either. That's the reality that I have woken up to.

I glance over at her. Right now, she's just trying to take this all in. She also has a new normal to accept. The only difference between us is that she has no sense of loss. Kayley doesn't know what she's forgotten. Maybe that's a blessing for her. Maybe it's better that she can't remember all her struggles or regrets.

I should accept that Kayley and I may never date again. That I may never again kiss her lips.

That we may never get married.

"I...I have so many questions," Kayley says, then turns to me and takes my hand. "And I'm sorry, Rance. I know what you just said before about us, but I just don't remember. To try to—"

"It's okay, I understand." I gently pull my hand from hers and stand. "I'm tired. I'd like to go to sleep now."

"No. Stay, please?" Kayley asks. "You've always been a special friend, Rance. I know you can help me remember."

Special friend. Afton and Nayla must see the agony on my face as they quickly move to my side and take me by my arms. I feel my knees get weak, and they adjust their stance to take my weight.

"Yeah, you look exhausted," Afton says. "Let's get you to bed."

"Yes," Doc Elizabeth adds, taking up the hint. "Sleep for the both of you will work wonders, I'm sure."

"But you'll come tomorrow, right?" Kayley asks, a hopeful tone in her voice.

"Let's just take things slowly, shall we?" the doc answers for me. I'm thankful. I couldn't have done it without breaking down.

The three of us stay silent as they return me to my room. Words seem useless to me, and the two of them are already saying as much as they can by being by my side.

Then, after they get me seated on the bed, I notice their hesitant loitering.

"Go," I say. "She needs you."

"So do you," Afton replies in a quiet voice.

"My troubles aren't solved so easily."

"Not true," Nayla says. "Something that once was can be again. Do not give up hope before trying."

Afton and I raise our eyebrows at her, and she returns a sweet smile.

"Come see me in the next day. I will have your readings prepared for you by then. I can help to make your path clear, Ransom Quigley He'."

Chapter Twenty-Seven

"Up and at them!"

My eyes fly open at the squeaky voice piercing my eardrums. I've never heard a sound so annoying. If its owner was intending to wake me up, it was a flawless execution of the plan. Not only am I awake, I'm terrified and ready to run.

I turn my head and catch Original Teddy standing at the side of my bed, watching me. He's never done anything like this before. Then again, I've never died before.

I wonder what he wants.

"Activity is recommended. Solution is offered," Original Teddy chirps.

"You want me to do something for you?"

"That is not accurate. Rancid will contemplate exertion with Teddy."

My forehead wrinkles. Even with Teddynet, I don't think I would have a real understanding of what he's talking about. It must be something new for him, too, because he's having trouble explaining to me what he wants me to do. I'll have to think through his words and figure it out.

I get he's offering to do some kind of activity with me. A game, maybe? No, that's not it. He said exertion—meaning something that takes energy. And what kind of activity is strenuous?

Exercise, that's what.

"Teddy, did Doc Elizabeth ask you to make sure I exercise?"

"That is accurate."

So a little physical rehab for me, then. I should, if I ever want to have any sort of normal lifestyle again.

Normal. Ha. After what happened between Kayley and me yesterday—no. Not Kayley and me. She doesn't understand what's got me so upset. It's not her fault, but that doesn't stop me from wishing I never woke u p.

"Thanks, buddy, but honestly, I'm not really feeling up to it today," I say.

"That's a pity." Original Teddy slides a tentacle under the blanket and grabs my ankle. "Nonacceptance is not possible."

He yanks on my ankle, and I slide off the bed with a yelp. Just before I smack the floor, his other tentacle catches me and spins me upright. I get dizzy and have to steady myself on the edge of the bed until the universe stops spinning before my eyes.

"Preparation is recommended," Original Teddy says. "Uniform is required."

I have a feeling he won't leave me alone until I agree to go with him. It looks like someone has laid out an exercise suit for me already, too. I suppose today was destined for me to do this.

"So what did you have in mind for an exercise activity?" I ask as I put the suit on.

"Teddy training."

"Yeah, can you elaborate on that?"

"Visual is best."

I guess I'll just have to see what he's got in mind, like he says.

It's not long before I find out. I follow Original Teddy to somewhere way aft in the ship. It's a long room, with a collection of panels placed on the walls, floor, and ceiling. A few other Teddys are there, including one blue buddy I recognize from our missions.

If I had to guess, it seems like some kind of Teddy maze. They must hone their mobility skills here. I'm surprised I've never seen it before, though it makes sense that they might have something like this on the ship to maintain their reflexes. If Original Teddy expects me to do the same, there's only one minor problem: I don't have tentacles.

"Teddy, you realize that I'm not capable of using this...facility or whatever you call it."

"Nonsense," Original Teddy replies and digs a claw into one of the many diamond-shaped holes in the walls.

A bell rings out, long and sustained. The Teddys waddle over to what looks like starting positions marked in red on a few panels. They latch themselves on and go still, as if waiting for something.

Then, without warning, the artificial gravity disappears. I lift from the floor, my arms flailing about for something to hold on to. But my sense of direction goes wrong. What was down is now left, and what was forward is now up. I feel my stomach get ready to release its contents. It's a good thing I haven't eat yet.

"Whoa! Hey!"

Original Teddy grabs me and flings me towards one of the unoccupied panels. I focus on clamping on to it as my sense of up becomes clearer. My training partner, or leader, passes me by and gets to the panel first.

"Follow Teddy," he instructs.

He launches himself off the floor panel and goes for one connected to what was the ceiling. The moment his feet touch it, he's off to the next one. He moves with such speed, he makes it seem like there's still gravity in here. I'm so amazed by his skill I forget to follow until he reminds me.

"Get a move on!" Original Teddy says.

I set my feet on the panel, bend my legs, and push off, keeping my eyes only on my target. If I look elsewhere, I'm going to hurl. I've always been afraid of heights, just not in the normal sense. Looking up for too long gives me vertigo. I've got to be careful of doing that in here.

The panel's closer than I judge, and I slam into it with my shoulder. I feel a shock run through me, and I clutch the panel for fear of floating off.

"Don't stop believing!" Original Teddy shouts. He's already halfway down the course. It shouldn't surprise me, but it does. I've got to catch up.

The next panel is a little easier, as is the next one. I'm think I might be enjoying this. Teddy was right to suggest it. Maybe I should get Kayley to try this, too. I bet she'd love it. She was always better in zero-g than I was.

My head smashes into the next panel before I realize it's there. I lost my focus thinking about Kayley.

Then the heartache comes rushing back.

For a few minutes, I was free of pain, just living in the moment and enjoying the challenge of following Original Teddy through the course. After that, I banged into and bounced off every panel I tried to target. It was a good thing all the Teddys had finished long before me. I would have just been another obstacle for them to avoid.

"Underwhelming," Original Teddy says as I tumble to the end of the course. "Concentration is recommended."

"Yeah, I know," I say, puffing.

"Again, Rancid."

With that, he takes off after the rest of the Teddys, who have already started their way back. I take a moment to catch my breath, then push off after him.

The course is just as new to me in reverse, and I'm already feeling tired. Doc Elizabeth was right to prescribe exercise for me. I need it. But I can't stop my mind from drifting to Kayley. I ache with every moment I realize that everything's changed.

Yet something gives me hope, however small. Nayla said something to me that's remained in my mind ever since she said it. *Something that once was can be again.* I'm reluctant to get my hopes up about what that means, but Nayla was confident in her statement. She knew, or at least believed, that Kayley and I could be together again. Maybe she's right. Then again, maybe she was just trying to put a smile on my face.

"Ouch!" I bang my head hard this time, and not even on a panel. That was the ceiling. I shove off the surface and stretch hard to reach the intended target. I chastise myself for my lack of focus and head for the next panel.

Despite my mind drifting away from the present moment, I make it to the other side of the course with less difficulty than I had the first time. I land in front of Original Teddy with a smile on my face.

"Deplorable," Original Teddy says. "Again, Rancid."

"Wait, let me catch my breath!"

"Denied." Original Teddy takes off again, this time snatching my arm and dragging me with him to a fresh starting point. I only have a second to react before I smash into the panel. He's really keeping me on my toes or, to be more accurate, my fingers. I don't have a moment to think about anything but my trajectory. Maybe that's what he wants.

By the end of this run, I'm so sweaty and fatigued I can barely hold on to anything. A green Teddy does me the favor of securing me to a rope so I don't float away. It's embarrassing, though. I feel like a helium balloon that's caught on a power line.

I am glad that Original Teddy made the effort to bring me here. I would have just wallowed in bed otherwise. That is not a healthy way to be, though I've never faced death and rebirth before. I doubt anyone has.

This reality has also smacked me in the face with a harshness that I haven't been able to recover from. I know everything just happened. Not just to me. Kayley too. She's trying to make sense of this new world. I hope that she's got someone looking after her recovery, too.

Maybe I should go talk to Nayla. I'm not sure I believe in all her hocus pocus, but it would be good to talk to someone, if nothing else. She's offering to help me, and I should accept it. It costs me nothing to listen, and I may just end up gaining some wisdom from someone who claims to have lived a thousand lifetimes.

"Rancid," Original Teddy says as he lands next to me. "Activity is not complete."

"Yeah, I know, I know. I just need a break. Dying makes you pretty tired, you know."

"Termination of life does not calculate in activity." He reaches out a tentacle and taps my skull. "Contemplation of alternate topic is liable."

I chuckle. How he knows I've got my mind on something other than physical activity is a wonder. Maybe the look on my face is just that obvious.

"Consideration for actuality is beneficial to destiny. Converge on actuality. Destiny will become conspicuous."

I blink. I understood him well enough. It's just that his advice is almost identical to a teaching of the Three Goddesses. I am awed another species would understand this teaching as well as humans do.

Or at least as well as I should.

That settles it. I'll go talk to Nayla tomorrow. Whatever she has to tell me, I'll try to understand it.

"Okay, I got it, Teddy." I smile. "Thanks."

"Well done." Original Teddy pats me on the back. "Now, Rancid."

"Yeah?"

"Again."

Chapter Twenty-Eight

I KNOW THIS IS just another berth in the Teddy ship, but Afton and Nayla have added so much décor that the moment I stepped in, the view transported me to another world.

Geometrically patterned drapes hang from ceiling to floor, covering over any Teddy surface in the room. They removed the bed in favor of a pallet, upon which a comforter full of moons, stars, and crisscross lines drapes. A small lamp even hangs from the ceiling. The colors are primarily blue and white, with some gold trim thrown in. It's not lost on me they chose these colors despite Nayla's turquoise and silver heritage.

Nayla herself sits cross-legged on a pillow, her trademark turban and robe adorning her. Before her is a deck of cards, a small globe of glass—possibly of crystal—and another pillow, which I assume is for me.

Even if it is, I'm not ready to sit. That she could tell me about my future with just some cards or some stones is unsettling. I already know what I want it to be. It could do irreparable damage to my psyche if she told me otherwise.

"Ransom Quigley He', you do not need a command from me to allow you to sit," Nayla says, patting the empty pillow before her.

"I will," I reply.

"And I cannot read your palm from over there."

"Didn't you just read it not that long ago? Why do you need to again?"

She gives me an annoyed look, one that I assume might come from Afton if she was here. Maybe the influence in that relationship is not as one-sided as I thought. At least Nayla won't just grab me and force me down if I continue to refuse.

"You know, I may no longer have a royal title, but I still expect people to treat me with respect. That includes you. Sit, or I cannot help you."

"I'm not sure I want you to," I say.

Nayla looks hurt at that response. "Why not?"

"Honestly? With all that's happened, I'm kinda scared about what you might have to tell me."

A warm smile comes to Nayla's face. "It is common to think that way." She pats the pillow again. "Do not fear. The future is not set."

Maybe that is what I'm most afraid of. Not knowing what the future holds. Of course, if it was already decided, and it was dreadful, that would be worse. I'm not sure how much more bad news I can handle.

Wait. I shouldn't judge the outcome before it happens. Not even Nayla knows for sure what will come to pass. I will sit and listen to what she tells me, and then I will decide whether to freak out or not.

"So how does this work?" I ask, crossing my legs and sitting down before her. "Do I pick a card or something?"

Nayla's hand flies out, grabbing the wrist of my right arm and yanking it towards her. I throw my left hand out to brace myself before my face smashes into her crystal ball. My nose stops just a finger's length away from its smooth surface.

"As I expected," Nayla says, dragging a finger across my palm. It tickles, but I try not to react. Moving might damage something valuable, me included.

"What is it?"

"It is not good." Nayla releases my wrist. I struggle but manage to sit upright again. "I am sorry, Rance. But..."

"What? What? What's not good?" I lean forward. "Are my stars still bad?"

"A moment."

Nayla pulls out a deck of the strangest cards that I've ever seen. They're nearly twice as big as normal playing cards, and the backs are adorned with what looks like hand-painted gold swirls, a representation of a galaxy or some other astral body. When she tilts the card, the galaxy seems to rotate in space. It's a pretty cool effect.

She puts the deck down and spreads the cards out in a semicircle before me so that each one overlaps the other.

"Choose three, and place them in a row," Nayla instructs. "Then turn them over, one by one, left to right."

I do as instructed and just grab any of them. Since I don't know what all this means, I choose at random, hoping that it's the right thing to do. I put the three cards down between Nayla and me and then turn the card on the left over.

On the other side is a picture of a man holding a stick and standing in a field of six other sticks. I stare at it, attempting to discern some meaning from it, but to me, it's just some random picture.

"What does it mean?" I ask.

"I will tell you, but not yet," Nayla responds, her face becoming a deep pool of sympathetic emotion. She smiles a little, perhaps to calm my nerves. It doesn't help.

I wonder just how bad things will get. They're already at the lowest that I could imagine. Then again, I could never imagine Kayley losing her memory.

"Turn the next card," Nayla says.

It's an image of an old man with a long beard, wearing a robe and holding a staff. It's strange, because other than in ancient pictures, no one in their right mind would dress like that, not even the loonies in government.

"Oh, it's upside-down," I say, reaching for it.

"No!" Nayla slaps my hand away. "Do not touch it. A card reversed also has meaning."

"So what's it mean?"

"I must see all three cards together to understand that."

"Is this really necessary?" I say. "Are a bunch of cards going to help me stop the conspiracy? Are they going to help me get Kayley to remember we're in love?"

"This is a difficult time for you," Nayla says. "You have experienced many changes already, and there are more to come. I am sorry to say that these are not changes that seem to benefit you, but that will depend on how you view them."

"What do you mean?"

"Change is inevitable. Everything changes, always. If we restrict ourselves to what has happened, then we will forever be upset by change. You must learn how to move with the flow of change, or else the flood of transformation will inundate you.”

“Whoa, whoa.” I hold my hands up. “You’re confusing me. Can you be more specific?”

“I will give you an example. Keep in mind that this is not how it will be, only how it might be.”

I steel myself for whatever comes next. Maybe what she says won’t happen, but it could. I’ve already been through a hurricane of change. More would be bad for my mental health.

My psyche is beaten and sore. That’s how I see myself—with a brain that is working at less than one hundred percent efficiency. A lot less. Except it’s even worse than that. Kayley has my heart, and even if she doesn’t realize it, I’m just a shell of myself without her.

“Consider your mission,” Nayla says. “You have already done great things for the Empire, Rance. But you cannot keep winning forever.”

“I know,” I reply. “I don’t expect to. We just need to win enough, anyway. Not all the time.”

“But your enemy is stronger than you think, and they will adjust their tactics to deal with the threat that they face. This is why they assassinated you. You were so sure of your ability to continue on the same path to victory that it blinded you to what was coming. A great obstacle has risen before you, and now you are suffering because you did not see it coming.”

“Hold on!” I pound my fists on my legs and point a finger at her. “You think that there was some way I could have seen that coming? Nobody could have seen that coming! Kayley and I were chasing after some guy. We were about to trap him, and then that crazy assassin showed up.”

“You expected you would capture him?”

“Of course! He’s the one who stabbed Kayley at the spaceport! They should have locked him up!”

“And did you ever suspect that something could go wrong?”

“We always do! Kayley is...”

I falter as I remember the moment she ran out of the alley and into the street. Kayley ignored her own rules of caution and put herself out in the open, where she became vulnerable to attack. I’m just as much to blame, as at that moment, I said nothing and then put myself at risk after the assassin shot her.

My body slumps as I realize Nayla has a point. I knew that exposing myself to attack was the wrong thing to do, but I did it anyway. I did it because I thought it was only that guy out there, and I didn't even consider it could have been a trap.

"So, what then? What do I do?" I ask.

"Turn the last card," Nayla replies, pointing at it. "Perhaps it will offer something to enlighten you."

The last card is easy to understand. It even looks like Emperor Joris sitting on his throne. Or at least the images of him that we've seen on vid. Of course, the image in the vid wouldn't be upside-down the way this card i s.

Nayla leans over the cards, staring at them. She says nothing, and that's when I feel my arms itch. I can't see any way that this is going to be good. It hasn't been so far. Every reading she's done for me has had some negative attachment to it.

"Okay, I know it's bad," I say and sigh. "Just tell me what it means."

"This reading is not about good or bad. It is about understanding your way forward and what paths you may choose to get there. It represents opportunity, challenge, and action. If you can persevere through your challenges, you may well succeed."

"Okay, that doesn't sound too bad."

"But, to succeed, you may need to face someone who has great power." Nayla taps her finger on the upside-down card of Emperor Joris. "This person may have abused their position for their own gain. It will not be easy to fight them."

I hope the person we will have to face isn't the Emperor, though why would the Emperor try to take the throne from himself? Authority figures don't scare me. And if this person had something to do with Kayley's and my assassination, I will be more than willing to do anything to take them down.

Maybe I was just scaring myself for no real reason. Sure, there's work ahead of us, but we already knew that.

"That's never stopped us before," I say with confidence. "We can handle someone like that."

Nayla sits back, folding her hands into her lap. She gives me a tight smile and shakes her head once. That's not promising. Does that mean that it actually *is* the Emperor we'll have to fight?

"I say it will not be easy to fight them, Rance, because you may have to do it alone," Nayla says.

"So that's it? I'm on my own on this one? You and Afton won't help? Grady? The Teddys?"

"That is only one interpretation. Afton and I will support you in whatever way we can. I fear whatever it is you will face is something you will also not see coming. Please be careful."

So much for my brief streak of courage. I was feeling alone even before I stepped into Nayla's room. Now...well.

I thank Nayla for her attempt to provide some clarity to my confused situation. She seems sincere in her concern and likely did her best to help. I should think a bit more about what she told me about the cards. Of course, they may mean nothing.

Still, if they are true, I don't want to be blindsided by whatever's coming.

Chapter Twenty-Nine

As I leave Nayla's room, a restless feeling runs through me. All my plans have taken three years' worth of steps backward, yet here I am, relaxing and playing cards. I should be doing everything in my power to drive our gains back to where they were and complete the Chamberlin's task once and for all.

I walk past the elevator and head down the corridor that leads towards the Teddy auditorium. That's not my destination—I don't have one in mind. I need time to think, and sitting still to do it is just not something I can do at the moment.

Maybe I could go up to the solarium. With the grass installed, it's serene and conducive to thought. Or not. At the moment, the only thing I feel like doing is walking. Blood pumping through my veins and bringing oxygen to my brain might be a good way to get the lump of pudding in my head to work better.

I recognize a familiarity about the corridor then and stop, coming to a halt right in front of a portal that is all too easy to remember. It's the portal to my berth. And Kayley's. Neither of us has been in it since the—since we died.

It won't be ours any longer. Kayley would freak if she found out we were sharing a room. There's no way she would agree to even try it. She won't even kiss me. I wonder how I'm going to explain that one to my mom.

I sigh. Mom. No one has heard from her. Not even Kayley's mom. She'd be the first person my mom would call if there was trouble. Wherever she is, I pray she is safe and well.

Just another problem I need to solve. And if Nayla's cards are right, maybe something I will have to do alone. I need to, but it's just another thing piled on top of everything else. If I didn't sense that she was okay, I'd be rallying the authorities to go find her.

And now, here I stand, staring at a dark gray panel that both reminds me of, and is a symbol of, all my challenges. If I go in, it will uncover all my repressed feelings about Kayley and me. Maybe that could be a good thing. We've got two decades of glorious moments together. It might help me remember some of them.

I lift my hand, ready to press the button that dissolves the portal and allows access to my happy memories.

But I don't. I'm not ready. And the moment that portal opens, the view could just as easily remind me of the current state of things.

Keep moving, Rance.

I turn and continue down the corridor. A few Teddys look up at me with curious eyes as I pass. There's another reminder of my disconnection from things familiar, from people and non-people who I care about.

To push those thoughts away, I keep walking, as if the physical distance will somehow create a mental separation as well. Of course, it doesn't.

So I walk more.

The Teddy ship is fairly large. It would take a long time for me to cover every corridor and space in it. I just might, if I keep this up.

So many images pop into my head, most of them bad. Parrish leaving. My home destroyed. The look on Kayley's face when I tried to kiss her. All of it haunts me. Even if things get better, I will never get any of them out of my mind. They've permanently burned themselves into my psyche.

This pity party has to end, though. I've got to figure out the next step for the team. What's left of it, that is. Grady, Afton, Nayla. Will they still have the determination to see this through, now that our gang has cracked and shattered?

When we first started, I really thought we could achieve anything. My dream was to fight for all of those who couldn't defend themselves. It was my father's dream, too. We were going to battle injustice side by side. Then, somewhere along the way, he chose self-ambition over truth. Now he's on a list of wrongdoers who are trying to take over the Empire.

That makes him our enemy.

I've faced my father before, and even though I have no love for him anymore, I don't wish to do it again. That's why we've avoided going after him. There are plenty of others to capture, anyway. The list has brought us no shortage of names.

But if it comes to it, if Nayla's cards are right, then I might have to take down that list by myself. If I don't, everything I've ever dreamed about goes down the drain.

I nearly slam into a pair of black and white Teddys as they pop through a portal. They give me a curious glance and continue on their way. Then I notice I'm in an area of the ship I've never been to and take a moment to look around. It's mostly the same as other parts of the ship, but I've noticed a red pattern appearing on the walls. No idea what it means. If I could connect to Teddynet, I'd know. I can't, so I don't.

Ah well. I'll just keep walking.

I rub my chest right over my heart. There's an emptiness there, a reflection of my life at the moment. Empty.

No. That's not true. I've got friends who care about me, and as much as it pains me to consider it, Kayley is one of those friends, just like she used to be before we became a couple. She cared about me then, and she cares for me now. That's not such a bad thing, but I doubt I could just leave it at that, knowing what I know and having experienced a most amazing time being her boyfriend. It could never be the same.

Maybe it wouldn't be so bad to just forget about all of this. Go home, rebuild the house. Make wooing Kayley all over again my regular pastime, though there wasn't much wooing. She punched me, and then she kissed me. I doubt it would be as effective if I tried the same thing. I could use all the things I've learned about her to my advantage. Somehow, I think she'd catch on to what I was doing.

The image of Kayley scolding me over it makes me laugh out loud. I laugh so much I get dizzy and have to brace myself on the wall. Which makes me laugh more. It's a good thing no one's around to see me. Then again, it would just be Teddys here. I'm already an oddity in this part of the s hip.

As I come to an area full of reddish light, I realize I'm lost. I must be way back in the tail end of the ship, but this isn't the same floor as the obstacle course Original Teddy took me to. I might find my way back from there.

Here is a big unknown. I don't mind so much. I'm in no rush. Not until I can figure out what I should be doing.

Which is…I don't know.

Spending my days chasing after Kayley and hanging with my buds, old and new, is tempting. Parrish and I would forgive and forget, Grady and I could visit his parents in prison, and I could recruit Afton to help me convert Nayla into a cinephile. Imagine the conversations we could have!

Who am I kidding?

A sense of despair hits me then. I press my back against the wall and slide down it, wrapping my arms around my legs.

I would just be pretending to be enjoying all that, while news vids would constantly report the results of my giving up. I would never get away from the reminder of what my decision had done to the Empire. I shouldn't care about that. Right? It's not my responsibility. I'm not even a citizen!

No, wait.

If I didn't care, then I would have never taken up the call to do any of this. I wouldn't have jumped out my window and gotten in the Teddy ship. I would have never agreed to help Danny Lecker, or Grady's parents, or the Chamberlin. I would never have gotten involved in anything.

My body shudders as if I just felt a chill. There is no backing out of this for me. I've got to see this through to the end or until I get killed again. I'm not sure what happens after that, but I've a feeling that I will never let this go.

I push myself up and reach inside for whatever courage remains there. There will be more sacrifices I need to make, and I must accept that. Things will be more challenging than ever, and if I must do this alone, then it will be next to impossible. But I have to. I have to do what's right.

I turn and head back the way I came. There's something I need to do before I talk to the others. Something I need to see.

Then I will be ready to move forward.

Chapter Thirty

With some luck, and numerous hand gestures, I find my way back to the corridor where I first started this walk into my thoughts. The Teddys I met along the way attempted to be helpful—after they realized I was asking them a question. Then they became even more helpful when they understood I needed directions. It would have been easier for me to call Original Teddy on the comm, but none of the units where I was had been modified for human use. I wasn't about to stick my finger into one of those diamond holes again.

I return to the portal of my former berth and stop, staring at it from half an arm's length away. The confidence I had just a few minutes ago quickly dissipates when the idea of entering becomes reality. I know what I will see if I go in. I'm just not sure what my reaction will be upon seeing it.

My and Kayley's berth is nothing like Nayla and Afton's cultured space. We've spent a good deal of time here, but it never occurred to us to decorate. Then again, Kayley and I had never lived together, not like Afton and Nayla, anyway. We were only thinking about things like that. Until now.

I raise my hand over the portal's open button, digging deep to find the will to press it. But as the seconds pass by, my hand gets heavier and heavier.

"Rance?"

I jump, hearing Kayley's voice, and spin. My face must have looked horrified because she gasps and steps back, her hand coming to her mouth. I sigh and deflate, despite my heart racing at an unhealthy rate.

"What are you doing?" Kayley asks. "This is my room, right? Were you looking for me?"

How do I answer that? I could just say yes, and it would be an accurate answer, depending on which question I was answering. It is her room, but the last person I would have hoped to meet here is her. It shouldn't surprise me Kayley's here. She has just as much right to enter as I do. It's just not in me to explain to her that this is *our* room.

"Well, kind of," I reply.

"Oh, well, come in, then." Kayley walks around me but pauses in a near repeat of my action. I wonder if it is the same fear that's causing her reluctance.

Then her hand wanders around the surface of the portal as if she's searching for something. So then, no. She's not afraid to go in.

"Um, how do you open this?" Kayley turns to me, a little wrinkle forming in between her eyebrows.

"Like this," I say and reach for the button. It's inset inside one of the original Teddy holes, so it's not obvious. Someone who lost their memory of how to do it would be hard-pressed to figure it out on their own.

I take a deep breath, then press the button. The portal dissolves in an instant, evoking a small chirp of wonder from Kayley. I fight to hold in a chuckle. It is pretty cool—no, it's really cool. Anyone who saw it for the first time would think so. I've seen it so many times that I'm used to it. Still, I have to remember that Kayley's lost these experiences. She's seeing much of the ship for the first time again. Which makes me wonder.

"Hey, how did you find your way up here?" I ask.

"Oh, Doc Elizabeth showed me the way," Kayley responds as she enters. "Come in."

We may not have decorated, but we humanized the tiny space at least. Before, it was just a pen with a thin mattress on the floor. The Teddys piled in and slept, and that was it. Kayley and I installed a platform bed, a small desk, and a tall cabinet for our clothes. Teddys don't have clothes, so they have no need of furniture.

It hits me then that my clothes and things are all over this room. It's too late to stop her from seeing them. I can only hope that her reaction to them being there is not as hard as me watching her wonder why.

"Rance, come in already!" Kayley smiles and shakes her head at me. "You're always so timid about bothering someone. I really wish you could get over that. There's no reason for it."

If she only knew the reason I'm having difficulty entering, she wouldn't say that.

"So what's up?" Kayley asks as she heads to a cabinet next to the wall. One side has my stuff, the other, hers.

"No!" I shout as she picks the wrong side. "Your stuff is there."

"How do you know that?" She frowns at me but moves to the other side as I point to it and opens a drawer, pulling pants and shirts out.

I keep my mouth shut, not wanting to make a habit of telling her half-truths or outright lying. If there's any possibility of her falling in love with me again, then that love needs to be based on the reality of what happened, not some made-up story that avoids all the difficult moments.

"Rance, you're awfully quiet for someone who has something they want to talk to me about."

"Sorry. It's just that—"

I thought Kayley was just getting clothes to change into, but she keeps piling more of them onto the bed. She's not getting something new to wear; she's emptying the entire cabinet.

"Hey, what are you doing?"

"Packing. What does it look like?" Kayley throws me a curious glance, then goes back to organizing her pile of socks. "Oh, shoot, where are my red-and-white striped ones?"

"At Grady's house. You know, you don't need to bring everything back down to the room. You can still stay here."

"I'm not staying, though. I'm going home."

She's what?

"Home?" My question comes out with such force that it startles the life out of Kayley.

"Rance, what's wrong with you?" But then she shakes her head and sighs. "Sorry. I've got to remember everything I've been told. It's a lot to consider. I think I may have already forgotten half of it."

That's true. I know exactly which half she can't recall. The years of memory that she's lost has got to make her day-to-day struggle that much harder. And here I'm about to drop even more past reality on her. I've got to remember to take it slow. For her sake.

"It's okay"—I wave a dismissive hand—"but don't you want to stay here? I mean, Doc Elizabeth is probably the best person to help you get your memories back, right? She's going through exactly what you are."

"Elizabeth was the one who suggested I return home, even though Afton told me someone planted a bomb in it. But Elizabeth says it might help my recall of the last two years. She doesn't think those memories are totally gone, just—"

"The important parts."

Like how we were putting a stop to a potential overthrow of the Emperor and a resulting civil war. Like how my clothes are hanging in the cabinet right behind her back. Or how she and I were talking about a future together. For the rest of our lives.

Kayley curls the side of her mouth down. No one regrets her missing memories more than she does. Kayley doesn't even know what she's forgotten, but I bet she understands it's a significant chunk of her life.

It pains me to see her despair like this, but I can't help wanting to fall on my knees and beg her to stay. She may remember things at home, but she could remember just as much here.

"Is one of those important parts the reason you know where my socks are?" Kayley asks. I have to look away. It's answer enough to her, I'm sure.

My throat gets tight, and I feel my eyes tear up—I can't help it. The fear over what happens after Kayley steps off this ship is overwhelming me. With her here, I feel there's a chance she and I could be together again. Back on Angelcanis, surrounded by all the things she remembers, being in love with me becomes a distant consideration for her. If it is one at all.

And what about her as team leader? Kayley's always been that to us. It's only become more of an official position since our first mission. I can't lead like she can. I can't lead at all. Grady, Afton, and Nayla might not even stay if she goes. Then everything I've fought for—everything we've fought for—ends.

"Rance, what's wrong?" Kayley comes over to me and guides me to the bed. "Here, sit down for a moment."

Kayley sits down beside me and takes my hand. Even that hurts right now. But I only hold her hand tighter. I want to believe so badly that she's still my girlfriend and not just my friend of three years ago. If I let go, that would be letting go of her, and I never want to do that.

"Do you really have to go?" I ask, choking up.

"Hey, I know," Kayley says, stroking my arm. "I'm going to miss you, too. But you'll come back soon, won't you? Isn't Mom missing you?"

She's called my mother *mom* ever since she was young. We differentiate by referring to our own mothers by calling them *my mom,* but the difference is only genetic. My mom loves Kayley like a daughter, and her parents, when they're around, treat me like family.

The reminder that my mother is still missing doesn't help. I wipe a sleeve across my eyes and nod. That's one thing I will hold off from telling her for now. She doesn't need to know it, and she'll find out soon enough, anyway.

"You should come home, too, Rance. I could use a friend around." Kayley pats my shoulder and gets up to continue organizing her clothes for packing. "I don't think Afton's going to be around much." Kayley chuckles. "I'm thrilled for her, but I still can't believe Afton and Nayla are a couple! No matter how many times they've explained it, it's still impossible to imagine Afton dating a princess."

"Former princess," I mumble and stare at the floor.

I haven't put up much of a fight to stop her from leaving. Maybe that's intentional. Maybe somewhere in the back of my mind I know it's better for her. It's desolation for me, of course. I'm losing someone else to this tragedy, and she's the last person I'd want to go. Kayley not only means the entire universe to me, but she's the most critical part of us completing this mission. Without her, we've got no direction.

I can't force her to stay. I can't manipulate her feelings by insisting we were so deeply in love that we were going to get married. Even though it's the truth, it would be wrong to try.

"Hey," Kayley says, pulling a wrinkled shirt from the drawer, then another. "This isn't mine. This one too. It's all boy stuff. It looks like something that you might even wear—"

She turns to me, eyes wide and jaw slack as she clutches the shirt. I feel a tear run down my cheek. Kayley's realizing my reason for being here. I wish she was remembering us, but she's only recalling what I told her three days ago.

"It really is true, isn't it?" Kayley whispers. "You and I?"

Her eyes get wet then, and that just breaks me.

"Rance, I'm so sorry." Kayley shakes her head, still clutching the shirt. "I'm so sorry. I wish I could remember something...anything."

"It's not your fault," I say, trying to hide my tears. "You can't worry about something that isn't in your memory, KayKa—Kayley. You should go home, see your parents, and don't worry about any of this."

"What about you?" She kneels on the bed next to me. "You've been through a lot, too...Goddesses, we *died*, Rance. How could that not affect you? You should come back with me, not stay up here in this...strange place."

"It's not strange to me."

Kayley frets over her poor choice of words. "Hey, listen, I'll make you a deal, okay? After I'm a little more together, why don't you and I go somewhere? Just you and me." Kayley shrugs. "Maybe it'll bring back some memory that's still there, and maybe it would be good for you, too. But only if you wanted to."

"I don't know." I sigh. "There's a lot more going on than just this."

"Which isn't your problem anymore." She stares at me for a moment, then says, "Just think about it, okay? We've been friends for a long time. We'll find a way through this. Together, right?"

All I can do is nod as I watch every dream I have crumble around me. I should go with her, but I can't. Not while there is even the smallest possibility that I could still complete this mission. I don't know how I will, but I know if I can, all our futures, including Kayley's, will be secure again.

Chapter Thirty-One

"Dude!" Grady shouts as he bursts into my new room. He's going so fast he slides into my bed. I stare at him and wait as he catches his breath. "You've got to come see this!"

"See what?" I ask, feeling my unease ticking up.

"There's a big fire in Bradbury!"

My eyebrow goes up. I was ready to jump out of my bed and race after him to the nearest Teddy vid globe. Now I'm thinking about throwing the covers over my head and getting back to my dreams.

"So?" I shrug at him and grab the edge of my blanket, ready to give it a sharp tug.

"It's the capitol!"

"So?"

"Dude!" Grady slaps the mattress and lets out a frustrated yell. "It's an attack!"

Maybe I won't be getting back to my dreams all that soon, not at least until I can get rid of Grady's over-hyped news.

"What makes you think that?" I ask.

"What else would it be? Come see and judge for yourself if you don't believe me."

"Fine." I roll my eyes and pull the covers off. He won't leave me alone until I agree to go see whatever he's so excited about.

Grady grabs a robe and helps me put it on. Once I'm ready, he ushers me at high speed to the Teddy auditorium. The screen is on, and the others—including Kayley—are already there. They're entranced by the news report, which is just a flyover shot of a burning building. To Grady's credit, it looks like the capitol. The bright burning orange of the flames sets the dark brick of the walls and roof off in a deep contrast.

"See?" Grady says in my ear as he directs me to a stool next to Afton. It's a good thing he does, because I'm getting sucked into the drama on the screen. There are people, maybe ministers, rushing towards and away from the blaze. Their movement is fast but erratic, as if they don't know where to go, but where would they go, other than away from the fire?

"I'm not seeing anything but a fire right now, dude," I reply. "And while that totally sucks, it's not any reason to worry too much. Fires start all the time. How'd you guys find out about this, anyway?"

"It interrupted an episode of *My Doctor, My Chef*," Afton replies.

Now here's the real thing to worry about.

"Wait, you guys were watching *My Doctor, My Chef* without me?" I give them the best shocked face I can muster. Likely they can't see it well. The only light in here comes from the screen, thankfully made flat for human viewing recently.

"We didn't want to wake you," Doc Elizabeth says. "You needed the sleep."

"What time is it, anyway?" The show is usually on in the afternoon. Does this mean I slept that long?

"Ship time or Bradbury time?" Grady asks.

That's a good point. When in synchronous orbit, we park right above our town and match time to our town's time. The capital is only a few time zones different, so if it's afternoon there, then I snoozed about twice as long as I normally do. And I even wanted to sleep more. Maybe I really needed it, after Kayley's news.

"Anyway," I say, "is it a repeat? How much time is left in the show?"

"It's almost over, I think," Grady replies, staring at the screen. Then he waves his hand. "No, wait, who cares? This is what we should be watching. Something is going on. I know it!"

"Dude, it's just a gigantic marshmallow roast," I say, turning around to walk out. "Let me know when you're having lunch. Or dinner. Whichever comes first."

"Why don't you stay?" Kayley calls after me. I freeze in place, as if her voice has some mysterious power over me. It does, of course. That's why I'm not moving, even though I know it will rip a hole in my heart to remain.

I want nothing more than to believe that Kayley's asking because she just realized she is in love with me.

But as much as I desire that to be the truth, it's not, and to go sit next to her—I have to, now that she's invited me to stay—as if everything is normal is an impossible task.

"Thanks, but I'm going to get more sleep," I say and wave like everything is fine. "See you at dinner."

"Wait! What is that?" Grady shouts. "What the hell is that?"

"Hilarious, dude," I say and glance back at him. "You're going to have to do better than that if you're trying to get me to—"

The moment my eyes see the screen, my heart stops. The zoomed-in shot of the inflamed capitol building has widened to show a mass of invading bodies rushing through a breach in the wall surrounding the campus. Flashes emit from the ends of dark objects in their hands. Pulses of light fly out, hitting the retreating politicians with such force that they seem to float before smashing into the graphcrete pavement, unmoving.

Plasma weapons.

"I told you it was an attack!" Grady says. "They hit the building to distract the guards, then they came in shooting!"

I don't need to know who he thinks *they* are. Only one group would be gutsy enough and capable of pulling this off. The conspiracy.

What is their plan? Why do something this obvious when all it will do is rally the entire military force on Angelcanis? They can't be thinking of starting a war on our planet, can they?

"Is this because of us?" Kayley asks, her voice shaking. "Did we provoke them into attacking our planet?"

"No," Afton replies. "We didn't do this. They're just bolder now that they think we're out of the way. They're sending a message to the Emperor."

We're coming for you. That's what they want to say to His Majesty. If they frighten him into stepping down, they'll win without ever having to attack Albion. The planet is a fortress, and even if they had half the military on their side, they'd be hard-pressed to fight their way down to the surface.

"We need to be there," Grady says, turning to us. "If for no other reason than to help. There's going to be a mass of casualties. We can help and maybe get some intel for Colonel Cortell. He's going to be full throttle after this."

"That's a great idea!" I say. That's the way we get back into this. Then maybe even Parrish and Kayley can lend a hand while we're there. Plus, I get to spend more time with her, like both of us want. At least I think so.

"No way," Afton says. "I don't care if it's the Prime Minister of Angelcanis. We're done. That is not our problem anymore, if it ever was."

"But they will need help," Kayley says. "It will take the rescue teams, even in the capital, a long time to organize that size of a response. We could go once the fighting stops."

"I could help to coordinate a triage station," Doc Elizabeth suggests. "We wouldn't need to be anywhere near the fighting."

"You are forgetting something," Nayla says. "Other than your parents, no one else knows that Rance and Kayley are alive. If someone spots them, or worse, catches them on camera, they will become targets again."

Everyone goes silent. I wasn't even considering that aspect of my murder. What happens when the conspiracy thinks they've gotten rid of us for good, then finds out they haven't?

"They'd come after us with everything," I say.

We have an advantage being dead, or at least the conspiracy thinking we are. We could plan and execute our strategy without fear of a counterattack—while still being careful, of course. All it would take is one of them recognizing us, and that would be the end of that.

"But I'm going home, anyway," Kayley says. "I could at least help in the hospital."

"You should rethink that," Afton says. "At least for now."

"But my parents are waiting for me!" Kayley says, sounding like she's reverted into a fourteen-year-old. The truth of it is not far off. Kayley's memories end in high school. "I really want to see them."

"Not a good idea. And that goes for you too, buddy." Afton points a finger at me. "Anonymous is the best name for you until you recover completely. And don't give me some nonsense that you feel fine. You're not, and you know it."

"When did that ever matter?" I shoot back. "We've gone on missions exhausted and hurt, and we still went through with them. How is this different?"

"The difference is that you're supposed to be dead, and if the person who wanted you that way finds out you're not, they're going to come after you, Rance, and make sure that there's no possibility of you getting up again." Afton rests her arms on her legs and leans towards me. "We lost you once. Isn't that already one time too many?"

I can feel Kayley watching me. She's expecting me to back her up, and the last thing I want right now is to let her down. That would be like walking away from any chance I have to win her back. Or, from her perspective, win her for the first time.

Afton keeps making sense, and that's hard to argue against. I hate the thought that people will die because we didn't put ourselves on the line to help them. But this is out of our hands.

"Alright," I say, dropping onto a stool. "I'll stay here like a good boy. But we've got to come up with a plan. All this sitting around will make me want to walk out an air lock one of these days."

"There's plenty of time to talk," Nayla says. "You are making a wise choice to allow it to happen."

"I guess I will, too," Kayley says, her eyes going hard. "For now."

Chapter Thirty-Two

I LET OUT A gigantic sigh once I know I'm out of earshot of everyone in the auditorium. The air pressure in that room just became overbearing to me. Of course, it's my fault for dreaming up situations that don't exist in reality. At least not yet, or maybe never, and that is another nightmare I've got to contend with.

My next breath is deep. I attempt to catch all the air that just left my lungs so I can get this weight off my chest. It's not working, but once I get back to my room, I can let it all out. And I'll need to. Kayley may not be leaving yet, but she will, as soon as Afton and Nayla will let her.

Which won't be long from now.

"Rancid," Original Teddy calls as he approaches me with a bit of speed. I stop in my tracks and wait for his arrival, which doesn't take long. "Menace approaching."

Teddy talk has little tonal inflection in it. They use other methods to express the details, which I don't know about, so I've got to figure out what he means on my own. Good thing I have experience.

"Are we being targeted?" I ask.

"That is accurate."

So much for my self-care. It feels like my blood pressure just jumped up to a dangerous level.

"What kind of menace, Teddy?"

An alarm sounds throughout the corridor. I'm reminded of the last time this happened. An Imperial cruiser was chasing us. I doubt that's the case this time.

The ship shudders and rocks before he can answer. I'm thrown into the corridor wall, wincing as my shoulder crunches against the hard surface. Teddy pulls me up from the floor and tugs me back into the auditorium.

The gang there are already taking action and securing themselves far away from walls and moving parts. Kayley may not remember the big hole that we had to seal, but Afton and Grady do. They wave us over when they spot Original Teddy and me flying in.

"What happened?" Afton shouts. "The engine didn't go again, did it?"

"That is not accurate," Original Teddy replies. "Menace has appeared."

It's clear now. We're being attacked. By whom, we don't know, but that doesn't matter all that much. Someone wants to blow this ship to bits—with us on it. I hope Captain Teddy has it under control.

"Let's blink out of here," I say. Maybe Original Teddy will pass that on to the captain. He's already thought of it, I'm sure, but a reminder doesn't hurt.

Another jolt of the ship sends us into the air. We float for a second before we slam back into the deck with a hard thump. It's as painful to my body as it sounds to my ears.

"That sucked," Original Teddy says.

"Sparkle drive!" I say. "Why haven't we used it?"

"Not available."

"What?" Grady yells. "I just helped you guys get it back online!"

This is bad. We've got no way to shoot back, and our best means of defense is to run. We might escape the attacking ship, but missiles and beam weapons are still faster. If one of those hits us, we're in trouble.

Same as it's always been.

"Get over here!" Afton shouts, waving Original Teddy and me over. There's protection in numbers, I suppose, though I don't get the chance to decide. Original Teddy coils a tentacle around my waist and flings me towards the others. I bounce once, then land with Afton's help as Teddy releases me into the group, dropping from his handholds on the ceiling.

The ship tilts hard to one side, and all of us slide towards the wall—along with a mass of stools and other objects. I'm reminded of what happens when you multiply mass and acceleration. It's not a pretty sight.

I find Kayley and cover her with my body, protecting her from what's going to be a painful collision—and it is. A stool pounds into my shoulder with a sickening crack. I cry out but hold still. I don't care if all the stools hit me. Nothing is going to hit her.

"You okay?" Kayley asks once the ship levels out. We're as close to the wall as we can be without going through it. There are still vibrations running through the ship. I hope that's just because we're still maneuvering and not because we've got a big hole in the hull.

"Yeah," I say.

"I'm glad." Kayley pushes her hands against my chest. "Can you get off me now?"

I feel heat come to my face as I comply. I took our past closeness for granted. Kayley's not comfortable with that level of intimacy anymore, and I just got a hard reminder of that.

"Come here, Rance, let me look at your shoulder," Doc Elizabeth says, coming to my rescue in more ways than one.

"Not recommended," Original Teddy says, grabbing debris off us as fast as he can. "Prepare for secure."

"Secure?" Grady says. "Why does that sound familiar?"

"Wait!" I shout. "That means we're about to push past light-speed!"

"Is that bad?" Nayla asks.

"Only if you're Grady," Afton responds, pulling her closer. "Keep your eyes shut until Teddy says it's okay."

"Hold on," Grady shouts. "We're not ready for this!"

"We've got no time to wait, dude!" I reply. "We've got to evade attack!"

"No, I mean, we've got to hold on to something!"

The Teddy ship may not have defenses, but it has one thing—speed, and lots of it. It's still faster than any Imperial ship, even with the improvements the Teddys shared with our engineers. The one small caveat in all that is, the faster the ship goes past the speed of light, the stranger things become. We've all experienced it before, save for Nayla, so we know what to do. But it doesn't solve our mass and acceleration issue. That annoying calculation is going to be the death of me.

"The back wall!" Kayley says. "Move against the back wall!"

Kayley's memory may end in high school, but at least she remembers her physics lessons well. We push ourselves up and find any method of motion to get there in haste.

"Scratch that," Original Teddy says.

"What? Why?" I look at my fuzzy friend with a wrinkle on my forehead.

"Engine is unavailable."

"But you just said the sparkle drive was unavailable! Now the FTL engine is busted, too?"

"That is accurate."

There's a thunderous bang aft of us, and the ship bucks, throwing us up into the air. We come down with minor damage but a lot more anxiety.

"Goddesses, now what?" Afton says.

Now what, indeed. If we can't outrun them and can't sparkle out to safety, we'll need another way to get this menace off our tail. But how?

"Okay, team," I say, rousing my inner Kayley power. She might not be able to lead us right now, but someone's got to if we want to get out of this without any more damage done to our bodies. "What assets does this ship have?"

Everyone stares at each other in silence. I expected as much. The two things we could have counted on aren't working, and I'm even wondering if there are any others.

"There are Teddys," Nayla says. "The ship has many of them."

"Yeah, that plan won't work in space," Grady replies, "not even if we had a thousand space suits."

There's another rumble, and an alarm goes off farther down the ship. It's my reminder that we've got little time, if we have any at all.

"Could we call another ship for help?" Kayley asks. It's not a bad idea, but who would come to our rescue? We can't trust any Imperial ships. They might be the ones chasing us.

"Any other Teddy ships available?" I ask Original Teddy.

"That is not accurate."

So we're on our own there. But Kayley's suggestion has lit a small ember in my brain, and I try to blow some mental breath on it to turn it into a raging idea. It's a slow smolder, but when it catches, it burns so fast I almost miss my plan.

"Teddy, can you ask the captain where the closest Imperial cruiser is?" I ask.

"Oh, dude," Grady says. "This is a bad idea."

"You haven't heard it yet. How can you know if it's bad?"

"I know you. That's how."

An alarm blares just outside the auditorium, and a pair of Teddys rocket by. I could be wrong, but it feels like our ship is slowing. If we're running out of thrust, then we're going to become an even easier target.

"Imperial cruiser is local," Original Teddy says. "Captain is requesting suggestions."

"Just tell us," Afton says. "It can't be worse than any other idea."

"Well, we can disguise ourselves, right? What if we got close enough to one of them and then turned into dust? They might think we sparkled out and then—"

Kayley yelps when the ship rocks hard from left to right. She smashes into Nayla, and they knock heads. Doc Elizabeth reaches out and pulls Kayley next to her as Kayley puts a hand to her head and winces.

"—and that Imperial cruiser might consider our pursuer a threat, right?" I ask.

If it wasn't for the screaming alarms and horrendous grinding sound happening above our heads, I'd be met with stares and silence.

"So you want—" Grady starts.

"Imperial is targeted," Original Teddy says, and Grady startles, looking over at him.

"So we won't vote on that one, then," Afton states and shrugs. "Fine by me. Let's hope it works."

I do too. We're not driving this ship, so all we can do now is sit and wait and pray as much as possible that it does.

Afton and Nayla hug each other and attempt to be brave. Doc Elizabeth holds on to Kayley and looks after the cut on her head. I watch the four of them with a small amount of envy. If things were normal, Kayley would have her arms around me, and we'd be comforting each other. If things were normal, we might not even be in this mess. Things are about as far from normal as they could be.

"What?" I ask Grady when I notice him looking at me. He shrugs and opens up his arms to me. I shrug back and slide over to embrace him. It's good I can always rely on my bud.

"Teddy, give us updates, please," Doc Elizabeth says.

"Approaching Imperial. Menace closing." Original Teddy decides he wants in on the human cuddle and drops next to us to wrap a tentacle around Grady and me.

"Can we make it?" I ask.

"Unknown. Ship is in pain."

I think he means we've taken a lot of damage. We'd better not be on a living ship, if there was such a thing. I'm not feeling up to contemplating that any more than I just did, however. Not while we're this close to getting blown away.

The next hit makes the ship twist, and we're thrown into the ceiling, only to crash on the floor. I somehow hang on to Grady, but the hit I took on my shoulder shoots a shock down my back.

"Are we there yet?" Afton says with a nervous laugh.

The ship becomes unstable, the floor trembling violently. I latch myself on to anything close by to stay upright. It happens to be Afton's arm. Nayla eyes me with a *get your own partner* look, and I give her an apologetic smile.

"Teddy, what's going on?"

"Engine is unhappy."

"That makes two of us!" Grady shouts.

"Standby."

"What else can we do?" Nayla asks.

The lack of information is killing us, me doubly so. With my Teddynet connection, I'd have a good idea about what was happening. Now I'm as confused as everyone else, save Original Teddy, and he's not all that great at keeping up the verbal communication.

How close are we to survival? Or death? If my life ends this time, there won't be a tub to bring me back.

If we manage to make it, I'm going to get rid of these conspirators for good. Whatever plan I need to come up with, whatever risks I have to take, I'll do it.

The ship shudders once, then slows. My body lifts from the ground, and Grady and I float arm in arm like a pair of ballet dancers. Our gravity may be gone, but we're still here. I think that's likely a good thing.

"Does this mean we're safe?" I ask.

"That is accurate," Original Teddy says, pulling Doc Elizabeth and Kayley to handholds along the wall.

There are sighs all around, and Grady drops his head on my shoulder. The Goddesses have seen fit to let us live one more day. I, for one, will not let that chance go to waste.

"This really is your normal life?" Nayla asks, more statement than question.

"Yeah," Afton answers. "Fun, isn't it?"

Chapter Thirty-Three

I GLANCE AROUND AT the landscape of Twyllodrus National Park, where Original Teddy and I have landed. It's as far from civilization as we can get on the primary continent of Angelcanis. No one will find us out here. No one will be looking.

After the attack, we limped back to Angelcanis orbit to repair the ship. That's when I sneaked—with Original Teddy's help—into the communications room and dialed up Colonel Cortell. I wasn't going to let us become a sitting target. Plus, I had an idea I wanted to discuss with him, something that would guarantee we'd never be targeted ever again.

"Teddy, are you sure this is where he said he'd meet us?" I ask. The terrain around here is flat. We should be able to see anyone coming towards us for a long distance. Yet all I can spot are a few butterflies and a pair of high-flying birds.

"That is accurate."

"Yeah, somehow I'm not getting that vibe."

"Sorry to keep you waiting!" Colonel Cortell says, coming from behind us. We turn to see him walking down from a small hill. I wonder why I didn't consider a hill as not-flat land. There's quite a few of them around. "My lieutenant needed to find a spot to touch down on where we wouldn't be seen."

"It's okay, we just got here," I say, even though it's not true. We'd been waiting an hour in this oven. He could have at least picked a shadier spot.

The colonel comes to a stop just before us with a heavy breath. He puts his hands on his hips and looks me over.

"Elizabeth told me about what happened to you and Kayley." He shakes his head. "I still can't believe you're standing here right in front of me. How do you feel?"

"Fine, I guess."

"I'm sorry about you and Kayley, by the way."

I nod my thanks to him, not interested in discussing it more. Besides, I didn't come here to have a pity party. I've had enough of that for the last ten days. I'm ready to get back at these bastards for doing what they did to us. And they will pay.

"So, what required us to meet down here, in the middle of nowhere and in person?" Colonel Cortell asks. "Shouldn't you be resting?"

"I'm done resting."

"Well." The colonel folds his arms and chuckles. "*You* may say that, but what does Elizabeth say? Did she give you a clean bill of health?"

"Yeah, sure she did."

"That is not accurate," Original Teddy says. I throw him a glare, but it's too late. The truth is out, and I may have just lost the opportunity to get things moving again. I'm going to tie his tentacles up in a bow, if that's the case.

Colonel Cortell smiles with the look of a commanding officer who knows when a subordinate is attempting to get one over on him. He may go a little easier on me because I'm a civilian, but I expect the outcome is going to be the same.

Now onto the lecture...

"Listen, Rance," the colonel begins, "I've got a lot of respect for all that you've done for my team. All of you have sacrificed your normal lives to bring peace to an Empire you're not even a citizen of. You've put yourselves at risk time and time again in the name of justice, with little benefit to yourselves. I can think of no more noble a group of individuals that have ever achieved what you have in such a short time."

And here comes the point where he tells me everything I'm doing wrong.

"As much as I'd like to see all these criminals get what's coming to them, I also think this is not the time for you to be pushing hard. Goddesses, Rance. They assassinated you!"

Colonel Cortell takes a moment to gather himself before he speaks again, this time using a less agitated tone.

"And I will be forever thankful that the technology existed to bring you and Kayley back. But there's got to be more than just physical wounds that need healing, not just for the two of you, but for the entire team. My recommendation to you is to lie low. Let us do what we can with the intel we've already gathered. Maybe we can slow them down for a while and give you time to recover."

I try to hide my anger, but I doubt I'm doing a good job of it. The colonel is too much of a professional soldier to react to whatever ugly thing is happening on my face. Still, he's laid his opinion down fairly thick. I won't be able to get his cooperation easily.

"I don't want to give them one nanosecond without feeling pressure from us. I want to see all their ugly mugs locked up with no chance of parole. Ever," I say.

"And how do you expect to do that without your team leader?" the colonel asks with a knowing smugness.

Well, that was an unexpected question.

"Yeah, I know about Kayley's memory loss. Believe me, I've got a lot of sympathy for you two. Especially her. You're a fighter, Rance. I've no doubt you'll bounce back when you're able. But Kayley?" Colonel Cortell shakes his head. "I don't even know how to *begin to* consider dealing with three years of missing time."

"But don't you see?" I shoot back. "That's why we have to do this now! For her! For Kayley!"

"You haven't answered my question."

I sigh and look down. I don't understand why he's making this so hard on me. We're on the same side, and we want to achieve all the same things. My mother gives me less of a lecture. Most of the time.

Goddesses. Mom. Yet another problem I've got to handle.

I take a slow, deep inhale to calm myself and gather my conviction again. If the only issue holding him back is who will be team leader, then that's an easy problem to solve.

"I'll be the leader," I say with a tight jaw.

"Rance, if you were on my team, I wouldn't put you out in the field until the med corps checked you out properly. Even then, I might wait a while."

"Why don't you listen to my plan first before deciding not to back me?"

Colonel Cortell tilts his head, evaluating my challenge. He'll know I'm not bluffing. I will lead the team if it comes down to it. The question in his head will be what happens if he lets me share my idea. Of course, I did bluff a little. I don't have a plan yet. Not a full one, anyway. I was hoping to discuss it with him so we could figure it out together.

"Okay. Let's hear what you've got." He wags a finger at me. "No promises, however. I'm not changing my assessment of you."

Well, here goes just about nothing. I might have to improvise a little. Or maybe a lot.

"So they're not afraid to come out of hiding, now they think we're out of operation, right? We can use that to our advantage. Their leaders will be bolder and may just allow us a chance to catch them out in the open."

Colonel Cortell nods as he listens. So far, so good. Keep going, Rance.

"We can create an opportunity they can't say no to. Like a high-value target. A person...or"—I snap my fingers as it pops into my head—"a way for them to get their forces onto Albion without losing huge numbers."

"You just made that up right now, didn't you?" the colonel asks.

"No, I didn't!"

"Fine. Then how do you propose to coordinate a strike that gets all their leaders at once? That's the only way we stop another retaliation from happening."

Great. Now I'll have to come up with an actual plan. I surprised myself with what I came up with so far. It sounded good to me, anyway. Perhaps there are a few major details that need to be worked out, but other than that, it could be a solid plan.

If Kayley were here, she'd have all of this down in an instant. There'd be no question about putting her plan into action. It would be who, what, and where, not how or why.

"So?" Colonel Cortell is staring now. If I don't give him an answer, I'm going back to the ship with no way to get my plan—whatever it ends up being—put into action. The colonel is right about one thing. Without him, all I have is me.

"Maybe..."

"*Maybe* isn't very convincing, Rance. Do you have a plan or not?"

"I do, but maybe it's two plans, not one. That's what I was about to say."

Phew, good save. I'll give myself one million points later.

"What do you mean, two?"

"Two parts of one plan might be a better way to say it. What we do is snatch up the top, top boss, then spoof the rest to make it seem like they're requesting an all-hands meeting to discuss the final assault on Albion. Then, when they show up, we get them all in one go. Problem solved!"

Colonel Cortell is back in assessing mode again as he rubs his chin. I'm hopeful that he buys my random idea or at least is interested in it enough that we can talk about it more.

"So how do we find and get this head conspirator?"

I swallow. He's always on about the details, though I guess he wouldn't be a colonel if he wasn't concerned about them. He may have a better idea on how to get that information, since he's got all the data and whatever other stuff he got from his prisoner. In fact, we may even have the name of their supreme leader because it could be on that communications list.

Wait. That list has another name on it that could be useful!

"Simple," I say with a smile. "We ask my dad."

The colonel presses his lips together while my fists tighten. I may have just found the ultimate key to this plan...or I may have just said the stupidest thing I've ever said—no. This wouldn't be the stupidest. There was that one time when I told Kayley—

I don't want to remember that. It's too embarrassing.

"Alright, Rance," he says, not sounding fully convinced. "Let me go back to my team and hammer out a bit more of the logistics of this, but this could be possible."

"Thank you...Harry," I reply. "Really. It means a lot to me you're willing to back me up."

"Not yet." He points at me. "Not until I turn your idea into reality. And in the meantime, you should really get back to the ship and stop disobeying doctor's orders. Does Elizabeth even know you're down here talking to me?"

"No," I mumble.

The colonel chuckles. "Yeah, I figured as much."

I'm not bothered by being caught. I've achieved my goal, and so whatever trouble I get in will be worth it.

Now all I have to do is convince the others.

Chapter Thirty-Four

Before I enter the canteen, I take a few deep breaths to calm myself, and I remember that this is just a room. One with a specific purpose. One that has been the scene of many terrible things, and still is, if I consider how and what Teddys eat. Even so, it is just a room.

Then why am I so nervous? Is it because my hopes and dreams all depend upon my buds agreeing to my plan? I know they will. I just have to present it to them properly.

Right?

"Hey, guys," I say as Original Teddy and I stroll in. Before we did, I begged him not to contradict me, and he promised he wouldn't, though I'm not sure I'm clear on if Teddys understand the meaning of a promise or not. They don't lie to each other—Teddynet makes that impossible—but humans have been rubbing off on them, and I think they understand the value of a little mistruth now and then.

"Hey, where have you been?" Afton asks. "We've been looking for you."

"Oh?"

"Yeah," Grady adds. "We were getting bored, so we were thinking about going for a hike in Twyllodrus National Park."

"What?" I shout. Everyone jumps. Doc Elizabeth gasps, and Afton has to throw her arms around Nayla to stop her from falling out of her lap. Only Kayley has a minor reaction to my outburst.

"Dude, are you okay?" Grady asks.

"Sorry. I just don't think we should go down planet. Even if it's in the middle of nowhere. We can't take any chances."

Of course, I was just there, and if they found out, they'd express their disappointment in me with some level of physical abuse. I've only gotten to feel normal again in the last few days. No need to make myself sore.

"Yeah, well, it was just an idea. Afton suggested the Teddy course that you've been doing, but most of us aren't so...you know..." Grady shrugs. "We hate exercise."

"There are many ways to maintain one's health beyond physical activity," Nayla says to Afton's dismay. I know they practice that yogurt thing together. Or is it yoga? Kayley used to join in, before she forgot how.

"Rance, you look worried about something," Doc Elizabeth says. She's always observant of her patients. I've been one most often, so she knows me well. "What's going on?"

"No, not worried," I say, waving my hands. It's not true, but that's the path I'm taking. "Actually, more excited than anything."

"What about?" Kayley asks.

"Well, I've put a plan together. With Colonel Cortell's help, we might just be able to capture the entire leadership of the conspiracy...starting with the big boss!"

My buds share a look of confusion with each other before turning back to me with various states of raised eyebrows, all except for Afton, who's giving me an icy stare.

"I told you we're out of that, Rance," Afton says. "We're caring for ourselves now."

"Who put you in charge?" I counter.

"I did."

"That's not how it works!"

"Deal with it."

"But this is our chance!" I reply, my hands flying around for emphasis. "Just let me explain my plan to you, and you'll see how good it is!"

Afton rolls her eyes, but Nayla chides her for dismissing me. In reflex, I look to Kayley for support, but she only smiles. It's something, just not what I was hoping for.

"Well?" Afton turns to Grady. "What do you think?"

Grady shrugs. "I could use some entertainment. Have at it, dude."

I give him a *thanks for the no support* glare before beginning my explanation. I stumble through a few details but then get back on track, putting as much enthusiasm into it as I can. There are a few spots where I embellish a little, but that doesn't matter. We can always make changes. The point of this is to get them to agree, and then we can mold this plan into a real winner.

To their credit, everyone listens attentively and waits until I'm done before even making any sign of a response. I'm hopeful. I gave it my best effort, and I think my plan is solid. There should be no reason why they'd turn me down.

Then they dash my hopes completely.

"No," Afton says. "Just no."

"I agree with Afton," Doc Elizabeth says. "I can't recommend you put yourself at risk. We still don't know how the therapy is going to affect you long-term, so I'd prefer to keep you nearby, Rance, in case something happens."

"This sounds really dangerous," Kayley says. "I'm not ready for anything like that. I don't know if I'll ever be."

I just stand there, frozen. Some doubt would be normal, but this is outright refusal. There's nothing I can use for a counterargument. It's just done, and I can't believe it. This can't be the way we go out.

Are we really stuck on this ship for who knows how long, waiting for the conspiracy to either take over or be arrested?

I look to Grady for support, but he only shrugs. So much for his help. Now all I've got is Original Teddy, and I'm not sure he's going to back me up, either. He turns to me, and I give him a hopeful look. Then he glances at the others, observing them for a moment before turning back to me.

Original Teddy curls his tentacles into a ball. It reminds me of human fists, as if he's trying to give me strength. Then he says, "Fighting!"

I'll take it. I've got nothing else.

But when I look at my buds, I sink. Any of Original Teddy's energy that he may have hoped to give me just dissipates, and I'm lower than before.

Still, I can't give up. No matter how bad I feel, I've got to make this happen.

"Guys," I say, stepping up to them, "this may sound silly, but we could be the last line of defense. We've already proven that we're more effective than the Emperor's own troops! If we don't do this, civil war could break out. Millions could die!"

"Hey, hey, hey." Afton holds up a hand. "Don't try to guilt-trip us. We've got every right to be..."

Afton looks up at Nayla, a question in her eyes.

"The huntress of our own destiny," Nayla says, smiling down at Afton.

"Yeah, that." Afton turns back to me. "So I'm going to do whatever I want. Got it?"

"You've always done whatever you wanted," Grady mutters. But before Afton can reply, Nayla puts a hand on her shoulder and shakes her head.

I don't like where this is going, and for this argument to happen here in the canteen is like reliving a nightmare that I've had many times over, except this time, we're not talking about how we can make a plan work. This is about whether anyone even wants to continue this fight.

So much has happened in the last few months that it's hard to keep track of it all. Doc Elizabeth says my memory hasn't been affected, but sometimes I wonder if I'm missing some important piece of time that would explain why Afton and Parrish are choosing the way they have. Parrish is already gone. There's no bringing him back. I can't lose Afton, too.

"Guys, this isn't the time to be arguing among ourselves," I say. "We've got a lot of questions to solve and not that much time to do it in. I understand you're worried. Just consider what happens if we don't do this!"

"What happens is we get to live," Afton says. "And so do you."

"Yeah, but what kind of place would we live in?" Grady counters. "Is it really better to be alive if you're living on your knees?"

"A fair point," Nayla says. "Yet one thing others will never control is your inner peace. It could be the best of times or the worst. How that affects your happiness is up to you."

"Even if someone has a gun to your head?"

"Guys, come on," I say, waving my hands to get them to focus again. "We don't need to be so philosophical about this. Of course we don't have to let bad things affect us. That's not the point. Terrible things are going to happen to others who can't do that! Those who can't protect themselves. That's why we started doing this in the first place, isn't it? We have to fight and protect those people!"

"We're not superheroes," Afton shoots back. "We can't snap our fingers and change everything. Or even half of everything. Get it in your head, Rance, you're just a normal dude. Stop trying to save the galaxy."

I don't think I'm going to convince her, which means Nayla's also out. She might be our spiritual adviser or something—not sure how valuable that is. I need someone who can run and fight faster and better than I can. That bar isn't too hard to achieve, but Nayla won't hit it, even if she wanted to.

"Dude," I say to Grady, "you're with me, right?"

"Sure." Grady swallows, and my muscles tighten. He must have noticed, because he races to add, "I mean, I'm scared, dude. I don't want to get hurt, or lose my memory, or anything like that."

"You won't, dude. I promise."

Afton snorts, and I throw a glare at her. Nayla slaps her arm with a gentle hand. She wants to be the peacekeeper and support Afton at the same time. It's considerate, but what she should do is try to convince her to help me.

My eyes go to Kayley, who's been pretending to pick at the celery and cabbage on the table. I know she's been listening. What I'd really like to know is what she thinks about all this. What I'm afraid of is Afton's influence on her thoughts. Kayley's vulnerable right now and might choose to hide away rather than face trouble. But I know her. Kayley will step up when faced with a challenge, dangerous or not. She's done it before, and she'll do it again.

"What about you, Kayley?"

"Hey, keep her out of this," Afton says, more pleading than threatening.

"Yes," Doc Elizabeth echoes. "This discussion is not for her."

"It's okay," Kayley says, looking up. "I know Rance only wants to do the right thing. And I can speak for myself."

Now there's my KayKay. And I like how she's starting off, too. If she gets behind the idea, that might pull Afton back to the right side of things.

"So what do you think?" I ask with a hopeful smile.

Kayley's lips remain flat as she looks at me. "I think you need to step away from this, Rance. You may have changed from my memories of you, but the Rance I know wasn't someone who could handle a plan on this scale. Maybe no one can. So I think you should forget about all of this. Better for you to be safe."

Well, at least she's consistent with dashing my hopes just like everyone else has, save Grady. But even he's on the fence.

I may have to face going this alone, and I really hate that idea.

Chapter Thirty-Five

"There's something else that I wanted to tell you," Kayley says, looking at me and only me.

"Just me?" It's my turn to swallow. What would she want to say to me directly? Certainly not anything I might hope she'd say about us becoming a couple again, but I can wish.

"No, this is for everyone."

The sound of shifting bodies and repositioning seats fills the air for the next fifteen seconds before everyone has turned to face her. Even Original Teddy has taken position up on a stool so he can see Kayley better. I remain standing. There's no way I could sit at a moment like this.

Kayley's eyes widen a little. Maybe she didn't expect all the attention. My Kayley wouldn't have so much as flinched. Then again, the scarlet-headed woman I see before me isn't exactly my Kayley. I've got to keep reminding myself of that.

"I've been thinking," Kayley begins, "and it's been hard, even with all your help, to understand what is going on. But I have decided one thing, for certain."

"What's that?" I say, jumping in, overeager to know what that one thing is.

"I'm going home. Today."

There's a host of *absolutely nots* and *you can'ts* that come from everyone, save for me. Kayley may not know the person I've become, but I know her. From our senior year in high school until three months ago, I've spent nearly every moment watching her, falling ever deeper in love with the person I knew I would spend the rest of my life with. Kayley has almost always taken time to come to a tough decision, but once she did, there was no changing her mind. I can tell that's where she is now, and try as my buds might, they are like flies against a gale-force wind.

"At least tell us why," Doc Elizabeth pleads. She is more distressed than I've ever seen her, and she never gets that way.

"You've told me I'd be safer on this ship, but that attack on us yesterday proves to me you don't know any better than I do where safe is. At least at home, I'd be around my family. And I don't plan to leave my house. Not for a long time. Not until I can understand what I've lost."

Kayley looks up at me then. I step back, unsure of what she wants and terrified that she might not want anything from me.

"I was hoping to convince you to come with me. I need your help. If we were together, then you were the one who knows me best. You'd know what memories I'm missing, and I want those memories back. I really want them back, Rance. I feel incomplete without them."

"KayKay," I whisper, my lips refusing to say anything more. What do I even say to that? Yes, with no conditions or stipulations? Just yes, I will do anything you want me to, until you are whole again?

My heart aches. If I could want only that. If all the universe wanted from me was that, I'd agree to do it in a microsecond, as best as I could and for as long as I was able. I should want nothing more. But that is far from reality.

"I suppose that's just as well," Nayla says. "We were planning to go home, too."

Grady turns his head towards them. "To Angelcanis? Would you make sure the house is clean, then?"

"Not there," Afton says. "We want to patch things up with Nayla's mom and, if that works, with mine."

I should have known it would come to this. They didn't want to be a part of the plan, not because they were worried about getting killed. They didn't want to because they had already decided that it wasn't what they wanted to do. I have to let them go, because I can't argue this on two fronts. It's not my preference, but I have little choice.

"What about your mom, Rance?" Afton asks. "Don't you want to see her?"

If she's still alive, that is. Afton deftly leaves that condition out of her words. I suppose I should be glad about that. I don't want to hear anyone say I will never talk to my mother again. I don't even want to consider that option.

"Of course I do, but she's not there. There's no one there. That's not my home anymore. I don't have one other than this."

"You could stay with us," Kayley says with hope in her voice. I wonder if she remembers her house is as much of a wreck as mine, though her parents would have rebuilt already. My mom would have too, if she were home. But no call or text has ever gotten through to her. I just have to hope she is somewhere safe. I can't accept any other possibility.

It's not Kayley, or even Afton, who is forcing me to choose between comfort and danger. I am the only one stressing myself out like this. But walking away is not an option. I've got to put my own personal needs and desires aside for the good of everyone. If I don't, how do I face my mom, or Parrish's mom, or Kayley's parents? How do I explain to them we had the chance to stop all these terrible things from happening, but we were selfish instead? Would they understand? Or pretend to?

No. I must fight to save the Empire. But all I can think about is going home with Kayley. There's no vision of me winning the battle against the conspiracy, but there's a ton of images in my mind of Kayley and me spending time together.

Maybe there is a way.

"I really want to help you, Kayley. I want to help you more than any-thing," I say.

"Then come with me!"

"No." I shake my head. "As much as you think it is, your parents' house is not the place for you. Not because it's not safe. It's because your life has been here. Not there. We've been here nearly a year. Other places, too, but most of it away from home. This has been your home, Kayley. This is the place where you'll be safest and the place where you will find your memories again."

If that's even possible. Doc Elizabeth has only remembered a few things about her past, and she's had much longer to recover. Of course, I don't want to mention that to Kayley. I want her to have hope, because I want to have hope, too.

"Rance is correct," Doc Elizabeth says as she nods in agreement. "I have nothing against the doctors on your planet, but they've never encountered what you are going through. Only I have. Don't misunderstand. I believe that spending time with your family will be good for you. That time is not now, however."

I stand up tall and smile. Doc Elizabeth clears her throat.

"But if you choose to spend your time here, we will fill it with healing, not fighting. I can at least promise you that."

"What if fighting *is* the thing that brings her memory back?" I ask.

Several glares come my way in answer to my question. Their involvement may be up for discussion, but talking about Kayley doing the same is right out. I can agree, with several layers of reluctance attached. None of us really has a clue what might bring her memories back. Not Doc Elizabeth, not the Teddys. No one. Everything is just a gamble, and a bad one at that.

"Thank you, Rance," Kayley says. "Thank you for wanting to help me. I know you care about me, but this ship is not where I should be. I have no doubts about that. And you should leave, too. I see the stress it's putting on you to be here. Please reconsider your choice to stay here."

My blood must be draining from my body right now. I can barely feel my fingers and toes. Kayley is going home. That is as certain as the stars in the night sky. I cannot change her mind. I'm not sure I even want to.

I glance at Afton and Nayla. Wrapped in each other's arms with such a level of ease between them, they give off the appearance of a couple who've been together for years. I am both envious and happy. All I want is to have what they have. I did, once.

There would be a great deal of happiness, spending time with Kayley, even if it was only as friends. It wouldn't matter. We'd be together, and all of this political nonsense would disappear from our minds.

At least for a short while. It would find us eventually, and we would never escape it.

That is what I am fighting for. And if I can protect Kayley by keeping all of it away from her, then I'm willing to sacrifice my happiness for her security. I just have to learn to accept that I will never feel joy the way I did before.

"I can't go with you, Kayley. Up here, I know I can keep you safe. Even when you're down there," I say.

Kayley looks at me for a long time before nodding. Then she approaches me. I freeze, unsure of what she might do. Somewhere in the back of my mind, there's a small crumb of hope that she will do or say something that changes everything we've been talking about.

Of course, that's only a dream.

She gives me a hug and kisses my cheek, then departs. As ecstatic as I am to receive it, I know it's different. It even feels different. Gone is the familiar comfort of two people who have fallen in love. Gone is that electric intensity I used to feel when she was near. Kayley's hug might as well have been from a stranger.

I feel my heart crumble as she walks out of the canteen. I may never see her again, and I don't know if I'll be able to handle the reality of that for long. All that means is I need to win this fight against the conspiracy as quickly as possible. I'm not sure we can win at all.

We? It'll just be me and Grady, if Grady is still willing after all of this.

"Ransom Quigley He'," Nayla says as she slides off Afton's lap and approaches me. "Remember what has been foretold. Remember your reading. In it is your truth, and in it you will find the answers you need."

She hugs me, then signals to Afton to follow her out. Before Afton does, she comes over to me, too, and wraps an arm around my shoulders. Then she turns to Grady and motions for him to join us, putting her arm around him, too.

"I love the hell out of you guys. You know that, right?" Afton says, the tone of her voice strong but on the edge of breaking. "I really wish you'd reconsider this and just go home. The universe won't end if you guys just did that."

"Maybe not," I reply, "but if we can give you and Nayla some comfort by keeping them off your backs, then no matter what happens to us—"

"Don't say that," Afton growls. "You're coming home. Maybe not today, but one day. We're going to see each other again."

I feel Grady wrap his arms around Afton. She pulls him in and kisses the top of his head. Then she turns to look me in the eye.

"For Kayley," Afton says. "No matter what else you do, you stay alive for her. Got it?"

"Yeah, I got it."

Our eyes connect in silence for a long moment, then without another word, Afton slips away, following Nayla. I could be mistaken, but just before she walked away, I thought I saw her eyes tearing up. Mine certainly are.

"Well, boys," Doc Elizabeth says with a sigh. "I guess it's just the three of us again, hmm? I suppose I'll need to go prep my surgical tools. Try not to make any foolish plans too quickly."

She ruffles Grady's hair, and then she is gone. Now there's a hole in my chest where my heart should be. It feels larger than the galaxy is wide. Whether it'll be filled again is now up to me, and possibly Grady.

"You still want to do this, dude?" I ask.

"Rance," Grady says in a soft voice. I turn to him, curious why he's using my actual name. "I get why you want to do this. That's why I'm with you. You don't even have to ask."

I give Grady a wistful smile and gently clap my hand on his shoulder. I wish he didn't have to choose this. I wish none of us did. But I also know if we didn't, we'd have very little to hope for. And I refuse to let any of us suffer like that.

Win or die, I'm doing this.

Chapter Thirty-Six

I HADN'T EXPECTED TO get a message from Kayley, at least not one so quickly. She had only been gone for two days. I was bursting with excitement. Did she remember something about us? Did she realize she made a terrible decision and want to come back?

Nothing like that.

It was a simple message.

KAYLEY: Parrish's mom. Please come.

There was only about five seconds between my reading of the message and my telling Original Teddy to get the shuttle up and running before we were heading down to the surface.

I rack my brain, trying to recall what Parrish had told me. I remember—his mother is terminal. In a few months, she could be gone. I don't want to believe it's already happened, but Kayley's message has left me with a lot to wonder about.

As fast as the Teddy shuttle is, it still takes twenty minutes to get through the atmosphere and then find a drop-off point that was close to the hospital. I can feel my stomach getting tighter and tighter as I pace across the shuttle's deck until Original Teddy reminds me to secure myself before I become a ceiling pancake. We're going to do a few tight turns to drop onto a local street so we won't have far to run.

I burst into the hospital lobby, stopping only to ask for directions. It isn't long before I speed into the correct wing and find Kayley and Parrish standing outside a darkened room. Their surprised looks are a good sign I arrived exactly when I wanted to.

"Well, your note didn't say much," I say, looking at both of them. "What's going on?"

Parrish gets choked up before he can reply. His head drops, and he turns away. I get a sick feeling in my throat, watching him, and fear the worst.

"Is she...Is she?"

Kayley shakes her head, offering a reassuring smile. I release the air that was caught in my lungs, thankful that's not the case. Parrish has got enough pressing him down without having to deal with his mother's funeral.

"Where's Grady? Elizabeth? Did you get in touch with Afton?" Kayley asks.

"They didn't want to delay me. Teddy is going back up to get them. I asked Grady to get Afton and Nayla a message, but they're days away at best."

Rather than wait for the sparkle drive to be repaired, they just took standard transport to Canis Ludis. Even at their fastest speed, it would be a week and a half before they'd arrive there. I don't even know if those kinds of ships have carrier wave communication while traveling FTL. There may not be any way to get in touch.

Kayley nods, disappointment covering her face. Afton's sudden departure must have shocked her, too. Other than her family, Kayley has no one to turn to here. Parrish won't be available often, and Grady and I have made our choice.

A thought runs through my mind then. However ridiculous it may be, dread runs through me as it hits me. Kayley only remembers dating Parrish. What if, in their moment of mutual need, they get back together? I clench my fists and push that out of my head. I made my choice. If it happens, there's nothing I can do. That won't stop me from hating myself, however.

Enough selfishness. I'm here to support my bud. That's why I came. Well, also because Kayley asked me to. Even if she can't remember, or winds up with someone else, I will always come if she needs me. That might make me a fool, but it wouldn't be the first time. I've been an idiot most of my life. It's only been a recent thing that I've woken up.

"Can we see her?" I ask Kayley quietly.

Parrish's embrace is the answer I get. It catches me off guard, as I didn't think he was listening.

"Thank you," Parrish says. "Thank you for coming. I'm sorry...I just..."

"It's okay, dude," I reply. "I get it. That's why I'm here."

He sniffles and stands up straight with a nod. Then he motions to the door and ushers me in, keeping an arm around my shoulders. I should reciprocate, but he's taller than me, and it would be awkward, so I just do my best to connect with him any way I can.

His mother's room is dark, save for the light that radiates from a screen showing her vital data. Maybe Kayley can understand what it says, but I've no clue. All I know is that no alarms or buzzers are going off, so I suppose that's good.

Parrish's mom lies on the bed, her face at ease. It's a reflection of when I last met her. She may have been tough on her son, but she always treated me with as much love and kindness as I have ever known. My mother cherishes me, too, though she's never been slow to discipline me if I was out of line. And I got out of line often.

"What did the doctors say?" I ask in a whisper.

"They're still doing tests," Parrish replies and sighs. "Always tests. It's like they can't make a decision unless they check every possible thing there is to test on a human being. You'd think they'd know what they were doing, but they're as clueless as we are about what to do."

"They're just being thorough, Parry," Kayley says. "They're looking for clues. Something that might tip them off as to a course of action."

"What are they, detectives?" I ask.

"Kind of."

To think that doctors might not understand what to do is a strange idea. A scary one, too. My only experience has been with Doc Elizabeth, and she's young for a doctor. I suspect she's much older than her appearance may hint at. But just like Kayley, any memory that might tip her off to her actual age is gone, or at least buried deep in her mind.

A tone sounds off, coming from the terminal next to the bed. It's like a long, sustained whistle. The three of us stare at the panel. Something is blinking next to a long straight line that crosses the screen.

"What's that mean?" I ask.

"Parry..." Kayley says, her voice getting worried. "Parry...get the doctor! Get the doctor!"

"No," I say. "You guys stay. I'll go."

Before they can answer, I burst out of the room, looking for the nurse's station. Someone's got to be there. They'll know what that alarm means.

I dash down the hallway towards what looks like a desk. It's the right place, but no one is there. Maybe they're at lunch? No, that makes no sense. Someone should be here to care for the patients!

"Hello?" I shout. Maybe someone will hear me.

Or maybe not. It's a big hospital. I bet there's a nurse in one of the patients' rooms, though.

But as I search each one, I realize nobody's around. Many of the rooms have no patients, and it's obvious they haven't had anyone for a long time. This is really odd.

The front reception desk. That's where I'll go. They'll know how to get in touch with someone.

As my legs burn and my lungs catch fire, I race to the front lobby, nearly knocking over a janitor. He cries out and throws himself against the wall to avoid my extreme pace.

"What the hell are you doing?" he shouts after me. "No running!"

"It's an emergency!" I shout back, unsure of why I would even need to explain that. It's a hospital.

When I get to the front desk, there's a line of people waiting to ask questions. I can't wait for that. I head straight for the receptionist, ignoring the comments as I cut to the front.

"Hey, you can't do that," the receptionist says. "You've got to wait in line."

"Please," I say, slamming my hands down on the desk. "I need a doctor!"

The receptionist stares at me, then asks, "For yourself? Or someone else?"

"A patient! Something's wrong! Some alarm went off, and nobody came! I checked the nurse's station, but there wasn't anyone around! Please! I think she needs help now!"

"Are you sure?" he asks as he frowns. "If an alarm went off on the monitor, it would alert the medical team in the department. They'd come right away."

"Nobody came! Nobody is there!"

There's another moment of staring before the receptionist picks up a comm and taps in a number. As he talks in a low breath, all I can think of is how terrified Parrish must be at this moment. We don't even know what the alarm means, but I've got a horrible feeling it could be really, really bad.

"What room number?" the receptionist asks.

"What?"

"The room number, for the patient! They need to know where to go!"

The number evades my mind as I reach for it. The receptionist shouts at me, demanding the number again with a slam of his fist on the desk. People behind me are getting restless as well. One of them even accuses me of being a liar. I'm in a near panic.

Then it's there, at the forefront of my mind. I yell it out. The receptionist jumps, then speaks it into the comm. Before he even gives me a confirmation, I'm racing back to Parrish and his mom, praying that the medical team is already there.

Maybe this is all just a big mix-up. Maybe she's just fine. Maybe I'll get there and she'll be awake and talking with her son.

Goddesses, I wish I could believe that.

As if I'm experiencing déjà vu, I catch Parrish and Kayley outside of his mother's room. The lights are on, and the two of them stare in as blue-gowned medical staff rush in and out of the room. A nurse approaches them and presses them away from the door with a gentle hand, then disappears inside.

"What's going on?" I ask in between wheezes. "Why weren't they around before?"

"This team is from a different floor," Kayley explains, guiding me to a seat. "Kwanon, I'm glad you're here, Rance. I had to stop Parrish from getting hysterical. There was no way I could have gotten the crash team and helped him at the same time."

As I nod and catch my breath, Kayley goes to Parrish and takes hold of his arm, the way she used to with me. Parrish doesn't even notice. His focus is still inside the room.

Two minutes later, a female doctor comes out, wiping her brow with the sleeve of her gown. It's such a clichéd moment, I feel like I'm watching a cine. I wish I was. Then Parrish's reality wouldn't have to be so tragic.

The doctor blinks a few times, then searches the hallway. I expect she's looking for next of kin. Kayley raises her hand and catches her attention.

With a grimace, she approaches the three of us. I stand, ready to face the news that none of us want to hear.

"Your mother's heart failed, and it had stopped beating for several minutes," the doctor explains. "We could not resuscitate her because of her condition. I'm sorry."

"Where were you?" I charge. "That alarm should have alerted you right away!"

"Us?" The doctor looks shocked. "The crash team from this floor should have been here."

"Where are they?" Kayley asks. "Why didn't they come?"

"I have no idea. No one's been able to locate them."

All I can do is shake my head.

Chapter Thirty-Seven

WHILE PARRISH WAS TAKING a moment to say goodbye to his mother, Kayley offered to walk me to the exit. When I expressed regret about not being able to stay longer, she told me not to worry, because she would keep Parrish company for as long as necessary and help him get through this, though she suggested I should visit as much as I could. She embraced me, pressing her cheek against mine, then turned to go.

I watch her walk back through the big sliding doors of the hospital, the pain in my chest fighting with the hot spot on my cheek for dominance of my emotions. Kayley is just being herself, yet every cell in my body wants to beg her not to spend time with Parrish. It wouldn't be right for me to ask that of her. One thing that made me fall in love with her is her deep care of others, not just me.

To calm myself, I try to focus on one of the main precepts as written in the book of the Three Goddesses: it is acceptable to look back on the past, but it is impossible to relive it. Or something like that. Maybe that's not it at all. I just know that the direction I've chosen is taking me away from her.

I send a message to Grady, telling him what happened and not to rush. I'd suggest he not come at all, but he wouldn't listen. He'd want to comfort his friend. Doc Elizabeth should come, too, if for no other reason than to ensure that I returned to the ship.

Then, because I was thinking of my mother, I try calling her Sergo again, hoping with some strange concept that she might answer this time. To my surprise, someone answers. My body goes still. Are my prayers answered? Is she safe? I have no right to hope for that, not when Parrish's mom just died.

"Hello?" I ask tentatively. "Mom?"

"Rance honey! Long time no talk, darling! How are you?" a woman's perky voice says.

I know that voice. I almost dread it. But if Danny Lecker is picking up my mom's Sergo, that means they're together, and that also means—

My mom is okay.

"Put my mom on!" I shout. She meets my demand with a yelp of surprise. There's a rumble of sound, and then my mother comes on. I become so overwhelmed with joy that I just drop onto the hospital lawn. The fear of losing her, combined with the sorrow of Parrish's loss, turns my eyes into fountains. I have a hard time controlling my emotions.

"Rance? Are you okay?" my mom asks, no hint of distress, other than for me, in her voice. "I was worried about you."

"Mom...it's so good to hear your voice! Where are you?" It doesn't sound like she knows about the house.

"Oh, just helping Danny on a case. What's the matter? You sound upset."

Parrish's mom and mine weren't close, but they were both single parents. They'd often trade ideas and suggestions on how to raise a child on a single income. They had a mutual respect for each other, even if they had little else to talk about besides their children.

"Parrish's mother just passed away."

There's quiet on her end for a minute. I wonder how she's taking it. It really wasn't how I wanted to break the news to her, though there's never a good way to disclose something so sad.

"Make sure you light incense and say a prayer," she says. "And let me know when the service is. I will go with you. And I hope you're spending time with Parrish. He's going to need your support."

I'm not even sure how to reply. So much has happened in a short time, it would be hard to explain. Or has it? No, it only seems short to me because I was dead. How do I tell her that?

Before I can, someone calls my name, and a chill goes down my back. Of all the people I want to run into at this moment, he's among the very last. I don't want my father to see me like this. I don't want to see him at all.

"Mom, I've got to call you back," I say and disconnect. I better make a quick excuse to get out of here.

"Rance," my father says as he approaches, confusion crossing his face. But when I catch his gaze, I see more than that behind his eyes. I see fear.

I stand and brush myself off, running a sleeve across my eyes just to be sure he doesn't notice my tears. It only helps my self-esteem, not my face. My eyes must already be puffy from crying.

"Who were you talking to?" he asks—a strange first question for someone who's likely noticed their child has been crying.

"Just a friend."

"I see." He shakes his head and glances around as if looking for something. "What are you doing here? Were you a patient?"

"Patients spend their time in their rooms, not out on the hospital lawn."

He nods, then motions to his two men to step away. I don't like the looks they give me before they follow his order. Their eyes are full of some deep-seated kind of anger or hatred. If it's for me, it's strange. I've never met them before. With their combat pants and military-issue sunglasses, they look more like mercenaries than assistants or even bodyguards. Not sure what my father would need men like that for.

"You seem upset. Did something happen to Kayley?" my father asks. It could just be in my mind, but he almost sounds hopeful.

"No. Parrish's mom..." I have to take a breath before I can continue. "She was sick, but none of us expected her to get bad so quickly."

"Yeah, what happened is really terrible, isn't it?"

I tilt my head at him, suspicious of his tone and his words. Did he know before I told him? And if so, it just happened. How could he know?

"Anyway, why are you here?" I ask, my eyes narrowing as I watch him.

"Me?" My father waves a casual hand—not one of his regular motions. "Just getting a checkup."

"At a hospital?"

"Sure. It's what worked out for my schedule today."

"And what's got you so busy you can't see your doctor during his regular office hours...on Albion?"

It's his turn to narrow his eyes at me. Sure, he might wonder why I know his primary doctor is on the Empire's capital planet, but he's forgotten he recommended I go see him about the plasma wound on my shoulder. Of course, there's not one trace of it left on me now that my body's rebuilt.

"I had business here on Angelcanis, so it was convenient," my father replies. What a nonsense answer. I had suspected him of wrongdoing well before this conversation. All he's doing is adding fuel to the engine exhaust. He knew about Parrish's mom, and he made a guess about Kayley without even asking how she is. I need to find out more.

"What business?" I ask.

"Why do you care?" he replies with a shrug. "If I remember correctly, Rance, our last conversation had you insisting you knew how to keep yourself safe, as if you knew better. In fact, I'm surprised you're still in one piece."

I narrow my eyes at him. Did my father just insinuate that he expected me to be hurt? Or wounded?

Or dead?

Wait a second—did he know about the assassin? Is that why he tried to warn us?

Did he give the order himself?

"Is that what you were hoping would happen?" I ask, the edge in my words more than apparent. I'm taking a risk, but if he knows something, then it's worth it.

"Why would I hope that? You're my son."

"As if that has some meaning these days."

He snorts and shakes his head. "Just because you can't understand a simple message doesn't change the fact that I am your father! It's you who has ignored the obvious. Not me. I never wish danger on you, Rance, but honestly, if someone had shot you and Kayley in the head, it wouldn't have surprised me at all. The two of you have put yourselves in a dangerous position."

Kayley? Why did he just bring her into this? He must know what happened. He may have even received confirmation of our deaths. That would explain his surprise and confusion at seeing me here and his odd tone when he asked about her.

As much as I despise him, the thought that he could have ordered my death is painful to consider. All he has ever told me is how much he cares about me, but was it just a lie?

Despite my anguish, another idea pops into my head. Bailiff Daughtry hired the Emperor's assassin to kill us on Canis Ludis, so she must have been one of the top leaders. How can my father do the same thing if he's just a minor boss? Am I wrong about that?

Could *he* be the boss of the entire conspiracy?

There is only one way to find out, though I am reluctant to try it. I'm not sure he would even admit to ordering the death of his son. He may not want to admit to himself that he did that. Despite his desire for power, he may have never expected me to get in his way. There was a time not that long ago when he'd asked me to join him. Of course, I refused. I don't share his ambition to rule the galaxy, if that's what he's after.

"Why bring Kayley into this?" I ask, my body tensing as I wait for his response.

"Rance, we both know who leads your little team, and it's not you," he answers.

"So you ordered your assassin to take Kayley out and I just happened to be an inconvenient liability?"

That scored a point. He takes a step back, then his hands clench, and his face gets red. I can almost see him getting angrier by the second.

"I told you not to get involved!" My father throws a finger at me. "I warned you because you're my son and I care about you. But that wasn't enough, was it? You pushed and pushed until someone pushed back. You should have taken my advice when you had the chance!"

There's silence between us then. He just came this close to admitting he gave the command to kill Kayley and it was okay if I died in the process. My father wants power so badly, he will let his own son die just to get it. I wonder what he is expecting in return for such a sacrifice. Maybe he wants to be Emperor, after all.

Right now, I cannot hate another person more.

"You're the one who ordered our assassination," I say, my voice steady but ready to unleash an explosion of threats and insults should he choose to fight me with words. "You wanted Kayley dead and me along with her."

"No! The only thing I ever wanted was for you to join me, like we had always planned! We were going to change the Empire for the better, Rance! You and me! But somewhere along the way, you got lost, and as much as I tried to bring you back, you resisted. If you want to blame anyone for your assassination, blame yourself."

Now I know. He's never cared for me in the way he pretended to. He's too full of his own desires to have a meaningful relationship with anyone other than himself. Maybe I've always known that, but to hear him all but admit it makes my body cold. He hasn't been my father for a long time. It still hurts like hell to realize it.

"That's all I am to you, isn't it? An obstacle to get out of your way? Then, once I'm dead, you've got nothing to stop you from overthrowing the rightful ruler of the Commonwealth."

"You know what?" My father sighs. "Perhaps I've been going about this the wrong way. I'll show you everything that you think you know. Then you'll understand."

He turns around to his two men and says, "Try not to hurt him. He's still my son, after all."

So he means to capture me. Maybe I should...

Chapter Thirty-Eight

Run.

That's all I can think of as I spin and burst back through the hospital's entrance and dart towards a passage I hope will get me away. The receptionist shouts after me, screaming some angry words I wouldn't repeat to my mother. I couldn't care less. I'm not stopping for anything.

My father's goons won't catch me. I can't let them. If he was fine with killing me before, there's no telling what he'd do to me now. I know too much, and he'll want every last piece of intel I can give him—even if he has to kill me again to get it.

The passage leads through a laundry room and out onto another medical floor. A nurse startles and yelps, gripping her patient as she helps him walk. I press my hands together in apology and rush off.

I'm halfway down the corridor when there's a bang behind me. The nurse screams. That wasn't a gun, only a door slamming open. Not that it matters. I just learned how hot on my trail those goons are. Besides, they won't fire their weapons here. Firearms and pure oxygen are a dangerous mix.

I dodge through hospital orderlies and elderly people in wheelchairs, trying my best to keep the distance between me and my pursuers. My new body works well, but I've got to find a hiding place or an escape route before I run out of power.

"Watch out, they've got guns!" someone cries. Great. They've got them out. No big deal. They're just trying to scare everyone.

A whine pierces the air, then something impacts the wall, sending sparks everywhere. I throw my arm up for protection, hoping to avoid catching fire. Another whine squeals past my ear, forcing me to duck. I smash into a medicine cart, sending pills and liquids across the hall. I stumble but stay on my feet.

So they're not afraid to use their guns. At least they're not plasma weapons. I still don't want to get shot.

I find a side corridor and fly down it. This one is less occupied—good. I won't have to worry about avoiding people who are trying to recover from injury.

"There he is!" one goon shouts. They're still right behind me. My feint didn't work. Keep going, Rance. Really. Move it.

My body complains about this constant sprint. I feel the fire in my lungs building. There's got to be somewhere to hide from these guys.

For now, I've got to keep moving. Stopping is capture, and capture means I lose, and so does the Empire.

Another shot burns past my ear. I'm glad it's difficult to aim on the run. There's only so much I can do to dodge fire I can't see coming.

I notice a pair of double doors up ahead. A janitor just came from there. That could be a way out of this hospital. Maybe I can find a constable and get their help. But who knows if they'd believe me on the spot? These goons are dangerous. They might just shoot the officer and me at the same time.

I'm right. Behind the doors is a loading dock. And freedom.

No one questions me as I rocket towards the exit. They're too busy with loading and unloading hospital stuff. Besides, I'm running out, not in. They won't stop me, but they're not going to stop a pair of tough guys with guns, either.

Where to go from here? Hide in the trash compactor? No. Bad idea. There're all sorts of strange things in there. I need a better option.

I spot a small shed close to the dock. It looks like a security booth. That might be my spot—if I can make it there without getting shot.

With a quick check behind me, I use as much strength as I've got left and dash to the shed. The door is on the opposite side. I duck in and slide it shut, trying to be as silent as possible. Then, once I'm in, I crash to the floor, gasping for air.

The police will be here soon. Maybe even military troops, after what happened at the capitol. If I can hide out here long enough, those goons will have to flee with all the heat they've brought down on this place. It's their own fault—what kind of jerk fires a weapon in a hospital, even if it was only a stun gun?

I wonder how Parrish is doing. Did all of this ruckus disturb his last moments with his mom? Goddesses, I hope not. I've already been a source of his distress. And what about Kayley? Is she with him now, staying close as a good friend should be? I should be there, too, not hiding away from my father's goons like some fugitive.

This is not the right time to start feeling sorry for myself, but with nothing else to do but consider my situation, it's hard to keep the mood away. I don't regret the things I've done...well, most of them. It's more the things I didn't do that bother me, like how I didn't stop Kayley from putting herself out in the open to get shot. How different would things be if I had done that?

Okay, it's been long enough, and it's still quiet out there. I think I can risk a peek out of the window.

Shoot! They're right there!

Those two goons are orbiting the shed, pretending like they're security agents or something. Either they're not worried about getting caught or the proper authorities haven't shown up yet. It makes me wonder if they've bothered to check this shed. I'll need to get out of here before they do.

If I can.

While their focus is aimed away from me, I take a quick glance around, looking for my next step. Then I just need to wait for the right moment and go. I pray that my moment comes before one of them gets curious about my hiding spot.

There! Not far away is a hedge that will cover my exit. All I need is to get there from here. It sounds easier than it will be, but I risk more by staying. I won't be my father's prisoner. I've already been that for most of my life, thinking he was some kind of hero. He's as far from that as anyone could be.

I peek out again to check the goons' position. Still there. They're keeping an eye out for something that hasn't arrived yet. Okay. This is my chance. I take a deep breath, then slowly slide the door open.

There's no way they won't notice me, but they're not leaving. I have little choice, and I stopped believing government agencies would protect me long ago. This is my opportunity to save myself.

I check them again, then bolt. My aim is the hedge. I've got my escape if I can make it there. All I need is for those two jerks not to notice me.

No luck with that.

"Dammit!" one of them growls. "Shoot him!"

Gun blasts fill the air as I dive towards the hedge. There's no time to go around. I've got to go through. Or under. Any way I can get to the other side, I'll go.

I bury myself into the hedge, the branches scraping at my face, and push through. The bush gives way easier than I expect, and I keep going, hopeful for escape.

It's deeper than I realized, and now I'm forcing my way through with no idea where the other side could be. Maybe it's better if I don't go straight across. They might expect that. This hedge wasn't designed for crawling around inside of it, however.

"Do you see him?" one goon shouts.

"Stop talking, you idiot!"

Well, I guess one of them is smart enough not to give away their position. Does that mean they may also realize I won't just come out the opposite side? I hope not.

It's difficult to move and remain quiet. I try to listen for their footsteps, but even the most minimal of movements from me clouds my ears in a wash of shaking branches. I'm going to have to do my best to find a way out of this bush trap and pray they're not just waiting for me on the other side.

With a little effort, I can see beyond the hedge. There's a road and a garden on the other side that leads to a small wooded area. If I can get there, I might have my chance.

Sirens sound in the distance. That's good and bad. I could try to wait it out, but I'll bet these goons will get more aggressive with their search. They might find me before the authorities arrive.

It's now or never.

I break from the hedge and scramble to my feet. A second later, I'm dashing across the road with a grin on my face. I've done it! I'm scratched to heck from all the pointy parts of the branches but otherwise fine. Freedom, here I come!

There's a shout behind me and the whine of a stun gun. That's okay. I've got a lead on them now. I can make it.

Then my body goes stiff, and I crash to the ground, landing hard on the graphcrete sidewalk. My face scrapes across the rough texture of it, and pain runs down my body. Or it should, if my nerves and muscles were working properly.

"Quick, drag him into the garden!" the lead goon hisses, grabbing my ankle.

"But he said to try not to hurt him!" the other says, grabbing the other side.

"So we tried! Now move!"

They slide me into a secluded area and make quick work of binding my legs and feet. My body is slowly returning to normal, and the reality of my capture seeps into my brain. I'm in a serious situation, but I'm not ready to give up yet. Maybe I can bargain with these guys. If I can scare them enough, they might release me.

"We know everything," I say, my voice shaky. "You won't win. And I will make sure your heads are on the chopping block first."

"You got a gag?" the lead goon asks the other.

"No."

"This will have to do." He takes out his stun gun and presses it against my chest. "Nighty night."

I guess they're not willing to bargain.

Chapter Thirty-Nine

I have no idea where I am when I come to. At least it's not a cell. I'm tucked into a modest yet comfy bed in a small room not unlike my own. There's a small table with a sofa and a desk with a rolling cover. It really feels like my bedroom, or what was my bedroom. That's destroyed now, thanks to the conspiracy and, likely, my father.

It seems like someone cared enough to clean me up and take care of my scratched face. There's a bandage across one cheek, and they've tended to my other scratches as well. I also spot a pitcher of water and a small bar of food on the table.

I'm not in a prison, but I am a prisoner. For what reason, I've yet to find out. If he had wanted to kill me, I would be hanging out in heaven with the Three Goddesses instead of being here. Since I'm not, I'll assume I still have some use to him.

There's a knock on the door, and it creaks open. In enters the man of all my current rage—my father. We lock eyes as he looks in on me. Then, once he sees me awake, he enters and closes the door behind him.

"You should be thankful you're not dead," he says, his face plain. If I had expected some other reaction from him, I would have been lying to myself.

"Sometimes death isn't the worst thing that can happen," I reply, matching his flat tone.

To my surprise, he smiles and lets out a chuckle.

"That is true." He crosses the room to the sofa, eases into the seat, and throws an arm over the back. For a moment, I notice a melancholy look in his eyes. Then they harden, and my father becomes all business again.

"You've caused me a lot of trouble, Rance. More than I expected. If you hadn't put a real wrench in my plans, I would be proud of all that you've accomplished. You stopped my attempt to smuggle the portals onto Albion, took down my associate at the Anti-Sedition Ministry…even captured my second-in-command. I have every reason to end you, but I've had a difficult time accepting that conclusion. Despite what you must think and feel about me, you are still my son, and I love you."

His confession burns a fire through my body. Whatever he expected to happen when he said it has only strengthened my resolve to see him gone. For the first time, I realize, to get what I want, I may have to do what he has done to me. I might have to kill my dad.

"I can see you're angry with me, and likely you should be. But the reasons for it are wrong. You think I want to rule the Empire because I desire power? No. I have no interest in being Emperor."

"So why do it?"

"Because the concept of one man having so much power is obsolete. The politicians on Albion are disconnected, out of touch. They have little care for the people of this Commonwealth. We need a new form of government, one that works for the will of the people, not the other way around."

I feel a tugging on my heart. It sounds so similar to the ideas we used to discuss. Of course, they were mostly his ideas. I was only twelve, and he was everything to me back then. I dreamed about the two of us doing great things in the name of justice. Those dreams turned sour when he walked out with not even a word or a message to me for years. It took Grady's parents getting arrested to bring us together again.

"Think about it, Rance," he says, his enthusiasm stirring. "It's what we've always wanted, and it's in our grasp! Real justice for all!"

"And you think that taking the Emperor from his throne is going to bring about this new era?"

"It's the first of many steps, yes." He shrugs off my concern. "I never said it would be a simple task."

He hasn't thought this through as well as he thinks he has. Since he's letting me, I'm going to continue to press him. Then I'll figure out how to escape. I can't wait around to find out what he's going to do to me.

"How do you know everything will happen the way you want it to? What if not all the Central Planets get behind you? What if you cause a civil war?"

"War isn't inevitable, but if it happens, then so be it. That will be the way we have to go."

I stare at him, the shock of what he just said hitting my brain like a comet into an asteroid. I want to deny what I just heard, but I know he'll just say the words again, as if there is no issue to be concerned about.

"Do you realize how many people would die in a war?" I ask.

"People die, Rance. That is the normal course of things. To bring about this kind of change will require a great sacrifice from many. There will be resistance to letting go of the old ways. I've planned for that. Some can't take part in this new era. It's better if they just step aside, but we both know many won't. There is only one recourse for people like that."

"So you're going to kill anyone who gets in your way? Like you did me? Do you plan to assassinate half the Commonwealth?"

"Don't be so melodramatic. Use that anger for something productive, like helping the people!"

I remember him saying that to my mother a few times, mostly when they would get into a fight about things he did that gave me the wrong ideas. He would always just deny her concerns, like they were nothing. I thought little of it then, but now that I realize his manipulations, I wonder what else he's done to my mother.

Was my father ever the good man I thought he was?

"I've been helping the people," I say through my teeth. "You've only been helping yourself."

My father tilts his head and gives me a look of dissatisfaction, as if I had just shown him a poor grade I got on a test. Maybe that's why he came in here—to test me. To see if I might understand his reasons and realize he's right and I'm wrong, then choose to be his ally instead of his enemy.

But any desire to be like him died when I did, and there was no hope of that resurrection once I figured out he was the one behind my murder. If he still expects me to join him, then he's more delusional than I thought.

"You know," my father begins, drawing his words out, "I am making an effort here, Rance. I'm taking the time to explain myself to you so you can see this is the right way. And the right way isn't always the easy way."

"As if I need you to tell me that," I spit back at him. "You have no idea what my friends and I have sacrificed. We have been through so much pain, but you'd never know that. You've never been around long enough to ask!"

"Is that what this little rebellious moment is about? You're still bothered that I left?"

"You want to know what I'm upset about? You tried to kill me, and it doesn't bother you at all! That's what upsets me!"

My shout fills the small room, reverberating off the walls and back into our ears. A long silence follows where the two of us just stare at each other. If I hadn't already given up on him, I might be feeling the sting of rejection. But all he's done since he's returned to my life is prove I've chosen right. Once he left us, he became someone else entirely. Someone who is not my father.

He leans forward, resting his hands on his knees but never taking his eyes off of me.

"Alright. You want me to admit I gave the order to have you removed? I did. I would have done that to anyone getting in my way. I've no regrets about it. And you've only yourself to blame for getting on the wrong end of things. Understand me, Rance. Nothing will stop this new era from happening. Not my son. Not anyone."

He throws a hand up before I can speak.

"I *am* glad you're not dead, in case you're wondering. As I said before, you're my son, and that still means something to me. Unlike you, I can separate politics from family business."

If my jaw wasn't already tight, it would be on the ground. How he can justify killing his own son and then blame me in the same breath is impossible to fathom. When every sense of right within me is screaming *wrong*, I don't even want to try to understand this.

"You are so beyond deranged, I can't believe I attempted to have a conversation with you! Now that I know what you really are, I can't stand to be near you for another second. You are not my father. You are nothing but the enemy! And the enemy needs to be stopped!"

I watch him, waiting for the moment when he shows a sign of being hurt by my words. But he has played this game for far too long to ever admit I, or anyone else, have affected him. And maybe that's what this all is to him, a big game.

It doesn't matter. I am done caring what he thinks.

My father stands, taking a moment to adjust his suit and flatten down his jacket. He puts more care into that than he has me. It only proves my point.

"Well, you may say that now, but you'll reconsider, if given long enough to think about it." He turns to the door and grabs the handle, then looks back at me.

I only glare at him, my hatred of the man I see before me moving up through me and firing from my eyes like plasma beams. I can only hope it burns him and burns him well.

"And if you don't," he adds, twisting the doorknob, "then you can just stay in this room and rot for all I care."

He moves through the door, slamming it behind him. I stare, then crash back down on my pillow, hoping oblivion will take me.

Chapter Forty

It doesn't.

Maybe that's a good thing. I've had enough, anyway. I've spoken to my father for the last time. He is not my parent anymore. A man who shows no remorse for attempting to end his son's life can't be called a father. And despite my hatred of him, I still feel utter despair when I recall the moment he admitted I was in his way because I was nothing more than an annoyance to him. That's why he had me assassinated.

I need to get out of here, and I don't expect it to be easy. He's wary of any escape attempt, I'm sure. I bet there will be plenty of countermeasures in place. That won't stop me from trying. I'd prefer death over having to be around him any longer.

So how do I get out of this antiquated room? There are no windows or vents that I can crawl through. I'm sure that was deliberate. The only way in and out of here is through the door, which could mean there's a guard just outside, or it could mean they don't need to waste a person on that. Of course, it won't really matter unless I can unlock the door.

I don't know how to pick a lock, so that's out. Bashing it down would bring too much attention and put a hard stop on my escape. Still, there might be something with the hinges or the lock that I can undo without much racket.

A quick examination of the knob shows what I'd expect to be a standard-issue door. Standard for where, though? I have no idea if I'm even still on Angelcanis. I don't recognize anything as being from my home planet, but then again, I've not been everywhere on Angelcanis, either.

What is of interest is the small sliver of light peeking through the lock jamb and the door itself. I can see the latch bolt, and I think if I could just pry that open, I could be free.

Provided there are no other locks or latches on the outside. I didn't hear any when my father walked in, so maybe not. I will feel quite stupid if I attempt to undo this one lock, only to find I'm still trapped.

I press my ear up against the door, listening for footsteps or other noise. There isn't any, not even the sound of shuffling feet. That worries me a little. I can't make any sort of plan until I open the door and look outside.

And that's the biggest problem I have right now.

There's nothing in the room that would make for an obvious tool to wedge into the bolt. All I would need is something flat and strong. Too bad I'm striking out in that department.

For now, I'll have to try another way. I stare at the door and the frame, searching for another option—there! I can pull the pins out of the hinges. I grab the cover off the pillow and quietly slide the chair up to the edge of the door frame.

Then I cover the top of the bolt with the pillow case and find the edges of its top. Metal on bare fingers is not a pleasant feeling, and the cover is rough enough to provide some grip. Now let's see if my fingers are strong enough to hang on while I pull this thing out.

I grit my teeth and yank. It's hard, because even while standing on the chair, I've got to raise my arm to shoulder height to get to the bolt. I try again with two hands, putting myself in a precarious position. It's okay. I can manage it. The middle one and the lower one should be easier.

But I get overconfident and use too much body movement. The chair tilts, and I lose my balance. I try to grab on to something, but my hands only find air. With a flail of my arms, I topple over, bounce off the bed, and hit the floor with a heavy grunt.

Shoot—I just made a very loud invitation for any guards outside to come check on me. I race to put things back to normal, pushing the chair up before I hop to my feet. But a wave of dizziness hits me, and I flop back onto the rug that the table sits on.

My eyes scan the door, waiting for an irate, burly dude to barge in. Yet no one does. Good. I'm glad I won't need to answer questions about why I'm on the floor with half of my body under the desk. Maybe I can tell them I was admiring the undersides of the furniture, with its fine woodwork and metal straps—

Wait, one of them is loose! And I bet it's thin enough and strong enough to wedge a space in between the latch bolt and the latch. If I can pry it off, I could be free faster than I expected.

I reach up and pull it towards me. My position on the floor makes it easy to apply a slow, steady force, with a bit of gravity assist. The strap bends, and I get my other hand on it for even more power.

The wood of the desk groans, and with a percussive pop, the strap snaps off the desk. I wait a moment, checking the door to see if that sound gets any attention. Then, when I'm clear, I scramble to the door and insert the tip into the crack.

Once I feel the resistance of the latch bolt, I put my weight behind it and push. The strap wiggles a little but then moves forward with a soft rumble. With my head filling with hopes of a mad dash out the back door and to freedom, I grab the knob and open the door a crack.

Well. That's why I got no noise complaints from the guards. There's no one out there. Still, I'm suspicious. My father wouldn't be so easygoing about the security surrounding me.

I open the door wider and peek out. There's a long corridor outside that appears to join a larger room at the end. Filling in the space between is a massive man who might be a guard. Okay, so that's why I don't have a door monitor. He's more like a hallway monitor. Fine. I will go the other way.

But when I check the other end of the corridor, I see another guard there toting a heavy rifle. So my father isn't slacking. He might even be on the edge of overkill by using these two.

Now here's the big question: Which way do I go? Can I rush the rifleman fast enough to beat him from taking a shot at me, or can I outwit the big guy into letting me just walk by? I'm not crazy about presuming a big dude has weak brain muscles. I've seen too many exceptions to that stereotype to just make an assumption like that. I've only got one chance at this.

Yet when I size up the rifleman again, I feel my confidence falter. This has got to be a highly trained soldier. I might surprise him, but I doubt that advantage would last for long.

With a sigh, I turn down the corridor and head for the big guy, not making any sort of attempt to be stealthy. The moment this dude spots me, I've got to look like I'm supposed to be out here. He's going to be suspicious enough about my intentions, and I don't yet have a plan in place.

Well, it's going to be interesting, if nothing else. I could sit in that room and scheme, scheme, scheme until I felt completely confident in what I was doing, but by then they might have changed my entire security. And while I'm here dreaming up complex scenarios, my father is busy destroying the Empire.

"How did you get out?" the big man bellows.

"Uh, it was unlocked?" I answer, pointing back to the door. "My father left it that way, because he asked me to join him."

"He didn't tell me that."

And there it is. I'm not giving up yet, but if I don't come up with a good reason for walking past him, I'm getting thrown back into my room, and the guard may just see why the door is unlocked. Then I'll have a real problem.

Yet my father placed these guys at the end of the corridor, not right at my door. Whatever orders he must have given them likely included a little leniency. Especially if my father still hopes to recruit me to his cause. That's something I can use!

"Why would he?" I ask.

"What are you, stupid?"

"Listen, if he wanted to keep me in that broom closet, he would have locked the door, right?"

"Yeah, so?"

"So did he tell you to not let me out?"

"Why would he have to tell me that? I'm , kid. I understand the mission without it having to be spelled out for me."

Ah, a know-it-all elite. Perfect. I think I just found my angle on this guy. It's not his intelligence; it's his ego that I'll use against him.

"Okay," I say, folding my arms. "If you're so smart, you tell me why I'm just able to stroll out of the room and have a conversation with you."

The big man frowns down at me. He's going to think this one through, just because I've challenged him.

"Hey, what's going on?" It's the rifleman, come to see what all the noise is about. "How'd he get out?"

"Your buddy here is keeping me from an appointment with my dad, that's what," I say. "He doesn't appreciate me being late. If I tell him you're the reason..."

"He won't do squat," the rifleman replies. "Now how'd you get out?"

"He says it was unlocked," the big man says.

"That so? Maybe we should check that out."

My arms get all itchy. I can't let them look. They'll find the strap just sitting inside the door, and then I will go to see my father, only to be shot when he finds out I tried to escape. I've got to play it cool.

"Do whatever you want, I'm going." I make a move, but the big man drops a hand on my shoulder and stops me cold. I feign getting hurt and fall to my knees with a cry.

"Hey, what are you doing?" the rifleman asks. "We were told not to hurt him!"

No use of force, eh? This is all coming together better than I could have expected. I keep the charade going by rubbing my shoulder and wincing. The big man grabs my arm with a sound of annoyance and hauls me to my feet.

"Did you really have to do that?" I whine. "That's my bad shoulder."

"This kid is a wimp," the big man says. "I barely touched him."

"Is this how you have fun?" I ask as I look at both of them, doing my best to play victim. "Beating on defenseless people?"

"Hey, you listen here." The big man thrusts a finger at me. "I am one of the most decorated vets in my division. I've beaten entire squads by myself."

"Yet here you are, fighting a guy without even so much as a pillow for a weapon."

The big man's face goes red, and his eyes get big. That's the reaction I was looking for. He's heading in the exact direction I want.

"You want to fight, kid? I'll show you—"

"Hey, hey, hey, enough," the rifleman says and holds up a hand. "Keep it together. He's just a kid. The *boss's* kid. Let's just let him go see his old man. He'll probably be back here in two minutes."

"Yeah, it's not like I can escape from this place." It's just a guess, but if they believe I'm familiar with the location, it might help me convince them.

"That's right, you're never getting out." The big man towers over me to emphasize his point. It works. I don't even have to pretend to be intimidated.

After a moment of looking between me and the rifle guy, he sighs and waves a hand. "Fine, go. But when you get back, we're locking you in."

"What if I need to use the toilet?" I ask.

The big man leans down and gets into my face with a big grin. "Then knock, sweet pea, and maybe, if you're lucky, we'll let you out."

"I'll escort him," the rifleman says, reaching out to grab my arm.

"Don't bother," the big man replies. "Just like he said, he's never getting out of here."

Oh, how wrong you are, Mr. Highly Decorated Braggart.

Chapter Forty-One

WHILE MY GUARD WAS wrong about me escaping, I haven't yet accomplished that. So, for the moment, he is right. I hope that won't be for long.

I take a corridor that looks like it might go deep into the reaches of this place, which, I'm figuring out, is a base of some kind, possibly underground. The walls, floor, and ceiling are all made from graphcrete, and not a single window exists here. That's a bit of an issue, because I can't tell where the base is or even what time of day it is.

Several guards and military aides pass by, yet none of them even look my way more than once. Maybe that's because they recognize me and don't want to be seen interacting with me. That might get them in trouble. Fine by me. It just makes this easier.

At the end of the corridor is a pair of doors and a vent large enough for me to fit through. I'd prefer not to go that way, even if I can get the grating off. No cine I've ever watched has a good outcome when the characters choose that path.

The doors are locked, of course. As much as I had hoped otherwise, I'm not surprised. If they just left all the doors unlocked, people like me would get into the places they want to keep me out of. They might as well just show me the exit and let me walk out of it.

So, to my displeasure, the vent is my only choice. I could go back and try to find another way, but that just adds the risk of someone stopping me, as it becomes obvious I have no idea where I'm going.

I do a quick scan of the grate—no bolts or latches. That could mean it just pops off. Only one way to find out.

"It *is* you!" a female voice says, full of amazement. My head spins towards the sound, and I gasp.

The assassin!

My fingers tense around the holes in the grating. I check to see what weapons she's got, but if there are any, they're hidden on her person. It's better to assume they're there than make the mistake of thinking she's unarmed. Now I need to find something to defend myself with. And quick.

"You are some miracle," the assassin says, stopping a few steps away. "I put two tipped TSX rounds into your chest. They should have made a mess of your insides. How did you survive?"

"I don't need to answer you," I say and plant my back foot to pull the grating from its housing. It's a bit unwieldy, but it could save me if I come up against her blades.

"Hey, hey, I'm only asking questions," the assassin replies, raising her hands. "We get to have that chat we didn't have the last time. Or are you that ready to die again?"

"Do I have a choice?"

"Well, not really. I have a reputation to uphold. No one wants to hire an assassin whose targets don't stay dead." She leans in, her eyes narrowing. "You're not some kind of robot, are you?"

"You saw the color of my blood."

"Yes, I did, and let me say, I thought it was really poetic how it mixed with your girlfriend's hair. It was so—"

I rip the grating from its frame and turn towards her with it. The assassin blinks and steps back, her hands coming to the ready. Good. I'm glad she gets I'm serious. She doesn't get to talk about Kayley, not even if she bows down and begs forgiveness.

"What are you going to do with that?" the assassin asks.

"You'll find out."

She sighs and moves to lean on the wall, crossing her legs at the ankle in a casual slouch.

"You're always in a rush to do things, aren't you?" she asks, nodding at the grate. "Are you sure you don't want to have a little chat first? We've met so many times now, it's like we're getting to be friends. I'd love to know what you've been up to."

"I've been planning your demise."

That gets a chuckle from her. Then she smiles, and I seethe. I don't understand how she can be so at ease before attempting to kill someone. Is she that lonely that she enjoys whatever company she can get? Even if that company is her victims?

She'll get no enjoyment here. This evil woman nearly killed Grady and actually killed Kayley and me. I will make sure she knows my rage for destroying my life.

I'd prefer not to fight her, of course. She's an expert in murder and has beaten me twice already. If we do battle, she's going to win again unless I come up with something that will distract her long enough for me to get away.

"Hey, can I be honest for a moment?" she says, pushing herself off the wall. "I don't hate you, Rance. There's nothing personal about this, you know. I've got a job that I'm good at, and I take pride in my work. If someone hadn't hired—"

"You mean my father."

"Oh? So you know it was him?" The assassin nods. "Well, I guess that explains why you're here, then...As I was saying, if you and your girlfriend hadn't become targets, we might have been friends."

"I doubt that."

The assassin's forehead wrinkles, and she tilts her head at me.

"I would have expected you to have a stronger response when I brought your girlfriend up." Then she makes a long gasp. "She's not dead either, is she?"

I tighten my jaw, unwilling to give anything away, but it seems I may have just spilled everything without even knowing. Now I've got to stop her, or else she'll be hunting for Kayley again.

With a cry, I swing the large grate at her. Her eyes go wide, and she backpedals, easily evading my attack. I swing again, but she's ready for me this time, swinging her leg to kick the grating. The force of it throws me back. I regain my balance, preparing for her next strike.

Which doesn't come.

"I'd really like to know who your doctor is," the assassin says, drawing a hand across her chin. "Someone who can rebuild both a brain and a heart with no signs of damage remaining must be some kind of genius. They might be useful in my line of work."

I seize the moment and come at her, this time tilting the grate so it has less air resistance and more speed. She drops to her knees and folds under my swing. She kicks, but her leg can't get me. The grate gives me more reach, and she's not exactly tall.

The assassin brushes herself off, then charges me, stepping off the wall to gain height. Then she comes down with a fist to my face. I react, swinging the grate at her and catching her in the side. She cries out but lands on her feet.

Her blades come out then, smaller versions of the ones I've seen before, yet still as deadly. She slashes and stabs, pushing me back into a wall. Then she spins and stomps on the grate, pushing it into my body.

I push the grate back just enough to avoid sudden death by stabbing, but while I'm distracted, her heel drives into my leg. I drop to one knee, and her blades come again, thrusting at my head. I raise the grate, and she slices my finger.

"You know I'm better at this than you are, right?" the assassin says with a grin and thrusts again.

I'm too busy defending myself to answer. She's not wrong. Even the anger inside of me won't overcome her skill. This is a losing battle, but I'm not going down without a fight. Not this time.

I see an opening, and I take it. It's a dumb move; the assassin would never consider it. As she goes in for a kick, I swing the grate at her back leg, dropping her but leaving my body open. It's only by sheer luck I dodge her foot.

The assassin lets out a hoot and springs to her feet. I rush her, grate ahead of me. She drops under it. It still catches the top of her head, whipping it back. I fly over her and hit the floor in a roll. I let the grate go so I don't crush my fingers.

Before I can recover and pick it up, the assassin is there. She looks ready to strike, and now I've got nothing but my hands and legs to stop her. Then she puts two fingers on the top of her head. They come away with red dripping off of them.

"You made me bleed, Rance. Good job, but I wish you would have hit me elsewhere. Do you know how hard it is to put stitches in your own head?" Then she smiles. "But it is really fascinating to be fighting you right now! I was certain you were dead. No one gets up from the job I did on you, and

I double-checked to make sure. I mean, what kind of assassin would I be if I didn't review my work?"

"Like I care."

Then that pout I saw last time—just before she ripped me apart with two high-powered bullets—comes out. I'm no less confused than I was then. How can she be disappointed? She gets to do the same job twice.

It's strange that I'm not more afraid of her killing me. Maybe it's because I feel like I've already lost everything. My relationship with Kayley is gone. My fight against the conspiracy is in ruins. What is it I should hope for?

Or is it because I've already died once? Dying a second time is not such a big deal. I can stand to risk it all. Again.

"Okay, I understand," the assassin says, digging into her pocket and pulling out a card. "You don't think you have any chance against me. I'll take that as a compliment. Last time was kind of easy, I'll admit. So I'll tell you what. If you can get this pass card from me, I'll—"

I plow into her, and we topple. Her arms fly up, and I press down the one with the card in it. I cry out as her blade slices across my back, but I keep going. That passkey is my way out of here. I'll endure any wounds to get it.

My fist meets her face, and she lets go of the card. I snatch it up and jump back, but the assassin gets me across the chest before I can get clear from her. She may have even stabbed me, too. There's heat and stinging all over my body.

"That wasn't fair," the assassin says, breathing heavy. "I didn't finish telling you the rules."

"You didn't care about fair when you killed me," I say. "Why should I?"

"Don't think you can just run away now, Rance. I'm not done with you. If you turn your back on me, I'll put both of my blades in it."

I believe her. I won't make it three steps before she cuts me down. That doesn't leave many options.

My eye catches the open vent. As much as I dislike the idea of sliding into darkness with no understanding of which way to go, that may be my only salvation. Let's see if I can come up with enough of a distraction to get me in there.

"Hey, are you listening to me?" the assassin shouts.

"You know what your problem is?" I shout back. "You want someone to talk to, but you don't even bother to listen! And now when you think I'm abandoning you, you threaten to kill me!"

"I don't listen?" The assassin blinks and pulls back, insulted.

"If you did, you wouldn't have to ask that question!" I take a step towards her—and towards the vent. "Listening isn't just about hearing what the other person says, it's about understanding their words!"

Thank you, Kayley, for that important lesson that may just save my life.

"Huh?" The assassin's brow winkles, trying to follow my words. It's not that hard of a concept to get, but this psychopath is struggling with it.

I move.

Three steps and a jump sends me into the vent. The assassin shrieks behind me, my deception clear. I scramble into the darkness, feeling my way to the first junction. When I hit the corner, I slide into it and stop, hoping she won't pursue.

"How dare you escape me!" the assassin cries and pounds on the metal sheet of the vent. "This is not over, Rance! You and I are not finished talking! I'm going to find you and nail your hands to a wall so you won't get away next time! Do you hear me, Rance? This is not over!"

Then, as she walks away, I think I hear...sniffles? This lady is seriously disturbed. I'm not having a next time with her. I didn't want a first time.

Now on to getting out of here.

Chapter Forty-Two

Once I'm sure Little Ms. I Will Kill You if You Don't Talk to Me is gone, I slide out of the vent and pick a door to use her passkey on. It doesn't matter which one for now. If the guards chase me, they'll think I went through the ductwork. At least that's what I'm hoping.

I take the first door—fail. It's just a utility closet. I've already spent time in a closet here. I'm not looking to do it again.

The second door shows more promise. It's a stairwell that leads down. That might be the wrong direction, but I won't know unless I try. So, stairs it is.

As I descend, the thought occurs to me that the assassin might alert my father to the fact that I've got her security key. Then I'd get caught again. Of course, that's no guarantee she'd get what she wants, which is...what, exactly? A chat? I think she's in the wrong business if she's the lonely type. Imagine meeting all these people, some fascinating, some not—it's the not knowing that'd make it exciting—and then murdering them. That would sure put a damper on your social life.

Whatever. I've got to get out of here the fastest way I can. Even if they find me, I still have a chance to slip past. I'm getting free, no matter what.

And then what? Flee as far away as I can and put this all behind me? There are a lot of complications that come with that. Kayley...and my mom. My friends. They'd have to run and hide with me, or they risk becoming hostages of the conspiracy. That's a lot of convincing I'd have to do.

The stairwell ends in another door. I crack it open and peek through. There's a passage that opens up into a large room. It looks a lot like a canteen. That's mostly because there's about fifty soldiers sitting down and eating. Okay, not that way. Definitely not that way.

I crack the door just enough to slide through and head away from the canteen. The corridor is clear—for now. I'll have to think fast if I hear someone coming.

Static crackles from behind a door, and I jump. Whoa. I'm a bit too on edge. It's just the comms room. Someone in there has got the sound turned up more than might be healthy. At least they won't hear me walking by.

So getting a friends and family plan together doesn't sound realistic. What should I do, then? Rally the troops and bomb this base to hell? As much as I hate my not-father right now, I'm not so sure I'd want to kill him, even if I'd be justified in doing it. And not everyone on this base is as equally deserving of the death sentence. All the canteen chef did was cook a bunch of meals for some bad people. His offense is worthy of a slap on the hand compared to what others have done.

Still, for the good of the Empire, this conspiracy must be stopped.

Footsteps approach from around a corner. I freeze, searching for a hiding place. There! I rush to a door just ahead on the left and slip the passkey into the reader.

But when I swipe the key, I only get a blinking red light. Shoot. Where's Grady when I need him?

One problem at a time, Rance. Someone is about to find me fiddling with a door I have no authority to open.

With a quick spin, I hit the door across the hall, swiping again. It works! I push it open and rush through, closing it gently once I am in. My ear goes against the door, listening for the footsteps to pass by. But rather than a single pair of feet, I hear multiple. And they stop nearby! Now I'm stuck in this room until they're gone.

In the near darkness, I search the wall for the light switch and turn it on once I find it. Once my eyes adjust to the light, I'm presented with—another closet, though this closet is much larger than the one I was in.

And it's more interesting.

The shelves are full of electronic equipment, some old, some new. I search for anything that might make a useful tool of defense—something small and compact. A duct grating was the worst possible thing I could have chosen for fighting. It served me okay in the end, I suppose. My other option would have been air.

Further searching only gives me a rusty screwdriver and a battery-powered injector that hasn't seen use since I was born. If this is the best I'm getting, then I'll have no other choice but to accept.

Then, I see it—a comm system! I rush to grab it from the shelf and plug it into power. Maybe I can get Colonel Cortell on the line and he can zero in on my location and send a ship to pick me up! Then I'm gone from here for sure!

Despite my attempts to power it on, however, I'm unable. It was a reach, anyway. This room looks like a repair facility now that I see the workbench at the end. I go there to check for anything, but unless I prefer a new driver to a rusty one, my luck is no better.

I take the new one, anyway.

So I'm back to running out whichever exit I can find. I don't even know where to find one. There's no map, and it's not like I can just smile and ask the nearest guard which way is the easiest for me to escape from.

I check the corridor and slip out into it once it's clear. My pace picks up, as I'm eager to be free from this place. Free from my father's grasp.

And, of course, free to become burdened with all the problems my new life brings. Deep down, I know most of them get solved by stopping my father. But I'm here alone. What difference can I make? I'm no fighter, and I just got lucky when I outsmarted those guards. I'm a flea trying to take down a bear.

Oh, there's a sign at the end of the hallway. An exit! A clearly marked emergency exit! Of course, there would have to be one. The people who designate those sorts of things weren't thinking about me when they planned it, yet it's perfect for me. Escape is what it's for.

I take off towards the sign just mere milliseconds after I recognize it. There's an unlocked door behind which are stairs leading up. I was right. This base is underground. It doesn't matter anymore. As long as they didn't build it on some snow planet, I'm out of here!

As I rush up the stairs, I have a sudden realization. This flea can beat the bear. Not by fighting it head-on, but by calling for help from the other fleas! I had the right idea to make a call to the colonel before, just the wrong reason to call him. If I can get him to trace my call signal, he'll know where I am. Then the entire Imperial military—at least the loyal ones—will smash this place to bits and arrest everyone.

But will it work? Can I sneak back down and into that comms room without being spotted?

I touch the emergency door, knowing all I need to do is push it open and I'm out of here. But then my father will get away with everything. He's too close to launching his ultimate plan. And I can't forgive him for ordering the hit on Kayley. Or me. I can't let him kill anyone else.

A sign on the door reads: *Alarm will sound if door is opened.* It makes sense that an emergency door would sound an alarm if there was an emergency. Phew. I'm glad I didn't open it, then.

Wait a second.

With both arms, I shove the door open. Then, as promised, a Klaxon goes off. I scramble down the stairs as fast as I can and rush back to the comms room. They'll figure out soon enough that it's a false alarm. It still should give me enough time to make the call.

There's already an organized rush to get out. The mass of people moving by makes getting back to the comms room a challenge. Still, I get there in less time than I expect.

I count down from three and rush inside. As expected, communications equipment fills the space, with banks of receivers, transmitters, encoders, and decoders covering the walls. And I'm in luck. There's only one comms tech in here. He's about my age, which means, like me, he could be a little gullible.

"Back away from the terminal," I growl as I press the screwdriver against his throat. He better be appreciative I brought the clean one.

"Dude! What are you doing?" the tech cries out and throws his hands in the air. "We're in emergency mode!"

"Dude?" I pause. The accent sounds familiar. "Where are you from?"

"Angelcanis."

"Where on Angelcanis?"

"Yeomanry. Don't you know where you are?"

"This is…Yeomanry?"

"Totally. How'd you get here if you don't know that?"

"Never mind! I want you to make a call."

"But you just told me to get away from the terminal."

"Holy Sophia, dude!" I bump him on the head with the base of the driver. "Don't listen to what I said. Listen to what I'm saying! Now key in this number, and once the call connects, you'll put in the message I tell you."

The Klaxon halts as the tech punches everything in. A little earlier than I wanted, but my plan is almost done. No matter what happens to me after this, Colonel Cortell is going to bring every military division he can round up down on this place. It's not a bad thing that the location is convenient.

"Dude, are you sure you want me to send this?" the tech asks, his finger hovering over the button.

"Oh yeah. Now send it before I bash you!"

He sighs and presses the button. Then, before I can stop him, he swivels about in his seat. I jump back, ready for a fight. But then he looks at me, and his eyes go wide.

"Hey! Dude!" He shakes a finger at me. "I know...I know who you are!"

Shoot. He does? I tense, ready to fight or run, whichever comes first.

"Can I have your autograph?"

"What?" I blink. "Um...sure. Be glad to."

He hands me a tablet and marker, and I scrawl something illegible on it. It's not far from my actual signature. I never did well with writing manually.

"Thanks, dude!"

"No problem. Now remember, don't tell anyone I was here or that you sent that message, or else." I shake my driver at him to emphasize my point, then head for the door.

"Aww, no worries, dude. I don't really like this job, anyway."

Chapter Forty-Three

I'M ABOUT TO DO something really stupid.

With the message sent and my fan satisfied, I could run. But no. I need to make sure my father sticks around long enough to be arrested. That means I need to keep him occupied with something without that something becoming me. I'm not looking to get captured again, though there's always the possibility that he orders his guards to shoot me instead.

Before any of my plan becomes reality, I've got to locate him first. This is a big base, or at least what I've seen of it so far. He could be anywhere. But I bet he won't. If I know my father, he'll likely be right in the middle of the action, wherever that is.

I head back towards the canteen, the area clear of personnel now that the alarm has been silenced. It won't be long before they investigate and find me waving to the camera. I don't want to be anywhere near that door when that happens.

There's got to be a central command area or a suite of offices somewhere. That's likely where he'll be. Not sure what I'll do once I get there…maybe just lock him inside. It could be enough.

Only one sad-looking soldier glances up at me as I pass through the canteen and turn right into a corridor that looks a bit more my speed. I turn left and end up at a bank of elevators. Great! There's a directory here. And, of course, the command offices are on a lower level. But it's not a great place to get off the elevator.

Ah—there's a mezzanine! I'll go there. It could be a good place to get a view of what's happening.

An officer and his aide walk up to stand beside me as I devour the contents of the directory. I'm so wrapped up in my study, I don't even notice them staring at me.

"Lost?" the aide asks.

"Huh?" I pivot to stare at him, freezing the moment I realize I'm caught.

"New recruits are up on the first floor."

My jaw drops open, but a second later, I come to my senses and snap to attention.

"Yes, sir! Thank you, sir!" I salute as the aide raises an eyebrow. But then the elevator opens, and the officer pats his aide on the shoulder as he steps in.

"That's better," the officer says, turning around in the elevator to look at me. "Get your hair cut, son. We don't allow slackers into this organization."

"I'll do it right now, sir! Thank you, sir!"

I hold my breath until the door closes, then I pound the call button for the next elevator. I've got to hide before another interaction like that happens. My luck might not last for a next time.

As the door opens on the mezzanine, I scan for the darkest shadow and dart into it. There's still a good view over the rail from this position. Good. I'm ready.

Below is an oval lobby, which is fronted by three sets of heavy metal doors. They might lead outside or, more likely, to some secure part of the facility, like a staging area or a hangar. A group of guards approach the doors and open the center set, lining up along the sides once they do.

And through one of those metal doors comes my father. Yes! I couldn't be luckier today! I guess all the bad stuff that's happened is getting balanced out by some good stuff. Praise the Goddesses! I'm going to make this happen!

"I thought I recognized you," a male voice says, one I just spoke with. "You're the commander's son."

I spin to see the aide I just met staring at me with a *I know what you're up to* sneer. For the moment, he's alone, but that could change in an instant.

"What are you doing up here?" the aide says, stepping closer, his hand sliding down to the weapon in his hip holster.

"Waiting for my dad, of course." I point down at the lobby. The aide's eyes follow, but his hand remains on his gun—no chance to tackle him. Yet.

"So now he's here...shouldn't you go say hello?"

"He seems kind of busy at the moment."

"I can solve that." The aide leans over the railing and cups his hand to his mouth. "Commander! I found your son! He says he's up here waiting for you!"

Oh shoot!

I spring forward, throwing my shoulder down into the aide's side. He goes down with a grunt. I catch his leg and stumble. I'm up again in a microsecond, dashing towards the elevators—and past. No way I'm going to get caught in a trap like that.

There's a door just past the elevators. I swipe the passkey across it in record time and rip it open, stopping only to disable the lock after I fly through.

That won't hold them for long, if at all. They know this base, and I don't. There's likely ten ways to get around that door. If I'm going to be a distraction, I'd better get creative. Just running won't cut it. They'll have me surrounded and captured in a matter of minutes.

Start a fire? No. I'd be putting myself in danger, though I already am. Big time. I need something better.

I spot a hallway just off the main corridor and dart down it. I've no idea what I'll find, but anything is better than what I've got, which, right now, is nothing.

A whooping alarm goes off, and red lights on the walls flash in sync. Is this for me? I'm flattered if it is. It's too soon for Colonel Cortell to arrive. Hours too soon.

Oh no. This hallway's a dead end! Nothing down here but a trash chute, and I'm still not desperate enough to go there. Yet another cine bad idea.

But as I come back to the main corridor, I halt. The thunder of many pairs of boots rumbles my way. I need to hide—but where? There are no doors here.

Too late! They're on me. All I can do is slip deeper into the hallway and hope they don't notice. It's a horrible plan, but I've got little else.

"Search everywhere!" someone in charge cries. "You two, check that hallway!"

Oh great. I hope they're small.

Instead of waiting to see if they come all the way down, I sprint directly at them, stealing the frenzy of the moment to use to my advantage.

It works. The soldiers freeze as they see me flying towards them at my fastest speed. One gets his senses back and levels his gun at me.

"Halt or I shoot!" he shouts in typical soldier form.

I keep coming, but before he can take aim, I drop to my side and slide between them and surge to my feet in a single motion.

The main corridor is empty, save for the officer, but he's watching for his soldiers as they scour the rooms and closets for me.

Only one move here—I make like Parrish in a powerball match and grab the officer's ankles from behind, jerking them back towards me. The officer flops forward, and I'm on him. I snatch his gun from its holster and keep moving.

"Dammit!" the officer shouts. "He's here! He's here!"

"Keep back!" I shout as the nearest guards pop back into the corridor. "Or I shoot!"

"I can take the shot, sir!" a soldier yells.

"No! Stun weapons only!" the officer says. "The commander wants him alive!"

Well, that's one thing I don't have to worry about. I grin and fire a few rounds into the floor to keep them back, then take off with them in pursuit a respectful distance away.

Still, there's no way I'm going to lose them. There's too many after me, and I won't be able to keep this up for long. My rumbling stomach is the first hint of that. I haven't eaten in a long while, so whatever single-digit calories I've got left in my system are all the power I have left.

I skid around a corner and dig my heels into the carpet to gain more distance, but the soldiers grow braver the longer they chase me. Soon enough, they're going to try something, and I don't know if I'll have the energy to fend them off. It could be high time I do something drastic.

One more turn, then I dart into a meeting hall full of tech people. Perfect. This could be my opportunity.

"Stop him!" one soldier cries, but the tech-heads are so focused on the lecture, few notice. I burn down an aisle towards the group, snatching up a lab coat along the way.

A soldier fires his stun gun. Then he shoots again. The bolt catches the coat and burns a hole in it. Now the tech-heads wake up. Heads spin towards the sound. The lecturer glances up from her lectern. Then, a second later—

Panic.

"Stay down, stay down!" the officer shouts. Some obey. Others fly from their seats and fill the aisle. I throw the lab coat on and blend in with them, hoping to pass through to the exit on the opposite side.

"Where is he?" a soldier yells.

I duck and make my way through the mass of bodies rushing to get out. There's an older woman calmly making her way through the confusion—I'll follow her. She seems to know where to go.

Yes! She's headed towards a set of doors just to the side of the stage. If I keep my head down, I'll be there in a split second.

The soldiers continue to push through the tech-heads by force or threat. There are yelps and screams behind me as they check every white-coated individual to see if it's me. Good. The longer they spend doing that, the more time I have to get free.

"Jane," a woman's voice says. "Who's that behind you?"

When the woman I've been following stops and turns around, I realize her name must be Jane. I give her a friendly smile, but she only responds with a glare.

"Do you know what you've done to my lecture?" Jane asks.

"I'm sure it's just temporary," I reply.

"He's here!" the other woman shouts. "Over here!"

"Nice to meet you," I say and jump up onto a table, dashing down the center.

"There!" a soldier yells, and I hear a rush of boots heading towards me. I slide off the table and, with a glance behind me, slam the door open and rocket through it.

Straight into a group of soldiers.

I collapse to my knees and slump. My chase was never going to last long. I only hoped it would have lasted long enough for my rescue to arrive. Who knows if Colonel Cortell is even coming?

"Rance!"

My head jerks up to see the assassin, smug in her victory over me as she prances forward, stopping just in front of me. I'm forced to bend my head back so I can see her face. Not that I want to. The haughty way she looms is making me ill. Or maybe that's just my hunger coming back.

"I told you, we weren't finished," she says.

"No, you said, 'this is not over.' Which is different."

She chuckles, then slips her blade from its sheath and presses it against my neck. "Oh, I am really going to miss you for the second time. Now where's my passkey?"

I reach into my pocket and hand it to her—not without making her work for it, however. She grunts and rips it from my hand, then puts it away. A second blade comes out, and that crosses with the other one across my throat.

"Any last words?" she asks.

I hear the soldiers whispering to each other, catching enough words to understand they're confused about why the assassin gets to kill me when they're forbidden from harming even my pinkie. I'd like to know that, too, but it doesn't seem like I'll have the chance to find out.

"Aw shucks?" is all I can say to that.

I get a laugh out of her again, and she shakes her head with a smile.

"A comedian to the last," the assassin says. "Okay, comedian, I'll make this painless for you."

I sigh. No luck for me this time. I don't regret my actions or my choices. I did what I thought was right. My only wish would have been to see Kayley again and, whether she accepted it or not, tell her how much I love her.

"You ready?" the assassin asks, looking almost disappointed she must dispatch me. But I put on a brave face and look her right in the eye.

"Yes."

Chapter Forty-Four

"No, stop!"

It's my father. He looks out of breath, as if he's just run all the way from where I saw him last. That's a far way. I know. I just ran it. He lays his eyes on me, inhaling and exhaling deeply. His face is passive and betrays no hint of emotion. Other than him stopping my execution, I don't feel any sense of fatherly love from him. That's fine. I've got none to give to him either.

"Goddesses, what now?" The assassin drops her blades from my neck and turns towards him. "Do you want me to do this or not?"

"You'll get your chance," my father replies with a glare. "But only when *I* say. He needs to tell me something first."

"And if I don't?" I reply.

"Ooh! Would it be torture?" the assassin asks with a bit too much enthusiasm.

"You just stand back." My father jabs his finger at her. "You've already caused too much trouble by letting him get your passkey!"

The assassin pouts but retreats. Then my father turns to me, his stare piercing. I wonder what he wants. Information? He knows about how I got around the base. Does he know I did something in the comms room?

"Who did you send a message to?" he demands.

Yep. That was it.

"No one." My reply isn't a lie. I wasn't the one who sent the message.

My head jerks to the side as my father backhands me across the face. I drop to my side, catching myself and my breath along with it. That was a surprise. He never struck me when I was a child. Not that I can remember. He must be really pissed.

"I know you sent a message! Tell me who received it!"

"I didn't send a message, so hit me again if you want. It won't help you—"

Sparks fill my sight, and this time I hit the floor. Now I know I've got no love for him anymore, but for my father to kill me and then smack me twice without provocation is pushing my tolerance level right up to the red line. He'd better not do it again, or I'm going to swing back. I don't care if I get shot. He's going to know he can't do that to me and get away with it.

"That message that you did not send was government encrypted." My father paces, but his gaze remains locked on me as he moves. "Did you think I wouldn't find out?"

Before I can answer, a whooping alarm goes off, followed by those flashing red lights. The eyes of the soldiers dart about. They weren't expecting this. Does it mean what I think it does?

"Attention! Attention! There is a critical foundation instability in the base that could affect the core reactor. All personnel must evacuate. Repeat. Evacuation procedures are now in place."

"Bring him!" My father snaps his fingers at two of his men, then turns to the assassin. "You. Stick with me. Your skills might still be required."

"My name isn't *you*," the assassin growls. "It's Dylan! Dylan Estrella Thomas!"

As a pair of soldiers grab me by the arms and all but drag me after my racing father, I catch a glance from the newly named Dylan the assassin. Her lower lip continues to push forward in protest of an opportunity taken away from her, at least for the moment. Still, with a name like that, she could fit right in with the hand-hunter crew at the Sin & Bone on Canis Ludis. Wait—does that mean? No...no way. She's even too nuts for them.

We move with all haste back towards the hangar. At least I think that's where we're going. Are we evacuating? Maybe. He might just be locking me up somewhere for safety. Either way, I won't make it easy for him.

I let my feet fall out from under me and jerk my body down. My guards stumble and fall, releasing me. I'm back on my feet in a microsecond, racing the opposite way. They give chase, and we're back at this game again.

Two flashes fill the corridor, followed by a percussive boom so powerful it knocks me on my face. Rapid gunfire follows. I throw my hands over my head, as if that's going to protect me. Another pair of distant rumbles shakes the base. I'm pelted by debris falling from the ceiling and realize my crash position was the right thing to do.

Bombs like that can only mean one thing...I'm saved! Right?

Someone grabs my arms and jerks me to my feet. Maybe I've jumped to conclusions. Saviors usually don't handle people so roughly.

But then I'm spun around to face my captors.

"Billie? Danny?" I blink as the two hand-hunters grin at me. "I was just thinking about you two."

"I bet you're always thinking about us, aren't you, honey?" Danny Lecker replies, brushing dust from her power suit.

I sigh, relieved to be in safe hands. Still, I should have known it was them. No one makes an entrance like Danny Lecker.

"You didn't bring Mom with you, did you?" I narrow my eyes at her.

"Of course not, silly. She's got her card game today."

"How did you find me? I mean, how did you know my exact location?"

"Your little fuzzy buddies made a Rance finder." Billie holds up her Sergo with a very Teddy-like map on it.

"Let's get him out of here," Danny says. "We've got to rendezvous with the others."

"Others?"

"Well, of course. All your cute little friends are here, precious," Billie replies.

"All?" I ask as we jog back the way we came. Does that mean...they came back to rescue me? Grady? Parrish? Afton and Nayla? The Teddys?

Kayley?

"Well, one ship and a bunch of fuzzies, anyway," Danny replies, putting her suited hand on my head and then lowering it. "Keep your pretty little head down. We don't want it to get shot off."

I duck as ordered, and none too soon. The smoky haze before us erupts in flashes, followed by the deep rattle of automatic weapons. Danny shoves me back and opens up with her, should I say, rather enormous gun. Billie does the same, though hers is a bit smaller.

I find a doorway to duck into and stay out of sight. Better I'm not something for them to worry about. But wait...I realize Danny said one ship! Does that mean Colonel Cortell didn't come? That's bad. Very bad! My father will get away! I've got to stop him!

"Let's go, honey!" Danny calls and waves as our opponents press their attack. "We can't play with these guys all day long!"

"No...wait, we've got to go after my father! He's the one behind this!"

"Are you serious?" Billie says. "We can't get him and get you out of here. Not with what we've got to work with!"

"Well, even if you wanted to, you're not following him." Danny points back at the collapsed roof of the corridor. She's got a point. It'd take a month for us to dig through that, even with her power suit.

"Here, discuss it with your friends." Billie plugs my ear with what I realize is a Teddy comm, like everyone else but me wears. At least until now. My built-in one fried, along with my connection to Teddynet. I've got to fix that. Just not right now.

"Hello?" I say.

Danny grabs my hand and yanks me up, charging towards whatever group of standard-issue soldiers remain to face us. Billie lays down covering fire and moves up behind. Between the two of them, they send more blasts down the corridor than an entire squadron. I can only wonder what's happening on the other side.

I don't have to wait long. Our attackers' fire gets sporadic and less accurate. It's not that they've got terrible aim. It's that Danny is nearly bulletproof. Plasma weapons would have been a better choice had they known what they'd be up against.

"Dude!" It's Grady! "Are you okay? We've been so worried about you!"

"Yeah, fine. Mostly. Who's we? Is Kayley with you?"

"Kayley is here, and I'm glad you're okay, Rance," Kayley says, if a bit stiffly. Still, my heart skips a beat, and a wave of joy runs through my body like I haven't felt in months.

"KayKay!" I hesitate, wanting to say so many things but unsure if they'd be appropriate. Instead, I say, "You're the boss! Give everyone the order to capture my father. He's the one who ordered your assassination, and he's the head of the conspiracy!"

"Rance...I can't do that."

"What? Why? You're our leader!" I drop to the floor as a volley of rounds hits the wall nearby. Danny fires an explosive projectile, pushing me aside to continue her fight.

"No, she's not," Afton says, hopping on the comm. "I'm in charge, and the only thing we're doing is getting you out. Then the Imperial household can fight its own battle."

"Who put you in charge?"

"I did. Are we really going to go through this again?"

I grit my teeth. It may be the safe thing to do, but it's not the right thing. We have to get my father, or he'll be gone before any Imperial troops ever show up. If they ever show up. No one's told me they would yet.

"I can't just let him slip away," I say. "If he does, we're not safe. The Empire's not safe!"

"Screw the Empire!" Afton shouts back. "What have they ever done for us? Get your butt to our meetup point, now!"

Danny jumps and curses as a handful of plasma bolts fly past her. Billie lets loose with a response that causes something down range to burst into flame. I can't tell what it is. It's still so hazy from all the smoke and debris in the air.

"Rance," Kayley pleads. "We've all risked ourselves to rescue you. We'd be taking too much of a chance to go after your father. Please, just let's get out of here."

"We have to get past these jerks first," Billie says as she reloads her weapons.

Kayley may have lost her recent memory, but her voice hasn't changed. When she asks me like that, it's near impossible for me to say no. I'm torn between giving in to her and doing what I know will make us all safe.

I fall into a dream of remembrance. Kayley and I, together, sharing a moment of simple happiness. No conspiracy. No danger. Just pure elation.

But there's no going back there. Not for now. I've made my choice, and my father is my target.

If only I could convince them.

With a quick check of the surroundings, I gauge the distance to the next corridor ahead of me, then spring up, crossing the hallway in a time that rivals Afton's record. I hear Danny call after me, but she's too busy fighting off the rest of the battle unit that attacked us.

"Rance, come on!" Afton shouts through Teddy comm. "Stop being selfish! You're endangering us!"

"That's a big word for you, Surela," I reply. "Did your girlfriend teach it to you?"

"I did not," Nayla responds. "Please do not talk about me as if I cannot hear you."

"Rance, please. We've got to get out of here," Kayley says.

I shake off the temptation to turn around. This has to be the way—my own needs be damned. I glance down a side corridor and do some quick calculations in my head. If I can pick the right way back through the canteen, I can get to the lobby, and my father, in no time. I just have to keep my pace up.

"Great Durga!" Afton shouts when I don't respond. "Parrish, go get that idiot before he kills himself again!"

"On it," Parrish replies. "Rance, hold up. I'm coming to you."

Great. I could use a partner, and I'm glad it's him. It will be good to know how he's doing after his mom's passing. I will be the first to go see her memorial and spend as much time with him as he needs.

As soon as I bring my father to justice.

Or kill him.

Chapter Forty-Five

As I BURN THROUGH a room with doors on both sides, I recognize the hallway I first came down before reaching the canteen. Perfect. Just go through there, hit the elevator, and I'll be at the lobby. Of course, I haven't exactly figured out what I'm going to do there. My father is likely to be surrounded by guards, and Dylan may still be with him. I don't even have a stone I could throw.

That hasn't stopped me so far. I might be out of Goddess points, but I still think I can pull something out of my back pocket when I need it.

I listen to the communication running across Teddy comm as Afton tries to coordinate a meetup between her, Kayley, Billie, and Danny. The hand-hunters have demolished their foes and are making their way some-what towards me, while Afton and Kayley are somewhere in the base that I don't get. They're not under fire, so they must be in a location that's far from anyone. Wherever that might be.

Okay, the canteen's cleared. Here I come, elevat—

"Ah!" I cry out as someone's shoulder slams into my side. Someone big. I take flight, in the air for a respectful distance before slamming to the ground and skidding another few steps.

My ribs scream with pain. I writhe as a burning ache runs through me, but I know I've got to get to my feet. Whoever pounded me like a mallet into a sweet potato has got some weight behind them. Likely some muscle, t oo.

"Get up!" Parrish says and grabs me by the shoulders to stare at me. His eyes are full of fire, and he's nearly growling at me. "Do you have any idea how stupid you're being?"

"Yeah, it's nice to see you, too, dude," I reply, pulling away from him. "How about, we were worried about you, Rance. I'm so glad you're not hurt, Rance. Good to see you in one piece—"

"Don't give me that! I postponed my mother's memorial for this! Now you're putting us all in danger because you've got some score to settle with your dad!"

"He's not my dad," I reply, my voice pointed. "He's not even my father anymore. And this isn't just some revenge plan! Millions of people will die if he attempts a coup! We've got to stop him!"

"Why does it always have to be us, Rance? Why are we so cursed that we've got to sacrifice everything for an Empire that looks on us like we're nothing?"

"I see Afton's been bending your ear." I sigh. "We're not doing it for the Empire, Parrish. We're doing it for the people. And we're doing it for us. Don't you want to be free of this mess?"

Parrish backs off, considering that for a moment. It gives me a chance to turn from him and head towards the elevators.

A deep rumble shakes the floor under my feet. So Danny and Billie are still having some fun destabilizing the base. Good for them. I'm more glad neither of them are hurt.

"Where do you think you're going?" Parrish challenges.

"To end this, just like I said I would," I reply.

"No...no, you're coming back with me, and we're leaving."

"Try to stop me."

"Rance, I swear I will knock you out if you don't come now."

"Go for it."

Parrish's pounding feet come up fast. He grabs my arm and spins me around to face him. His hand is balled up in a fist, his arm back, ready to strike. I just stare, waiting for him to do it. But the longer we look at each other, the more reluctant he seems.

"We've both have lost too much, Parrish. All I want is to rebuild my life, hopefully somewhere close to what it was. Or better. I want that for Kayley. And for you. And for Grady."

Parrish releases his grip and drops his hand with a deep exhale. "What about Afton?" he asks. "Don't you want all that for her, too?"

"Honestly?" I smile. "I think Afton's the only one of us who has it together. She doesn't need me to cover for her. Though if what I'm about to do helps her, too, then that's just another candle on the cake."

"You know I can't let you do that," Parrish says, though all the rage in his voice is gone. "We've got to go. Don't you want to see Kayley?"

"More than anything."

"Then?" Parrish motions with a sweep of his arm back the way he came. "Let's go, dude."

I take a step back, uncertain. Parrish waits. For a moment, I just look at him. His face is drawn and weary. There are bags under his eyes where there never used to be. Even his commonly sharp haircut shows neglect. I try to remember a time when he didn't look like that and have to dig into my memory to do it.

Then the elevator bell rings, snapping me back to now and reminding me of what I have chosen.

"I'm sorry, Parrish," I say. "This really is for you."

I jump through the opening doors and slam the first-floor button, then the one to close the doors. I catch Parrish off guard, but a second later, he curses and jumps in after me. He grabs me, and we scuffle. I lose my balance and slip, hitting the floor hard. He pulls me back up again with disappointment all over his face.

Before he can yank me out, the doors close and the elevator drops. We stare at each other, our breath heavy.

"All of that was just a lie, wasn't it?" Parrish asks between gritted teeth.

"Not a single word."

The elevator door opens, and we react, first taking cover in the elevator cab, then darting out and ducking behind one pillar that holds up the mezzanine walkway.

It's quiet in the lobby. All the desks and guard stations have been abandoned. I'm worried I've already missed him. Maybe he's still in his office, whichever one that might be.

I slip over to the edge of the corridor that leads to the office area. There are lights on in a few of the offices, and I track some motion. The only way to find out who's there is to go see. It shouldn't hurt to take a peek, and besides, Parrish has a gun. I'm surprised he hasn't used it on me yet.

"Hey," Afton says over Teddy comm, breaking the silence. "Are you guys almost at the meetup point?"

"Nope," I reply, fully knowing it's going to piss her off. She will take it out on me later. If there is a later.

"Parrish, are you with him?"

"Yes," Parrish replies in a hushed tone.

"What are you waiting for? Shoot him in the leg and carry him back!"

"I can't do that at the moment."

"Goddesses, why not? Are you on his side now?"

"No, but if I fire a gun, the soldiers down the corridor are going to hear it."

"Oh, Holy Sophia! That's it, I'm coming to you! Danny. Billie. Meet me there."

I glance at Parrish, wondering if he's lying now. Sure, there may be soldiers down there, but we can't tell that through the translucent windows. I don't even see the shadow of a gun.

Maybe he is coming around to my side of things. Maybe it wouldn't take much to get him there. I should try, but I'll need to be quiet about it. If Afton hears what I'm attempting, she'll shoot me in the head and leave my body to rot, for sure.

"Dude," I say and point down the hall. "My father could be down there, and we could capture him, just like that. We could take him by surprise, and all this would be over. We'd be heroes to the Empire, and then we could ask for whatever we wanted."

"There are some things that you just can't get back, Rance," Parrish replies. "You should know that."

An ache runs through my chest as I remember all the people and things I can't get back. One of them is not that far away. Another is only slightly farther than that and headed towards me. People change, but this is a further turn than anyone should have to experience.

Kayley might come back to me if I try really, really hard. My father never will. I don't want to even make the attempt with him, because I know it would be a wasted effort. I've said my farewell to him, at least in my mind. I could never say those words to Kayley, in my head or otherwise.

"Even so, Parrish," I say. "If we take him down, we stop a lot of other people...millions of them...from losing things that are precious to them.

We have an opportunity that we have to take, if for no other reason than we are here now. And like I said before, this is for us, too. Putting him away ends everything for us."

Parrish looks at me as I watch the moving shadows in the offices. They seem to get hastier about whatever they're doing. Maybe packing stuff up to take with them? I can count about five people in one room and two in another. Eventually they're going to come out. I want to be ready for them when they do.

"How can you be so sure?" Parrish asks. "How can you be sure that putting your father away in jail will end all our problems?"

"Because I know my father," I reply. "He needs to be in control. He needs to be the one holding the strings. Even if he isn't the big boss, which I doubt, he's positioned everything around himself in such a way that if he falls, the conspiracy falls with him."

I turn to Parrish then, who still continues to struggle with what he believes is the right choice. I can see it in his eyes, the same agonizing over a choice to help just his friends or everyone.

"Dude, please believe me," I say. It's my turn to plead. "I would want nothing more than to just go home right now and to stop worrying about everyone and everything. I just want Kayley to let me hold her again without freaking out about it. What would be better than that?"

Parrish thinks for a minute, then he says, "I think we'd all want that kind of happiness again."

"Exactly. Now you understand why I'm choosing this."

He looks me in the eye, and I gaze back. I can see that noble part of him returning. He always was the one of us who believed that virtue was its own reward. I have a deep respect for him for that. Parrish has set me straight on many an occasion. That's why he's here now. He's trying to do what's right.

If I never get Kayley back, I could think of no one better for her to end up with. He always has and always will treat her right.

"Okay," Parrish says, nodding once. "Let's do it."

Chapter Forty-Six

With a nod to Parrish, I slink across the corridor to get a better view of the inhabitants of the offices. Parrish pulls out his pistol and takes up a position just behind a storage cabinet at the entrance to the offices. I don't have an exact plan of what we're about to do. We're working at this moment by moment. The only thing we won't do is run. I'm determined to do this

An office door opens. A soldier and a woman in a business suit hustle out. I signal Parrish and press against the wall behind another cabinet. He'll take the soldier, and I'll...stop the woman from clomping away in her heels. She's carrying some kind of briefcase. There could be important information in it.

"Hands up!" Parrish shouts with more rage than I've ever heard him express before. His gun is in the soldier's face before the man even realizes what's going on.

"I'll be taking that," I say to the woman, who's frozen stiff staring at Parrish, and rip the briefcase from her hands. My next motion is to take the soldier's gun from his raised hands.

Then the next three—two soldiers and another business type—pop out from the same office.

"Drop your weapons!" one soldier shouts. Both raise their rifles as the business dude takes cover. He's also got a satchel, which I would like to have, and not for its cosmetic appeal. There's got to be documents of the conspiracy in there—valuable evidence we'll need to take my father down.

"No, you drop yours!" a female voice shouts. It's Afton! She must be here with Kayley, and hopefully they've brought guns. I'd check, but I think turning my back on weapons pointed at me is a bad idea.

Five against four now, but only two of them have guns. Granted, they're more powerful than the pistols Parrish and I have. And we'll be the first to get hit if they squeeze their triggers. Maybe Afton's got an assault rifle.

She doesn't.

"What have you gotten yourself into, galactic idiot?" Afton says as I catch her slide up to me from the corner of my eye. Her gun is at least a plasma weapon, but it's no assault rifle.

"Lovely to see you, too, darling," I reply, my eyes steady on our opponents.

"Stuff it, Rance. I am going to beat you within an inch of your life and then jam you back into that tub until I'm old and retired."

Afton can say whatever she wants. I don't care as long as she's got our backs. And she will, if only for the pleasure of smashing my brains in later.

Doors bust open behind us, and feet, booted feet, stomp into the lobby. I can't tell how many, but it's over two. And they'll be well armed. Advantage soldiers once again.

"Weapons down, or we shoot!" a man, more than likely a soldier, shouts from behind. "You have two seconds to comply!"

"No, you drop yours, or I'm going to turn you into donuts!" a woman's voice replies. Danny! And Billie! We're back on the winning team!

There's shuffling and repositioning in the lobby. The floor shakes as Danny steps closer in her power suit. I'll bet she's moving to protect our backs, which is good. We'd be wide open otherwise.

Still, this has become a complex situation. All the soldiers—I'm guessing there's another five now—versus Parrish, Kayley, Afton, and me. We might have the advantage in weapons, but Danny and Billie are only two. They might have more firepower, but they could get surrounded by too many opponents.

"Danny, how many?" I call.

"Five jerks who should think twice about facing off against us. Especially after we just demolished an entire squad of their buddies!" Danny shoots back.

"Hold steady!" one of them shouts. "There's no proof of that."

Silence comes over us then. Sixteen people, with varying levels of combat experience, tense and prepare for a complete onslaught. If this becomes a firefight, we're all going to get shot, and a few will die.

"Holy smokes!" Dylan cries out and unsheathes her blades. She must have just stepped out of the other office.

Along with my father.

"What are you waiting for?" my father yells, staring at me. He glares and grits his teeth, and every cell in my body screams *move*. "Shoot them!"

As the first gun goes off, I dive right, slamming into Kayley and pressing us both against the wall. She shrieks and drops behind a cabinet. I spin back towards the fighting and unleash a hail of bullets down the corridor.

The soldier I took the gun from is already on the floor, unmoving. I can't tell where the rest are. Plasma bolts fly back and forth at a dizzying rate. Moving from my position is a guarantee of pain.

"Kayley, reload this," I say, exchanging guns with her. She's too shocked to fight. I don't even know why Afton let her come. I think I'm going to have a word or two with Afton about that.

But later.

Danny and Billie are doing a decent job of keeping the other soldiers pinned down. Anytime they lift their heads, they're pounded with an array of weapons from the hand-hunters.

I take a chance and peek out. My father's nowhere to be seen, but Dylan the assassin is still here, ducked behind a desk, awaiting her moment. I fire two shots at her, and she hits the ground. But I can see her glaring at me. Good. I want her to know who it was who tried to take her out.

Bullets ricochet off the cabinet, spraying sparks into my face. I throw my hands up to protect myself. Someone else must have seen me fire. I drop the barrel of the gun on the edge of the cabinet and shoot a spread down the corridor.

Something taps my leg—Kayley's reloaded the gun for me. Good! At least she's functioning enough to do that. I snatch it up and return to the battle.

A blade slices through the cabinet and nearly impales me. I jerk back into a seated position, scrambling to get my weapon up. Then Dylan appears, a bloodthirsty grin on her face.

"You missed," she says, stabbing at me. I duck, but she still gets my shoulder. My gun is up in the next second, firing, but she's gone before I've even squeezed the trigger.

I suck a breath in through my teeth at the burning on my shoulder. I can't tell how deep it might be. It certainly hurts enough. Then I feel hands there, examining.

"Does it hurt?" Kayley asks. "Hold still."

"In the middle of a battle? Are you kidding?"

"Do you want to bleed out?"

There's a groan from across the corridor. Dylan's there! She slices at Parrish, who blocks her attack with the barrel of his gun. Afton turns and fires, but just like a ghost, the assassin is already gone.

If this keeps up, we're going to lose through attrition of blood. While we're pinned down like this, Dylan is free to use hit-and-run tactics as much as she wants to. She can just slice and dice us until we're so bad, we can't even fight back.

"Dammit. Grady, why don't we have any Teddy backup?" I shout into the Teddy comm.

"There are no Teddys," Grady responds. "Their ship got called away. All we have is Original Teddy and the shuttle."

"What?"

"And I'm working from my house."

"Goddesses, could this get any worse?"

I hear a cry from behind. A woman's cry. It sounded like—

"Billie!" I shout into the comm.

"It's alright," Danny says. "They didn't get her too badly. But you bastards will pay for that!"

An explosion rips through the lobby, throwing dust and debris at us. Kayley presses down on top of me, wrapping her arms about my head. What is she thinking? She can't protect me. I'm not sure anyone can right now. We're in a bad spot, waiting for more disaster to befall us.

There's no way we can fight Dylan unless we can face her in the open. That's never going to happen with all these bolts and bullets flying in the air. We need to put our focus elsewhere, like somewhere we might have a chance.

"Danny, we need your help!" I shout into the comm. "The assassin's hit Parrish and me. We can't fight her pinned down like this. Let's swap!"

"What about Billie?" Danny says.

"I'll help her," Kayley says, then pats my back. "Just get me there."

"Deal!" I say. "Afton. Parrish. Let's retreat."

"We're moving," Afton says. They don't have the problem of crossing the hallway to reposition against Danny's opponents.

I throw a volley down in case someone was thinking about going after them. A spray of gunfire flies back in response to my shots. Then it doubles up as the two soldiers down there realize they're only fighting one person. Which means Dylan will return any minute.

Or sooner.

I sense her blade even before she swings. It comes from behind. There's no way for me to defend against it. I wince, ready to take the hit.

But it never comes.

"Dylan?" Danny says, staring at the assassin as she clamps down on Dylan's blade with the glove of her suit.

"Danny?" Dylan's eyes go wide.

Wait. They know each other?

"Oh, you bad girl," Danny says. "You hurt my friends! I'm really pissed at you!"

No time to stick around and find out.

I grab Kayley and haul her away. We don't want to be in the middle of that fight. Neither do the soldiers down the corridor. They've stopped firing. Either they're confused or they want to watch. I send a few shots their way just to remind them there's still a battle on.

As we move to join Afton, Parrish, and Billie, the shriek of metal on metal fills the air as Dylan and Danny face off. I find cover with Kayley as the two of them clang and clash in a battle of titans. The assassin, nimble but unprotected. The hand-hunter, slow but tough.

I have to take my attention away from them, though. There are three soldiers left across the lobby, and they're not out of the fight. They're just being judicial about their use of ammo and placement of shots. We fire back less sporadically, keeping their heads down.

"Patch me up quick," Billie says, clamping down on her leg with a grimace. "I'll take care of those jerks down the hallway."

Kayley presses her lips together and nods, then she grabs a pair of tools and some gauze from a waist pack I missed and sets to work. Maybe I misjudged her. She's not as helpless as I thought. Then again, Kayley never panicked the way I've done.

"Here." Billie presses a grenade into my hand. "Send them my love."

I smile, remembering how she told me she was a hopeless romantic, though a hand-tossed explosive is a strange way to show someone you care.

"I'll countdown to three, then I'm throwing it. We move up once it detonates," I say to Afton and Parrish. They nod in return, but Afton gives me a curious look. I bet she's wondering who put me in charge. That's easy: I did.

"Three...two...one!" I hurl the grenade at our opponents, then duck as they try to take a shot at me. They scramble the moment they notice the grenade. Afton fires as they flee, taking one down. Parrish gets another in the leg.

The explosion blows apart the desk they hid behind. Splinters fly everywhere, impaling the walls and the desk we're sheltering behind.

Dylan shrieks and drops to one knee. I'm not sure if Danny got her or if it was the shrapnel from the grenade. Either way, she doesn't look like she's interested in fighting any more. She holds up a hand to Danny, as the other clutches her side.

Danny, for her part, is merciful. She only stands guard over the assassin, while Dylan doubles over in agony. It's a strange that we took out such a dangerous woman so easily, especially after everything that she's done to us. Stranger still is that I feel any level of sympathy for her pain. I won't be so compassionate in bringing her to justice, though.

"Surrender!" Afton shouts as she and Parrish advance on the wounded soldiers. "Weapons down, hands up!"

With little other choice, they submit, tossing their weapons towards Afton, who kicks them out of the way. Once they're clear, Kayley runs to Dylan, getting her to lie down so she can look at her wound. The assassin blinks and stares at Kayley as she follows her directions.

Oh shoot! I almost forgot about the two other soldiers! And my father!

"Billie," I hiss. "Did you get them? Was my father there?"

"Nope. Nobody there, precious," Billie replies.

I mutter a curse under my breath. We may have given the conspiracy a few serious punches in the face, but without my father's capture, this hell is just going to continue.

Just then, the elevator bell rings.

Gunfire erupts from it, striking Kayley and forcing Afton and Parrish to the floor. I spin to see the two soldiers and my father burst forth, firing like madmen. I fire back, my body slow to respond. My shot hits the closest soldier, and he drops.

Then my father notices me, and he turns, ready to fire his rifle and kill his son.

Chapter Forty-Seven

His first shot hits my arm, sending my pistol flying. The second scores a line across my face. I twist and tumble, landing hard on the floor. Gunfire erupts, then stops. I don't know who's shooting or who got shot, but I fear the worst. I grimace and turn myself over, only to find my father's gun in my face.

"All of you, guns down, or Rance dies!" my father shouts.

"Kayley!" Parrish cries and drops next to Kayley to check on her. It's not clear where she was hit. Dylan has an arm around her shoulders, as if protecting her. If I wasn't in such pain, I might have more brain capacity to ask why.

But as it is, my vision is fuzzy, and I'm struggling to catch my breath. The barrel aimed at me is taking most of my focus, yet I don't have it together enough to be angry about it. Kayley is all I can worry about.

Afton still has her gun. So does Danny. I don't suspect they'll be dropping them soon. That doesn't bode well for me. If my father shoots first, I can only hope they get their revenge for my death.

"I said drop the guns!" my father yells again.

"And then what?" Afton shoots back. "We let you go? No. I don't think so! There is no option where you get to walk away from this."

"Then say goodbye to your friend."

"Are you so ready to kill your own son?" Parrish says. "It wasn't that long ago when you wanted him to join you!"

"That was before all of you messed with my plans! If Rance dies, it will be your fault!"

"Do you really not love your son?" Danny asks. She looks down at Dylan when she says it. Boy, do I hope I can stay alive long enough to know what's going on there.

"He stopped being my son the moment he went against me," my father says.

I just stare at him, amazed that his words still hurt me, even as he points a gun at my face. When he squeezed the trigger before, he was shooting to kill. There's no doubt of that. It's only by the grace of the Three Goddesses that my father never learned how to shoot well. Otherwise I'd be with them n ow.

I'm glad that our relationship is over. There's no way this is going to end happily, and whether my father kills me or someone kills him, I don't want them to feel remorse for doing it. The only thing they need to be thinking about is the fate of the Empire. My life is unimportant compared to that.

A bang comes from nowhere. My father jerks and stumbles, dropping his gun and crashing against the wall. Three shots blast from Afton's weapon. The soldier flies back, hitting the doors of the elevator, then crumpling to the floor. It happens so fast I didn't see who shot first.

Then it's over.

A second later, Afton is next to me, lifting me to sit. She asks if I'm okay. More than once. But I'm lost, my eyes locked on my father as he slouches against the wall, holding a hand against his side. All I can think of is that's a strange place for him to have been hit. Afton couldn't have done it from where she was.

But if she didn't do it, who did?

He stares back at me, fire burning in his eyes as he struggles to breathe. Even at his last, he still thinks he's right. He still believes that his way is the only way. Now I know that's why he left us eight years ago. Not because someone offered him a promotion, but because he was ready to begin his plan that would bring him to this moment. I also realize, despite my hatred of the idea, that I wouldn't be here facing him had he not left that day.

There's a gasp. I break my gaze to look. Parrish is supporting Kayley as the two of them approach. One side of her head is covered in blood from where the bullet grazed her. My jaw goes slack at the sight, but that's not what really shocks me.

In Kayley's right hand is Parrish's gun. It becomes clear then—Kayley's the one who shot my father. Questions fill my head. Just moments before, she was cowering beside me as the firefight was in full blaze. How did it come to this?

"Kayley, why?" I ask.

"Because he was going to kill you," Kayley answers a bit too plainly for my comfort. "I had to stop him."

Her eyes glaze over as she stares at me. Maybe she's in shock over what she did. Maybe I am, too. The Kayley I knew before wouldn't have done this. The Kayley who loved me would have found another way. What does that mean for her?

"Are you happy?" my father blubbers in between tight breaths. "Satisfied with your minor victory? That's all it is, so celebrate while you can. As long as we are all oppressed, others will rise to take my place, until one day the Emperor is overthrown. What will you do then when someone who doesn't have the interest of the people in mind gains control? You should have let me win."

"Shut up!" I shout, my voice breaking. "The only interest you've ever had was your own! You're telling me about some other tyrant? That tyrant is you! If I had just stopped you—"

"Look out!" Parrish cries. It's then I notice the gun in my father's hand. He struggles to raise it at me. I'm frozen in the moment, unable to respond.

But Afton is up, kicking the gun away before he can lift it far. Then she stomps on his hand to dissuade him from trying again. My father growls, jerking his hand up to his chest.

"Disgusting!" Afton says to me. "Even like this, he's still trying to kill you! Are you sure you want to let him face a jury? What if he's found innocent? Or what if they let him out early? He's never going to stop coming for you, Rance! You should take care of the problem while you can!"

Afton leans down and grabs my hand, slapping her gun into it. I stare at it as her meaning becomes clear. My eyes rise to look at my father. Must I watch my back for the rest of my life? Will I never have peace as long as he's alive?

No. I refuse to live like that.

The rage builds inside of me, and my hand tightens its grip on Afton's weapon as my desire to see the true end of this grows.

"Surela, no," Nayla says over Teddy comm. Until she spoke, I had forgotten she was online with Grady. "This is not the way. No peace of mind can be achieved through violence."

"Stay out of this!" Afton shouts back. "You're going to confuse him, Nayla! There's a time for your way, but it isn't now. No crystal is going to save Rance's life if this bastard tries again!"

When Nayla continues to try reason, Afton rips the Teddy comm device from her ear and throws it at the wall. Then she turns back to me, her face full of fury.

"He's not your father anymore, Rance," she says. "He is only an obstacle to your freedom. Do it. Do it quick, and rid yourself of his curse. I don't want you to suffer anymore."

My hand shakes as I hold the gun out, and Afton drops next to me and helps to steady it. I lean into her support, more content to be near my friend than to see my father dead. Afton cares about me, more than she's one to say. I should trust her, right? If she tells me to do this, I should. She's right. I wouldn't be killing my father, I'd be ending my suffering.

And I've suffered enough. We've all suffered enough.

"Rance, no," Kayley says, surprising all of us. "You don't need to do this."

"Hey," Afton responds. "I know you're trying to help, but you're not. You don't remember how much we've been through. You don't understand how much he's endured, and you don't even realize how much he's hurting now."

"That's not fair," Kayley says back. "Just because I can't remember doesn't mean I don't know, or did you forget I've been friends with Rance since we could talk? I haven't forgotten that. You may know him better now, but I've known him longer. This won't stop his pain. I know how Rance feels about me. I may not feel it, but I know it. He can't do this. It will only complicate things!"

I suck in a quick breath. Did Kayley just say she knows I am in love with her? Of course, I told her, but she said it like she truly understood. That's different from just knowing the fact. But how is that useful to me?

"He can, and he will!" Afton says, breaking me from my wandering mind. I've lost blood, but it's not the only reason I'm getting spacy. This entire situation is surreal.

"Dude, are you sure about this?" Grady asks. "I mean...he deserves it, but...it's still your *dad*."

I squeeze my eyes shut. There are too many words to consider, too many opinions. I just want to be done with this. All I have to do is fire, and I should. The man before me is a criminal. A plague on the Empire. If I could just find that last pinch of strength to do it, this could be over.

"Rance," Nayla pleads. "Consider the future. Your future. You will not walk away from this easily."

"Would everyone just be quiet?" I yell. "This is my decision to make, and it's not up for debate!"

As the others go silent, my father chuckles. It's more of a strained cough than a laugh, but I have no sympathy for his pain. If anything, I may hate him more.

"What are you waiting for, then?" he says. "This is what you wanted, isn't it?"

"Do it," Afton whispers in my ear as she guides my arm right at my father's heart. "Squeeze the trigger, and let's go home. Okay? End your agony, Rance, and I will be here to support you all the way."

My eyes dart to Kayley, who's watching me with uncertainty. Parrish, too. Maybe in this moment, they don't know me. They don't know what I will do. I don't, either.

I want to give in to Afton's urging. I so desperately want this to be over so I can get on with my life. But can I? Will this solve everything that's given me pain? My father has been the source of so much of it, it's hard to tell where his fault ends and another one begins.

My finger makes contact with the trigger. I feel its weight and the consequences of squeezing it. It's an easy action, to fire the bullet that will end my father's life, just like he ended mine. And Kayley's. But there will be no coming back for him. If I shoot, that's it.

As I look upon my father, I see what a sorry state of an individual he's become. He's so wrapped up in his own delusion that he got beaten by a bunch of post-teenagers just beginning their climb into adulthood.

We were nobodies before this. Now look at us. We took down an entire conspiracy. Just us and a few of our friends.

I realize then that no matter what he tried, my father could never hurt me again. We'd just beat him a second time, and a third. And he knows I understand that. My finger moves away from the trigger, and my arm relaxes. I won't be killing my father today. Or any day after.

"Rance...Rance, no! What are you doing?" Afton says, fighting to keep my arm up. "Hold steady!"

"It's okay, Surela," I reply, using her first name not in jest, for once. "I don't need to do it."

"Are you sure?"

I nod. "He can't hurt us anymore."

I look him right in the eyes when I say it. He holds my gaze for a moment, his face softening. Defeated. Maybe if there is still love in him for me, he might find it in himself to be proud of all I've accomplished. It's the last happy thought that I will ever have about my father.

Then he turns away, staring at the floor.

The doors to the lobby burst open, and soldiers pour through them—Colonel Cortell's soldiers. One of them calls to him the moment they lay eyes on us, and the man himself comes forward, shouting for a medic before turning to us.

"I guess I missed the party," the colonel says. "Sorry about that. Stretchers are coming. We'll get all of you evacuated to the nearest military hospital ASAP."

"Danny and Dylan," I say and nod towards the last known location of the hand-hunter. But when I look, they're both gone. Billie, too. I have no idea when they disappeared. Maybe they want to handle their wounds on their own. But why take Dylan with them?

"You," my father says, raising his head to eye the colonel. "You were on their side?"

"Every step of the way. You should have known better than to go up against these kids. I've never seen a crack military unit like them."

"You hear that?" Grady asks. I can hear him grinning across the Teddy comm. "We're a crack military unit!"

"Maybe. Something is definitely cracked about us," Afton adds with a chuckle. "That's for sure."

Parrish and Kayley drop next to Afton and me. Kayley wraps her arms about me and, in doing so, hugs Afton at the same time. Parrish covers the three of us with his long arms. Then I find myself in the middle of a four-way embrace. I close my eyes and let it happen.

It feels different, as if it lacks something. My first thought is Grady, but it's not him. He'd be here if he could, and I know even halfway around the planet, he's still with us. No, it's not that. It's more like I've got my arms wrapped around different people. That's not bad. What we've gained is far more than what we've lost. And even though my heart aches when I remember Kayley is not in love with me, I feel like that might only be temporary.

But who knows? If my current self visited my old self before all this happened and told me all the things I'd go through, I'd never believe it. I would never have believed that Kayley and I would be together, yet it happened.

And if it could happen once, it might happen again.

EPILOGUE

"You've kept me quite busy, my little darlings," Doc Elizabeth says as she drops herself into a chair next to my medical bed. She wipes her forehead and sighs, but then smiles. "Please do me the favor of not getting tangled up with any more conspiracies, alright? I don't think I can handle the stress anymore."

"Hey," Afton says, sitting across from me on Kayley's bed. "Don't blame me. I came out nearly unscathed."

"Nearly," Grady echoes.

The military hospital they evacuated us to was close to the conspirators' base, which turned out to be a former research facility. No one had suspected it because of its odd location on Angelcanis. Apparently the top brass of the Imperial military were aware of the potential but dismissed it because it was on a colony planet, and who'd want to put their base there?

"So does that mean we're ready to get out of here?" I ask.

"How about a *'thank you, Elizabeth, for fixing us up for the billionth time'* and a *'we promise never to do it again, Elizabeth'* first?"

"If that is what you are expecting, then I have a bad omen I must share with you," Nayla says, floating into the room. "The doctors here are so impressed with your skills they want to hire you."

Elizabeth frowns. The military medical staff let her take care of us only when Captain Teddy intervened on our behalf, claiming a diplomatic priority. Plus, we're not citizens, so they didn't have any real say over what care we received. They still watched Doc Elizabeth's every movement like my neighbor watches people near his lawn. Until they saw what she was capable of, that is. Then she was free to do whatever she wanted, with the occasional intrusion by a nurse or a patient aide.

"Well." Doc Elizabeth leans forward to examine the bandage on my cheek. "You both seem to be healing, so I'd say you could be out of here as soon as tomorrow. I'd like to keep Kayley another day, however."

"No!" Kayley protests. "I'm done with hospitals! I want out!"

"I'll stay and keep you company," I offer with a hopeful smile. Kayley smiles back, but I can see her reluctance to take me up on that offer. I suppose there's a conversation waiting to be had there that she's not ready for. It's fine. I won't press her.

"Nayla and I will hang out," Afton says, to which Nayla replies by chewing on her lip and narrowing her eyes at her partner.

"Ah, I should mention," Nayla says. "Parrish and Mr. Pink are bringing a guest with them. They should arrive any moment."

By Mr. Pink, I think she means Original Teddy. Nayla's gotten into the habit of naming them all Mr. So and So. I don't know how she remembers every name. Maybe it's a skill learned from years of being in the public eye. I hope she realizes they're not all misters.

As if right on cue, Parrish and Original Teddy arrive with Danny Lecker, sans power suit or trademark bodysuit and jacket. With the comfortable pants and oversize shirt, she looks more like she's about to spend the afternoon—

"Croquet is my new favorite game!" Danny says to Parrish as they enter. "So that's why I started a hand-hunters league."

"Weapons are banned, right?" Parrish asks, to which Danny frowns.

"Of course! Do you know how much a croquet ball costs to replace?" Then she turns to me. "Hiya, honey! Feeling better?"

"Sure, but..." I shake my head. "Where did you disappear to?"

"Oh, well. Just a little interpersonal business I needed to take care of. You kids had everything under control, so I thought it was a good time to split."

"Where's the assassin?" Afton asks.

"Assassin?" Danny thinks for a second. "Oh! You mean Dylan!"

"Yes, Dylan Estrella Thomas," I say. "The one who shot Kayley and me! Where is she? She needs to pay for what she did!"

There's an echo of support from the others. My father may have given the order, but Dylan pulled the trigger. And once she found out we were still alive, she was ready to do it again. She needs to be locked up, if only so the Empire is safe from a dangerous woman like her.

"Thomas?" Danny shakes her head. "That's not her name."

"It's not?" Kayley asks. If there wasn't a big bandage wrapped around Kayley's head, I'd see her forehead wrinkling. As it is, she reminds me of orange Teddy veggies with her hair popping out of the top of the bandage like that. Afton did her best to help but gave up once she realized the futility of her efforts.

"No! It's Lecker, like mine. Dylan Lecker. Our parents liked the letter *D*, apparently."

"Wait—" I'm stunned into silence, my brain trying to accept the reality of Danny's statement. "She's...your sister?"

"The assassin is Danny's sister?" Grady shouts. Parrish frowns at him for making too much noise.

"Where is she?" I ask, my heartbeat rising. "Did you turn her over to the authorities?"

"What authorities?" Danny replies. "She works for the Emperor. Who's going to arrest her?"

All of us slump in unison. I should have known the Emperor would protect his assets. Even if they arrested her, there would never be a trial. She likely knows way too many secrets to ever appear in a public forum, and no way would they'd ever place her in a common prison facility, though I fear more for the inmates than I do for Dylan.

"*Bzzzt*," Original Teddy says.

"What's up, Teddy?"

"*Bzzzt*," Original Teddy says again and points to Nayla, who stares at him until she realizes the meaning.

"Ah," she says, digging into a pocket in her voluminous dress. "I have a call."

I often forget how sensitive Teddy hearing is, though they also can dampen their ears if sound gets too loud. They just don't enjoy doing it.

"It's for you," Nayla says, holding her Sergo out to me. I motion just to put it on speaker because, other than my mom, everyone I want to speak to is here. It must be some kind of solicitation.

"Hello, Mr. He'? Ransom Quigley He'?" a woman's voice says.

"Yes, I'm here. Go ahead."

"You have put me on speaker? Very well. This concerns everyone in the room."

We eye each other silently. I suppose whomever it is can hear the background noise that speaker mode creates, but how does this person know who's here?

"I am Sarah Peredur Leigh, bailiff and senior aide to Chamberlin Tyrwhitt Sitwell Egerton."

"Oh, congratulations on the promotion!" I say.

"Pardon me?" There's a brief pause. "I see. You are referring to the removal of my predecessor in the position, Bailiff Daughtry. You are mistaken. The Chamberlin did not promote me. This position was merely mine to fill once it became empty due to Bailiff Daughtry's unfortunate...departure. I must apologize for my predecessor's actions, by the way. What she did was unbecoming of this post."

"That's okay. Nobody really liked her anyway," Afton mutters.

"Well, what's the reason for the call?" Then I remember the deal we had with the Chamberlin. "Wait, don't tell me! I already know!"

"You do?"

"Yes, you're calling to coordinate the clearing of our records and also find out what letters of recommendation we need written!"

"Letters of recommendation from the Lord Chamberlin?" Kayley's eyes light up, thinking of all the possibilities for her. I'm glad. After all, that's what we've sacrificed so much for. To have this moment where our futures could be anything and everything we could dream about. The letters would see to that.

But when silence is the only reply we get, I turn suspicious.

"Bailiff Leigh, the Lord Chamberlin is going to clear our records, right?" I ask. "And write us letters?"

"I'm sorry, Mr. He'. You must be mistaken. His Lordship has mentioned nothing of the sort," she replies.

"Then why are you calling us?" Afton shouts.

"I have a message from the Lord Chamberlin for you," the bailiff replies.

"Well, out with it, then!" Afton shakes her head and sighs.

"Of course. His Lordship congratulates you for a job well done. You have done a great service to the Empire by stopping a plot by such a well-organized group of seditionists to overthrow His Majesty."

"Great," I say. "How about a reward, then?"

"Unfortunately, that will not be possible."

The volume of our collective *what?* is so loud that Original Teddy jabs his tentacles into his ears and a nurse steps in to glare and shush us, followed by a second one a moment later.

"Allow me to explain," the bailiff says.

"Oh, you'd better do more than that," Afton growls. Nayla moves to sit next to her and puts a calming hand over Afton's mouth. If I wasn't so angry at the moment, I might have laughed. Nayla's really becoming one of us.

"There can be no connection between you and the success of this mission. If the Emperor's enemies were to find out that his own legions could not remove the conspirators, the attempts to dethrone His Majesty would increase. That would destabilize the Empire, and we cannot have that. Therefore, the credit will go to the newly appointed Deputy Minister Cortell, the new head of the Anti-Sedition Ministry."

"Well, at least he got something good out of it," Parrish says.

"But what about us, then?" I ask.

"As it is, with the current...problems on your records, it would be better if you were to lie low for a while. Any remaining pockets of conspirators could target you, and that would cause difficulty. I would recommend moving away from Angelcanis to somewhere more...remote."

"For how long?" Kayley asks.

"Perhaps about five years would be best. Give us time to remove any last dangers to His Majesty, and then we will send for you."

"Five...years?" Parrish shakes his head. "No...no, I can't do that. I've got to get a job and pay for my house."

"Yeah, and my parents will get out of prison in two years!" Grady says.

"I'm not leaving," Afton says. "Queen de Avila will protect us."

"Ah yes...the princess," Bailiff Leigh says. "Or should I say *former* princess? As far as the Empire is concerned, you are still a fugitive. Your mother may forgive you, but she hasn't pardoned you yet, has she? I believe it might even be in her best interests not to."

"You have no idea what you are saying," Nayla says, clearly hurt by the bailiff's words. "My mother will protect us."

"If you say so," the bailiff replies. "You may want to call her first to confirm that."

"So is that it?" I ask. "You just want us to run away and hide until you decide we're no longer an inconvenience for you? The Chamberlin made us a deal, and we did more than hold up our end! Do you have any idea what we sacrificed to make this happen? No! Of course you don't! All you care about is that it's done! Now we just get swept under the royal carpet and forgotten? No way!"

"I would be happy to inquire with His Lordship about your status as citizens...and the benefits that come with it."

"Benefits? I don't need to become a citizen to have this benefit!"

I pound on the call disconnect button, cutting off any more comments from the bailiff, or any government agent, for that matter. I'm so entirely fed up with the Empire that I might just take their advice and get as far away from any mention of them as possible. But then I couldn't be near Kayley, my buds, or my mom. If that could all get figured out, I think I'd be well on my way...somewhere.

"So..." Afton says, turning to Nayla. "Your mom hasn't pardoned you?"

"Of course she has," Nayla says, sounding like she's attempting to convince herself of that. "She must have done it."

"Have you spoken to her about it?" I ask.

"Well." Nayla looks down. "I was going to contact her once we arrived in Canis Ludis' orbit. I would not be allowed on the surface otherwise."

Afton sighs but slides an arm around Nayla's shoulders and pulls her closer. At least they can still stay at Grady's house.

"How serious is this threat to our safety?" Kayley asks. "I thought we'd be fine once Rance's dad—"

"Father," Grady corrects, "though I doubt he even wants you to say that."

When Grady and Kayley look at me for confirmation, I just shrug. What someone calls my relation, or lack of one, to my father is trivial compared to us no longer having a future to look forward to.

"I'm sorry, everyone," I say. "This is my fault. I got us tangled up in this mess when we should have stayed far away from it. And then you had to drop everything and rescue me when you were all about to start your lives up again."

"I didn't drop anything," Parrish says. "And I'd come rescue you time and time again if you needed it, because I know you'd do the same for me."

"Yeah, Parrish, but your mom—"

"Hey," Afton says. "Knock off that nonsense. Do you really think you're the boss of me? Of us? *I* choose my own actions! I am the—"

"Huntress," Nayla says.

"Yeah, that." Afton pecks Nayla on the cheek and turns back to me. "And don't you dare discount what you mean to us, Rance! Don't you dare consider yourself worthless in our eyes. Even when we were walking away, you stayed to fight. You were ready to give up everything so that the people in this Goddess-damned Empire could live their lives and be naïve of the danger they were in. It's because of *you* we came back."

"But that still doesn't change the fact that we're worse off than we were before all of this started," I say. "How are you guys going to live your lives always looking over your shoulders?"

"Who says?" Grady shrugs. "We could go live on Deeneehaan for a while. Or...better yet! Let's build some huts and live on the beach on Littus!"

"That's not a horrible idea," Parrish says, considering. "I'd have to sell the house, but..."

It's not the best, either. Five years on a beach is not my idea of fun. Even Nayla will get bored of communing with the sea life and rocks after a while. The other colony planets aren't really much of an option, either. Most of them are in the very early stages of colonization. Life would be hard, and we'd all struggle to fit in with a different breed of people built for the harsh life. I'll be the first to admit Angelcanis' conveniences have spoiled us.

Plus, we'd be doing nothing but trying to survive. If we've got to lie low for five years, we should take a clue from the Teddys and get to work on something for our future. When they left their planet, they did so with the notion to explore and create alliances with other like-minded beings. Heck, if we had our own Teddy ship, we could go do our own exploration and come back as heroes of the Empire. Imagine what we could learn just by going to the Teddy—

Wait a minute!

"Teddy," I say. "You're leaving soon, aren't you?"

"That is accurate. Transit is forthcoming. Teddy is ready to split."

"Oh sure. I heal your wounds, and now you're looking to get rid of us," Doc Elizabeth says, half joking.

"Not get rid of you. *Go* with you."

Original Teddy whirrs and twists his tentacles together—a sure sign of emotional excitement. Parrish and Grady look at each other, their eyebrows raised. Parrish offers him a question with a shrugged shoulder, and the edges of Grady's mouth turn upward.

I grin, too. I knew I could count on them. If I hadn't thought of it, Grady may have. Parrish likely was just looking for an excuse to get far away from his troubles. This could be his fresh start.

"What do you think, darling?" Nayla asks, watching Afton, hopeful. "A romantic notion if ever there was one, yes?"

"You mean going to some strange planet as the first humans?" Afton chuckles. "Sure, but it doesn't really matter."

"What do you mean? Are you not excited about the idea?"

"I'm excited about being with you for the next five years." Afton's cheeks take on a rosy hue, and Nayla smiles. The two of them get close, their lips connecting for a long, passionate kiss. The rest of us suddenly find interest in the nearest inanimate objects we can spot. I'm glad they are so comfortable with each other that a little public display of affection doesn't bother them. It doesn't bother me, either. I just don't want to be the pervert who's staring at them while they share a moment.

Kayley gasps, catching my attention. Her eyes have gotten big, and I see the gears in her head are churning overtime. I wonder what she might be considering.

"Teddy," she says. "If Elizabeth were to go home with you, might your scientists there have a solution for her memory loss?"

"I *am* going with them," Doc Elizabeth says.

"Possibility abounds," Original Teddy says. "Kayley can qualify."

There could be a way to get Kayley's memories back? I hadn't thought of that. Does that mean she wants to come?

"Then I'm going, too!" Kayley says.

She does!

"KayKay, are you sure?" I ask. "Don't you want to spend time with your parents?"

"Yes, but"—Kayley presses her lips together—"honestly? I had little hope they'd be able to help me. I don't know why, but I feel something good might happen if I go."

I cannot help but smile. It might be contagious, because everyone else does, too. At least the ones I can see in my periphery. Right now, I've only got eyes for Kayley. Five years is a long time to rebuild a relationship. It may even be enough to grow one.

"But what about Mom, Rance?" Kayley asks. "Will she be okay if you leave her for so long?"

"Are you kidding? Nothing's going to happen to Tzu-Yu!" Danny answers. "Not while I'm around. She's been cooking for the girls every Sunday, and they absolutely cannot get enough! I don't know how you're not twice your size!" She grabs me into an embrace, pulling my head down into her chest and rocking me back and forth. I'm caught off guard and struggle to get air, my arms flailing about, though I dare say it brings back memories. "You go do your thing, sweetie. I'll protect her with my life!"

"Hey!" Kayley shouts. "Hands off Rance!"

"Why?" Danny asks, dropping the embrace to turn to Kayley. She keeps a possessive arm around me, and knowing what I know about Danny now, I think I understand her little ploy.

"Yeah," Afton says, catching on. She grins and pivots to face Kayley. "What's your objection?"

"Well," Kayley stammers and thrusts a finger at Danny. "Didn't you see that? He couldn't breathe! You should be more careful!"

There are a few chuckles and not a few *mmmhmms* from everyone.

"Kayley," Original Teddy says, "jealousy is unbecoming."

Grady and Danny snicker, though Kayley still doesn't get the joke. I hope one day she will, and we'll all have a big laugh about it then. I look forward to that day.

That's the other thing that the Teddy world might bring us. Hope. Something that we all could use a great big helping of. Because where there's hope, there's action. And where there's action, there's change. Change for the better. Change for those who couldn't change their circumstances. Change to give each and every one of us a little brightness in our lives.

And that, I think, is what I really want most. To be an instrument of positive change. For everyone.

Books by Marc B. DeGeorge

Origin Story Series

The Starship Sneak

The Reckless Rescue

The Traitors' Trial

The Conspiracy Clash

Air Born Series

A Call to the Sky
A Challenge in the Sky

About the Author

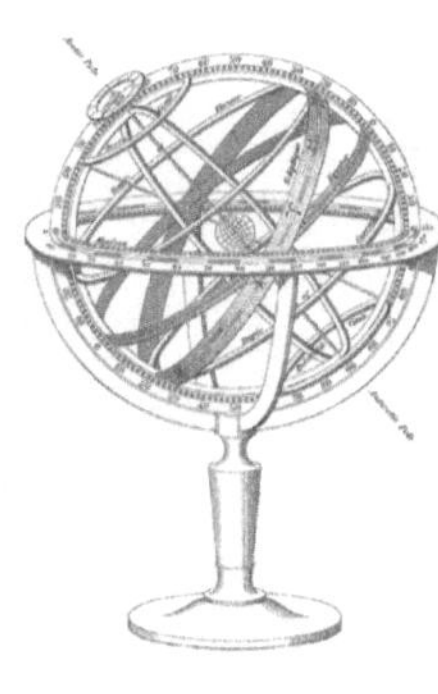

Marc B. DeGeorge has made every attempt in his adult life to maintain a balance between how much science and how much art he dabbles in. Sometimes, he's even successful. When he was young, he wanted to be an astronaut, and then an aeronautical engineer—he even went to Space Camp! But then he learned how to play guitar and his space dreams took a back seat. He spent a decade playing professionally in bands and studying music in college (university only took five years). These days, things have come round full circle, and Marc envisions the future by writing books that imagine what challenges humanity may face, and what we might accomplish together.

When Marc isn't writing, he performs traditional Japanese music on shamisen and writes, shoots, and edits performing arts photos and documentaries under the MuseMarc Studio name.

 amazon.com/Marc-B-Degeorge/e/B09LDCNVHV/ref=aufs_dp_fta_dsk

facebook.com/MarcBDeGeorge

instagram.com/marcbdegeorgeauthor/

goodreads.com/author/show/22081012.Marc_B_DeGeorge

9 781956 487138